A DETECTIVE INSPECTO

HUNTER HUNTED

NEW YORK TIMES #1 BESTSELLER **TONY LEE** WRITING AS

JACK GATLAND

MEDIA

INSPIRATION • PRODUCTION • PUBLICATION

Published by Hooded Man Media.

First Edition: February 2021
Second Edition: September 2023

Before LETTER FROM THE DEAD...
There was

LIQUIDATE
THE PROFITS

Learn the story of what *really* happened to DI Declan Walsh,
while at Mile End!

An EXCLUSIVE PREQUEL, completely free to anyone who
joins the Declan Walsh Reader's Club!

Join at bit.ly/jackgatlandVIP

Also by Jack Gatland

COVERT ACTION

COUNTER ATTACK

STEALTH STRIKE

DAMIAN LUCAS BOOKS

THE LIONHEART CURSE

STANDALONE BOOKS

THE BOARDROOM

For Mum, who inspired me to write.

For Tracy, who inspires me to write.

CONTENTS

PROLOGUE

OF ALL THE LIVERY COMPANIES IN LONDON, CHARLES BAKER reckoned that the *Worshipful Company of Stationers and Newspaper Makers* was the most pointless.

Usually known as the *Stationer's Company*, they formed it way back in 1403, although it had to wait until 1557 for its Royal Patronage. Many people claimed it was an Elizabethan patronage, and this was the start of the Elizabethan "Golden Age", but the fact of the matter was that 1557 was still very much in the time of her sister, Mary I. She was better known as *Bloody Mary*, a nickname given mainly because of her persecution of Protestant heretics, burning hundreds at the stake during her reign, and therefore this long-established printing and stationer guild's "Royal Patronage" had been bathed in infamy from the very start.

Charles was a fan of the earlier versions of the guild; illuminated manuscripts were beautiful things, and Charles was very much a fan of beautiful things. It was just that once technology (in this case the simple printing press) replaced the art of calligraphy, a kind of crassness came into the industry. The stationers stopped non-members from having the right to copy texts; that's where the term *copyright* came from. Then from the printers came the publishers, and the publishers created the newspapers.

Charles Baker hated the newspapers.

Nowadays, though, the Stationer's Company represented more of the *content and communications* industries. This included digital media and software, and worse still, advertising and PR. Probably not what the poor buggers who created the guild over six hundred years ago had ever envisioned; that their beautiful, artistically designed manuscript guild would one day be filled with bloody Instagram influencers, science-fiction authors, and people like Rupert Murdoch and William sodding Hague.

But, as much as he despised many of the members, he couldn't fault the fact that they threw a damn good party.

In fact, it was a party that they threw that Charles Baker now found himself at, standing at the head table in the Livery Hall, with dozens of Freemen of the company and Liverymen watching him as he prepared to speak. It was an amazing location for a speech: deep mahogany wood panelling covered most of each wall, with a variety of hand-lettered members lists, portraits of liverymen, flags or even coats of honour adorning each one, with the top third of the wall (and the ornate ceiling above him) painted cream and gold, with guild flags hanging above heraldic shields. When the windows weren't looking out onto London, they were replaced with beautiful stained glass windows of ancient printers such as William Tyndale or William Caxton, given the same reverence that a church might give to a saint. It felt religious. It felt as if he was giving a sermon.

Which, in a way, he was.

'Thank you, Master of Company,' he said to the wizened old man in the tuxedo who now sat to his left, 'for that wonderful introduction, and thank you,' this was to the hall itself, 'for giving me such a warm welcome.'

There was a small smattering of applause at this. Charles forced a smile.

'As a Member of Parliament, I have had an interesting history with the Worshipful Company of Stationers and Newspaper Makers,' he said. 'In fact, I think that all Members of Parliament have, at times, had a similar situation.'

There was a low rumble of polite laughter. Charles allowed it to build and fall before he continued.

'When I was a child, printing fascinated me,' he continued. 'To be able to place words onto paper and change a single mind in the process was nothing short of a miracle to me, and it probably was the one thing that set me off on the career path that I chose.' He paused for a moment, allowing the silence to fill the room. 'But, although it set me on my journey, it hasn't been that kind to me.'

The room was still silent, but now the atmosphere had changed, as if the other invited guests had realised that this *wasn't* the speech that they had been expecting.

'As many of you know, a few weeks ago my beautiful, wonderful wife, Donna, passed away,' Charles continued, allowing a hint of emotion to creep into his voice. 'She had suffered from mental issues for much of her life, including clinical depression. So, when the national press started attacking me, started commenting on a child I'd had out of wedlock a life ago, before we even met, a child that I hadn't known that I was the father of, it proved too much for her, and she took her own life.'

There was a muttering in the hall after this. Charles had

never publicly spoken about how Donna had died. They had believed it was because of illness, not because of an overdose, or a noose in the underground garage of the Baker's house. Charles carried on.

'It's true,' he continued, 'and I will never forgive you, the ones that did this. I will hunt you down and I will destroy you.'

He was enjoying this.

'I look up and I see Caxton and Tyndale, the fathers of printing and I wonder, what would they say if they saw this travesty that sits here before them? Would they, like Doctor Frankenstein, be appalled at the monster they had created?'

The murmuring was building now, an angry rumble, as the people sitting at the tables now realised that this wasn't a simple after-dinner speech. This was a spanking.

'I may not be the Secretary of State for the Home Office anymore, but I still read the briefings,' Charles said. 'I've seen the rising gang war that is occurring between Birmingham and London, a war that you yourselves have given life to, after your reckless reporting of the murders of Angela Martin and Gabrielle Chapman in the national press. You cannot run unchecked—'

'But that was stopped!' A portly man at one of the closer tables shouted out. 'It was on the news tonight!'

Charles paused. The man spoke with such conviction that for a moment Charles wondered if he'd been mistaken. Glancing down at his phone, turned over on the table and switched to silent mode so as not to distract him, he picked it up, abandoning his speech for the moment as he turned the phone in his hands and saw the notifications of missed calls and left messages. Reading them, he nodded to himself.

'My apologies,' he continued. 'I was in session directly

before this, so I hadn't seen the news. And yes, it seems that both the Delcourt family and the Byrne family have been taken into custody following a police raid on a Beachampton residence earlier today.' He straightened his shoulders, giving the appearance of someone proud.

'I'm happy to say that the unit that solved this case comes from the City; in fact, their offices are less than a mile from here. Actually, the arresting Detective Inspector is the same one that saved my own life several weeks ago. Our police are a credit to us, if woefully understaffed. But that doesn't stop the fact that this wouldn't have escalated so fast if there had been some order, some regulatory aspect to your radical news agenda.' He was back on track now, casting aside the bad news as he pushed forward. 'If I ever get the chance to make such a change, I will ensure that all media, be it traditional press or digital, will follow the rule of law. I hereby put you on notice.'

With that, to a cacophony of complaints from guild members as they rose from their tables, Charles Baker placed his phone into his jacket pocket and, his work done here, turned to leave the table. However, blocking his way was the man who'd introduced him, the Right Reverend Doctor Reginald Walsingham, the current Master of Company.

'Interesting speech,' he whispered. 'If we'd known you were coming to tell us off, we would have called the current Home Secretary to replace you. I mean, we invited you when you still held the role, not when you became nothing more than a backbencher.'

'I'm far more than a backbencher,' Charles replied with a smile. 'You think these articles, these news reports hurt me? Things that I did when I was young and single, that I was never informed about. Follies of youth.'

'How about the reports of Devington Industries working with you on arms contracts? Or the rumours of illegal arms trades? Of Rattlestone?' Reginald raised an eyebrow. Charles laughed at this.

'Walk into the House of Commons on any Prime Minister's Question Time and throw a stone,' he said. 'I guarantee that whoever you hit on whatever side will have the same industry-related skeleton in their closet. Yes, I have made questionable choices in my career, but I have something better on my side.'

He leaned in.

'I have public sympathy.'

Reginald stared coldly at Charles for a long moment before speaking.

'You almost sound like you killed her deliberately to gain the widower vote,' he said.

'Old man, that's a very cynical view of life you have there,' Charles replied. 'But rumours are rumours and facts are facts.' He looked up to the stained window where a Latin phrase was emblazoned under the image of a man arguing with another over a proffered piece of parchment.

'*Verbum Domini Manet In Aeternum*', he said. 'Interesting motto.'

'The word of God remains forever,' Reginald translated.

Charles nodded. 'I know,' he said. 'I'm not a pleb. I did Latin at Harrow. I was just considering that you might think about changing it.'

'To what?'

Charles leaned in.

'The word of law remains forever,' he finished before patting the shoulder of the Master of Company, waving to the room of dinner guests and, with his Special Branch guards either side of him, marched determinedly out of the hall, the sound of angry diners rising behind him as he left.

'Where to, sir?' his bodyguard asked as Charles climbed into the back of his Ministerial car. He might have been nothing more than a backbencher to the public now, but that was for the masses to believe. He was destined for far greater things, and the party knew this; they had made concessions for him.

'The George,' he said, checking his watch. 'I'm running late.'

———

THE GEORGE INN WAS A PUB OFF SOUTHWARK HIGH STREET, just south of the Thames. It was an old medieval coaching inn where Charles Dickens had once drunk, although that debatable claim could probably be given to most of the pubs and taverns in London. A long, white-painted, galleried and timber-framed pub, it was mainly a series of interconnected bars with a restaurant and function room upstairs. It was to the latter of these that Charles, now in a thick coat, scarf and hat to disguise his identity, made his way up rickety stairs, opening the door on his left and entering a small, quiet room with windows along one wall.

In the room were four other people, all Members of Parliament. Malcolm Gladwell was the trouble-shooter of the Conservative Party, and the MP for some pokey little Berkshire dump that had been too stupid to vote him out in the last election. Stick-thin and with curly ginger hair, Gladwell was a sickeningly fit, bio-hacking ultra-runner in his late forties who looked a decade younger, thanks in part to the multitude of expensive supplements he sucked down every day. Like a cockroach, he'd most likely survive everyone.

Next to him sat Tamara Banks, one of Charles's rivals for the Conservative throne; in her early forties and resembling the bastard daughter of Cruella De Vil and Heinrich Himmler, Banks was a toxic Thatcherite, more right-wing than most of her party, a woman that had gained power and influence during the Vote Leave campaign, but was distanced enough to keep her reputation once Brexit polarised everyone.

Watching out of the window was Jerry Robinson, an Ulster Democrat. Squat both in stature and intellect, and patting down his greasy, dyed-black hair as he stared at the young, attractive women in the beer patio below, Jerry was a devout creationist who didn't believe in dinosaurs, believing that they were a test from God to see if humankind's faith was strong enough.

Charles thought that Jerry Robinson was a test from God. That, or a rather annoying joke.

The last person in the room was a Labour MP, one that Charles had known back when he was on the red side of the Commons. Norman Shipman was old, ancient even, nothing more than a well-dressed skeleton under stretched-tight skin. He'd been an MP back when Jim Callaghan was in charge in the seventies and every battle, every fight was etched into his face. He'd spent his entire political career on the back benches; but Charles knew from experience that this was where he did his best work.

In the shadows, in rooms like this, and with people just like the ones that Charles faced right now.

'You're late,' Tamara complained. Charles didn't bother to reply. Complaining about someone when they arrived was simply Tamara's way of saying hello to them.

'I see your man's in the news again,' Malcolm smiled. 'If he keeps this up, we might have to promote him to DCI.'

'He's not my man,' Charles poured himself a wine from a bottle on the side table before turning to face the others. 'Also to be honest, I'd have preferred it if he delayed a few days.'

'So where are we on these?' Straight to business, Jerry drank from his bottle of tonic water. He didn't use a glass, just the tiny bottle. It looked ludicrous.

'Do I have permission to move on with the target I informed you of during the last session?' Charles asked. Malcolm looked at Norman, as if waiting for guidance. Even though he was of a different political party, Norman Shipman was the obvious leading force in the room.

He nodded.

'I call this session of the *Star Chamber* open,' he said, his voice cracked with a mixture of age and far too many cigarettes.

Charles released his held breath as he leaned onto the table he sat beside.

'As I said last time, I put forward an extremist terrorist to include in the lists,' he spoke carefully, ensuring that he didn't mis-speak, or understate anything that he was revealing. 'We believe she was radicalised in Syria two years ago and, since returning to the UK, she's been running as part of a terrorist cell in South West London with a UK-born and radicalised, London-based handler.'

'Do we have any idea about what her plan is?' Tamara asked. Charles shook his head.

'All I know is that after we investigated her, she met with my wife the same day ... the same day that Donna killed herself.'

'You think this extremist caused your wife's death?'

Tamara seemed appalled, but Charles guessed it was a more mawkish curiosity.

'I do,' he nodded. 'I also believe she is a danger to our Government.'

'We shall put the name into the lists for consideration,' Norman nodded slowly, looking to the others. 'Any refusals?'

As the other MPs in the function room agreed to this decision one by one, Charles quickly tapped off a text on his phone under the table, sending it off before Norman looked back to him:

flick the switch

'What's the name to be added?' Norman asked, returning Charles to the conversation.

'Taylor,' Charles Baker replied. 'The extremist terrorist's name is *Kendis Taylor*.'

THE MAN WITH THE RIMLESS GLASSES SAT IN HIS CAR, PARKED on the pavement at Tudor Street, deep in the City of London. He'd been there for close to an hour now, watching the evening trade at the wine bar to his right as, ahead of him, he monitored the white-bricked, arched entrance into Temple Inn. There was a large, black gate and a yellow and black barrier blocking his way into the Inns of Temple, and the guard would be in the cabin to the side of it. That said, people walked in and out all the time with no issues, and the man with the rimless glasses knew the guards paid them no heed, especially when they dressed in overcoat, scarf and suit.

His phone beeped with a message; glancing down, he read it. The man with the rimless glasses didn't recognise the number, but he knew who the order had come from. He'd known ever since he'd moved allegiances, since they had freed him from custody under ministerial conduct subclauses, creating this new legend, this new identity of sorts for him.

He knew what the order meant.

Leaving the car, the man with the rimless glasses made his way through the entrance to the right of the arch, past the notice that stated that *only residents could bring their dogs through* and, keeping his head down he passed the guard who didn't even glance at him in passing, reading that night's edition of *The Evening Standard* and ignoring the suited man who continued down Temple Lane, and out into King's Bench Walk.

Turning right as he entered the large courtyard, the man with the rimless glasses carried on along King's Bench Walk, stopping when he reached a particular door. It was late in the evening, and he knew that nobody else would be in; the target was still there though, as his car was outside, parked in a bay opposite the entrance. Checking to ensure that nobody was watching, the man with the rimless glasses entered the City of London police's Temple Inn Crime Unit, otherwise known as the offices of the *Last Chance Saloon.*

DETECTIVE CHIEF INSPECTOR ALEXANDER MONROE WAS TIRED, but he didn't want to sleep, scratching at his short, white beard as he stared at his laptop screen, trying to will the words on it to stop swirling around the display as he tried to type. Earlier that day they had drugged him while in Birmingham; a nasty little bugger named Gamma Hydroxy butyric

Acid, better known as Liquid Ecstasy on the club scene, given to him by an equally nasty little bugger, the corrupt police officer Detective Inspector White, shortly before White himself had been killed like a dog in the street by Birmingham gangsters. Monroe had woken up in a basement in Beachampton, rescued by his *own* Detective Inspector, Declan Walsh. After wrapping up the case with the help of a large amount of bravado, bluff and a simunition grenade, Monroe was checked over by the Divisional Surgeon, Doctor Rosanna Marcos, who had fussed over him like a bloody mother hen before allowing his team to take him back to the office. He'd sent everyone else home, saying he just wanted to finish up before leaving, but the fact of the matter was that Monroe didn't want to go home. He didn't feel safe anywhere outside of his own office right now.

Also, when he closed his eyes, he had a fear, an irrational one, that he would wake up like last time.

Handcuffed and gagged in a basement.

So, Monroe had started this letter, trying to take his mind off the gnawing terror in the pit of his stomach. He'd already tried napping on the office sofa to see if that helped; it didn't.

However, the sound of someone walking up the stairs into the primary office stopped him.

Rising from his desk, he walked into the open-plan office, watching the door. Nobody was due back, and the steps were heavy. A man's shoes.

The man with the rimless glasses emerged through the entrance into the room, stopping when he saw Monroe watching him. Middle-aged with short, dark-brown hair, the man with the rimless glasses looked more like an accountant than an assassin.

'I know you,' Monroe intoned. 'We arrested you in Devington Hall.'

The man with the rimless glasses nodded, sauntering towards Monroe. He also knew that Monroe had been spiked earlier that day; he was relying on this to slow the old man's reactions, to make him an easier target to take down. Monroe however hadn't finished, still trying to clear his fuddled brain.

'You're the one that attacked Declan outside his apartment,' he continued. The man with the rimless glasses nodded once more, still continuing towards Monroe. He jerked his right wrist, and a vicious looking extendable baton flicked out.

'If this means anything to you, it's nothing personal,' he said as he raised it.

Alexander Monroe nodded, already realising that he wasn't fast enough to stop this attack, especially with the remnants of the GHB still in his system.

'So this is how it ends, eh laddie?' he asked calmly. The man with the rimless glasses thought for a moment, considering Monroe's last words.

'Yeah, pretty much,' he said.

Then he struck.

1

NEW BEGINNINGS

DECLAN HADN'T MEANT TO STAY THE NIGHT.

The whole evening had started off innocently. Fresh from Beachampton, having solved the case and completed the arrests of the people involved, Declan had sent Kendis a text, saying that he wanted to see her. This was, of course, only after she'd texted him, saying that she believed that her future wasn't with her husband, Peter.

This *wasn't* an affair.

Was it?

Declan laid in Kendis's marital bed, staring up at the ceiling. They'd intended to share a celebratory drink, nothing more. Declan had promised to keep Kendis in the loop, to give her the exclusive story, and that's how the evening had begun. Kendis had suggested a Chelsea pub, and they'd met there around eight. But, as the evening progressed, they'd drunk more, reminiscing about their past and toasting people like Patrick Walsh, Declan's late father, who had been working with Kendis on his memoirs before he died. That had led to more toasts, and then a conversation where Kendis had informed Declan conspiratorially that Peter wasn't at home that night, that he was in a conference in Hull for the next day or so.

Things weren't supposed to progress this fast.

But progress they did, and by midnight Declan and Kendis were back at her house, pulling off their clothes, as they pawed at each other like the teenagers they had been the last time they had been this intimate.

It was only afterwards that Kendis had mentioned that she hadn't yet discussed her problems with Pete, and that this evening was something that even she hadn't expected to happen.

This *was* an affair.

Declan was angry at himself. Earlier that same week he'd expressed jealousy at Lizzie, his estranged ex-wife, going on a date with another man. She hadn't even gone on it yet, and he was jealous. How would he have reacted if this had been the other way around, and that she had slept with someone?

He glanced over to Kendis, still asleep in the bed next to him, her bare, dark-skinned shoulder visible under a mass of curly black hair. She was facing away and breathing heavily in her sleep, seemingly a lot more comfortable about this than he was right now.

He couldn't help it; he smiled. Kendis had always been the one that had got away, and that there was a chance, no matter how small, that he could regain something believed lost made him excited, and gave him butterflies. But he knew that this had to build with time. *This was too fast.* However, what was worse, if it came out that they had slept together before Kendis and Peter filed for divorce, this would give Peter a far greater advantage in any court proceedings.

He was an idiot for doing this.

His phone, currently in his trouser pocket halfway across the room vibrated, the faint buzzing audible in the quiet morning. Declan looked to the clock beside the bed; it wasn't even six in the morning. Calls before six were never good.

Climbing carefully out of the bed so as not to awaken Kendis, Declan pulled on his boxers and knelt beside the trousers, pulling out the phone. It was Anjli, but it had already gone to voicemail. Now awake, he pulled on his shirt and socks, hearing the faint ding of a message on his phone, informing him he had a new voicemail. Connecting to it, Declan sat on the floor of the bedroom for a long minute as he silently listened.

It was another minute before he disconnected the call and texted one simple line back.

On my way

This done, he looked back to Kendis, still asleep. He couldn't wake her with this news; he'd explain later. Having pulled on his trousers, he made his way out of the bedroom carefully, closing the door silently behind him, gathering his discarded clothing, often entangled with items that had been discarded by Kendis and pulling them on as he paused by the front door.

There was a photo on the side cabinet, one of Kendis and Peter at some event. Maybe their wedding, or some kind of gala. They looked happy. Looking back up the stairs, Declan wondered what right he had to stop this, to end this happiness. Who could tell if Kendis wouldn't change her mind? That she'd stay with Peter and class Declan as a simple one-night stand?

Shaking off the thought, Declan emerged from the house

into the cool morning air. It was just gone six in the morning now; the street was still empty, the morning rush hour having not yet started in Putney. However, as he started down the path towards the street, an elderly woman was walking towards the house next door. She was small and frail, a mop of white hair under a scarf worn over a purple coat, and in her hand was both a bottle of milk and a newspaper. Declan assumed that she'd been to the corner shop early, perhaps to pick up supplies for her morning tea or coffee, and now she looked blearily up at Declan as he passed.

'Morning, Pete,' she said before continuing with, 'ooh, sorry.'

'I'm his cousin,' Declan lied quickly with a smile. 'Had a bit too much. Stayed the night.' He didn't stop, but carried on past her, hoping that she wasn't so close to Kendis's husband that she'd mention *the strange man that came out of his house at six am*. The woman seemed to accept this story, however, continuing into her house without a second glance. She didn't watch Declan stand on the street, confused where his car was until seeing it a few yards away, realising that he must have driven back to Putney well over the legal limit.

He didn't look back to her, either.

Which was a shame, as if he had, he might have looked up at the bedroom window, seeing Kendis Taylor, wrapped only in the duvet, staring down at him.

THE DRIVE FROM PUTNEY TO THE ROYAL LONDON HOSPITAL IN Whitechapel was just under ten miles, mainly along the Battersea Park Road, following the Thames eastwards through Battersea, Vauxhall and Kennington, circling the annoying roundabout that enclosed the Elephant and Castle Shopping Centre before heading north across Tower Bridge and connecting to Commercial Road. In a normal car, driving at rush hour, you could expect to do this in just under an hour; with the lights and siren on, Declan was there in twenty-five minutes.

Pulling up outside the main entrance with a squeal of braking tyres that most likely woke the whole neighbourhood, Declan ran from the Audi without locking it, sprinting towards the modern-looking, red-brick and glass building, continuing through the glass-doored main entrance, waving his warrant card at anyone who looked official.

'Where's the ICU?' he yelled at practically everyone as he paused in the reception area, a wide expanse of glass and marble that, with its high glass ceiling, felt more like an airport terminal than a medical institution. Although many were confused by this strange, bedraggled man in half-dressed clothes, his shirt undone and his tie hanging loosely around his neck, eventually he was pointed down a corridor and towards some elevators, informed that here, the Intensive Care Unit was the *Adult Critical Care Unit*, and was on the fourth floor of the South Tower, which involved Declan crossing the Stepney Road and heading for a place known as *Lift Core 5*, whatever that meant.

Eventually finding it and taking the time to reassess himself while waiting for the elevator to reach the fourth floor, Declan tried his best to smooth down his ruffled brown hair while straightening his tie. But, as the doors opened, he put his sartorial needs aside and emerged out of the elevator. Finding himself in a shared waiting area, he followed through a door to the right that led into a bridge corridor, the windows that showed the outside world ignored by Declan as he continued at speed through a set of double doors, now in a corridor with two options: one was to Ward 4E on the right, and on the opposite side, around a corner to the left was Ward 4F. Both were apparently ACCU wards. Luckily, there was a police officer, a young man no more than twenty, standing guard at the junction.

'Is he in here?' Declan asked. The officer nodded. He didn't have to ask who Declan meant; he wasn't the first person to come running up and ask the same question that morning. Declan showed his warrant card for identification, and was pointed to the left, and Ward 4F.

The ACCU was filled with more officers and detectives than the average crime scene. There was a small sign on the wall beside Declan stating that there were twenty-two beds in this ward; four-bedded bays of four beds each, where privacy was nothing more than a screen around the bed, and six side rooms for single patients. The rooms to the sides were closed, the blinds down, but one room, a single patient room had the door open, a continual movement of officers and medical staff passing in and out. Declan took a breath in as he looked around; there was a sickly sweet, antiseptic smell that made him shudder with suppressed memories from his childhood. He'd always hated hospitals.

Standing outside the door, looking up as Declan arrived was DS Anjli Kapoor. She was also in a suit, her short black bob pulled back, but like Declan gave the impression of someone who'd dressed in a hurry.

'How is he?' Declan asked as he approached. Anjli looked back into the room for a moment before looking back to him.

'He's in a coma,' she replied. 'Bugger's lucky to be alive.'

'Do we know what happened?' Declan tried to look through the door but there were too many people in his way to gain a glance at the figure in the bed. Anjli pulled out her notebook, flipping it open.

'Doctor Marcos is going over the crime scene now, but it looks like someone or some *ones* came into the Crime Unit around ten pm last night. Monroe was the last person out, and it looks like that he emerged from his office to confront them, in the process being attacked.'

'He was the target?'

'No idea yet,' Anjli said, looking up from the notes. 'He had defensive wounds, but there was nothing that stated that he had been specifically hunted.' She looked back down to the paper, mainly to hide the fact that she was close to tears.

'Anyway, there was a fight, and he lost. Badly. Marcos said that the amount of GHB in his system would have slowed him right down; he wouldn't have had a chance. They slammed his head through one of the glass partitions, Declan. You know when you see someone go through a windscreen? Crime scene apparently looks like that. He lost so much blood that they must have thought he was dead, and they left before security arrived.'

She looked away now, trying to gather her emotions, but the main one, anger, was there in force.

'We took down two of the biggest gang leaders in the UK yesterday,' she said. 'We bloodied The Twins' noses too. Then, eight hours later Monroe's beaten almost to death. It can't be a coincidence.'

'Why was he still there?' Declan was angry too, angry that he hadn't stayed to ensure that Monroe was alright, angry that he'd left to meet up with what had turned into a one-night stand. Anjli shrugged.

'Probably didn't want to go right home,' she said. 'I mean,

when you're drugged and almost killed, you probably don't want to be in a place where it can weigh on you.'

'I need to see him,' Declan went to enter the room, but Anjli raised a hand to stop him.

'There's a Guv here that wants to see you first,' she said. 'Wanted to speak to the most superior officer on the team—' she frowned as a thought suddenly struck her.

'How did you get here so fast?' she interrupted herself. 'There's no way you made it here from Hurley in half an hour.'

'I was in the apartment in Tottenham,' Declan lied quickly. 'I give the keys back soon, so needed to check it out. Dozed off there.'

'That explains yesterday's clothes, then.' Anjli seemed content with this explanation and pointed over to a man in the middle of the ACCU corridor, currently talking to two assistants. He was tall, with short grey hair, whiter on the temples and had thin, black-rimmed glasses. Jacket-less, he wore the white shirt and black tie of a police officer, but the diamonds on his black epaulettes gave him the rank of Chief Superintendent. Looking up, he noticed Declan's gaze and waved him over.

'You DI Walsh?' he asked. Declan nodded.

'Yes, sir.'

'I'm Bradbury,' the officer continued, and Declan didn't need to ask anything more. Chief Superintendent David Bradbury controlled the City of London's police force. Effectively, he was Declan's boss's *boss's* boss. 'Terrible situation we have here.'

'Yes, sir,' Declan replied. 'We're ready to start on the case. Our divisional surgeon is already examining the crime scene, and we believe that—'

'Don't flim-flam me, Walsh,' Bradbury replied. 'You just got here. You don't know what your team believes.'

'With respect, sir, I know the team, and I trust their opinions,' Declan stated. 'We've solved crimes with less than we have right now.'

'But that's the problem,' Bradbury said, leading Declan to the side, away from the other officers. 'You don't yet know what you have here. I'm guessing you believe that it's connected to the gangs you put away yesterday?'

'That's a possibility, sir.' Declan was wondering what kind of conversation this really was. 'Unless you know of another?'

'I do, actually,' Bradbury nodded. 'How well do you know a reporter named Kendis Taylor?'

Declan paused for a moment, blindsided by the question. 'I, that is we, Monroe and I know her,' he replied. 'She grew up in my village.'

'You can vouch for her character then?' Bradbury enquired. Declan wanted to scream, to shout that *of course he did, he loved her,* but he stopped himself.

'I would prefer to answer that when I know what else you have here, sir.'

Bradbury nodded. 'Monroe was apparently working on a document when he was disturbed,' he explained. 'One that stated that there is a strong possibility that an extreme terrorist faction radicalised Kendis Taylor while in Syria for *The Guardian* newspaper.'

Declan wanted to laugh at this, but the dead-pan manner in which Chief Superintendent Bradbury had explained it stopped him. This was real. They genuinely believed that Kendis could have attacked Monroe.

Did she take Declan home with her to provide an alibi? Was this the reason she'd insisted so heavily on that pub?

No, he had to stop himself believing that this could even be remotely true.

'Where did the report come from, sir?' he asked, keeping his face void of emotion.

Bradbury shrugged. 'Your lad, the pretty one in the posh suit is looking into that,' he replied. 'But here's the problem, Walsh, and I know that you've already worked it out.'

'I'm not the right person to lead the team with Monroe out of action,' Declan whispered. 'First, I'm a Detective Inspector, while you need a higher rank. Second, I have a personal connection to one suspect. And third—'

'Third, your whole department is made up of cast-offs and screw-ups,' Bradbury stated. 'Without Monroe to vouch for you, there's a chance that Temple Inn, regardless of the outstanding work you've done so far, will be closed and the officers reassigned.'

Declan nodded, trying to stop the worry in his stomach from rising to his face. 'Do we know who'll be leading us, sir?' he asked.

'Jesus, Walsh, it's seven am,' Bradbury exclaimed. 'We only just learned about the attack. We'll decide today and the transferred DCI will make themselves known to you by tomorrow, I'm sure.'

'Yes, sir. Thank you, sir,' Declan replied woodenly. 'With your permission, until they do arrive, I'd like to continue our lines of enquiry.'

Bradbury nodded, already checking an iPad screen passed to him by an aide.

'I worked with Monroe,' Bradbury said. 'Strong, obstinate bugger. If anyone can survive this, it's him. Once that happens, then we can talk about the Unit's future.'

Declan nodded as Bradbury, surrounded by his aides and

assistants, walked away, most likely trying to work out how to spin this in the inevitable press conference. Declan looked over to Anjli and forced a smile, but there was no humour in it.

His mentor, his friend, had been critically injured in a baseless and cowardly attack by as yet persons unknown.

And Declan Walsh was going to find them.

2

CRIME SCENES

DOCTOR ROSANNA MARCOS AND DC JOANNA DAVEY WERE
hard at work when Declan arrived at the offices of the
Temple Inn Command Unit.

'Feet!' Doctor Marcos cried, throwing a small bag at
Declan as he walked through the door. Opening it, he pulled
out a pair of disposable shoe coverings. Placing them over his
own brogues, he pulled out a pair of disposable latex gloves
from a pack in his pocket, pulling them on as he continued
into his workplace.

The offices were modern for the building that they were
in: downstairs was a forensics lab with an examination table,
but the upstairs area was very much an open-plan situation,
set in rows of desks: seven with an eighth desk loaded with
printers. Three of the desks were where Declan, Anjli and
Billy Fitzwarren would sit, while the other desks sat empty
for the moment. There were three closed-off glass offices on
one end, each with solid walls dividing them. The first was
Monroe's office, currently being examined by PC Davey,
moving around the desk with what looked like an old-school

magnifying glass in her hand while Billy examined the laptop on the desk, his blue latex gloves irritably tapping on keys, while the middle was a briefing room with a plasma screen on one wall, and the third was a single desk with two chairs either side of it, utilised mainly as an interview room, although most of the interviews had been performed at other locations. All the rooms had ceiling to floor blinds on the glass that could open or close when needed, most of which were pulled down for privacy. However, in the middle of the interview room's glass frontage the blinds were broken, the damage most likely caused by the shattered hole in the middle of it.

The hole that Monroe's head had most likely gone through.

Declan stared at the hole, at the blood that pooled around the bottom. *What force was required to slam a human head through such glass?*

'Bastard,' muttered Doctor Marcos, staring down at the broken glass next to Declan. 'They just left him there.'

'Can you go through what you've worked out yet?' Declan asked.

Doctor Marcos nodded, pointing to Monroe's office. 'Alex was working in there,' she said. 'Something's happened to the laptop and Fitzwarren's trying to fix it, but I don't think that was anything to do with this. He was in his office when the bastard arrived.'

'That's the second time you've said that,' Declan commented.

'What, bastard? Because they were. A right royal one.'

'No, that you say it singular. *Bastard*, not *Bastards*. You don't think this was more than one person?'

Doctor Marcos shook her head. 'Even from a cursory

examination, I'm seeing one person, not two,' she said. 'Plus Alex would have been slow, still slightly drugged from earlier. Even Billy could have taken him.'

'I heard that,' Billy said, walking out of the office, Monroe's laptop in his hand.

'Oi!' Doctor Marcos snapped, seeing this. 'No moving things!'

'Come on, this isn't part of, well, this,' Billy replied as he waved his hand around the office. 'I need to work on it separately. Use some specific tools.'

'What's the problem?' Declan asked. Billy shrugged.

'Don't know yet, and I don't want to restart it until I do.' He looked down at the laptop. 'Bloody thing's frozen.'

Declan looked back to Doctor Marcos. 'So one man enters?'

'Guard claims he saw a man in an overcoat walk past late in the evening,' Doctor Marcos replied, glancing at him. 'Actually, he said that from the style of coat and the walk, he didn't really look up because he thought it was you.'

Declan looked surprised at this.

'I didn't come back after Beachampton,' he admitted. 'I ...' he paused, only a momentary one, but enough to throw a stutter into his reply. 'I went home.'

If Doctor Marcos picked up on this, she didn't respond, already walking to the main entranceway.

'The bastard entered the office and DCI Monroe emerged to confront him,' she explained, and Declan noted the more formal way she named Monroe now, as now all business, she forensically went through the events. 'I think Monroe knew his attacker. He had enough time to run, or to call for help. He could have moved back into his office and barricaded the door, but he didn't.'

'The drugs in his system?'

'Maybe. But I don't think so.' Doctor Marcos shook her head. 'I genuinely think he was surprised at this arrival, but not threatened.'

'He's Glaswegian,' Billy suggested. 'He doesn't do well with threats.'

'Anyway, he's facing, well, whoever it is, and then he's struck.' Doctor Marcos showed her forearms. 'We have several welts on his arms, around here, as if he's thrown them up to block a strike from some kind of baton, or staff.' She pointed over to a spare desk, the sheets of paper that were on it scattered to the floor. 'He's then grabbed and thrown over that table. At this point they strike his face badly, and he bleeds from the lip and nose.'

Declan was angering more now as he listened. 'And then?'

'Then he looks to attack his assailant with a keyboard,' Doctor Marcos pointed to a broken one on the floor, a marker next to it. 'It's blocked but effective. The attacker loses ground. I think Monroe went to run at this point but was tripped, and fell over there.' She pointed to the floor by the broken glass. 'We have a small amount of trace blood there, and then I think the noise gains attention. Our attacker knows they don't have long. They grab Monroe and physically slam his head into the glass window.'

'Then it breaks?'

'Christ, no,' Doctor Marcos shook her head, kneeling beside the impacted glass. 'This is impact resistant. He slammed the poor bugger's head into the glass three, maybe four times until it shattered.'

She stood up.

'Guard said he heard glass smashing and ran to see what it was. Thought it was an external window, it was so loud.

The attacker would have known that his time was up. His target was, for all intents and purposes, dead. When they found Monroe, he was in a pool of blood. It must have looked horrific. Job done, our attacker leaves. Moments later, the guard arrives, calls an ambulance.'

'Any idea how the attacker got out?' Declan was already pacing the scene, trying to work out in his mind the battle that Doctor Marcos had just described. She rubbed at her chin as she considered this.

'Probably waited downstairs in the examination room until the guard passed and then slipped out,' she suggested. 'We're looking for CCTV that could help us.'

Declan looked to Billy. 'What's frozen on the screen?' he asked.

Silently, Billy opened the laptop. On the screen Declan saw an image of Kendis Taylor, taken on a zoom lens camera, walking down a street and on the phone.

'It says that while in Syria for *The Guardian* she was radicalised by an extreme terrorist faction,' he explained. 'But there's no proof. Just conjecture. It says they believe she has a UK handler, but doesn't mention his or her name or where they're based.'

'What's the rest of it say?' Declan stared at the screen. 'It looks like there's more on page two?'

'That's the problem,' Billy closed the laptop back up. 'The laptop is frozen. It looks like it was sent to Monroe but by who, how, or even when I don't know.'

'You don't want to restart it because?'

Billy made a face at this. 'Everyone always goes "turn it off and on" as if that's a magical answer, but if I turn this off, we might lose this file. I don't know what server it was on, or where he downloaded it from. I'd rather see if I can back up the hard drive first.'

'Kendis isn't a terrorist.' Declan spoke it as a statement. Billy shrugged.

'Someone seems to think so, and whether she was or wasn't, she was being watched.'

'She *wasn't*,' Declan insisted again, more forcefully this time. Billy quietly nodded and walked over to his desk, pulling out a USB drive and slamming it into the side of the laptop with a little more force than was usually required.

'You're not the only one pissed at this,' Doctor Marcos said. 'We're all angry.'

Declan nodded. 'I know,' he said. 'I just … the thing here with Kendis, it seems off somehow.'

'Then prove it,' Doctor Marcos walked off now. 'Don't just shout it at people.'

Declan stood alone now, staring around the office. There was nothing he could do here; perhaps he could check into the external CCTV, see if there was anything that he could find.

His phone buzzed. He hadn't realised that he'd placed it on silent, and he pulled it out. There were three unread messages on it, all from Kendis over the last hour.

> We need to talk

> Call me when you get this

> Dammit this is important you dick

Looking back to Billy, still working on the laptop, the image of Kendis still visible, Declan looked back to the phone. He didn't want to call Kendis in the middle of this. He needed to convince himself that she wasn't a part of it, even in some small way. Even though he'd known her all of his life, there had been a good decade where the two of them hadn't spoken. Hell, he'd only called her after his father died because she'd been working with him.

No. Kendis wasn't a terrorist, no matter what anyone said.

There was movement from the entranceway, and Declan turned to see Will Harrison, the special advisor to Charles Baker, enter the room. Overweight as ever, Harrison was in his early thirties, his hair cut short at the side, maybe a number two razor setting even, and left long on top in that 'Peaky Blinder' style that seemed trendy with people half his age. It was a style that didn't match his shape of head or body and didn't really match with his expensive charcoal-grey suit. He was sweating, probably from the effort of walking up the stairs, and obviously didn't want to be here, paling at the sight of Monroe's blood. Seeing Declan however gave him purpose and shaking off whatever trepidations he had, he started striding over.

'Oi! Shoes!' Doctor Marcos yelled, and Harrison immediately stopped, as if realising the floor was lava and that he was on a small island. To ease the tension of the moment, Declan walked to him.

'Mister Harrison,' he said cordially. 'What brings you here?'

'Charles Baker is in his car out front,' Will Harrison replied, slowly backing back out of the office, his eyes on Doctor Marcos, glaring at him beside the broken glass. 'He asked to speak to you.'

'Then he can come in and speak to me.'

'He can't,' Harrison replied. 'He's a backbencher now. He can't really be seen here before a Minister for State appears.'

Declan sighed. He understood a little of how the Government worked, and things like this, the bureaucracy issues, annoyed the hell out of him.

'Fine,' he said, indicating the doorway. 'Let's go chat to Charlie.'

OUTSIDE IN THE CAR PARK, DECLAN SAW THE MINISTERIAL CAR waiting, the driver emerging as he saw Will Harrison exit the building. The driver opened the back door and Charles Baker climbed out, straightening his jacket as Declan approached.

'Detective Inspector Walsh,' he said, offering his hand.

Declan took it, shaking it. 'Charles,' he replied.

If Charles was irritated at the informality of Declan, he didn't show it, staring instead at the building behind him.

'Terrible thing,' he said. 'Do you have a suspect yet?'

'We're still examining the scene, and you know we can't discuss ongoing investigations with members of the public.' Declan noted a small wince when he said this; Charles Baker might have the staff and the car, but he was still a simple MP these days.

'I'm here as a friend,' Charles insisted. 'Your team saved my life a few weeks back. I want to help.'

'And it's appreciated,' Declan replied. He didn't like or even trust Charles Baker, and the last thing he wanted right now was to be in the man's debt.

'Have you seen Kendis Taylor recently?' Charles continued. Declan paused before replying.

'Why would you ask that?' he asked carefully.

Charles shrugged. 'Oh, I don't know,' he smiled. 'Maybe

because you were childhood sweethearts, maybe because she worked with your father, or maybe because you gave her the story of when I was saved on the roof of Devington House.'

'I didn't give her anything,' Declan lied. 'She had been working on a piece on Andy Mac, if I recall.'

'A piece that not only used my son as bait, but resulted in his death.'

'I don't think anyone knew he was your son at that point,' Declan replied. 'Yourself included.'

Charles nodded, conceding the point. 'I'm just saying that you need to be wary around her,' he said. 'Speaking as a friend.'

'Oh, we're friends now?' Declan smiled. 'What do you know that I don't?'

Charles looked around the courtyard as if considering what to say.

'It's nothing but conjecture, but I've seen things,' he said. 'Reports ... and she visited Donna.'

'Your wife? Why?'

Charles shrugged. 'I genuinely don't know,' he replied. 'All I know is that she spoke to Donna and then, within a few hours Donna hanged herself.'

Declan went to say something, to state that Donna's suicide wasn't connected to Kendis, but then stopped. *He didn't know this.* But, before he could continue, he saw a group of reporters and news teams enter Temple Inn from the Tudor Street entrance, all making a beeline towards Declan and Charles.

Now Declan understood why Charles Baker hadn't entered the crime scene.

It was contained. It was controlled.

More importantly, you couldn't do a press conference there.

'Mister Baker!' One reporter, his cameraman behind him, almost ran at them, microphone in hand. 'Is it true that you've called for the police to have more support from Parliament? That you've asked for private firms like *Rattlestone* to gain more powers?'

Will Harrison moved forward, blocking the reporters.

'I'm sorry, but this is a personal visit, and we'd prefer some privacy. This is also an active crime scene, so please give us space.'

'Why are you here, Mister Baker?' another reporter shouted.

Again, Will spoke for Charles. 'Mister Baker is visiting with friends,' he said. 'As you know, the Temple Inn Crime Unit saved his life a few weeks ago, and now with the cowardly attack on one of their own by suspected terrorists, he's come to give support.'

'With that we must leave,' Charles said, looking to Declan. 'I'm sorry. I didn't mean to bring the circus to town.'

'I almost believe that,' Declan replied.

As Charles and Will climbed into the car and drove off, the reporters seemed to dissipate, a single police detective not as exciting as the possible next Prime Minister on a joyride, and one glance at Declan's furious expression was enough to ensure they kept away. Left alone, Declan turned to return to the Crime Unit, but was bumped into by a reporter as they passed. Looking up, watching them walk away, he realised it was Kendis, tapping into a phone. He moved to follow her, to call after her, but a vibration in his jacket pocket stopped him.

That wasn't where his phone was.

Reaching into the pocket, he pulled out a small, cheap burner phone, obviously planted there during the bump. On it was one message.

> In danger. Need to meet. Keep this on. Text you place.

Staring in confusion at Kendis, now walking out with the other reporters through the Tudor Road gate, Declan scratched at his head. His boss was critically ill, his one-time girlfriend, who he'd recently slept with was now believed to be a terrorist who was apparently in danger, and Charles Baker was telling everyone that they were friends.

Ignoring the calls of the last reporters, Declan walked back into the Temple Inn Crime Unit, pulling off the plastic booties. He'd need new ones now he'd been outside.

Also, the last thing he wanted was Doctor Marcos shouting at him again.

————

3

VISITING HOURS

IT TOOK ANOTHER HOUR FOR BILLY TO GET MONROE'S LAPTOP working again; and when he did, the document was no longer there.

'Maybe we can at least learn where it came from?' Declan asked from his own desk, where he was currently working through the Temple Inn CCTV files to no avail. 'Was it emailed? Did he find it on the internal network?'

'There's nothing on any internal networks,' Billy leaned back in his chair, staring at the ceiling in frustration. Doctor Marcos had allowed them to sit at their desks once more, as long as they promised not to move around too much. 'I've searched everywhere. If that document was real, then it was created by someone outside of the police.' He stared at his own laptop where an image of Monroe's screen, a screenshot from before the document had disappeared, was displayed. The image of Kendis, walking and taken from a distance was visible.

'You think it could have been MI5? Or worse?' Declan asked. Billy made a noncommittal face as he shrugged.

'They'd be my first guess. Or maybe it's another agency. An external one, or someone private. Another country, Interpol perhaps?'

'This is an old school friend,' Declan muttered, omitting the recent change in developments. 'I can't believe she's some kind of terrorist sleeper.'

'She's also a journalist who tried to take down ex-politicians, and was the first to contact you about Derek Salmon murdering Angela Martin,' Billy replied. 'She seemed remarkably well connected.'

'Says the guy who had a breakfast meeting with a source who stated that Baker's office was targeting us,' Declan added.

Billy nodded. 'True,' he replied. 'But then I don't trust my source as far as I can throw them. How much do you trust yours?'

Declan went to reply but then stopped. Billy was right. How much did he know about Kendis, other than that she was having a bad time with Peter? Was that even true? Had Declan been an alibi for the night before?

'Okay, let's look at this,' Declan continued. 'Kendis is a terrorist. Let's just say that for the moment. She's being watched. Monroe has a dossier on her on his laptop when he's attacked. Why does he have this and why does she want him killed?'

Billy stretched. 'No idea,' he admitted. 'But let's be honest, he was never a fan of hers. I heard him shout *Kendis bloody Taylor* at you on multiple occasions.'

'You think he might have been doing his own, off the books investigation?' Declan looked over to the office.

'Makes sense,' Billy said. 'As I said, this could be some kind of private security company's dossier. There's a watermark I can't quite make out, but that could give us an idea. Monroe may have ...' he trailed off as he examined the screenshot.

'Yeah,' he said. 'This could have been a private security file. That would explain why nobody has it.'

'Can you get that off a photo on a screen?'

Billy smiled. 'I've done more with less,' he said. 'The watermark uses a particular font. That gives me a comparison search. Give me an hour. Let me see what I can work out.'

Declan looked to his watch. It was almost lunchtime. 'I should go back to the hospital, check up on Monroe and Anjli,' he said.

'Is she still guarding him?' Billy was already typing on his laptop as he spoke.

'Wouldn't you?' Declan rose from the chair. Billy turned to face him.

'For what it's worth, I don't think that Kendis is a terrorist,' he said. 'However, Monroe was looking at her file, so there's a fair chance that she's involved somehow. Be careful.'

Declan nodded, very aware of the burner phone in his pocket. It was the second burner phone he'd had in as many days.

He hoped it wouldn't become a habit.

BY THE TIME DECLAN ARRIVED BACK AT THE ACCU UNIT AT The Royal London Hospital, this time using the far easier entrance on Stepney Way, normality seemed to have returned, with the multitude of police that were there earlier now visible by their absence. Even Chief Superintendent

Bradbury and his entourage were missing. Anjli was still there though, sitting on a chair in Monroe's side room, alone, and seemingly asleep.

She jerked awake when Declan walked into the room. He waved her back down and passed her a coffee he'd picked up downstairs.

'Any change?' he looked at Monroe, still unconscious as Anjli shook her head.

'He's in a coma,' she replied. 'Something about blood on the brain and pressure and hell, Declan, I've got no bloody clue what they were talking about. All I know is that he's got a fifty-fifty chance of dying right now.'

'Why don't you go home, freshen up?' Declan asked. 'I can take on guard duty for a while.'

'You need to be finding his attacker,' Anjli sipped at the coffee.

'We'll both find the attacker,' Declan suggested. 'Billy's already in the laptop and Marcos is examining every inch of floor. Currently, our prime suspect is a single male who looks like me. Height and clothing wise, at least.'

'So a badly dressed divorcee,' Anjli forced a smile. 'That could be anyone in London.'

They sat in silence for a moment.

'When they called me yesterday, when Monroe was found missing in Birmingham, I thought he was dead for sure,' she eventually said. 'When Billy and me ... when we drove to Beachampton, I was already writing his eulogy out in my head, and then he was fine.'

She looked at the bed.

'He wasn't supposed to do this,' she muttered.

'He means a lot to you, doesn't he?' Declan asked. 'I mean, I knew him all my life thanks to Dad, but you ...'

'He met me when I was in Hendon,' Anjli whispered. 'Like a thousand years ago. I didn't remember it at all, but he reminded me of this when he took me in.' She took another sip. 'After Mile End, I thought I was gone for good. I mean, I know I worked for DCI Ford and she was crooked as shit, but she played the game, you know? By the book.'

Declan took a sip from his own coffee. 'I don't want to ask, but Monroe never told me why you ended up in the Last Chance Saloon.' He tried to plan his words carefully. 'Was it The Twins?'

Anjli froze as the coffee cup moved towards her mouth. The previous day, she'd finally admitted to Declan that she was in debt to Johnny and Jackie Lucas, the "Twins" of East London, and in doing so had passed on information on Declan to them. Unlike DCI Ford though, who Declan had learned was in their thrall because of gambling addictions, Anjli had needed help with her mother's breast cancer treatment. That she had offered to resign because of this had stopped Declan reporting her. There was more mileage in keeping her as a double agent.

'Mariella Hudson,' she replied. 'Married woman, two kids, prick of a husband. He'd been beating on her, but he worked for some mechanic who knew The Twins, so we weren't allowed to do anything. Orders from on high and all that.'

'Ford?'

'Yeah. Anyway, one day Mariella turns up in hospital. *Fell down the stairs*, she says. But they live in a ground-floor flat. I sniff around.'

'Bet that went down well.'

'That wasn't what did it,' Anjli actually chuckled at this. 'I found out that she'd been beaten half to death by the prick for burning his sausages. His sausages, for God's sake. So I popped over and kicked the living shit out of him. Claimed I was taking him in but he resisted arrest, and I broke his collarbone in two places.'

'So, that's why they kicked you out?'

'That's why they kicked me out,' Anjli nodded. 'God, Ford was livid. She wanted me gone. Fired. Out. The Twins were getting shit, so *she* was getting shit. Anyway, it goes up the chain and then a week later I get a call from Monroe. We meet, he reminds me we met at Hendon and he asks me why I did what I did. I answered honestly.'

She looked to the bed, a faint half-smile on her face.

'Next day he requested my transfer. Best boss I've ever had,' she said. 'He gives me space, you know? He allows me to make my own mistakes and, in doing that, I make my own successes.'

Declan nodded. 'Yeah, he's good at that,' he replied. Sighing, he leaned back in his chair.

'He'd better get better soon,' he muttered. 'This is going to be a sod of a case to solve without a witness.'

'You think Kendis was involved?' Anjli asked, warily watching Declan. He shook his head.

'If she was, she wasn't there to see it,' he admitted. 'She ... she was with me.'

'Until when, though?' Anjli was already running the incident's timing through her head. 'I mean, if he—'

'All night,' Declan interrupted. 'She was with me all night.'

There was a long, uncomfortable silence.

'Isn't she married?' Anjli eventually asked. Declan nodded again.

'It was an accident,' he sighed. 'We were drunk.'

Anjli considered this. 'We were, or you were?'

'What's the difference?'

'*We* implies that both of you had been drinking. But if she was more sober, then she could have let you drink until you passed out, and then left you. Unless you remember the entire night?'

Declan shook his head. 'No.'

Then he shook his head again, more vehemently.

'No.'

'I get it,' Anjli steepled her fingers in front of her chin as she continued. 'You don't want to think this. But why did Monroe have her file on his laptop?'

Declan couldn't answer the question. Silently, he looked back to Monroe, the tubes and wires in his arms making him look like some kind of bed-ridden cyborg.

'Don't make me choose,' he said as his phone buzzed. Pulling it out, he glanced at the name on the screen.

'It's Jess,' he said as he rose to take the call. 'Back in a minute.'

Walking into the central area of the ACCU, Declan answered the phone call as he walked to the exit at the end, away from the main entrance to Ward 4F and through a pair of heavy, grey double doors that led into a junction corridor and a stairway. 'Everything okay?'

'We saw you on the news, Dad,' Jessica Walsh's excited voice spoke down the line. 'People at school think you're a rockstar right now.'

'That's why you phoned me?' Declan almost laughed at this. 'To tell me I'm suddenly your cool dad?'

'I didn't go that far,' Jess laughed. 'But I wanted to call because I saw about Mister Monroe. Is he okay?'

Declan looked through the windows in the doors, back

into the ACCU. 'Not really, but he's a fighter,' he said. 'He'll be okay. I'm sure of it.'

'Was it because of the book?' Jess continued. She'd been helping Declan try to solve the murder of his father, her grandfather, and in the process she had not only worked on Declan's crime board, but had also read Patrick Walsh's likely edited memoirs.

'I don't think so,' Declan replied. 'But as soon as I know, I'll come back to you. Love you.'

Disconnecting the call, Declan thought for a moment, standing alone in a hospital stairwell. Could this have been The Twins? Could The Seven Sisters have pushed for revenge? More importantly, was there someone else from Monroe's past, someone who was in Patrick's book that could have arrived late in the evening and taken down the already tired and battered DCI?

There was a vibration in his pocket, and Declan pulled out the other phone, the one he'd gained from Kendis earlier. It had received a single message.

> Brompton Cemetery N entrance 3pm. Don't drive. Avoid CCTV. Don't be recognised.

Declan stared at the message in confusion. He could understand Kendis being annoyed at him for stepping out that morning without saying goodbye, but this was becoming more and more suspicious by the second.

Putting the phone back into his pocket, he forced a smile before re-entering Ward 4F. He could spend a little more time with Monroe before he started playing spies with his possible-terrorist, newspaper journalist mistress. Anjli, however, was already grabbing her coat.

'Everything okay?' she asked. Declan forced a smile.

'She saw me on the news,' he replied. 'Suddenly I'm the cool one.'

Anjli shook her head. 'It's hard to believe that twenty-four hours ago we were bringing down crime syndicates,' she laughed. The laughter stopped though when she stared back into the side room, and the unconscious Alexander Monroe.

'You sure you can stay?' she asked. 'It's just that I could do with a shower.'

Declan nodded. 'If I need to go anywhere, I'll call a uniform in,' he said. 'I'll catch you later.'

As Anjli walked out of the ward, Declan wandered into the side room, sitting beside the unconscious Monroe. His head was bandaged, most likely from when it had been slammed through the glass, and a wicked-looking black eye was already forming around his left orbital bone. Declan couldn't help it; he laughed.

'You've never looked more Glaswegian, boss,' he said as he picked up his lukewarm coffee from the floor beside the chair and sipped at it.

He would deal with Kendis later.

4

WALKING THE DEAD

DECLAN HAD TAKEN THE MESSAGE THAT KENDIS HAD SENT HIM to heart; he understood why she didn't want him to use the Audi as it would have had a tracker installed in it, as per all police cars. Which meant that if he'd driven to Brompton, there would have been a record of the journey. What he couldn't understand was why she needed to have Declan do this off the grid, avoiding CCTV and in disguise. He guessed that this was possibly to do with ensuring that Peter didn't find out somehow, although he didn't know how that could ever happen. So, he dutifully waited in the ward room with Monroe until two pm, called in a uniform to take over his shift and made his way out of the Royal London Hospital through the basement exit, passing through the staff changing rooms and the locker areas; doctors and nurses needed a place to change out of dirty scrubs, after all. Here he acquired a pair of cheap looking aviator glasses and a baseball cap for some American team out of open lockers as he passed through; he felt bad for taking them, but had ensured he took nothing that looked expensive. Eventually, stopping at his car and swapping his coat, jacket and tie for a pale-grey hoodie and a black bomber jacket that he'd found on the back seat when he'd inherited the car on his first day, adding the baseball cap and the stolen sunglasses, now covering the top half of his face.

He felt a buzzing in his pocket and pulled out his phone; it was a message from Billy. Apparently the fonts on the watermarked file matched ones used by private security companies Hamilton Securities, Dowson and Rattlestone. Firing off a reply of thanks, he left his phone in the car's boot, locking the vehicle before he made his way out of the car park and north to Whitechapel Underground Station.

Once there, and paying for a Travelcard by cash from the machine, Declan found he was warming to this *spy* nonsense. He didn't look up at any cameras, keeping his head and cap down and his hands in his pockets. He could have been anyone. He was everyone.

It took over thirty minutes to get to Earls Court, and from there it was a half-mile walk down to Brompton Cemetery, arriving just shy of three pm. Stopping at the North entrance, he took a moment to look around, pulling the hoodie up around his neck. Kendis wasn't anywhere to be seen.

Declan had never been to Brompton Cemetery before; it was very much a *Chelsea* place. Even both the founder and the first manager of Chelsea Football Club were buried here, among a multitude of equally famous people. Declan didn't know who, and the sign beside him didn't give any more light on the situation, instead informing him only that Brompton Cemetery was the burial home for over two-hundred thousand people, with over thirty-five thousand gravestones and monuments held within. Doing the maths here, Declan already knew that there were therefore a lot of unmarked graves within the walls. Tens of thousands of unmarked graves, most likely common people who'd been buried on top of each other, the coffins piled high, their names never shown.

He didn't know why, but the simple thought of this, to be buried in an unmarked grave terrified him.

As he idly read about a volunteer organisation called the *Friends of Brompton Cemetery,* there was a buzz in his pocket. Pulling out the burner phone, he read the message that had just arrived.

> Passing you in a moment. Count to twenty then follow.

Looking up, Declan saw Kendis walking towards him from the left, most likely from West Brompton Station. If she recognised him she gave no sign, strolling casually past Declan and through the narrow, high arch of the stone gatehouse that provided entrance to the cemetery. Declan placed the phone back into his pocket and slowly counted to twenty. He'd reached fifteen before he decided that he'd had enough. There was nobody following her, and he was tiring of the cloak and dagger games. Heading through the arch, he found himself in the cemetery itself; a long, south-facing, tree-lined tarmac avenue was laid out in front of him, with mausoleums and gravestones on either side. There were paths off to the east and west, likely to other areas of the cemetery, but his target was continuing down the primary route, and so Declan started following, speeding up his pace to catch up with Kendis.

He knew from the map at the entrance that this was The Avenue, and led to a more public area known as The Grand Circle, but he didn't expect Kendis to stay in the public areas. When they reached the first crossroads, she turned left, heading eastwards towards the older graves. Declan hurried to catch up with her, and caught up beside a tall, broken-down mausoleum on the right-hand side of the path.

'You look stupid,' she said as a hello. Taking off the aviator glasses, Declan shrugged.

'You made a point about not looking recognisable,' he replied. 'Can you honestly say you would have picked me out if I hadn't been meeting you?'

'Fair point,' Kendis glanced around to ensure that they were alone. 'I needed to speak to you, and it had to be somewhere private.'

'A cemetery was your first choice? Not really a place for a political reporter to hang out.'

Kendis looked around the cemetery. 'Don't belittle the dead,' she smiled. 'Some of Westminster's biggest and brightest have plots here.' She pointed to a square, stone mausoleum across the path, about fifty yards away and under an overhanging tree branch. 'That's the one for the Gladwells. Over there is the Harrison family.'

'As in Baker's adviser? Didn't realise he came from money.'

'They all come from money, Declan,' Kendis replied sadly. 'Even the ones that claim that they don't.'

Declan passed her back the burner phone. 'Here, next time just call me on my normal one, yeah?'

'It's not that easy,' Kendis replied as she wiped the phone down before placing it in her pocket.

'Look, if this is about this morning—' Declan started, but stopped when Kendis raised her hand.

'What? You mean when you snuck out of my bedroom

like a sodding burglar?' she asked. 'Don't flatter yourself. There's more to life than you, Declan.'

'I didn't want to wake you,' Declan continued. 'I had the call about Monroe.'

'I know,' Kendis wearily leaned against a stone cross as she pulled out a cigarette, lighting it. 'Just like I know that if you *had* spoken to me, we'd probably have had some talk about how we were moving too fast or similar.'

'We are,' Declan insisted. 'Christ, Kendis. Have you even told Peter you want a divorce?'

'I told you last night that I'd broached it with him,' Kendis snapped. Declan frowned. He couldn't remember the conversation.

How drunk had he been?

'Look,' Kendis was looking around the cemetery again as she spoke. 'As great as it is to see you, this is bigger. I had something posted through my letterbox this morning.' She pulled out a piece of paper, passing it to Declan. Opening it up, he read a sheet of Arabic writing.

'I can't read this.'

Kendis took it from him, glancing at it as she did so. 'I can,' she said. 'I learned the lingo while abroad. I'm not fluent, but I know enough to see the gist of things, and Google Translate is amazing for filling in the gaps.'

'And the gist here is?'

'This is a letter telling me it's time to see the Prophet, that it's time to strike at the infidels.'

'It's a martyr's call to action?' Declan stepped back from Kendis. 'Christ, are you really one of them?'

Declan saw Kendis's face pale as he spoke.

'How could you think that?' she asked.

'Monroe had your file on his screen when he was

attacked,' Declan explained. 'It stated a whole load of things about you, mainly during your time in Syria.' He paused, almost unable to continue. 'It said that they radicalised you.'

'What?' This stunned Kendis. 'And you believe that?'

'Of course not!' Declan snapped back. 'But then you show me Arabic calls to martyrdom sent to you, while having a secret meeting in a graveyard!'

Kendis thought for a moment, then, slowly, she nodded.

'I can see that,' she whispered. 'But it's not true. I'm in trouble, Declan. I bit off more than I can chew this time.'

'Then let me help,' Declan stepped forward. 'Whatever it is.'

'It's political,' Kendis replied. 'That you're here is help enough for the moment. Walk with me.'

They started down a smaller lane now, gravestones on either side of them as she continued.

'It began when I was researching into Andy Mac,' she explained. 'I found out things about Charles Baker back then. Then, when the Devington case ended I carried on digging.'

'Why?' Declan shook his head in confusion at this. 'He was done. Finished.'

'People like Charles Baker don't just finish,' Kendis continued. 'He's protected.'

'How so?'

'Have you ever heard of the Star Chamber?' Kendis asked, stopping beside a gravestone.

'I remember seeing a film about it,' Declan admitted. 'Something about people taking the law into their own hands.'

'They started it during the reign of Henry VII, back in the fourteen hundreds,' Kendis explained. 'They named it after the room that they sat in, in the Palace of Westminster. It had stars on the ceiling, you see.'

'Who sat?'

'Two royal judges and two counsellors to the King,' Kendis continued. 'It was designed to administer justice to cases that couldn't be heard publicly. Usually property matters, that sort of thing. But, by the time Henry VIII took over, he left it to its own devices as he couldn't be bothered to attend the meetings. It became autonomous to the Crown, and by the reign of Charles I, it was actively used as a tool of royal oppression, finding rivals to the king and torturing them, silencing them, or simply making them disappear. It was officially disbanded in the sixteen hundreds.'

'As great as this history lesson is, why am I being told about it?' Declan asked.

'Because unofficially, it never stopped. Removed from royal hands, it became a tool for Cromwell's Parliament. Even when Charles II took the throne, nobody informed him of this, and so on.'

'Until now?'

'It's never been busier than now.' Kendis took a long drag on the cigarette. 'It's Parliament based, you see, and to keep things equal its membership of five are taken randomly from all parties. You stay on it for five years, or leave earlier if you lose your seat. The longest serving member becomes the grandmaster of the chamber, replaced by the next longest serving member on their exit and on and on. Also, once you've been a part of it and left, you can't return.'

'Let me guess,' Declan said, considering this. 'Charles Baker is on it.'

'Came on after last year's election, when the Lib Dem for Bishops Stortford lost his seat and opened up a spot,' Kendis nodded. 'It's also the reason that, after effectively being moved from High Cabinet status and relegated to the back-benches, he still holds some ministerial privileges.'

'They're too scared to piss him off,' Declan mused. 'That makes sense. But surely he can't try for Prime Minister again?'

Kendis almost laughed. 'I think he's aiming higher. Prime Ministers come and go. Look how many we've had in the last decade outside of elections. All of them end up with nothing. Chief Whips and Chair people have the power these days.'

She shrugged.

'But then this is Baker. Who knows what he'll decide next week.'

'So Baker hates you for Andy Mac?'

'More,' Kendis said. 'I started learning that Baker was connected to illegal arms trades, and that he was being paid for these through fake lectures, paid into a shell company, one of two that his wife, Donna, owned. Baker made almost five million dollars last year for three "talks", each one a jolly on the taxpayer's expense. When I started checking into this, though, I found another name I recognised. Rattlestone.'

'The private security firm,' Declan nodded. 'I'm hearing their name a lot these days.'

'You'll be hearing it a lot more if Baker gets into power,' Kendis admitted. 'They're not like the usual private security firms. Those are all filled with ex-squaddies and officers. The US ones are all Marines and ex-Delta Force. This one's differ-ent. It comprises ex-Special Branch and Police Protection coppers, and spooks.'

'Spooks? You mean MI5?'

'I mean whoever they can get. Not just UK based. But the money Baker's been making for these talks in one shell company is paid to him from Rattlestone's one.' She shook her head. 'Not that they eat much of a loss doing that, as the contracts Rattlestone are going for are very lucrative.'

'What kind?'

Kendis stamped out a cigarette and immediately lit up a second. 'I was in the Balkans a few years ago,' Kendis continued. 'I saw a Peacekeeping convoy attacked by militants. Four soldiers died. After it happened, there were rumours that Baker was involved somehow, that his office – he was Under Defence Minister or something back then – leaked the itinerary out. He'd given information on troop movement to make them look bad, to fail, and then when the contracts were re-tendered, looking to private security firms instead, Rattlestone gained it.'

'Bullshit.'

'I thought the same. But, I looked into it and, as I did, it became clearer. I'm not a tinfoil-hat-wearing looney, Declan. This is serious. Moreover, they're only just starting.'

'Meaning?'

'Ministry of Defence properties.'

Declan shook his head. 'There's already a police force that looks after those.'

'Yeah, but think about it,' Kendis insisted. 'The Ministry of Defence police don't have an outstanding record, and they're classed as a separate entity to the Met. You guys even call them "Mod Plod" when they're not looking.'

Declan shrugged. 'Still doesn't explain the relevance here.'

'Their contract is up for renewal this year,' Kendis explained. 'If Rattlestone have Whitehall backing, they can take the contract instead. It's worth millions. Billions, even. Army bases. Nuclear power. Whitehall itself. They'd have power over the military. They could arrest whoever they wanted on Ministry of Defence land and that's not including the arms contracts and the power they already have.'

Declan considered this.

'Christ,' he said. 'If Baker controls these, and if he gains power, he'd have unlimited power. The Star Chamber could vote to do his bidding, Rattlestone could carry it out and nobody would know. He'd have his own secret police.'

'Enough to lead his own *coup* if he wanted.' Kendis took a drag from her cigarette. 'Declan, he has the dominoes lined up already.'

'He's going to create a dictatorship and we have to stop him.'

5

THE GREAT DICTATOR

DECLAN LEANED BACK AGAINST A GRAVESTONE AS HE TRIED TO take this all in. That a company like Rattlestone was making a power play was bad enough; that they had Baker's backing, and possibly even that of the highest levels of London politics was frankly terrifying.

'They know you're looking into them, don't they?' he said.

'How do you know that?'

'Monroe. On his computer, the file I mentioned. It was frozen on the screen, but the first page was there. Your radicalisation, how you have a handler, everything.' Declan raised a hand to stop Kendis replying. 'I know it's fake. But when I was coming here Billy sent me an analysis of the fonts used – I know, he needs to get out more – but he said that one of the three security firms that used these fonts was Rattlestone.'

'So they're starting a disinformation campaign,' Kendis mused. 'Figures.'

'How did Baker, or whoever it is, learn that you knew

this?' Declan asked. 'I'm guessing they did, and that's why you're being set up?'

'I was an idiot,' Kendis muttered into the remnants of her cigarette before tossing it aside. 'I got to know Donna while investigating. I liked her. Then, when I learned she was the signatory on Rattlestone, I knew she had to be a patsy. She didn't have a clue what it was. Said that the requests to sign the shell company documents came from Baker's office and was something boring and administrational.'

'You told her everything, didn't you?' Declan sighed. 'Jesus, Kendis! She would have gone straight to him with this!'

Kendis nodded. 'I think she did,' she replied. 'But not in how you think. She was furious when I told her. Realised that she'd been duped, that if it came out, she'd be the one doing time. She's the only name you can find on both boards, and you have to really know what you're looking for to find it.'

'And then she died,' Declan mused.

'No, then she was killed,' Kendis replied. 'Nobody believed it was suicide. Even my source said as much.'

'I thought Donna was your source?' Declan asked. Kendis shook her head.

'There was someone else, another whistle blower,' she replied. 'They came to me after the suicide, spoke to me by WhatsApp messages and I only met them ...' she paused, as if realising that she was about to give away a terrible secret.

'I only met them face to face for the first time last night.'

'Last night? As in when we had our drink. Is that why you chose The Horse and Guard?' Declan exclaimed. 'Christ, Kendis, was I nothing but backup for a story?'

'No!' Kendis replied defensively, crossing her arms as she did so. 'I was going there already, and then you sent that text, saying you wanted a drink! I thought it'd be easier!' Her voice softened. 'I knew Pete wasn't around, too.'

There was a silence.

'Did I see them?' Declan asked. 'The source?'

Kendis shook her head.

'I don't think so,' she replied. 'They were in a different part of the bar, and all we did was work out a code for meeting up in the future. Can we move on?'

'It's your story,' Declan muttered.

Kendis nodded. 'So, Donna had charity work that was important to her, and she knew that if any of this came out, she'd lose it all. She told me she was going to confront Baker about it, or at least check into this with his lackey.'

'Will Harrison.'

'Yeah. I told her not to, to wait instead, but she didn't listen.' Kendis sat down on the base of the stone cross, as if too weary to stand anymore.

'A day or two later, the news came out that she'd committed suicide,' she breathed, close to tears. 'She confronted Baker and then she died.'

'You don't know that's what happened.'

'Don't I?' Kendis looked up. 'I'm shooting in the dark, Dec. Donna could have helped me blow it all up, but she's gone. The day after it was announced that she'd died, the source appeared, wanting vengeance for the death. Said there's one voice behind Rattlestone, and hinted strongly that it was Baker. But this contradicted what Donna had said before she died.'

'What did she say?' Declan looked around the cemetery now, feeling as if he was being watched.

'When she talked about Rattlestone, she'd told me that all she knew was that Baker had come in after it was created, and the genuine power was some unknown guy in the shadows who named it with a bombing and some scrabble letters.'

'A bombing?'

'Yeah.'

'What do you mean, Scrabble?' Declan asked. Kendis shrugged.

'That's it,' she said. 'Simply that half a day, a bomb and a pack of scrabble letters would give me the truth behind Rattlestone.'

Declan stood silently for a moment, staring silently at Kendis.

'Anagrams,' he said.

'Of course it's bloody anagrams,' Kendis snapped. 'I'm an award-winning journalist and investigative reporter. I don't need the mighty detective brain of Declan Walsh to point out the bleeding obvious. Rattlestone's not even a proper word.'

She stopped, rubbing at her temples.

'Sorry,' she said. 'Anagrams are good and all that, but when you don't even know what you're looking for, every word made could be the correct one.'

'So we go through every word,' Declan smiled.

Then suddenly, whipping around, he called out to a tree fifteen feet behind him. 'You can come out now,' he shouted.

Slowly, and a little nervously, a slim young Indian emerged from behind the tree. He wore a denim jacket and black jeans over a graphic design band tee shirt, and over his shoulder was a canvas camera bag.

'Declan, wait,' Kendis rose from the base. 'He's with me.'

'He's with you?' Declan looked back. 'How many others are at this *secret* meeting?'

The Indian man reluctantly walked over, nodding to

Declan. 'Wasn't my idea, I promise you,' he said, holding out a hand. 'Nasir Gill. I work with Kendis. I'm a photographer.'

Declan shook Nasir's hand. 'Declan,' he said. Nasir laughed.

'Oh, I know who you are,' he said. 'If she's not going on about you, I just have to watch the news. You're either breaking up gangs, destroying politicians, or punching out priests.'

Declan couldn't help it. He laughed at this.

'I like him,' he said to Kendis. 'Now how about explaining why he's been stalking me?'

'I needed to make sure you were alone,' Kendis admitted. 'Nasir was part of the team that helped me with Donna. He's been watching Rattlestone for months.'

'That aside, why on earth would you think that I'd bring anyone with me?' Declan replied. 'You think I *want* people to know that I'm playing spies with you?'

'We're not playing anything,' Kendis snapped.

Declan showed the baseball cap. 'Really? Because so far, I've used a costume and a burner phone. If I don't go home with some kind of a cool watch that fires lasers, I'm going to be massively pissed off.'

'Insurance,' Kendis replied. 'I don't need the police involved, Declan. You need to find out who's attacking your own, anyway. But I've found out where the bodies are buried. I'll gain some information tonight that'll give me what I need to destroy Baker once and for all. Proof that he killed Donna, sold arms, sacrificed soldiers in the Balkans, everything. It won't end Rattlestone, but it'll be enough to ensure he'll go to prison, and have no power in Whitehall again. But I have to do it by myself, and it's helpful to know that if people move against me, someone like you is looking out for it.'

'Don't be an idiot!' Declan hissed. 'You can't take on someone like Baker on your own! Let me help!'

'You can't,' Kendis was sad now as she spoke. 'They're watching you. They already know your weak spots. Look at Monroe. You help me, they won't hurt you. They'll move higher. Maybe even get to you through Jess.'

Declan relaxed his grip. He knew Kendis was right.

'But I'm police,' he feebly protested. Kendis smiled.

'And you will be, once I get this out there,' she said. 'Next week, if all goes well, it'll go live. By then you'll have what you need to take down Baker and the buggers behind Rattlestone.'

'But what about this terrorist nonsense?' Declan asked. Kendis shrugged.

'Noise, nothing more than proof that they can get to me. Rattlestone want to scare me off, to get me to back down.'

She looked to the floor, back to the still smouldering cigarette butt.

'I'm not gonna do that,' she hissed. 'I'm not gonna betray Donna like that.'

Declan leaned in. 'And us?' he whispered. Kendis smiled, a sad, remorseful one as she stroked at his hair, protruding out from under the baseball cap.

'Once I do this, we can go away together,' she said. 'I'll tell Peter. It'll work out.' She kissed Declan on the cheek. 'Just watch out for me. I'll be off grid for a few days; then I'll bring the fireworks.'

With that, Kendis Taylor nodded to Nasir and walked off down the path, back towards the southern entrance of the cemetery. Declan looked back to the photographer.

'You're alright with this?' he asked angrily.

Nasir shrugged. 'You've met her, right?' he replied. 'You

tell her not to do something, it'll just make her more intent at doing it. I'll monitor her. It's my job.'

Declan sighed. Nasir was right. All he could do was wait now and hope to hell that nothing bad happened to Kendis Taylor before he killed her himself.

———

BILLY FITZWARREN SAT AT HIS DESK, EXAMINING A HARD DRIVE in his hands, turning it carefully around as he did so. This was the brains of DCI Monroe's laptop, and somewhere deep inside it was the clue that he needed to find, that explained how this random file had arrived on the screen.

He'd worked out that the file had been uploaded rather than downloaded, so perhaps Monroe had clicked onto a link that had provided malware to do so? *No, because that couldn't happen because of the firewall.* Billy had designed it himself, and would have ensured that strange files couldn't travel through it. Because of the firewall, you could log every keystroke that—

Billy almost dropped the hard drive as a thought came to him. Placing it aside, he opened up his own laptop, clicking on a homemade server application that he'd built from scratch a few months back, firing up the application. Taking the laptop into the briefing room, he attached it directly to the LAN network port, entering the router details. Then, bringing up a second terminal window, he started typing in commands at machine-gun speed, his fingers flying over the keyboard as he sent process after process into the system.

Eventually, after what felt like a dozen failed attempts, he stopped.

On the screen was a *terminal process receipt.*

'Jo, are you still there?' he called out.

'You meant "DC Davey," didn't you?' A voice called out from Monroe's office, where the forensics officer was still hunting for the smallest clues that could help.

'Sorry,' Billy replied. 'Can you confirm the time of attack again?'

'The guard claimed that he heard glass breaking at ten-twelve pm,' DC Davey now popped her head around the door, her frizzy ginger hair wild. 'Why?'

'The file didn't appear on Monroe's screen until ten-fifteen,' Billy replied. 'Which meant that Monroe never saw it, because by that point he'd been attacked.'

'The attacker put it on?'

'No, it would have been sent before then, but it'd been delayed in the server, like in some kind of command code limbo,' Billy spun the laptop to show DC Davey. 'Look, you see? There's a back door into our system. Someone opened it and entered our system at ten on the dot, and then attempted to upload it to a particular address, Monroe's laptop, a minute or so later. But then *here*, you can see that something else forced the network to freeze for ten minutes. Dumb luck, but they countered each other out. That's probably why only the front page appeared.'

'So the network freezing and the attack were two separate incidents?'

Billy leaned back in the chair, staring at the screen.

'Yeah, I actually think so,' he said. 'Which means this could have been two different people, working without knowledge of the other.' He smiled. 'But with this, I can now start trying to reverse the transaction.'

'Good,' DC Davey left the door, walking back into the

office. 'Can you do it outside? You're still trailing contaminates all over the crime scene.'

'But it's cold outside!' Billy protested.

'Then wear a coat,' Davey's voice shouted out.

'You know we're the same rank, right?' Billy folded his arms. 'I don't have to take orders from you.'

DC Davey's head popped around the door again.

'I know how to kill you and make you disappear forever,' she said, before leaving once more.

Billy shivered.

'I'll get my coat then,' he muttered.

———

In a small office in Portcullis House, Malcolm Gladwell sat at his desk, reading a daily report while munching on a chocolate digestive. It was his only vice, really. Everything he ate was organically grown and ethically farmed, but these bloody things were his Kryptonite. He'd finished one and was about to reach for another when a line in the report stopped him.

'Denise!' he shouted out of his door. A moment later a mousey blonde woman in her late thirties, slim but shapelessly dressed, appeared, notebook in hand.

'You summoned me, oh lord and master?' she enquired.

Gladwell glared at her.

'Why was I under surveillance last night?' he asked, pointing at a line in the report. Denise squinted, but standing across the room, there was no way that she could see what he was showing. Irritated, Gladwell looked back at it.

'It says here that security services were outside The Horse and Guard last night, while I was in there,' he muttered. 'Is someone making a bloody play for me? Have you heard anything?'

'Nothing on the drums,' Denise walked in now, snatching the report from Gladwell and reading it. 'Also, this doesn't say that they were surveilling you. Just that they were there.'

'It's a pokey little nowhere pub in the arse end of Chelsea,' Gladwell snapped. 'Nobody else would ...'

He stopped.

'Unless they were following who I met with.'

'Who was that?'

'Never you mind,' Gladwell rummaged through his desk. 'I don't need you now.'

As Denise wandered back out of the office, Gladwell pulled a cheap-looking burner phone out of his drawer. Turning it on, he walked over to his office door, closing it as he dialled a number. After a few rings, it went to voicemail.

'They're watching you,' he said. 'We need to talk as soon as possible.'

Disconnecting the call, Gladwell once more dismantled the phone, placing it back into his drawer. Sitting back in his chair, he leaned up, staring at the ceiling.

He was so close right now.

Nobody was going to stop him.

6

WINE BARRED

ANJLI HAD RETURNED TO TEMPLE INN AFTER A HASTILY grabbed lunch, and a change of clothes back in her shared apartment in Shoreditch. She hadn't been out the night before, but had thrown on the first things that she could find, half in the dark, when she'd heard the news about Monroe. Now she'd showered, imbibed a litre of the finest coffee she had in stock, checked in with her mum to ensure that the chemotherapy sessions were still going okay, and now had what she called her battle armour on: her most official looking suit and her *bitch please* boots. If anything or anyone came at her today, she'd give them a damned good kicking.

Billy was waiting outside the Crime Unit when she arrived. She didn't have a car because of a lack of parking around her home, so she often pooled any driving cases with him, including a terrifying, breakneck drive through country roads the previous day as they hunted the captured Monroe.

Fat lot of good that did.

'What have you got?' she asked. 'Or has Marcos kicked you out of the office again?'

'She's with Monroe right now,' Billy replied indignantly.

Anjli smiled. 'So it's DC Davey that's kicked you out?'

'Shut up,' Billy muttered. 'She scares me.'

'Everyone scares you,' Anjli replied, patting Billy on the shoulder. 'So again, what have you got?'

'Not sure,' Billy admitted. 'The file that Monroe had on his laptop, the one that had frozen it. I realised that there was no route for it.'

'What do you mean, route?' Anjli frowned.

'Journey, procedure, whatever you want to call it. To end up on Monroe's screen, there had to be a route. Either he had it emailed to him, or he downloaded it from a server, maybe even found it on a website, it doesn't matter. Files don't magically appear.'

'Except this one did.'

Billy nodded. 'You know when you're online and a cookie window appears, advertising something? That's exactly what happened here. Something or rather someone sent this to Monroe without him asking for it, and straight through the network.'

'I thought we had fail-safes on the network?'

Billy shrugged, looking around the car park. 'We're City of London police. We have exactly the same firewalls as they do. More so because I upgraded them. The only way that this could have come in was if someone had a backdoor in. So, I ran a few processes, and bingo. Someone used a backdoor to send this directly to his laptop. However, someone else seemed to have the same idea to hack our server at the same time, there was some kind of server blip when they did, and it broke the laptop.'

Anjli raised a hand to stop Billy. 'Someone with a backdoor ... are you saying this was Trix?'

Trixibelle Preston had been an intern at the unit a few weeks ago, but was forcibly removed when it was discovered that she was a mole for a suspect in a murder case, and had been working for Pearce Associates the whole time. She'd bugged the rooms in the Crime Unit when she was in the offices, so there was no reason she couldn't have bypassed the network.

'Possibly,' Billy said. 'But then I don't know how we'd find out. She disappeared off the grid after the Devington affair.'

'We should do something about that,' Anjli muttered. 'Okay then. Anything else?'

Billy shook his head. 'CCTV had nothing and nobody was in the other buildings.'

Anjli nodded, deciding. 'Right then, we need to sweep the area. See if anyone saw something suspicious.'

'There's a bar just outside the Eastern Gate,' Billy suggested. 'It's a long shot, but they might have seen the attacker enter?'

Anjli and Billy started down Temple Lane, out into Tudor Street. It wasn't worth driving, as everything nearby was within a short walk. There, exactly as Billy had said, outside the gates of Temple Inn was a wine bar. Walking across the road and up to the door, Anjli could see that the afternoon trade was already thriving. With Billy beside her, Anjli opened the glass door and entered.

To the outside it looked like a simple bar with blacked-out windows and minimal flamboyance, but once inside it was like a new world. Mirrors lined the walls, reflecting into the bar, with comfortable chairs and expensive-looking oak tables on either side of the hardwood floor. Along the top of the walls were old drinks adverts, lit by small lamps and a selection of fairy lights, stapled up so that they were strewn across the ceiling.

Walking through to the end, Anjli found that the wine bar opened up more as they passed into a larger back room, a long wooden bar to their left, and diners to the right sitting at small tables, deep in conversation. Behind the bar was a man in a black shirt, currently pouring a generous white wine for a group of ladies on the other side.

'With you in a minute,' he said, passing the glass over and taking a credit card. Pressing it to his card machine, allowing the receipt to go through, he passed card and paper to the ladies and, as they walked away turned his attention to Anjli.

'What can I do for you?' he asked.

Anjli showed her warrant card. 'I'm DS Kapoor, and this is DC Fitzwarren,' she said. 'We work in the Temple Inn Unit.'

The barman nodded conversationally. 'Do you want to see the manager?' he asked. 'I'm guessing this is a noise thing?'

'Actually, no,' Billy interrupted. 'There was an incident in the Unit late last night. They attacked one of our own. We believe the assailant entered through the gate, just outside, and we hoped that you may have a camera or something that we could check? Or perhaps someone was outside and saw anyone coming or going?'

'A lot of people come and go from that place,' the barman started drying a freshly washed glass as he thought. 'We have side tables down Temple Lane, but we don't have any CCTV as such. Just covering the door.' He shrugged apologetically. 'I could ask the staff who were in last night, see if any of them saw anything?'

'Please,' Anjli replied, passing a card over. 'This is my number. If you think of anything, call me immediately.'

'There was one thing,' the barman said as he pocketed the card. 'What time was this?'

'Some time around ten pm,' Billy replied.

The barman thought for a moment and then nodded. 'We had a car parked outside,' he said, pointing through the wall towards the approximate location of Tudor Street. 'Not outside us, but to the left, outside next door's office. It's a single yellow so you're allowed to in the evening, but it just felt odd. He was sitting there for a good half hour, maybe more. I came out around ten thirty for a smoke and it'd gone.'

'Did you see the man inside the car?' Billy asked.

The barman shrugged. 'Not really. I think he was white, dark hair? I know that's pretty much most people. Sorry.'

'What type of car was it?' Anjli continued the questioning.

The barman considered this. 'I don't know cars well,' he admitted. 'But it was grey and it had these four interlocking rings on the front grill. Is that Audi? Or Saab?'

'You saw a grey Audi parked outside for half an hour around ten pm?' Anjli was writing this into her notepad. 'Thanks, you've been incredibly helpful.'

The barman smiled, happy to be of service as Anjli and Billy walked back out of the wine bar. Exiting out into the street, Anjli paused, looking to her partner.

'What?' he asked.

'Just going through everything in my head,' Anjli replied. 'The guard said he considered nothing off about the man who passed last night, as he thought it was Declan.' She looked back to the junction of Tudor Street and Bouverie Street. 'What's more, apparently, a grey Audi waited just there before Monroe was attacked. Declan drives a grey Audi. We need to see where it was last night.'

'You can't seriously believe that Walsh did this!' Billy exclaimed.

Anjli shook her head. 'I don't, but I'm thinking that someone wants people to,' she admitted. 'Your source said that Baker is after Declan, and us by default. The same day you get this, we have a late night attack on Monroe, and circumstantial evidence is racking up against Declan. Something's off. There are too many things in play. I'm not sure who we can even trust right now.'

'We need a codeword,' Billy suggested. 'You know, so that when someone says, "this reminds me of Belgrade", we know what they really mean.'

'I've never been to Belgrade,' Anjli muttered as she started back towards the arched entrance to Temple Inn. 'What in God's name are you talking about?'

Billy smiled. 'Like in the movies. Spy codes. So when I say "this reminds me of Belgrade—"'

'But, I've not been to Belgrade,' she repeated.

'You don't need to, I mean that when I say the code word, you know I'm really saying "I'm gonna kill the man on the left and jump through a window."'

'Why in God's name would you do either of those?'

'I don't mean those exact actions,' Billy grinned. 'I'm going to work us out some.'

Anjli sighed. 'Can you do it after we've solved the attack on our boss?' she asked sweetly. 'You know, as that's the important bit here?'

Anjli knew she was right. Someone was trying to cause doubt on Declan. But then a memory came back to her.

'*How did you get here so fast? There's no way you made it here from Hurley in half an hour.*'

'*I was in the apartment in Tottenham. I give the keys back soon, so needed to check it out. Dozed off there.*'

Had Declan really been in Tottenham? What would his tracker say? How could she believe he would do such a thing when there were far more obvious targets out there?

Shaking her head to dispel the thoughts, Anjli followed Billy back into Temple Inn.

It was almost five when Declan returned to the ACCU ward, seeing Doctor Marcos alone beside Monroe's bed.

'Any change?' he asked as he entered the room.

Doctor Marcos looked up. 'A little,' she said. 'He's responding to stimulus, which is good. But we still don't know how bad things are in there until he wakes. It also impacted one of his teeth, so he'll need to see a dental surgeon. Probably at half-past two.'

'Why then?' Declan was confused at this.

Doctor Marcos gave a small smile. 'It's their favourite time,' she said. 'Two thirty.'

Tooth hurty.

Declan almost groaned, but saw that with the faint attempt of a joke over, Doctor Marcos' face had returned to the grim concern that it had been when he arrived.

'He'll be fine,' Declan stood at the end of the bed now. 'He's Glaswegian. This is a holiday.'

'If he'd just been attacked, I might feel the same way about the tough old bugger,' Doctor Marcos replied. 'But considering what he's gone through over the last couple of days ...'

Declan sat on a second chair, a small, rickety one, and stared at the bed and his boss. 'They're bringing in a DCI to look into this,' he said. 'I spoke to the Chief Superintendent earlier.'

'They should just leave it to us,' Doctor Marcos muttered. 'We'd work it out way faster than any clown they called in. Any idea who it'll be?'

'No idea,' Declan shook his head. 'Only DCIs I know are Bullman from yesterday, Farrow in Tottenham and Ford, although she's not police anymore.'

'I've already reached out to Bullman,' Doctor Marcos leaned across, checking Monroe's pulse with her fingers, as if not believing the machine beside her that showed his heart rate on the screen.

'You have? Why?' Declan was surprised at this. 'I thought you didn't get on with her?'

'I saw her when she thought Monroe was in trouble,' Doctor Marcos explained. 'She felt guilty for letting him get into that situation. I'm hoping that guilt still exists, because God knows we could use someone needing to prove themselves right now.'

Declan nodded, looking back to Monroe.

'I can take over for a bit?' he asked. Doctor Marcos shook her head.

'I'll do it,' she said, watching Monroe as she spoke.

'Does he know?' Declan rose from the chair.

'Know what?'

'How you feel about him.'

'Go home, you silly boy,' Doctor Marcos chided, but

Declan saw the hint of a smile as she spoke. 'I'll let you know if anything happens.'

Declan patted Doctor Marcos on the shoulder before walking out of the room. He stopped, however, at the door.

'The moment anything does,' he reminded her. 'Make me the first call.'

Doctor Marcos nodded absently, already forgetting that Declan was even there.

Realising that there was nothing left to do in the ward, Declan nodded once more and left.

He was so busy thinking about Monroe and Doctor Marcos, that he didn't see the shaven-headed man on the other side of the ward corridor door, watching him, and taking a note of the time in a journal.

7

POCKET PARKS

KENDIS TAYLOR KNEW SHE WAS BEING FOLLOWED. SHE DIDN'T know who he was, but she pretty much could guess who he worked for, and why he was there. Rattlestone were getting spooked, and they wanted to know who her source was. They wanted her discredited; that was pretty clear by the note passed through her door that day, and this apparent file that had been created and sent to Alex Monroe's desk, right before they attacked him.

Having left Nasir and Declan in the cemetery, presumably to decide which one of them was more loyal to her, she'd left through the south entrance, turning left up the Fulham Road. She'd stopped at a bagel shop opposite the Chelsea and Westminster Hospital, partly because she was hungry, but also to see who changed their rhythm behind her, and saw a man, stocky and balding, in jeans and a brown leather bomber jacket turn and enter a creperie on the corner of Hollywood Road, making the cardinal sin for anyone secretly following of continuing to watch out of the window at their target rather than pretend to look at the menu. She smiled, waved to the man and moved into the road, waving again to stop a black cab as it passed. Leaping in and giving directions, she watched the balding man run back onto the street, frantically making a call, most likely trying to remember the registration number of the cab as he hunted for one for himself to follow. Turning out of sight on Redcliffe Road, Kendis quickly paid the driver a tenner and leapt out, popping into a stationery store on the corner and waiting until a second black cab passed, the balding man sitting in the back as he spoke into a phone.

The threat now passed, Kendis walked back onto the Fulham Road and crossed over, heading south down Limerston Street to the King's Road, leaping onto an 11 bus to Liverpool Street. She knew she'd made a mistake the moment she tapped her Oyster card to the reader; that careless error meant that now they'd see she used it, and they could follow the bus. This was easy to fix however and, after carefully watching the passengers of the bus, she sat across from a teenager in a shell suit, letting her Oyster card accidentally fall out onto the seat, rising and moving to exit through the middle doors as the bus arrived at Victoria Coach Station. She wasn't looking directly at him, but through the window reflection she saw the teenager move past the seat, pausing momentarily to pick up the travel pass. He didn't move to give it back though, and she smiled. There was about twenty quid on the Oyster and he was welcome to it all, as long as he took a few journeys that day. It would lead anyone following the card on a wild goose chase, while Kendis carried on with her business, heading eastwards down side roads towards Vauxhall Bridge Road, walking against the traffic on Rutherford Street and turning down Horseferry Road. She hadn't seen anyone following her for a while now, so finally she relaxed, making her way to the meeting place.

She wouldn't have relaxed, however, if she'd known that Nasir Gill was already waiting for her.

MALCOLM GLADWELL WAS THE MP FOR WOODLEY, IN Reading, but he didn't travel home that much when Parliament was in session, instead preferring to stay in a small apartment in Westminster, at the junction of Page Street and Marsham Street. He felt a sense of nostalgia coming here; at one time it had been a *Star Trek* themed bar that he remembered attending in his early twenties before it closed, but he'd mainly picked the apartment because of the great running routes that were around there. Because of this, he'd often walk home for brief breaks between sessions, passing Westminster Abbey and the giant monstrosity of a building that housed the Home Office. Today was no exception; he had an eight pm reading on a Justice Bill addendum in the Commons, so had grabbed a late lunch, or rather a slightly early dinner at the apartment, while waiting for his guest to arrive.

However, as he walked up to the apartment block's entrance, he spied a piece of white paper taped to the door.

WINDOW CLEANING HALF PRICE

There was no number on it, but it didn't need one for Gladwell to understand what it meant. He'd only created the meeting drop idea the night before, after all. Glancing around, ensuring that he wasn't being followed, he turned away from the building and started east up Page Street, walking towards St John's Gardens.

Originally the burial ground for St John Smith Square back in 1731, this was another of these "pocket parks" that had appeared in the mid-nineteenth century, when the gravestones were removed or placed around the sides, the burials were stopped and people conveniently forgot there were thousands of dead bodies beneath their feet. Laid out in a symmetrical pattern; paths to the middle from each corner and two additional paths from the sides joining them at a large, circular clearing, a small circular fountain in the middle with trees planted equidistantly around it, the park was a well-kept green space, surrounded on all four sides by eight-storey buildings, created for locals and visitors alike to relax in, and take stock of their situations.

Sitting on one of the benches that surrounded the fountain though was Kendis Taylor. Gladwell sighed audibly and walked over, sitting on the bench beside her.

'When I gave you this way to contact me, I didn't expect you to use it immediately,' he stated irritably.

'I'd hoped to find you at the cemetery,' Kendis replied. 'You said you volunteer there.'

'I couldn't today. I have a session,' Gladwell explained irritably. 'I was hoping to make it there tonight. What's this about?'

'They're gunning for me,' Kendis replied, passing Gladwell the sheet of paper with the call to martyrdom written on it. 'I need to move on them now.'

'There's nothing I can do about it,' Gladwell replied. 'They're apparently watching me too. That is, they were watching the pub last night.'

'The Horse and Guard?'

Gladwell looked at Kendis. 'How many pubs do you think I go to in a night?'

'Well, I know you were upstairs in The George with Baker and a couple of *starry-eyed* MPs beforehand,' she smiled sweetly. 'You might have been on a pub crawl.'

'You checked into my movements last night?'

'Let's say I'm a little protective of my investments.'

'I'm not one of your bloody investments,' Gladwell replied. 'I'm a completely anonymous source, and that doesn't work when we're not being anonymous. Christ, Taylor. If they were watching me, then they'd have seen you there too!'

'Then I'd say it's more dangerous for me to be around you, than for you to be around me,' Kendis tossed some breadcrumbs from a bun she held to a pigeon. 'Besides, I saw who you were with in there. Interesting piece of political tittle-tattle, wouldn't you say?'

Gladwell took the bun from her, tossing it into a bin beside them.

'Don't do that,' he chided. 'They're vermin.'

He sighed, looking up at the trees that towered above him. 'Baker put your name forward last night. This is probably the start of a discrediting scheme.'

'Then I need to discredit him first,' Kendis leaned forward on the bench. 'I need to gain leverage on him, put the piece out and make this public.'

'It's not Baker you need to worry about,' Gladwell replied. 'It's his department. He's not the genuine power there.'

'I know,' Kendis nodded. '*Sir Hiss* has been asking about me all week.'

'I bumped into Harrison today, during lunch,' Gladwell looked across the park as he spoke. 'I've spent years keeping off their radar, and now I'm seeing them all over the bloody place. He knows my ... *astronomy* side, so I asked whether Baker's intel was credible.'

'On me?' Kendis smiled. 'Was it? Am I a terrorist?'

'He made a fairly credible argument,' Gladwell admitted.

'But you didn't shoot it down.'

'How could I?' Gladwell leaned forward to join Kendis, lowering his voice. 'I regret the Balkans, I really do. But it wasn't my mistake. Wasn't even my bloody department. When we spoke to Baker about the leadership, when I placed him in contact with the 1922 Committee, he said he had no skeletons. I assumed that it had been someone else, that he hadn't known about it, and took him at face value.'

'Then you learned he had a secret love child and had been blackmailed by Francine Pearce for twenty years.'

'Well, yes,' Gladwell finally smiled. 'He did shit the bed quite spectacularly there.'

'Do you know who leaked the schedule?'

'Of course. We both know. It had to be someone who could see an opportunity for Rattlestone.' Gladwell shook his head. 'And no, I don't know all the names of power there. I just know that Harrison and Baker were brought on board a year before the Balkans, promising big things.'

Kendis sighed. 'I need to know where the smoking gun is, Malcolm.'

'I'm trying to find it,' Gladwell hissed. 'But meeting me in secluded gardens right before you're possibly outed to the press as a terrorist sympathiser doesn't help! God knows who followed you here!' He looked around, glancing carefully at the others in the park as if expecting them to attack him at any moment.

'I know how to avoid a tail,' Kendis replied. She couldn't

help herself though, and she looked around as well; she paused as she saw the figure standing by the shelter. Looking back to Gladwell, she rose, pulling him up as she did so, patting at his jacket's pockets. 'Are you wearing a wire?'

'Of course I'm not!' Gladwell looked at the figure. 'Who is it?'

Kendis avoided the question. 'Get home. I'm going off the grid for a couple of days. If you can find out where they keep the evidence, you know how to find me.'

'What if they get to you first?'

'Then speak to DI Declan Walsh.' Kendis started walking away from Gladwell who, grateful for the end of this meeting, rose and trotted out of the park.

Kendis however wasn't leaving the park just yet. Opening up her hand, she glanced down at the wrought iron key that she'd just taken from Gladwell's jacket while patting him down. It had been a calculated guess to find it, especially after he'd commented about visiting the cemetery later. She needed to do what was needed and then return it back somehow, preferably before he realised it was missing. But now, she was walking over to the man watching her. A man who now looked incredibly embarrassed to be caught.

'What the hell are you doing here?' she hissed.

'I thought you might need backup,' Nasir explained.

'How did you know that I'd be meeting Gladwell here?'

'You mentioned it to me.'

Kendis stared at her photographer. 'This is the first time we've ever done this,' she replied. 'So how the hell would I tell you that?'

'I don't know!' Nasir snapped. 'Maybe you mentioned it when you were working it out! I came here to help you, Kendis. If you don't need me, then just tell me!'

'Did you at least ensure that you weren't followed?' Kendis snapped back, already looking around the park more carefully this time, her paranoia levels rising. 'You ensured you didn't use your credit card, didn't use your Oyster, didn't make sure that anyone could bloody follow you electronically and find not only you, but me?'

Nasir didn't reply, his silence answering the question.

'Christ, you're an idiot,' Kendis sighed. 'Go somewhere. Anywhere. Use the same card. Make it look like you're following me elsewhere. Lead them away from me.'

'But what will you do?' Nasir was apologetic, his tone nervous as he spoke. 'You could get hurt.'

'I've been hurt before,' Kendis replied. 'I'm a big girl. I've got a lead I need to check out in a graveyard and then I'll disappear.' She patted Nasir on the shoulder.

'Just like you should.'

Before Nasir could reply, Kendis was gone, running out of the park and back up Page Street, towards Victoria.

Nasir stood alone for a moment, taking in the park's silence.

Then he checked the photos he'd taken on his phone, deleted the ones that weren't relevant, and left.

JESSICA WALSH WASN'T A CHILD ANYMORE. SHE WAS ALMOST sixteen. You could join the army and be trained to kill people at sixteen. You could get married at sixteen. Ride a scooter or even fly a glider at sixteen.

But Jessica Walsh was almost sixteen. So, that meant that she still had to ask her mother's permission for things. Like, for example, going out with her friends that evening to a local board-game cafe.

'I don't know,' Lizzie Walsh pondered. 'Will that Owen boy be there?'

'Doesn't matter,' Jess replied. 'We're not dating anymore.'

'One date doesn't equal dating, young lady.'

'You know what I mean,' Jess slumped into the sofa. 'I'm not going with him. I'm going with Florence and Bianca.'

'Until what time?' Lizzie asked. Jess shrugged.

'About nine thirty?'

'It's a school night.'

'Come on, Mum. I'm distraught,' Jess did her best sad face. 'My break up with Owen was traumatic, and I need cheering up.'

'I thought you said that you weren't dating him?' Lizzie raised an eyebrow. Jess sighed. It was a loud *ha-rumph,* and audibly annoyed sigh.

'Nine,' Lizzie countered. Leaping from the sofa, Jess ran to the door, grabbing her jacket.

'Nine fifteen?' she suggested, opening the door.

'Nine!' Lizzie shouted back. Jess smiled back at her.

'You got it, Mum!' she said. 'See you at nine fifteen!' With that, the door slammed shut. Lizzie made a loud sigh of her own now, reaching for her half-finished glass of wine.

Still, at least Jess wasn't as bad as she was at fifteen.

Chuckling, Lizzie finished the glass.

———

OUTSIDE, JESS WAS SO BUSY TEXTING ON HER PHONE THAT SHE didn't notice the grey Audi across the road. She didn't see the man inside, cleaning his rimless glasses with a lens cloth before placing them back on, watching her as she walked off.

The man with the rimless glasses noted the time down in a notepad. Once he saw Jess turn the corner, he started the car and slowly pulled out into the street, following her. He couldn't help it; he gave a brief smile as he thought about what he was about to do to Jessica Walsh.

8

RAISE A GLASS

'You look like a man who won the lottery but lost the ticket,' Anjli said as Billy sat down at the table opposite her. They were in the wine bar that they'd visited earlier that day, but now, out of work hours, they'd grabbed a drink to discuss the case rather than continue in the office.

It still felt too *real* in the office.

'Got some news,' Billy said, gratefully accepting the gin and tonic that Anjli passed over to him. 'It's not good news.'

'Go on.'

Billy sipped at the drink, as if delaying the conversation.

'Declan's car, the Audi,' he started. 'The tracker wasn't on last night.'

'Why not?' Anjli frowned. Billy looked to the table, as if ashamed to look her in the eyes right now.

'Because I might have turned it off,' he muttered.

'Why the hell would you have done that?' Anjli exclaimed, her voice so loud now that several of the other drinkers at their respective tables turned and glared at her. Billy, ignoring this, shrugged.

'I was trying to help,' he said. 'Declan was being set up by Derek Salmon, and I knew that if he drove anywhere they'd find him with the tracker. So I hacked in and put a twenty-four-hour block on it.'

He sighed. 'I didn't know that Farrow would tell him to take the train.'

'Of course, the lock carried on until this morning,' Anjli nodded. 'What time did it restart?'

'About nine.'

'He was back in London by then.'

Billy looked up to face Anjli. 'I can find a way of tracking his phone,' he said. 'I might triangulate where he was—'

'He was with Kendis,' Anjli replied. 'He said he stayed overnight in Tottenham, but when he turned up this morning, you could tell that he hadn't showered, and he had the slightest traces of women's perfume on him.'

Billy's eyes widened. 'Bloody hell,' he said. 'No wonder he got so pissed when we said that Kendis was a potential terrorist.'

Anjli took a sip of her own drink. 'Your friend,' she said, 'the one that gave you the tip about Baker gunning for us. Do you trust him?'

'God, no.'

'Do you think he told you everything?'

'Probably not,' Billy looked around the bar, stopping at the wall beside them, a wall that earlier that day a barman had indicated to, when mentioning a car that had been waiting outside at the time of Monroe's attack.

'I can't believe he's still in a coma,' he muttered. 'Also, I can't believe we're still considering Declan.'

He raised his glass.

'To Belgrade.'

'I'm not doing this bloody code words thing with you,' Anjli muttered.

But she raised her glass all the same.

AFTER WORK, DECLAN HAD DRIVEN HOME TO HURLEY ON Thames, spending what felt like a good hour in the shower and finally changing out of his suit. The problem with one-night stands was the lack of a change of clothes, and Declan had already decided that a wise thing to do in the future, if things continued to progress with Kendis, would be to place an overnight bag in the car's boot for those unforeseen occasions.

Although today's unforeseen occasions eclipsed a single overnighter with a childhood sweetheart.

After showering, he'd spent a couple of hours in his father's secret study; he still hadn't cleaned out the room yet, and so the office area was still the equivalent of a modern day priest hole, created behind a fake wall and with a doorway hidden behind a slidable bookshelf. He still didn't know why Patrick Walsh had gone to such extremes here, but that someone had broken into the house two days earlier and stolen his father's iMac from the living room made him think that there was gold of some kind in the room. Not just a strange USB drive with a passcode cypher that now rested on the desk with WINTERGREEN written on it in his father's handwriting, the name of an apparent Detective Sergeant that once worked with his father, but who no longer seemed to exist in current records.

There was something more going on here.

He'd spent a good hour working once more through his

father's crime wall; photos of suspects and post-it notes with names and locations on, all linked with red string. He'd gone over this wall many times over the last few weeks, and each time he found something new, a different rabbit hole to fall down. But today his attention was distracted, and he moved to the bookshelf where he'd found another book, a fake one like the one he'd found that housed the WINTERGREEN USB drive. This one was *The Count of Monte Cristo,* and inside it was close to two thousand pounds in twenty-pound notes. Declan didn't understand why his father would have such an amount squirrelled away, and the recent revelations that Patrick Walsh had been less than clean returned to his mind.

Was this dirty money that Patrick was too scared to declare?

Closing it and placing it back on the desk, he continued to search for more clues, before moving back to the fake book and removing some notes, placing them into his wallet.

Funds were funds, after all.

He'd been looking for something, anything that could help him work out why Monroe was targeted. The attack could have been from friends or allies of the Delcourt family, Danny Martin or even the Byrnes in Birmingham, and that was only a list of people that had a problem with Monroe resulting from the last couple of days. He had decades of people hating him, as Derek Salmon had shown. Plus, if it had been a long-term grudge that had caused the attack, then surely Patrick Walsh, one of Monroe's oldest friends on the force should have known about it. Fastidious and organised as he'd always been, he would have noted it down in a journal or file somewhere.

But there were a lot of journals and files in this room, and over the last few weeks Declan had been through them all, most of the time with Jess beside him.

There was another option though; earlier the previous day, before everything happened in Beachampton, Billy had met with an informant who had told him that Charles Baker was hunting the *Last Chance Saloon*, and it seemed convenient that Monroe was attacked the same day they passed the news. But that didn't quite pan out right, as Billy had also been told that *Declan* was the primary target, so why would they attack Monroe? Also, this wasn't a beating, like the one that Declan had once had at the hands of the man with the rimless glasses outside his Tottenham apartment a couple of months earlier. This had been an attempted murder. One that needed to be solved before whoever had done this heinous act tried to finish the job.

Declan had decided that he'd be spending a lot more time next to Monroe in the next few days, in case the attacker returned. That said, Doctor Marcos was a suitable, and often creatively vicious defender. Declan felt sorry for any attacker who arrived while she was on guard.

At around ten pm Declan was feeling wiped, his eyes starting to unfocus with the strain of so much paperwork passing his vision and the lack of sleep the previous night; partly due to the events of the evening and partly because of the monstrous hangover he'd woken up with. So, with a yawn and a stretch, he went to bed. He wasn't a young man anymore, able to lose an entire night's sleep as he crammed for exams, or working a case that required constant attention and he knew that it'd be easier to work through these files in the morning, filled with coffee and with a better idea of what was going on following a night's sleep.

This plan was stopped however by a frantic Lizzie who called around ten thirty.

'You okay?' Declan asked, sitting up in the bed that he'd only just climbed into. 'You don't usually call this late.'

'It's Jess,' Lizzie replied. 'She was supposed to be back an hour ago.'

'She's probably lost track of time, Lizzie,' Declan rubbed at his eyes. 'We've all done it.'

'I've tried calling her,' Lizzie replied. 'She's not picking up the phone.'

'Not picking up, or the phone's going straight to voicemail?'

'What's the difference?' Lizzie was angry now, and her voice was rising.

'If it's the latter, she could be in a place where the signal's not good,' Declan replied calmly. 'She might not even realise.'

'What if it's the former?'

'Look, Liz,' Declan leaned back against the bed's headboard. 'She's a smart, intelligent girl, and she's had self-defence classes given to her by the best police instructors since she was six. She knows how to look after herself. There's probably a simple explanation to this.'

'The simple explanation is that she's bloody well grounded.'

'That's your right as a mum, but just remember when you yell at her, you did far worse at her age.'

There was a pause.

'I'm scared, Dec.'

'I understand that.' Declan looked at the time on the phone. 'Listen. If Jess doesn't return by eleven, call me again. I'll get the entire bloody police force out looking for her. But if you don't give her some rope, she'll always pull against what she has. She'll probably come back in half an hour and she'll have an explanation that answers everything.'

Lizzie reluctantly agreed and ended the call. Declan laid back in the bed and turned off the light, but couldn't sleep, waiting for a second call that confirmed the worst; that Jessica Walsh was missing, and it was all Declan's fault.

But the phone call never came; Jessica had obviously come home late and faced her mother's wrath; and happy to stay out of that particular family squabble Declan eventually slept fitfully through the night, waking up just before seven in the morning. He'd showered, shaved and dressed, grabbed some toast for breakfast and was on his second coffee, preparing to leave when the doorbell went.

Nobody called at seven thirty in the morning.

Suspicious and walking to the door, Declan stopped.

What if this was the same person who attacked Monroe, now attacking Declan?

He paused by the door, peering through the fisheye peephole. Surprised, he opened the door.

Trix was standing on the doorstep.

'Alright, Declan?' she asked.

9

SURPRISE VISITORS

DECLAN STARED AT THE YOUNG WOMAN STANDING ON HIS FRONT doorstep.

'You're bloody kidding me,' he said, looking around to see if anyone else was around who could have seen this early morning visitor. 'I thought you'd be locked away by now.'

Trix shook her head. 'I was being forced to do those things,' she said. 'But, when it all ended, they gave me a lifeline, a way out.'

'So what, you want your old job back?' Declan almost laughed. 'Yeah, I don't think that's going to happen.'

Trix stood on the doorstep silent for a moment.

'Okay, we can do this,' she said. 'You can be a prick and be all *holier than thou,* or you can get off your bloody high horse, let me in and we can talk about Monroe.'

Now it was Declan's turn to stand silently.

'What do you know about Monroe?' he eventually asked.

'Ask me inside.'

'What are you, a bloody vampire? Get in,' Declan moved

to the side of the doorway, allowing Trix to enter past him. 'So, what do you know?'

'More than you might think. I've been keeping tabs on you,' Trix explained. 'For someone in Whitehall.'

'Charles Baker,' Declan answered for her. 'Let me guess, he's the one who sorted your sentence out?'

Trix paused, as if unwilling to confirm this, before nodding. 'Like him, I was being forced to do things by Pearce. But unlike him, I didn't get away with things, so rather than going to prison, I'm working off a debt,' she said. 'Surveillance. Similar to what I was doing when I was under Pearce, to be honest, but I'm *Security Service* now.'

'MI5?'

'More a bastard offshoot. I was listening to you all the way through the Angela Martin case, and—'

'You can't have been,' Declan interrupted. 'Jo Davey swept the office for bugs every day. We found all of them.'

'Yeah, you found the *bugs*, but I wasn't talking about those,' Trix sat down on the sofa. 'Any chance of a coffee? I'm parched.'

Declan looked as if he was going to shout, but eventually, after a silent count to ten in his head, he nodded and walked into the kitchen. Trix carried on, speaking through the doorway.

'You've got laptops and computers in your office, and they all have webcams, microphones, yeah?' she said. 'Before you found me out, I'd put a backdoor into the server and executed a command that allowed me to operate any of these remotely.'

'That'll piss Billy off,' Declan shouted back. 'The server's like his bastard child.'

'I know,' Trix grinned. 'It's why I did it. I wanted a challenge, and the Met and City Police systems are usually so shit.' She stretched her arms. 'I couldn't turn the cameras, like physically move them, and I could only hear through the laptops and webcams when you were near one of them, but I could pretty much get the gist of most things.'

Declan emerged from the kitchen, a black coffee in his hand.

'You watching the night before last?'

Trix took the mug. 'Got any milk and sugar?'

'No.'

'Fair dues,' Trix leaned back. 'And yeah, I was.'

'Why?' Declan sat in an armchair facing her. 'Nothing on TV?'

'I told you, I was working off the debt,' Trix leaned forward, sipping at the coffee. 'I was told to upload a file. Because of that I was online, so to speak.'

'What do you mean, upload a file?' Declan leaned in to match Trix, his tone of voice darkening. 'Was it you? The file that Monroe had?'

Trix pulled back at this accusation.

'Yes, but hear me out,' she cautiously replied, reaching into her pocket and withdrawing a phone. Showing it to Declan, there was a single text message on it.

flick the switch

'That's the go order,' she explained. 'I was told by my boss that when this message arrived, I was to remotely ping a file to Monroe's laptop. No idea who created it, and I didn't see what the contents of the file were, just the name. *Kendis Taylor dot pdf.*'

'Was it supposed to freeze the laptop?'

Trix shook her head. 'No. It was an upload, nothing more. From what I could work out, some other outside source created it. Monroe was supposed to read it, and because of what it said, he would most likely distrust Taylor. You know, in case she came to you with any wild claims.'

'So, you have no connection with Rattlestone?'

Trix paused. 'Why would you think that?'

'Because we think they made the file. Care to confirm or deny?'

Trix sighed. 'Look, I don't work for them, but I know them. Have done for years. Pearce Associates often used them,' she admitted. 'Security, off the books things, things like that. Also, I know that they're connected to Whitehall somehow.'

'How?'

'Above my pay grade.'

'You don't have a pay grade.'

Trix grinned. 'Yeah, fair point.'

Declan thought back to the conversation that he'd had with Kendis the previous day. With the concerns that she had, he understood very much why someone would want her credibility questioned.

'What about the attack?'

'Nothing to do with me, I swear,' Trix replied. 'I was just to upload the file and drop out. But someone, not Whitehall sanctioned, was doing another op at the same time, and whatever they did to the network to jam it, well it kinda froze my systems before it fully loaded my file, locking me into the network. I was trying to exit the bloody thing when Monroe started talking.'

'Talking?'

Trix nodded. 'I had his laptop camera on at the start, but watching him staring at his screen meant he was effectively staring at me, so I'd disconnected the visual. He's a scary-looking bugger.'

Declan nodded at this. Trix continued.

'The other webcams in the office were all facing away, but the microphones were on. I heard him speak, and reconnected the visual to see what was going on, but he wasn't at his desk anymore. His voice was faint, in the main office, away from a microphone and I had no way to record, so I held my phone to the speaker on my computer. Because of that, I only got part of it, but I got enough.'

She pressed the screen of her phone, moving to the *Voice Memo* app. She pressed the start button and a voice, faint and distant, could be heard.

'If this means anything to you, it's nothing personal.'

Declan froze. He recognised the voice that spoke through the speaker.

The voice of the man with the rimless glasses.

'So this is how it ends, eh laddie?' Monroe again.

'Yeah, pretty much.'

Trix turned off the voice memo. 'That's all I got. There's a lot of crashing about afterwards.'

'I need that,' Declan reached for the phone. 'This proves who attacked Monroe.'

'Does it?' Trix pulled the phone away. 'Think about it. All I have is dialogue, and faint at that. It could be anyone. It could be you.'

'Me?' Declan sat back in the chair. 'What's that supposed to mean?'

'It's why I'm here,' Trix placed the half-drunk mug of coffee on the table. 'There are people out there who are seriously out for you.'

'Rattlestone?'

'Yeah.'

Declan sat silent while he processed this. 'Killing Monroe is part of that?'

'That wasn't part of what I was doing,' Trix admitted. 'But yeah, you've made a lot of enemies who'll go that far to hurt you. They've been waiting for you to slip up, and now they're taking matters into their own hands.' She shifted on the sofa. 'From what I could hear through the laptops, you were on the run after Derek Salmon's death. Someone in the office told you to take the train because there was a tracker on your car.'

Declan nodded. 'I kept off the grid until Beachampton. What of it?'

'Billy, probably thinking that he was helping, remotely turned off your car tracker, just in case,' Trix replied. 'But it was a day pass of sorts. Twenty-four hours.'

Declan thought for a moment. 'How does this affect me?'

'Christ, you're dense. Let me explain it so you might understand. I only get an hour a day when I can get away without being followed by other departments,' Trix explained. 'They all watch each other as much as outside threats. Anyway, I came here yesterday, same time. You weren't here.'

Slowly, Declan understood.

'I was—'

'Don't lie,' Trix smiled. 'You had your phone on you, and I tracked the cell towers.'

'Christ, Trix—'

'I know you were in Putney,' Trix continued. 'But nobody else does ... yet. What they know is that you were in a car that couldn't be tracked.'

'Billy and Anjli spoke to a barman in the wine bar,' Declan replied slowly as he worked through the revelation.

'They sent me an email about it. The barman said that a man in a grey Audi parked outside Temple Inn on the night. Also, that the gate guard didn't question him when he entered because he thought the man was me.'

'Bingo,' Trix nodded. 'There's no proof you weren't, unless you dob in the woman you had an affair with that night to be your alibi. Who might also be rumoured to be a terrorist, and therefore an unreliable witness.'

'You mentioned the cell towers.'

'That just proves your phone wasn't there. Not you.'

Declan rose now, pacing. 'Monroe finds a report, left on his laptop that states that Kendis is a terrorist, with a UK handler. Then a man, pretending to be me, attacks him.'

Trix rose from the sofa to face Declan, glancing down at her watch. 'Baker wanted Kendis to be ruined, but he didn't want her dead. That's not his style. He also didn't hate Monroe enough to do that. But here's the thing. Adding what happened to Monroe to what I was doing? It was genius, but had to be done by someone who not only knew that *Rattlestone* had created the file, but that Baker was having me upload it. It became a moment of opportunity, to not only go for you and the Unit, but pin this on Baker.'

'Because they can show you uploaded a file for him.'

'Yeah. People won't realise it's two separate ops. They timed it to the second.'

'You don't know who did this?'

'Not yet, but I'm working on it. It has to be someone who knows Baker, though.' Trix walked to the door. 'I've been here too long already,' she explained. 'Just be careful, eh? Someone's trying to rewrite your narrative.'

Now at the door, she stopped.

'Listen. Before you caught me, I had a way out,' she said.

'Never got to use it though. When I joined the Unit, I got hold of the building plans. The whole place was bombed during World War Two, and they kept the external walls, building effectively a whole new block within. Created a lot of crawlspaces.'

'So?' Declan was confused at this sudden architecture lecture.

'Your offices didn't have toilets originally, as they linked to next door. When the police were given the floors, they added them in, in the process bricking over a door at the back that connected to the next office via a back staircase.'

'There's only one staircase,' Declan corrected.

'Now there is, but originally there were two,' Trix continued. 'In the toilets, over the middle cubicle is a hatch into the crawl space between the second and third floors. Get in, crawl north five yards, and you bypass the wall. You drop into the corridor next door, leading to the stairway. Follow the stairs until you reach the top floor. Once there, follow the corridor west, to the front-facing windows, effectively skylights to the roof. Once on the roof, run north until the end, and drop off the western side onto the roof beside. West, north, and west again around Old Mitre Court, jump north onto the next building—'

'Jump buildings?' Declan almost laughed. 'I think we're falling more into the *Mission Impossible* school of escapes here.'

'Listen!' Trix's voice rose in anger. 'I'm not talking about me! I'm telling you in case you have to escape!'

Admonished, Declan stopped.

Trix continued. 'When you jump, carry on to the end, and up a set of white metal stairs to the white door. Code to enter is 5022. Once in, go down the stairs to the bottom. It brings you out on Fleet Street, beside Messrs Hoare Bankers. You've then got several routes of opportunity while they're still working out if you're still in the building.'

'Why are you helping me?' Declan asked as he opened the door for Trix.

She shrugged. 'When he hurt you outside your apartment, back at the start of all this, that wasn't supposed to happen. I realised then that people like Pearce Associates and Rattlestone believed they were higher than the law. What I did to your friend's reputation wasn't great, but she's a stranger to me. You guys? It's complicated.' As if remembering, she patted Declan on the arm. 'Behind the toilet in the cubicle is a taped burner phone. It has my number in it. I put it there last night. If it all goes wrong, call me.'

With that Trix walked over to her Fiat 500, parked half on the curb. Declan went to shout out after her, but his phone, currently on the coffee table, rang. Closing the door on Trix, Declan walked over to it, seeing on the screen that it was Anjli.

'Yeah?' he answered.

There was a moment of awkward silence, and then Anjli spoke. She was outside, and she was nervous, shocked even.

Declan had a sudden fear that Monroe was dead.

'We've got a body,' she replied. 'You need to come.'

'Where?'

'Brompton Cemetery, in Chelsea,' Anjli's voice was breaking. 'Declan, it's personal.'

'Who is it?' Declan thought back to the call last night, where Lizzie had claimed that Jessica hadn't come home. A sensation ran down his spine. The one that people always claimed was when someone walked over your grave.

'I don't want to say on the phone,' Anjli whispered. 'Just get here now.'

The phone went dead. Declan stared at it. Then, in a flurry of action, he called Lizzie.

No answer.

He called Jessica.

It went straight to voicemail.

Now suddenly scared, with the gut wrenching feeling that the sky was falling, Declan grabbed his coat and keys and ran out of the front door, locking up and clambering into his Audi. It was an hour to Brompton, but with the sirens on and his foot down on the accelerator, he could make it in twenty minutes.

He started the car but paused as his phone went. On the screen read JESSICA.

'Thank God,' he said as he answered it. 'Do you know how worried I've been—'

There was no reply. Just a slow, soft breathing.

A *man's* breathing.

A chuckle. A quiet, mocking one.

Then the phone went dead.

10

BAD DAY

Declan drove to Brompton like a man possessed. He couldn't get through to Lizzie, and Jessica's phone was now turned off. He left message after message as he sped down motorways and A-roads, his siren blaring and his blue lights flashing. He almost changed direction halfway along the route, driving directly to Lizzie's to see what was happening, but Brompton was closer and he knew that this couldn't, wouldn't be the worst-case scenario that he was thinking it could be. There were a ton of reasons why he couldn't get through to his daughter, or why a strange man had her phone—

He almost took out a car as he sped across a crossroads.

He couldn't stop himself. He started screaming with impotent rage.

Jessie was fine. Jessie *had* to be fine.

Pulling up outside the north entrance of Brompton Cemetery, Declan realised it had been less than twenty-four hours since he'd attended a secret meeting here with Kendis. He hadn't expected to be back so soon.

Waving his warrant card at an approaching Scene of Crime Officer, he was waved through the crime tape, past the curious bystanders and mourners currently barred from entry and started making his way down The Avenue towards the first crossroads where he could already see a gaggle of police officers and forensic teams gathering, the white crime tent already raised.

His phone buzzed; pulling it out, he saw with a mixture of relief and fear that it was Lizzie.

'Christ,' he said, answering the call as he walked past the graves. 'I've been worried sick! Is she alright? Tell me she's alright!'

'Of course she is!' Lizzie replied, far calmer than she had been the night before. 'She was a little shaken, though, because someone stole her bag in the cafe so she couldn't call home. Had to get a lift from a friend, and after they searched for the bag and tried to call her number and all that sort of thing, she eventually got back just before eleven in a bit of a state. And then my phone died, and I forgot to turn it back on.'

'Someone called me,' Declan was approaching the crime scene now, Anjli breaking off from a conversation, now walking towards him. 'Using her phone.'

'Probably kids, screwing around,' Lizzie replied. 'She's fine. Honest.'

'Gotta go. I'll call you later,' Declan turned off the call, looking at Anjli's concerned face. *If it wasn't Jessica, who was it?'*

'Why so secret?' he asked. Anjli pulled him to the side.

'I didn't want you crashing or anything,' she said. 'They found the body when they opened up. Doctor Marcos reckons it's been about twelve hours, so around eight pm last night since she died, and they brought her here post-death.'

'She?' Declan's gut churned again. 'Who is it, Anjli?'

'I'm sorry, Declan,' Anjli looked away as she spoke. 'It's Kendis Taylor.'

Declan stared at Anjli silently for a moment and then, without even realising it, he ran towards the crime tent. Billy, standing near the tent and talking to some officers, saw this and hurried to intercept him.

'Suit up first, sir,' he said calmly. 'I know she meant a lot to you, but you have to be *police* right now.'

Declan stared at the tent. This wasn't happening. This was a dream.

'How did she die?' he asked woodenly. Everything was fading; the colour was seeping out of the scene in front of him, the sound being replaced by a *whooshing* sound that filled his ears. He wanted to sit on the floor, to cut the string above his head that held him standing and just collapse to the ground.

But he didn't.

Billy was right. He had to be police right now.

Robotically, he gathered his white PPE suit, pulling it on, pulling the white boots over the bottom and the blue gloves over his wrists as Billy joined him.

'I hate these things,' Billy muttered. 'They always make me sweat in the worst places.'

'That's because you're always wearing tweed,' Declan replied in an emotionless monotone as they entered the tent. It was nothing more than a gazebo with sidings, and Declan saw that Doctor Marcos was standing by a gravestone, something that you didn't expect to see under the tarpaulin.

Next to the stone, however, was a body.

Declan knew it was Kendis the moment he saw it; she hadn't changed from the clothes she'd met him in earlier that day. He turned away, taking a deep breath. Doctor Marcos walked to him.

'You don't need to be in here,' she said soothingly. 'I can send you a report.'

'What do you have?' Declan's voice was still emotionless, even if his expression wasn't. Doctor Marcos looked back to the body, still being examined by one of the onsite CSI officers.

'Defensive wounds on her hands and arms, bruising around her neck, as if she was throttled.'

'She was strangled to death?'

'No, sorry. She was arm-barred during the struggle, I think. Forearm pressed against the throat. There are taser marks on her upper chest, so I think she tried to fight whatever was happening, and then was zapped. There's a cut to her head where she fell, struck it on something.'

'What then?'

'Declan, we don't need to—'

'*What then?*' Declan's voice had risen in volume now, and the other CSIs stopped momentarily to glance back at him. Doctor Marcos sighed.

'They stabbed her in the chest,' she replied. 'Small, thin blade into the lung. It would have caused an injury-related pneumothorax, a collapse of the lung itself. She would have passed out most likely, suffocated eventually.'

'She was killed here?'

Doctor Marcos shook her head. 'There's not enough blood,' she said. 'She was killed elsewhere but dumped here.

God knows why. Weirdly, they left her possessions too, purse and phones still in her jacket.'

'Phones, plural?'

'Yes, two of them. Not that uncommon these days.'

Declan moved past Doctor Marcos, past the forensic team who, realising that this was an important moment for him, stepped back to allow him some space.

Kendis was lying on her back, arms crossed, as if in repose. She had a blood covered chest wound, but her eyes were closed and her face looked peaceful. Declan knew though that this death had been far from peaceful, and he was going to make someone pay for this.

kissing in the living room as Kendis pulls back for air
pulling at his tie, sliding it out of his collar
tossing it to the carpet

Rising to his feet, Declan backed away from the body. 'Anything that connects this to Monroe's attack?'

'Nothing as yet,' Doctor Marcos replied. 'Joanna's with Monroe right now.'

Declan nodded, feeling hot. The walls of the tent were moving in on him.

pushing Kendis against the bed
fumbling for the clasp of her bra
laughing as they move together

'I need some fresh air,' he muttered.

'In case you hadn't realised, we're still *in* the fresh—' Doctor Marcos stopped herself. 'Of course. Let's move outside.'

Walking back out into the cemetery, Declan pulled off the PPE suit, gasping for air. The world was slowly and lazily spinning. He staggered across The Avenue, making his way towards a waste bin.

Kendis smiles as she says she loves me

'Guv?' It was Anjli, her hand on his back as he started vomiting into the bin. 'Let's get you out of here.'

No dammit, don't you dare pass out. Declan nodded, wiping his mouth with a napkin that she passed him. Looking up, he saw she had a bottle of water ready as well.

'We'll find the bastard,' she said. 'But we need you at your best right now.'

'Why?' Declan felt that there was more to this statement than just well-being. He didn't want to be at his best right now. He wanted to crawl into a hole and *die* right now.

Anjli indicated a group of detectives in the cemetery crossroads.

'Because that's who's taking over for Monroe,' she said.

Declan rose, sipping gingerly from the water bottle, swilling it around his mouth and spitting it into the bin as he looked across at the DCI leading the scene. He was over-weight, in his fifties, and bore the attitude of a man who didn't expect to be argued with.

He was also a man that Declan had met before.

In fact, DCI Sutcliffe had once stood on the doorstep of Declan's house with a full contingent of SCO19 officers and demanded a suspect who Declan had inside. If Monroe hadn't arrived, Declan didn't know what would have happened. But one thing Declan knew was that Sutcliffe was at the time connected to Francine Pearce, or Pearce Associates, because the man with the rimless glasses had also been there when—

The man with the rimless glasses was here.

He wasn't next to Sutcliffe, but he was to the side and back a little, speaking into a phone. Declan hadn't even realised that he was moving, his fists clenched into balls as he positioned himself to attack—

'Guv,' once again Billy had stepped in, blocking his way. 'Not now.'

Declan looked to Billy and was about to demand that he move aside, but seeing this Sutcliffe walked over to him.

'DI Walsh,' he said, offering a hand. 'We seem to meet at inopportune moments.'

Declan paused, but then took the hand, shaking it.

'DCI Sutcliffe,' he replied. 'I thought you didn't work for the Met?'

Sutcliffe forced a smile. 'When we met, I was working with an undercover unit that was examining corruption in the police,' he said matter-of-factly. 'In fact, if your suspect hadn't jumped off a roof back then, we'd still be there, gaining far more than you did.'

'We?' Declan was now staring at the man in the rimless glasses as he finished his call and walked over to Sutcliffe. It took every inch of self-control that Declan had to not leap at the man and attack him, to beat him like he knew he'd beaten Monroe.

'Yes,' Sutcliffe replied, showing the man with the rimless glasses. 'Meet DI Frost. He was working undercover in Pearce Associates for almost six months.'

'Apologies,' Frost, the man with the rimless glasses said as he held out his own hand to be shaken. 'I went a little too far undercover. I deserved the beating you gave me.'

Declan smiled as he took the hand, his expression hiding the dark fury he held. 'Yeah, you did.'

'Of course, I let you beat me,' Frost continued. 'I needed you to get up there before Shaun Donnal killed anyone.'

Declan's smile strained a little. 'I see,' was all he could say before looking back to Sutcliffe. 'I understand you're taking over the Unit until DCI Monroe recovers?'

'If he recovers,' Sutcliffe replied, raising a hand to stop Declan's immediate reply. 'I know, he's a fighter. But he's still in a coma. Once he's out, we'll assess how he is, and whether he'll be fit enough to return to duty.'

'He will,' Declan said, looking at DI Frost. 'When he wakes, we'll learn who did this to him ... and then we'll do the same back.'

Declan was sure that Frost flinched, the slightest of facial movements before Sutcliffe continued.

'We won't be playing eye for an eye here, Detective Inspector,' he said calmly. 'No matter how much you like punching suspects.'

'So what's the plan then, sir?' Declan asked, forcing himself to be professional.

'You knew the victim, right?' Sutcliffe asked, continuing before Declan gave an answer. 'You could speak to the next of kin then, see if they knew anything about her extremist tendencies.'

'Her what?' Declan could hear the whooshing noise in his ears again.

'She was a terrorist, Declan,' Frost said, intervening again. 'We've got files on her. She worked for some violent little rag-heads that wanted us all dead. Surprised you never saw it in her. Guess you're not as shit hot a detective as people say.'

Declan didn't mean to, it was completely instinctive; he went to swing at Frost, a vicious right hander that would have sent the glasses flying from his stupid, smug face. It didn't connect though, as Billy grabbed the arm, holding Declan back.

'You *bastard!*' Declan cried out at Frost. '*You piece of traitorous shite!* You weren't undercover! You're corrupt—'

'*Detective Inspector Walsh!*' Sutcliffe exploded. 'I'll let you off this time because you're emotionally connected to the victim. But I will not have this in my squad!'

'It's not your squad,' Declan muttered. 'It's Monroe's.'

'Monroe isn't here right now.'

Declan glared at Frost. 'We'd love to see the files,' he said, his voice ice cold. 'The ones Rattlestone sent last night froze on Monroe's computer when he was beaten.'

Again, another micro expression of surprise. Declan knew he was giving away ground here, but he didn't care right now.

lying in bed after

Kendis smiles and lazily drapes her arm across his chest

'I'll ensure he's okay, sir,' Anjli said, bringing Declan back to the moment. Sutcliffe nodded.

'I was actually hoping you could assist DI Frost,' he replied. 'He'll need some getting up to speed as he takes on the case.'

'*He's* taking the case?' Declan was appalled.

'You're too close, and we need a DI in charge,' Sutcliffe said coldly. 'You can carry on with the Monroe investigation.'

'I'll assist DI Frost,' Billy blurted. 'If that's okay?'

'Going full Judas on us, are you?' Still holding Declan, Anjli glared at Billy, who shrugged.

'We make our own choices,' he replied, staring directly at Anjli, as if daring her to reply.

'Then it's decided,' DCI Sutcliffe looked back to the tent. 'And someone get that bloody Doctor out of here, yeah? She's banned from crime scenes for the next five months, so I've been told.'

As he walked away, DI Frost and Billy following, Anjli pulled Declan back.

'You know more than you're letting on,' she said. 'We both know that your judge of character, although lousy, isn't that bad. So what's going on?'

'I saw Kendis yesterday,' Declan mumbled. 'Secret meeting, right here, in this cemetery. This morning Trix appeared at my doorstep, telling me that Baker and a security company called Rattlestone are trying to take out both Kendis and myself, seemingly unconnected to each other and ... and I heard a recording of that prick with the glasses attack Monroe.'

'Do you still have it?'

'I can get it.'

'So we find proof and we nail the bastard,' Anjli suggested. 'What do we do about Kendis though? I can't see you stepping back.'

'I'm not,' Declan replied. 'Someone wants to create a new narrative, one where Kendis is a terrorist sympathiser whose word is worth shit.'

'They don't want her being believed,' Anjli nodded.

Declan looked back to the tent, and to the hidden body of the woman he'd loved since he was a teenager.

'Charles Baker started this,' he hissed. 'So now he's going to pay.'

He pulled out his phone, dialling Jessica's number. Someone had taken it, and he wanted to know who, and why.

As the phone started to ring, however, Declan saw Frost stop, touching his pocket, as if feeling something vibrate.

Then Frost turned to Declan, looking at him across the cemetery.

And smiled.

The call, unanswered, went to voicemail and Declan stared at the man with the rimless glasses, once more in his life, knowing without a doubt that not only did he attack and almost kill Alexander Monroe, but he also stole Jessica's bag.

That meant war.

11

PAPARAZZI

It wasn't far from Brompton Cemetery to Kendis and Peter Taylor's Putney house, and so Declan and Anjli decided to make the journey there now, to see if Peter was back from the trip he'd taken. Not only did he need to be told of the murder, but as next of kin he needed to officially identity the body of Kendis Taylor.

There was nobody in when they knocked on the door. Declan was a little relieved at this though; the last thing he wanted was to face Kendis's husband the day after he'd left her bedroom in a walk of shame.

'We'll come back later,' he suggested.

'Billy and Frost can do it,' Anjli replied. 'Remember, this is their case right now. We're just doing this because Sutcliffe wanted to be a prick to you.'

'Is there a problem?' An elderly, female voice spoke from the side, and Declan turned to see a small, frail old lady, a mop of white hair on her head leaning out of next door's front door.

The one he'd passed the previous day.

He froze, completely sure that the old woman would recognise him, but after a moment he smiled and pulled out his warrant card.

'Nothing to worry about,' he said, showing it to the old lady. 'I'm DI Walsh, and this is DS Kapoor. We were just looking for Peter Taylor.'

The old lady squinted at the IDs as they were shown. 'Have we met?' she asked.

'No ma'am,' Declan lied. 'In fact, could you give us your name?'

'Edith,' she replied. 'Edith Langham.'

'Well Mrs Langham,' Anjli leaned in now, passing her business card over. 'When Mister Taylor returns, can you pass this to him and ask him to call us? We'd be very grateful.'

'Is this about the woman?' Edith read the business card, putting it away in her pocket.

'Woman? You mean his wife?' Declan asked.

'Yes,' Edith replied. 'Always out, she was. Didn't come back last night, neither. I would have heard her through the doors. Had men over, too, when he wasn't here.'

'Men?' Declan asked carefully. 'More than one?'

'Oh, yes,' Edith spoke with the tone of an expert in the subject. 'She claimed it was work related, but some were quite unsavoury. The swarthy one in the denim jacket was here yesterday morning, right after another man left yesterday morning, half dressed.'

'Half dressed?' Anjli glanced at Declan. 'Do you remember what he looked like?'

Edith looked at Declan. 'Like him,' she said. 'But older. Fatter maybe. Similar hair.'

Declan released a silent, held breath. 'So a tall, fat

Caucasian man with brown hair?'

'I know it's quite generic,' Edith continued. 'But it was early, and I hadn't had my tea yet.'

Declan smiled. 'Anything you give is helpful,' he replied. 'Please, pass that to Peter Taylor when you see him.'

With the conversation now ended, Declan and Anjli walked back to the car.

'You're a lucky bastard,' Anjli whispered as they reached it. 'If she clocked you, that could have been game over. I'm guessing it was you she saw?'

Declan nodded. 'And I think the *swarthy man* was Nasir Gill, her photographer,' he replied.

'Then you're bloody lucky that you look like shit first thing in the morning,' Anjli finished as she entered the car. Declan breathed out a pent-up breath of frustration, climbing into the driver's seat, and a moment later they drove off back towards Temple Inn.

Neither of them noticed the black Ford Focus with the shaven-headed man that was parked across the road, watching them leave and noting the time down in his journal.

WHEN THEY ARRIVED BACK AT TEMPLE INN, THERE WAS SOME kind of argument occurring with Sutcliffe, already taking over Monroe's office, screaming at Billy and Frost.

'I don't care where they got it!' he shouted. 'I want to know how it was taken in the first place!'

'Problem?' Declan asked as he and Anjli entered the office. Sutcliffe looked up at them.

'I'd say it was probably you, as you love leaking shit to the press, but your point of contact is the sodding story this time,' he said, spinning his monitor to reveal the front page of *The Daily Mail*'s website. On it was a photo of a man, standing outside Brompton Cemetery, baseball cap and aviator glasses hiding his face. It was a zoomed in photo, so the image was grainy and slightly blurred. Under it read the headline

FACE OF A KILLER
FACE OF A TERRORIST

'What the hell is that?' Declan exclaimed, moving in for a closer look. 'Who gave them this?'

'That, DI Walsh is the bloody *Daily Mail* telling the world of the death of a rival journalist and believed terrorist, and *that* is a picture of who we believe is her terrorist handler, moments before he met with her in a secret meeting.' Sutcliffe sighed. 'Now, thanks to the magic of the World Wide Web, everyone in the bloody world knows about it.'

Billy was reading the piece.

'They say she was an extremist,' he said.

'Where?' Anjli leaned in now.

Billy pointed to the screen. 'It says here they reckon that they have a source, claiming that when she was in Syria a few years back, an extremist Muslim organisation turned her. They write that this man may have been her handler, and that he killed her because she failed some mission.'

'This is bullshit!' Declan exclaimed.

'This is tabloid journalism,' Billy replied.

'Well, it's out there now,' Declan said. 'Let's move on and solve this before—'

'Oh, so you're still on this case?' Sutcliffe snapped. 'The one I specifically told you to walk away from?'

'Just offering to help,' Declan suggested. 'I assumed we'd have a briefing?'

Sutcliffe pointed at the briefing room, and Declan, Anjli, Billy and Frost entered it, with Sutcliffe walking in behind them.

'I don't know how to use this bloody plasma screen,' Sutcliffe muttered. 'So someone will have to work it for me as I talk.'

'I'll do that,' Billy started tapping on his laptop and the screen filled with *The Daily Mail's* website, complete with image.

Declan shifted uncomfortably in his chair, looking around. Nobody yet was staring at him, so he hoped the disguise would hold.

'So as we all know, journalist Kendis Taylor was found murdered in Brompton Cemetery today,' Sutcliffe started. 'She was killed by a stab wound to the chest, likely inflicted elsewhere around eight pm last night, and was brought to this spot under cover of darkness. The wound is apparently an interesting one, according to your team as it's double-edged, like a tiny sword and it left behind a strange residue.'

'Strange how?'

'Ruthenium,' Sutcliffe read the word from his phone. 'Which is one of the rarest minerals in the world, apparently, and used in solar cell batteries and electrical contacts.'

'So, someone stabbed her with a sharpened solar cell?'

Sutcliffe raised a hand to stop the conversation, waiting for silence before continuing. 'We've sent her personal items off to be examined, and hopefully we'll get something from them.'

'What were the items?' Declan asked.

'Two phones, a purse with twenty-five pounds in, some

credit cards and her NUJ card—'

'NUJ?' Billy looked up.

'National Union of Journalists,' Declan replied.

'She also had a notebook with pages written in short-hand, which we've asked her newspaper to translate for us and a post-it note with both *TOTTERS LANE* and *FOB C* written on it.'

'Totters Lane is in Shoreditch,' Billy said as he checked a page on his laptop. 'Nothing of note, got obliterated in the war. People literally vaporised.'

'Check if she had any connections there,' Sutcliffe ordered. 'It could have been her next target.'

Declan resisted the urge to respond to the comment.

'FOB C?' Anjli now looked up at the DCI. 'As in key fob?'

'No idea,' Sutcliffe replied. 'If it is, it's the third one in a series of fobs, so we need to work that out. Unless Mister Walsh, being our soldier on the scene knows?'

Declan looked to the desk. There was a term that he knew, used back when he was a military police officer.

'FOB can mean *forward operating base,*' he reluctantly replied. 'It's a military term, more used by the US army, but it means any secured forward operational level military position that's used to support tactical objectives and strategic military intentions.'

'Look at that,' Frost grinned. 'A known extremist having a piece of paper that—'

'She's not a known anything,' Declan snapped. 'As Anjli said, a key fob is just as possible.'

'Well, we'll know more when we get a report back,' Sutcliffe interjected.

'DC Davey could have done that quicker, sir,' Anjli spoke up.

'DC Davey is a jobsworth who only does what her boss tells her to do,' Sutcliffe replied. 'I'd rather a professional does it. Anyway, we have a rough timeline of her last day. She arrived at her desk at ten in the morning and was apparently quite agitated. She disappeared at around noon and turned her phone off, which is concerning.'

'Or she was conserving her battery,' Declan suggested.

'Let's go with the extreme terrorist idea first, shall we?' Sutcliffe threw back. 'Either way, she turned it back on around one thirty and sent a text message, arranging a meeting for three pm that afternoon at Brompton Cemetery, with this mysterious man, and a Nasir Gill, a co-worker with Muslim tendencies.'

'Muslim tendencies?' Anjli shook her head. 'Do you mean he is a Muslim? That's like saying someone has Christian tendencies.'

'I'm sorry, was my statement not woke enough for you?' Sutcliffe took a moment and then continued. 'She also met with Nasir Gill, a co-worker and *known Muslim*.'

'Who did she send the text to?' Declan asked. 'Maybe it can nail down the target?'

'Unregistered sim,' Billy replied. 'More importantly, it doesn't matter because it was one of the two phones she had on her body. The man must have given it back when they met. She then caught a taxi but almost immediately got off it, as if throwing someone off her trail, and then caught a bus to Victoria Coach Station with her Oyster card. We have the card being used again after this, but bus CCTV footage shows it being used by a young Asian man.'

'He stole it?'

'Or she gave it to him. This is still three hours before time of death. She then disappears from view until this morning when we found her. At some point she was taken back to the cemetery that she'd been in earlier.'

'What time does the cemetery close up?' Declan asked.

'Waiting to find out,' Sutcliffe replied.

'Two nights ago she used her credit card to buy a round of drinks in The Horse and Guard pub in Chelsea,' Frost spoke now. 'Apparently the bar staff remember her being there until closing, drinking with a tall, dark-haired man in his thirties or forties. Possibly the same man we have in the picture here. We're waiting to look at their CCTV footage.'

'What else?' Anjli was writing into her notebook now as Declan felt sick. *If the CCTV appeared of the night before, he'd be seen with her. Damned by association.*

Sutcliffe looked at his phone as he beeped.

'A message from Doctor Marcos,' he said. 'Apparently there were traces of semen in the body. With hubby not around, this has to be our guy's DNA.' His phone beeped again. Reading this message, Sutcliffe shook his head.

'No,' he simply said before walking out of the room, phone already to his ear.

'We went to the Taylor house,' Anjli continued in his absence. 'We met his neighbour, an Edith Langham. She said that she saw a man leave early yesterday morning. He was white, brown hair—'

'Bit like you then, Declan,' Frost smiled.

'My friends call me Declan, everyone else calls me DI Walsh,' Declan replied coldly. 'You don't get to call me anything. Yes, he looked like me. She told me that, before pointing out all the points where we differed.'

Sutcliffe walked back into the room now, seemingly chastened. He stared at the image of the man on the screen, as if staring through the glasses and the hat.

'It's *you*, Walsh,' he said.

Declan felt his stomach fall.

'Sorry?'

Sutcliffe turned to face him now, and the impotent fury was obvious in his body language.

'I said it's you,' he repeated. 'Lead on the case.'

'I don't understand,' Declan looked around, in case he was missing something. 'This is a murder case. A DCI runs that, and you told me that—'

'*I know what I damn well told you!*' Sutcliffe shouted. 'But that was Whitehall. Seems your friend Baker's pulled some strings, wants you running it. Claims you're the best detective he knows, and he therefore believes that you can solve this murder.'

Declan stared in shock at Sutcliffe. 'Baker asked for me personally?'

'Must be so great being special,' Sutcliffe snapped. 'Oh, and your boss, Monroe? He's woken up.' He raised his voice as Billy, Anjli, and Declan rose. 'Sit back down, dammit! We've got a murder to solve. Walsh, Kapoor, you're tagged in. Find out what you can. Frost, Fitzwarren, go see Monroe and find out if he remembers anything about his attacker.'

Frost and Billy rose and left the room, Sutcliffe returning to Monroe's office as Anjli looked at Declan.

'So what now?' she whispered. 'I mean, we can't hunt this guy down when he's you!'

'I know,' Declan rose. 'Let me think.'

Leaving the briefing room, Declan walked down the corridor at the back of the office that led to the toilets. Although it had several cubicles inside, it was a unisex room, mainly because of the small amount of officers working there. Entering the middle cubicle, Declan paused, leaned over the bowl and threw up anything that remained in his stomach. Images of the night with Kendis swum around his vision, forcing him to fall against the cubicle, while random thoughts flashed through his mind, striking at him as they did so.

Why did Baker want Declan to run the case?

Who killed Kendis?

Did Frost steal Jessie's phone, and if so, did this give him an alibi for the murder?

Who was her contact, and how could Declan get them to pass everything to him?

At the sink, splashing cold water onto his face and swilling out his mouth, spitting into the basin and watching it swirl into the plug hole, Declan felt a little more normal. He had to hold it together. He had to work out what the next stage was, because everyone would try to learn the identity of Kendis's terrorist "handler".

He knew, the moment they found out that it was Declan, there wouldn't be a trial.

Declan would be taken to a black site and forgotten.

He looked back to the cubicle, walking over to the toilet and flushing it once more. Then, reaching around the back of the toilet tank, he felt the lump of a phone taped to the back.

He could take it and run, leave now, find a bolt hole and hide.

No.

He had to solve the murder, find out who killed Kendis Taylor and possibly bring down a Governmental coup before the world learned his identity.

Because when they did, he was *totally screwed.*

12

BIPARTISANSHIP

CHARLES BAKER SAT AT A SMALL TABLE IN THE MEMBERS Terrace of the Houses of Parliament, eating an early lunch before the noon sessions began when Will Harrison, a face of thunder joined him.

'What do you have?' Charles asked between mouthfuls, ignoring his companion's expression. Will, turning on his iPad glanced at a page of written notes.

'Well, I think—'

'Please, for the love of God tell me you don't have the notes on that,' Baker pointed at the iPad with his fork. 'We said paper only, remember?'

'These are just notes,' Will replied. 'Nothing more.'

Charles stared at his advisor with the look of a man who desperately wanted to believe in them, but just couldn't. 'So, go on then. What do we have?'

'Someone's taking a shot at you,' Will started. 'I've ensured that our assets are on the case.'

'Not my bloody assets,' Charles muttered. 'If I find that they were involved in the murder—'

'She wasn't exactly our greatest ally here, Charles,' Will waved for a server. 'It's not a bad thing that she's gone.'

'There'll be a bloody investigation!'

'Then my men will fix this!' Will caught himself from raising his voice too much. Charles looked across the terrace dining area at Julia Roxbury, the Lib Dem MP for Christ knows where and faked a smile as she looked up.

'They don't need to,' he said through smile-gritted teeth. 'I've fixed it. I've arranged for DI Walsh to lead the investigation.'

'Why the ever-living fu—' Will caught himself, forcing his tone quieter. 'Why would you do that, sir?'

'Because I want the murderer found and I want this removed off my table,' Charles snapped. 'We had her ruined! Nobody was going to believe her word!'

'We didn't kill her,' Will replied. 'No command was given.'

'So, therefore, Walsh will find whoever did it, and it won't fall on us,' Charles repeated.

Will shifted in his seat. 'Have you lost faith in me?' he asked.

Charles placed his cutlery down, glaring at his advisor. 'Let me turn this around onto you,' he snapped again. 'Do you have faith in yourself? In your team? Because currently, I'm not seeing it. I might not have liked the Last Chance bloody Saloon, and they might have made my life a living hell, but they still saved my life and got me out of a decades long servitude agreement, so currently I feel a kinship for them. Also, if one of your men attacked Monroe—'

'Any order I gave was given by you,' Will replied carefully. 'It's not my fault if you were too vague to give the specifics.'

Charles stared at Will for a moment, open-mouthed.

'You little shit,' he eventually hissed. 'It was you.'

'I just pass your wishes on,' Will replied. He went to continue, but movement at the entrance to the terrace distracted him.

'And the charity case cometh,' he muttered to himself as a woman holding a box file hurried over to them. She was in her late forties, with dyed-blonde hair pulled back severely. She'd never mastered the art of makeup, and so her attempt was minimal, with a base foundation, lipstick and a deep-blue eyeliner plastered on so strong that she looked more like a stage performer than a civil servant. She was overweight but not incredibly so and fidgeted with her wedding ring once she'd placed the box file on a convenient chair.

'Laurie,' Charles said with genuine delight. 'How are you settling in?'

'Very well, thank you,' Laurie Hooper replied, still standing awkwardly. 'I mean, it's different to when I worked for your wife, but I'm grateful for the opportunity.'

'Talking of opportunities, I hear you met some other MPs,' Will said, looking up at her. Laurie flushed, twisting her wedding band even harder.

'I don't know what you mean,' she half whispered.

Will smiled. 'I heard you were in The Horse and Guard pub in Chelsea two nights ago with Malcolm Gladwell.' He noted Charles stop eating at this.

Laurie paled. 'Um, yes,' she replied. 'He asked me for a drink, to see how I was settling in.'

'You didn't think that was suspicious? That a rival MP invited you out?'

'He's a Conservative too,' Laurie argued. 'That's not a rival.'

'Depends on the job you're going for,' Charles muttered.

'Be wary of Gladwell,' Will said carefully. 'He's a party man. Which means he has no loyalty to anyone.'

'What did you talk about?' Charles asked nonchalantly.

Laurie shrugged. 'Things,' she replied quietly. 'He was worried about you.'

Charles almost laughed at this. Malcolm Gladwell barely spoke to him, even though they'd once worked in the same department. Although to be fair, Charles preferred it that way.

'Then he can come and speak to Mister Baker himself,' Will snapped. 'Remember that you're a married woman, *Mrs* Hooper.'

Laurie flinched at this, as if slapped physically by Will's words.

'We're just friends,' she replied, her voice only a whisper.

'There are no friends in Westminster,' Charles mused, continuing to spear at his salad with his fork.

'Was there anything you wanted, anyway?' Will enquired mockingly. 'Or did you just want to stand awkwardly over us?'

Without another word Laurie picked up the box, turned and stomped out of the terrace area. Charles looked at Will, currently basking in the point score.

'Bad move,' he said. 'We need her.'

'The only reason she's still employed on your staff is guilt, and you know it,' Will replied.

Charles finished his salad, dabbing at his lips.

'Loyalty is something I respect,' he said.

'As do I,' Will said, rising from the table as he did so. 'Anyway, I'm sorry for spoiling your brunch. I'll keep you in the loop on what happens with the investigation.'

'Do so,' Charles rose from the table as well now. 'Also check into why Malcolm bloody Gladwell is taking Donna's ex-PA out for drinks, yeah? Because it sure as hell wasn't to give an orientation.'

———

MALCOLM GLADWELL WASN'T AT PARLIAMENT FOR THE NOON meetings. He'd returned to his Page Street apartment, his stomach *flip-flopping* after the news of Kendis Taylor's death had fed through, looking for something that could settle it. The iPad that he currently stared at had *The Daily Mail*'s cover, with the image of a man outside Brompton Cemetery, and he had to place it back down to stop his hand shaking.

What if they learned it was him?

Kendis had been found in Brompton Cemetery, and from what the news outlets said, she had found her way in after hours. Even the police weren't sure how she managed this, but Gladwell knew.

She'd taken the key from him, after all.

He sat on his sofa, staring out of the window for the moment. He didn't have a magnificent view, but in all fairness, he wasn't really paying attention to it. She'd gone there to get answers and had only found death. Somewhere there was likely to be a Special Services report that not only showed her talking to him in a local park, but also visiting a pub near Brompton Cemetery with him the night before. As soon as the CCTV footage came out, they'd find a way to leak it.

He'd expected this, though. This was a power move and a *war*. So he'd spoken to a journalist? Everyone does in Westminster. And as to her being a terrorist? He never knew that when they met. Gladwell knew that the rumours of extremism were just that, created to throw doubt on her.

They didn't expect a murder hunt and a terrorist plot suddenly being thrown upon the British public.

He started visibly when his buzzer went. Walking to the door, he saw on the video screen a woman, looking around nervously. Allowing the downstairs to open with a click of a button, Gladwell walked to the door and opened it. A moment later a visibly distressed Laurie Hooper entered, passing Gladwell as he moved aside, closing the door behind her.

'What's the matter?' he asked.

'Harrison knows we were together,' Laurie whispered. 'He said that you're a party man. Which means you have no loyalty to me.'

'Harrison is an overweight fool who's one more Big Mac away from a coronary,' Gladwell replied, forcing a smile. 'Perhaps if we cross our fingers and hope really hard, it'll happen soon.'

Laurie couldn't help it. She laughed.

'When will you tell me what really happened?' she asked. 'What Donna really said to you on her last day?'

'When I'm a hundred percent convinced I'm right,' Gladwell pulled Laurie into his arms, embracing her. 'Then we'll both gain revenge for her.'

Laurie looked up, her eyes wide and innocent. Gladwell almost wished that he had the same innocence, long washed away by the Thames under Westminster Bridge.

'I want you now,' he whispered, kissing her hard on the lips, feeling her melt into him as she complied.

She always complied.

ALEXANDER MONROE HAD BEEN HAVING THE STRANGEST DREAM. He couldn't remember it now, as he lay in a hospital bed with tubes attached to every part of his body, but he remembered snippets. A moment of incredible pain to his skull. A man he thought he'd never see returning into his office, but dressed like Declan. A teenager with a gun to his gangster father's head. A paint grenade going off.

Much of this he knew were scenes from the day, his muddled, drug-addled brain trying to put them into some kind of organisation, but one moment, one scene from the dream was still clear, and certainly hadn't happened. He was standing on a beach, facing Kendis Taylor. She was wearing a large, slightly oversized parka, zipped up tightly, and they were arguing. He couldn't remember what about; that part of the dream had disappeared. All he remembered was Kendis saying that she was sorry, that this wasn't her fault, the coat opening and a bomb vest being seen underneath—

Then he woke up in what was apparently an Adult Critical Care Unit, with Rosanna Marcos sitting on a chair beside him reading a magazine. Obviously, once she realised he was awake, the magazine was thrown to the side and a flurry of medical staff were around, prodding, poking, asking questions, shining torches into his eyes ... Monroe believed it was then that he passed out again, but when he awoke the second time the room was quieter, with Doctor Marcos now taking his pulse while ignoring all the machines that told her the answer.

'Does it match?' he whispered with a smile. Doctor Marcos saw he'd woken and leaned closer to him.

'Stay quiet,' she said. 'If they hear you're awake again, they'll start prodding and poking all over again.'

Monroe chuckled at this but stopped when a wave of pain

slashed through his skull, like they had placed a metal band around it, set to constrict quickly.

'How bad?' he whispered, reaching up and feeling the bandaging around his head.

'You're battered, but you put up a good defence. Your head, however … you lost a lot of blood, Alex, and for a while we didn't think you were coming back.' She grabbed his hand, squeezing it.

'I'm sorry …' Monroe said, looking up at her. '… but do I *know* you?'

Doctor Marcos stepped back in horror, but her expression turned to anger as Monroe laughed again, a wheezing, sporadic one that started and stopped as the pain in his head slashed at him in intervals.

'Oh, you little shit,' she snapped. 'I've been worried sick, and that's what you do.'

'I'm sorry,' Monroe croaked. 'It was too good an opportunity to miss.'

Doctor Marcos sat down beside Monroe again.

'You know that with one pinch of these tubes going into you, I can ruin your day real fast, yes?' she muttered. 'Do you remember what happened?'

'Someone kept ramming my head into a glass door, I think,' Monroe replied. 'Can I get a sip of water?'

Doctor Marcos passed a sippy cup over, holding it for Monroe as he took a small mouthful. 'Do you remember who did this to you?'

'That's what we were going to ask,' Billy said as he entered the room, a broad grin on his face. 'Good to see you awake, Guv.'

Monroe smiled and was about to reply when the second man entered the room.

The man with the rimless glasses.

'Good to see you awake, DCI Monroe,' he said. 'I'm DI Frost. I've been seconded to your unit.'

Monroe looked to Billy, wondering if this was some kind of hallucination.

'It's true, Guv,' Billy replied. 'The DCI who's running the case is DCI Sutcliffe. You met him during that armed stand-off in Hurley. Frost here was working undercover for Pearce Associates during that case.'

'Sutcliffe is working my case?' Monroe was still confused.

'No, sir,' Frost stepped forward. 'You're one of two cases, this and the murder investigation on Kendis Taylor.'

'Kendis is dead?' Monroe looked to Doctor Marcos, who nodded. 'How long have I been out?'

'Only a couple of days,' Billy replied. 'But we need to find the man who did this to you. If you remember anything, it'd help, Guv.'

Monroe remembered everything. He remembered the man with the rimless glasses, who was now apparently called DI Frost, attacking him with a baton he kept up his sleeve. More importantly, judging from a quickly taken glance at him now, moving to bar the door, Frost was about to attack again the moment Monroe spoke.

Also, he knew that Doctor Marcos and Billy would suffer this time.

'I'm sorry,' he whispered. 'I don't remember anything after being drugged in a car. Doctor Marcos has been explaining what happened in Beachampton.'

'You remember nothing?' Frost moved closer, suspicious.

Monroe shrugged. 'Sorry, not a thing,' he lied.

Watching him, Doctor Marcos nodded.

'Short-term amnesia is common in head trauma,' she

explained. 'A few days of bed rest and I'm sure it'll come back to him.'

'Well, we'll leave you alone now,' Billy was still smiling. 'It's really great to see you awake.' Monroe forced his own smile as Billy and Frost left the room, slowly turning his head, fighting the pain to look at Doctor Marcos.

'I need to speak to Declan,' he said. 'I need to speak to him *now*.'

13

TICK TICK TICK

DECLAN STARED UP AT THE HORSE AND GUARD PUB, SHAKING back the fear that this could be the moment that ended his career, that had him named as some kind of extremist terrorist handler rather than the slightly more innocent, but no better explanation of a man and a woman having an illicit affair.

'You want me to do this?' Anjli, climbing out of the passenger side, turned to ask. Declan shook his head.

'No,' he replied. 'It's fine.'

It was a small pub, completely detached and at a corner of the Fulham Road and a gated entrance to a small cul-de-sac. To his back was a brick wall made of old, blackened bricks, as if built during Victorian times but recently renovated to fit the local aesthetics, easily eight-feet high that ran the length of the red-brick, six-storey apartment complex behind it. To his right, and further on from the complex was a church, equally cleaned of the dirt and soot that came from a hundred years of pollution, its sandy-coloured bricks gleaming in the sun and now converted into a very expensive house, with likely some kind of swimming pool or cinema or even both in the onetime crypt.

Looking back to the street in front of him, Declan saw it had two personalities; on the right-hand side of the cul-de-sac was a series of design studios, accountants and estate agents, the two-storey buildings above painted white, straight edged and well maintained, while the left-hand side, the side that held The Horse and Guard pub was built in a different style, the bricks stained, the corners rounded, and a ten-foot gap in between veterinary clinics, junk shops, beauty salons and the pub; blocked off with a tall fence, covered in the same black-painted style as the rest of the building, covered in posters that told of exciting televised sports and even more exciting food available inside. At the front was a metal hatch that led to the beer cellar, one side open, as if waiting for a delivery.

Declan stared at the pub for another long minute.

'Are you really sure that you don't want me to do this?' Anjli asked again. Declan smiled.

'I'm good, I promise,' he replied. 'It's just that there's something, a half remembered moment ...' He stopped. 'There was someone else there. Kendis seemed distracted. She was happy to sit and talk, and then I went to the toilet ...' He furrowed his brow as he tried to remember. 'I think I went to the toilet, and when I came back she was different. Wanted to leave there and then. I thought at the time she just wanted to go somewhere quieter, but I'm now wondering if I missed something.'

'Can you remember the person?' Anjli asked. Declan shrugged.

'There were a few people in there, and I wasn't on a case,' he admitted as he closed his driver's door and, checking the traffic, crossed the road, heading towards the building. 'Maybe the CCTV will show what happened.'

'Maybe the CCTV will show you, though,' Anjli was walking to catch up with him now. 'How do we explain that?'

Declan stopped. 'At that point you arrest me,' he replied. 'As I'll be a suspect at that point.'

'Come on, Guv!' Anjli protested, and Declan couldn't help but smile. She only called him 'Guv' when she was trying to be official. 'They can't think you're a terrorist!'

'They can and they will,' Declan retorted. 'That's why we need to finish this first.'

Declan stopped before entering though, looking back across the road, down towards the onetime church and the shops that faced it. Parked up on the pavement opposite the church and facing them was a black Ford Focus car, currently stopped on the single yellows that fronted the shops beside it. Inside, the shaven-headed man that had been watching them now looked elsewhere, as if unaware that Declan was even staring at him.

'That car's been following us all day,' Declan whispered. 'It was across the road at Putney, and I think he was at the hospital.' He started towards the car, picking up speed as he walked determinedly past the shops, pulling out his warrant card as he did so, Anjli following him.

'Oi! Police!' he shouted. 'Out of the car now!'

Ignoring Declan, the shaven-headed man pulled out his phone, making a call. As Declan ran to the side of the car, tapping on the glass, the man looked up, pointed at the phone as if to say 'hold on I need to take this' and then looked away. Declan was about to bang on the window again when he noticed the journal on the passenger seat. It was open, tossed aside the moment that the man had grabbed the phone and there was a collection of jumbled notes visible on the pages. The first couple were about Declan; the times that he was at Kendis's house, who he spoke to, and also when he arrived at the hospital.

But it was the last two notes that Declan saw that made him step back.

The first was a simple note; it read

N GILL New Change 1pm take out

The second was more worrying, as it read

Monroe awake clean up ASAP

'Get out of the car now!' Declan screamed at the man as he reached into his pocket and pulled out his pen. It might have seemed like a pointless gesture, but the pen was a tactical one, from his days in the Military Police, and was titanium built with a steel tip on the end; a steel tip that Declan spun in his fingers to face the car as he gripped the pen hard, slamming the steel tip against the driver's window, the impact shattering the glass into tiny pieces as he did so.

'I said *do it now!*' the shaven-headed man screamed as Declan grabbed at him. Anjli was already running towards them—

Then the world exploded.

It wasn't, but it felt like it. The Horse and Guard pub's ground floor erupted in a brief flash of light and sound, as a detonation occurred; the windows exploded outwards into the Fulham Road as flame and smoke burst through, an ear-splitting *foom* and blast of hot wind slamming through the air a split second later. Anjli, closer to the exploding pub than

Declan was found herself thrown to the pavement, blown off her feet by the force of it. Declan meanwhile slammed against the Ford Focus, stumbling to his knees as the shaven-headed driver now wrenched the car into first gear and, spinning the steering wheel, sped off down the street away from the explosion. His ears ringing, Declan caught the licence number of the vehicle before he fell back to the road, jotting it on his hand with the pen before turning to face The Horse and Guard pub.

There wasn't much of the original external decor left; the windows were now shattered and the pub sign engulfed in flames. Staggering to his feet, he ran towards it. He didn't know if the pub had been open, or whether anyone had been inside when it exploded, but he knew he had to try something, anything to help.

It was Anjli though who pulled him back.

'Don't be a fool!' she cried out. 'They're dead. Anyone in there? No hope.'

Declan pushed Anjli aside and ran to the door on the corner, pausing as a piece of burned paper lying on the ash-covered floor beside it caught his eye.

CLOSED FOR DELIVERY

Declan allowed Anjli to pull him back, staggering back to the Audi, now covered in debris and broken glass, already pulling out his phone.

'Call it in, we need ambulances on the scene,' he commanded as he turned back to the phone. 'Dave? Declan Walsh. Yeah, hello mate, long time. Look, my computer whiz is busy and I need a favour. Could you run a plate for me? Cheers.'

As Declan gave the licence plate currently on the back of his hand to the voice on the end of the line, he looked across to Anjli.

'He did this,' he said. 'The man shouted to *do it now*, right before the bomb went off.'

He turned back to the phone call.

'It is? Brilliant. Thanks.'

He disconnected the call, moving back to the now burning pub, peering down into the beer cellar.

'Anyone in there?' he shouted. There was no answer, but there was no smoke, either. Anyone down there would be injured at best, and the fire brigade could sort that.

Now in a hurry, he ran back across the debris-strewn road, cars at either end stopping as drivers climbed out of their cars to stare at the burning pub, and pulled open the driver's door of the Audi.

'What are you doing?' Anjli exclaimed. 'You can't leave the scene of crime!'

'That car is licensed to Rattlestone Securities,' Declan replied. 'Also the guy had two notes I could see written. One of them was that Monroe was awake, and they needed a clean-up ASAP.' He winced as he looked back at the flames. 'Call Doctor Marcos, get her to find a way of getting the Guv out of there before they come for him.'

'But he's still critical!'

'Better critical than dead!' Declan snapped. 'I need to get to New Change Shopping Centre by St Paul's. The other note said that Nasir Gill is there in ...' he looked to his phone, '... about half an hour. All the order said was "take out".'

'As in kill?'

'They're a secret police made up of coppers and spies,'

Declan climbed into the car. 'I don't think they're considering taking him to *Wagamama's*.'

'What about the pub?'

'It was closed for deliveries,' Declan replied through the open window, starting the engine. 'With luck, this means that nobody was upstairs. At least it wasn't open, and it's not connected to the buildings beside.'

Anjli went to reply, to state that even closed there could have been several staff inside, but the Audi was already driving off, blue lights flashing as it drove eastwards to St Paul's.

Sighing, Anjli looked back to the pub as, in the distance, she could hear the sirens of fire engines. 'Well, I reckon the CCTV records are probably gone,' she muttered to herself before turning to the road, walking into the middle of it and waiting for the emergency services to arrive. Pulling out her phone, she dialled a number.

'Rosanna, it's me,' she said when it eventually moved to voicemail. 'When you get this? Call me. Or get Monroe out of there now, whichever's easiest.'

Disconnected, she considered calling this in, but she still didn't trust Sutcliffe or Frost to cause some kind of issue there. She guessed that this was why Declan called in a favour to gain the car registration details rather than call Billy.

Dialling another number, Anjli waved the fire engines to the burning pub, waving aside some shopkeepers and visitors who'd stopped to watch, and who were now blocking the way of the lorries, showing her warrant card to a police car as it pulled up beside her in a screech of tyres.

'Pull the crowds back,' she shouted, turning back to the

phone as it was answered. 'Jo? Anjli. Get to Marcos right now.'

She looked to the firefighters, already preparing the hoses.

'Someone's coming to kill Monroe.'

14

RACE THE CLOCK

DC Jo Davey wasn't a fan of running. She'd spent most of her life avoiding the act, and so the fact that she was now sprinting down the Victoria Embankment wasn't lost on her as she waved down the first black cab she could find, clambering wearily in and sending them to The Royal London Hospital. Doctor Marcos still hadn't checked her emails or voicemails, and the calls were still going through to the annoying bloody voice that stated that '*blah blah blah* number' wasn't available right now.

The least she could have done was make a funny answerphone message.

Out of the car, DC Davey now started reluctantly running again, her frizzy ginger hair blowing out in the wind as she pushed her glasses back up her nose. She'd been here several times over the last couple of days so, unlike Declan on his first time there, Davey knew the quickest and exact route to Ward 4F, entering through the Stepney Way entrance, running past the Air Ambulance kiosk and through the double doors on the far side. Here she ran up some stairs and took another right to the elevator, already out of breath, running up to it, yelling 'hold the doors!' as they closed and sliding into the cramped enclosure between three burly men in bomber jackets.

The button to the fourth floor was already pressed, and she went to say nothing, but there was something off about the surrounding men, and so she pressed the button for the floor above, smiling at the man closest to her. He was close-shaven, giving him a bit of a "spray-tan Jason Statham" look. The man to her right was dark-haired and Asian, while the man behind her, from the brief glance she'd given as she entered had looked to be the oldest of them all with peppered-grey hair cropped into something similar to a buzz cut, but at the same time not. Which was lucky because buzz cuts were really tragic.

The button for the ACCU dinged, and the doors opened. Smiling, Davey stepped back into the elevator, allowing the men to leave, watching them as they entered the shared waiting area and walked off to the right. She held the <> button for a moment, keeping the doors open for a count of five and then, peeking around the door and seeing they were now out of sight, she slipped out of the elevator and moved quickly across to the main door, letting them walk across the bridge corridor and through the other end's doors before making her own move to the end. There had been a police officer there the last time she'd been there; through the double windows in the door she could see that he was still on duty, rising to his feet to confront the three men, who seemed by their postures to be quite relaxed at this, pulling out warrant cards and showing them. The police officer relaxed, and now seemed to chat happily to them, indicating to the left, and the corridor that led to Ward 4F.

But there was still something wrong here, and once they moved on Davey entered the junction, waving her warrant card, the three men already around the corner and out of sight.

'Call backup now, armed if possible,' she whispered to the officer, turning right and entering Ward 4E. It was almost a mirror image of the other ACCU ward, running parallel with it to the doors at the other end. Running faster now, the adrenaline fuelling her legs, she shot past the confused consultants and nurses in the central area and slammed through the double doors into a white-walled corridor that led to the stairs and the rear entrance of Ward 4F. Arriving at its double doors, she stared through the window into the central area.

She was too late.

As she looked through the pane of glass, she saw the three men walk into Monroe's side room, one of them stopping and standing outside as a guard.

She went to open the door, steeling herself for a fight she likely couldn't win but then, a moment later, the other two men walked back out, looking around the ward, now looking confused. Davey ducked back, so that they didn't see her and almost punched the sky in delight.

Monroe and Doctor Marcos weren't in there.

She probably would have done this, if the hand hadn't snuck around from behind and clamped over her mouth.

'Shush,' Doctor Marcos said as she pulled Davey through another set of grey double doors, entering a side room, barring the door behind her. 'What are you doing here?'

'There's three men here to kill Monroe,' DC Davey said, seeing him sitting in a wheelchair, an IV bag on a pole above his head. 'Should he be out of bed yet? I guess you got my messages?'

'No,' Doctor Marcos said, already grabbing Monroe's wheelchair and moving off towards the back of the room. 'To both questions.' They were in a sterile-looking storeroom, which looked very much like a kitchen in a school or college. Davey assumed it was where the meals for the forty-odd ACCU patients were made.

'How many?' Monroe asked, his voice dry and raspy. 'Out there?'

'Three,' Davey replied. 'But they looked military. Or something.'

'Something?'

'I think they had warrant cards,' Davey explained, opening a door so that Doctor Marcos could wheel Monroe through, closing it and barring it behind her. 'The officer on duty seemed to be okay with them.'

'Everyone these days has a bloody warrant card,' Monroe muttered. 'How did you know about this?'

'DS Kapoor,' Davey said. 'There was an explosion at a pub. Some guy drove off, the car was connected to Rattlestone and there was a written order that DI Walsh saw that said to kill you ...' she paused. 'How did you know, if you didn't get any of the messages?'

'Billy and that DI Frost came to visit,' Monroe explained. 'All smiles, said they were going to catch my attacker. I told them I couldn't remember anything. Thing is, I remembered everything, including the fact that it was Frost, or whatever his bloody name is that attacked me.'

There was a hammering on a door back from where they had started.

'They've worked out where we are,' Doctor Marcos

shifted the wheelchair as they started running down another corridor, this time heading through what looked like a radiology waiting room.

'Great, more running,' DC Davey breathed before starting after them.

EVERY DAY, NASIR GILL TOOK HIS LUNCH AT ONE PM, AND MADE his way to a new location in London to take photos. They weren't for his personal collections and they weren't for the newspapers, but they were a solid if small additional income for him. Nasir took dozens of photos of places, of people, people in places, it didn't matter. Twenty, thirty in a go and then, in the afternoon he'd edit them, pick the best five or six and upload them to stock footage sites. There was good money in those these days. More so than working as a photographer for a newspaper.

He hadn't been to work today, but still he spent his lunch in One New Change, a small but affluent shopping centre to the east of St Paul's Cathedral. From his perch on the first-floor balcony he could see the people entering and exiting; a mixture of tourists and city workers on their lunch.

People with money.

He snapped a few images, looking around for something new to shoot. He tried not to take closeups of people as they always had to sign image waivers, and likeness rights were an absolute pain. He liked to find alternative ways to take the images, ones that showed the people while *not* showing the people. He'd done the same yesterday when he'd taken some artistic shots of Brompton Cemetery. He expected some good paydays from those. People always used cemeteries in their blogs and articles.

Looking through the viewfinder rather than staring at the screen on the back of his Canon, he stopped, zooming in as he focused on the entrance of the shopping centre. Two men in bomber jackets were entering, looking around for someone. Nasir snapped off a couple more shots and then turned to leave, only to find Declan standing in front of him.

'How—' Nasir started, but Declan grabbed him by the arm, pulling him to a side pillar.

'People are after you,' Declan explained. 'They had your location written down. Lucky for you, I got here first.' He looked over the balcony, down at the men who now stood on the escalators, moving up to their floor. 'Just about, anyway. Come on.'

Moving quickly, Declan and Nasir made their way through the lunchtime crowds, stepping onto the escalators to the upper floor.

'What's the rush?' Nasir asked.

Declan looked to him, surprised.

'You didn't hear about Kendis?' he asked.

'I've been off the grid,' Nasir explained. 'I haven't heard anything.'

'They murdered her.' Declan pulled Nasir into a shop entranceway as he watched the escalator.

'Oh.' Nasir seemed neither stunned or nonplussed by this. Declan looked at him for a moment.

'You *knew*,' he hissed.

'I didn't—' Nasir started to protest, but Declan rammed him against the door window.

'I used to work for the Military Police,' he explained, pulling out his warrant card and waving it to a concerned shop assistant through the window. 'I hunted down and interrogated a lot of suspects. Over the years, I got a kind of sixth sense for liars.'

'I don't know what you mean!' Nasir cried out.

'You were a friend of Kendis, but when I said she was dead, you didn't react.'

'Shock!'

'Also, you didn't ask how she died,' Declan continued. 'People can't help themselves, especially with people they knew. They have this morbid curiosity. Unless they've seen the news, and they know the story.'

He paused.

'The message said *take out*. But they weren't killing you, were they? They were *extracting* you.' His forearm resting against Nasir's throat pushed harder.

'How long have you worked for Rattlestone?'

'I don't know what you're talking about!' Nasir pleaded. 'I was brought in by Kendis!'

'Did you deliver the letter to her house?' Declan asked. 'The call to action sheet? Her neighbour seems to think so.'

Nasir just stared silently at Declan.

'The photo of me at the entrance, the one that's all over the Internet,' Declan continued. 'You took it, didn't you?'

Nasir nodded.

'What did Kendis do after meeting us?' Declan hissed. 'Did she find the source? Did she go to the cemetery again?'

Nasir was trembling now. 'I have a family,' he whispered.

'*I* have a family!' Declan snapped back.

'You should have thought about that when you did what you did with her!' Nasir almost shouted. Declan went to reply but forced himself to relax. He wanted nothing more than to punch Nasir's face through the glass, but that wouldn't get them anywhere.

'Who's the source?'

Nasir looked away, as if deciding whether to say. Declan pushed harder with his forearm.

'*Who's the source?*'

'Some woman named Pearce,' Nasir eventually replied.

'Francine Pearce?'

'Yeah,' Nasir was looking to the escalators. Following the gaze, Declan saw the two men arrive on their floor.

'She's in prison,' Declan replied.

'No, she's under house arrest until the trial—'

Nasir didn't finish the line as his head snapped back, a *phut* sound echoing around the balcony level, and a bullet smashing through his skull, dead centre of his forehead, killing him instantly. As he fell to the floor Declan looked back to the two men, one of which held a pistol, the silencer now aiming at Declan.

Grabbing Nasir's camera by the strap, Declan moved quickly, leaving the body and zig-zag running towards the man who, surprised to see his target come at him rather than run, fired blindly at him, the almost silent bullets missing Declan and scattering the shop window as he moved in close and swung the camera at his attacker, connecting hard with his head, sending him to the ground with the side of his head busted open from the impact.

The second man looked down in horror before reacting, pulling out a KABAR assault knife, but the momentary pause was enough for Declan and he pivoted, using the camera strap, wrapping it around the man's wrist before he could use the blade and spinning around, twisting the strap, snapping the wrist in one quick motion, flipping the second attacker onto the floor.

By now the shopping centre was emptying as people ran for the main entrance, the screams echoing around the shops. With both men now down and Nasir dead, Declan stared at the remains of the camera now hanging from the strap. Discarding it after removing the Micro SD card, Declan rose. He could see an Armed Response Unit entering the main entrance; being close to St Paul's, there was always going to be a unit within screaming distance and, pocketing the card and pulling out his warrant card, he waved it at them.

'Up here!' he cried. 'Detective Inspector in need of assistance!'

The SCO19 officers saw him and, still holding their rifles at the ready, made their way to the upper floor. Slowly and carefully, his arms up to show that he had no weapons, Declan walked towards them.

'I'm DI Walsh,' he said. 'The two men there killed my informant before—'

The butt of the assault rifle striking his head was unexpected, and he stumbled backwards.

'Get on the ground!' the assaulting SCO19 officer screamed, rifle now aimed at Declan who, checking his temple for blood but finding none, dropped to his knees, his hands in the air.

'I said, I'm Detective Inspector Declan Walsh,' he continued. 'I was defending myself and my informant.'

The SCO19 officers were already at the two attackers, the first responding leaning over them as he checked their pockets. Pulling out a wallet and riffling through it, he looked to the officer beside Declan.

'It's them,' he said.

'Them who?' Declan had a sinking sensation in his stomach. This wasn't going the way he expected. The officer before him stared down coldly.

'The two men you assaulted were Special Branch officers, here to take into custody a terrorist suspect,' he said. 'A suspect that you apparently attacked and murdered before they arrived, according to witnesses.'

Declan glanced to the shop where, a phone in her hand, the shop assistant that he had shown his ID to was watching, terrified. *Great.*

'It's not what it looks like,' he said.

The officer smiled. A dark, cold one. 'It never is,' he said before kicking Declan hard in the ribs, sending him to the floor. 'Now, resist arrest, you terrorist piece of shit, so I can shoot you legally.'

Declan laid on the floor and stared up at the ceiling. He'd learned who Kendis's source was, but he would never be able to do anything with it now.

His race was over.

15

INTERVIEW ONE

Declan had expected to be dragged to New Scotland Yard itself, but instead the SCO19 officers waited with Declan by the entrance to the shopping centre. They'd handcuffed him, but they hadn't searched him or even read him his rights. It was as if Declan was in some kind of strange limbo state.

It wasn't long before Declan saw why he was being held. A black BMW pulled up to the kerb, followed by a police car. DCI Sutcliffe climbed out of the BMW, staring coldly at Declan.

'Christ,' he muttered.

'Those bastards aren't Special Branch,' Declan said. 'They shot my informant before I could speak to him.'

'If they did, then the fingerprints will back you up,' Sutcliffe said nodding to the SCO19 Team Leader. 'Thanks for keeping this under wraps.'

'Under wraps?' Declan exclaimed. 'They dragged me out to the front of the shopping centre and hanged me out for everyone to take photos! No thought for my rank or even the truth of the situation!'

'The situation is that you killed a man and almost killed two others,' one of the SCO19 officers muttered.

'The situation is you're a cretin,' Declan snapped back. 'Ask the witness! How did I shoot Nasir when the gun was in a Special Branch officer's hand? Magic?'

'We'll take it from here,' Sutcliffe turned to Declan. 'Get in the car.'

'Uncuff me.' Declan held his arms out. 'You either believe me or you don't. If you do, then prove it. If you don't, then at least give me my call to a solicitor.'

'Your solicitor is already waiting for you,' Sutcliffe looked back to the other car where two police officers walked to Declan.

'You're bloody kidding me,' Declan hissed. 'I knew you were corrupt the day I met you in Hurley.'

Sutcliffe leaned in close.

'You were a prick then, and you're a prick now,' he hissed. 'The only difference is that now, you're a prick in handcuffs.'

He nodded to the police officers, and they grabbed Declan, one on either side, walking him back to their police car.

'Am I arrested?' Declan yelled. 'Are you going to read me my rights? What about *do your job*? This is a setup!'

Now sitting in the back seat of the police car, Declan looked to the car's roof and sighed.

'Damn,' he whispered. One of the two officers, now in the passenger seat looked back to him.

'Sir, I'm sorry about this,' he said. 'If it means anything, we're fans of your department, and if that man needed killing—'

'I didn't kill him,' Declan replied. 'But I appreciate the comment.'

He leaned back, watching the crowds, all taking photos with their phones as the car drove off.

He would be Internet famous within the hour, it seemed.

TO HIS SURPRISE, DECLAN WASN'T TAKEN TO SOME KIND OF terrorist black site, and he felt a surge of relief course through him when he realised he was entering Temple Inn as he looked out of the window of the car. That said, the faces on the officers as they climbed out of the vehicle and pulled him out didn't seem that happy to be here; Declan assumed they knew something that he didn't.

There was a small group of photographers at the sides of the entrance, shouting out questions and taking photos as Declan was marched past them. He couldn't help but note that if someone wanted to completely discredit his testimony in the same way that they had been discrediting Kendis, this was the exact way to do it.

Entering the main office, Declan saw that Frost and Billy were there, while Anjli was conspicuously absent. The two police officers walked him into the glass-walled interview room, where he sat on a chair, holding out his handcuffs.

'Sutcliffe got his photo op,' he said. 'I don't need these on here, especially as I still haven't been arrested.'

One of the officers nodded and pulled out a key, uncuffing and then taking away the handcuffs. Declan rubbed life back into his wrists as he looked out of the window at Billy and Frost.

'How's Anjli?' he asked. 'And the pub?'

'They were lucky,' Billy replied after looking quickly to Frost. Although his friendship was to Declan, his loyalty was to his career, and Frost was his superior. 'They were in the beer cellar, awaiting a delivery when the bomb went off. Ground zero seemed to be the security room at the back, which was utterly destroyed. Also, the upper floor was pretty much undamaged, the buildings around only suffering external glass damage, with only the external frontage of the pub permanently ruined. It was almost as if they did it for show.'

'We don't know that,' Frost added. 'We don't know what Taylor's plan was.'

'Still keeping that narrative?' Declan asked. 'Top points for consistency. Where's my solicitor?'

'Do you need one?' Frost enquired. Declan shrugged.

'Sutcliffe said there was one here.'

'*Detective Chief Inspector* Sutcliffe must have been mistaken,' Frost replied. 'Or, he wanted you here with a minimum of histrionics.'

Declan nodded, looking back to Billy. 'And how's *Detective Chief Inspector* Monroe?'

'We don't know,' Billy admitted, ignoring the jibe. 'He seems to have gone missing with Doctor Marcos. DC Davey told an officer to call for armed backup but when they got there, all three were gone.'

'DC Davey is a hysterical idiot,' Frost muttered. 'Sooner she's suspended for wasting police time, the better.'

Gone was good, Declan thought to himself. *Gone meant no dead body.*

There was movement from the door, and Sutcliffe entered the main office.

'Stop talking to the suspect,' he snapped at Billy and Frost. 'Fitzwarren, you're in with me.' Entering the interview room with Billy, Sutcliffe sat down opposite Declan.

'I don't know what you're playing at here, but it looks real bad for you,' he said, leaning over to the recorder, clicking it on. There was a long beep and then the device started recording.

'Interview with Declan Walsh—'

'DI Walsh,' Declan interrupted.

'Interview with Detective Inspector Walsh,' Sutcliffe amended, looking to his watch. 'One thirty-seven pm, DCI Sutcliffe and DC Fitzwarren in attendance.'

'Shouldn't we be waiting for his solicitor?' Billy asked nervously.

'Don't need one,' Sutcliffe smiled, his eyes not leaving Declan's face. 'We're just having a friendly chat.'

'Then turn off the recorder,' Declan replied. 'Because friendly chats aren't admissible in court.'

'Guilty conscience?' Sutcliffe asked.

'Not at all,' Declan replied, leaning back in his chair as he measured Sutcliffe. 'I'm guessing this is all a power play because you were told by a Tory MP to let me take over a case that would have made your currently limited career for you.'

'Interview paused,' Sutcliffe stabbed at the recorder as he turned it off. 'How dare you!'

'How dare I?' Declan leaned forward now, his face a mask of fury. 'You left me to stand in the open while everyone with a smartphone uploaded me to the internet! You've blamed me for a murder I couldn't have committed, ignored injuries I took while defending my life from armed insurgents and a bomb that almost killed me, and labelled my girlfriend a terrorist, when you damn well know this is a campaign by either Charles Baker or Rattlestone! Tell me, Sutcliffe, which one of those is paying your mortgage these days?'

Sutcliffe stared at Declan with a cold, hard hatred.

'So, she's your girlfriend?' he asked.

Declan leaned back, calming down. 'She was, many years ago,' he replied carefully.

'You know nothing about the pub she was in last night?'

'No,' Declan lied. Sutcliffe nodded, looking to Billy, who reluctantly pushed a closed manila folder over to him. Opening it, Sutcliffe read from a page.

'The Horse and Guard pub. Chelsea. A favourite drinking spot for Chelsea Pensioners. Strange that she's there the night before a bomb goes off.'

'A bomb that doesn't actually kill anyone and destroys security footage.'

'Incompetence isn't proof of innocence.'

'Neither is hearsay,' Declan shook his head. 'I don't get this. Why are you so convinced to paint her as the enemy? Why are you doing your best to discredit me in the process? You know damn well that I didn't kill Nasir Gill.'

'What were you talking about before he died?' Sutcliffe closed the folder.

Declan shrugged. 'He worked with Kendis. There were people going to kill him.'

'Ah yes,' Sutcliffe smiled, looking to Billy, who currently wore the expression of a man who really didn't want to be there. 'The mysterious man, in the mysterious car, with the mysterious note.'

'Nothing mysterious about him,' Declan replied. 'The car registration showed that it's a Rattlestone fleet vehicle. Therefore, he's a Rattlestone employee.'

'One that's been following you and you alone?'

'Maybe. Or it's the team. I saw him at the Taylor house, and I recall a man looking like him when I went to the ACCU.'

'Convenient that nobody else did,' Sutcliffe mused. 'Or that DS Kapoor didn't hear this alleged Rattlestone employee yelling into his phone, nor did she see these notes that you saw so well in what, the half a second you had there? And it was *so* convenient that he'd left it open and angled so you could read them.'

'Convenience doesn't equate to lies,' Declan replied. 'That he yelled into a phone for someone to "*do it now*" seconds before a pub we were about to enter exploded is fact, not speculation.'

'Fact by you, an unreliable witness.'

'Why am I an unreliable witness?'

'Come on, Walsh. The murder victim, the extremist—'

'Alleged.'

'The *alleged* extremist terrorist was a close friend of yours and you're telling me you never once picked up on these personality shifts in her, these changes?' Sutcliffe tutted to himself. 'You're a shit detective, or you knew about it and lied.'

'First off, I haven't seen her for years,' Declan replied heatedly. 'And second, *she's not a goddamned terrorist!*'

'What did she say to you?' Sutcliffe asked softly. 'In the cemetery?'

Declan faltered. *How did Sutcliffe know of the meeting?*

'Who?'

'DS Kapoor, when she pulled you away.'

Declan relaxed again. 'You'll need to ask her that.'

'Oh, we will, as soon as she's back from the crime site,' Sutcliffe looked to his watch again. 'Shall we reconvene—'

He stopped as the door to the interview room slammed open and a woman filled with righteous anger stood there. In her late fifties or early sixties, her short blonde hair peppered with flecks of grey, this wasn't a woman who worried about her appearance. She wore a smart charcoal-grey suit worn over a white blouse, her makeup was minimal and she was flushed, possibly from running.

'What the hell is going on?' she asked, looking to Declan. 'Are they interrogating you?'

Declan kept quiet as Sutcliffe rose from his chair, turning to face the intruder.

'Who the hell are you?' he asked.

'I'm DCI Sophie Bullman,' she replied. 'And I'm DI Walsh's Federation Representative.'

'We don't need a Federation Rep in here,' Sutcliffe looked back to the table. Billy however shook his head.

'He has the right, sir,' he said, glancing at Declan as he spoke. 'If Declan – I mean if DI Walsh – wanted DCI Bullman to rep him, she'd be within her rights to stay here.'

'Who called you?' Sutcliffe asked. Bullman smiled.

'I was in the area,' she said.

'You're a West Midlands copper, aren't you?' Sutcliffe continued. 'You worked with Walsh on the Beachampton case.'

'Actually, she worked with Monroe on that case,' Declan added from the chair. 'We barely met.'

'The world's a big planet,' Bullman said to Sutcliffe. 'Birmingham's only a couple of hours away. In the globe scheme of things, anywhere in England is in the area.'

'I'd like DCI Bullman as my Federation Rep, please,' Declan said.

'Is he under arrest?' Bullman folded her arms.

'Not as yet—'

'Is he suspended from duty?' Bullman interrupted, glancing at Declan. 'I mean, is he suspended again?'

'Not as yet—' Sutcliffe repeated and was interrupted at the same moment.

'Then why the hell is he stuck in this room and not sitting at his desk solving this crime?'

'There was an incident at a shopping centre,' Sutcliffe was angering now. 'He's a suspect in a potential murder.'

'Bullshit,' Bullman stepped to the side of the door, indicating for Declan to leave. 'If he was, you'd have taken him somewhere with a cell. This is just targeted harassment. Go on, Walsh. Shoo.'

Almost wanting to not miss the ensuing conversation, Declan reluctantly rose from his chair, but Sutcliffe stopped him.

'We have information that leads us to the fact that Walsh here is more than he says,' he said as he looked out of the door towards Frost, now watching in. 'That he could indeed be the mysterious handler that we see in a photo that the press have, who was witnessed leaving the house of Kendis Taylor the same morning of her death and from his cell phone location records, we know he was in The Horse and Guard pub with Taylor the night before it exploded.'

'So I'm supposed to be in a pub *and* here attacking Monroe?' Declan snapped back. 'Because we all know that's a narrative you've been playing with.'

'You could have done both,' Billy muttered into his chest. 'We could only track the phone, not you.'

Declan looked through the open door at Frost's desk. On the screen was a photo of the baseball-capped, sun-glassed man, positioned next to the police ID photo for Declan. You didn't have to be Columbo to realise that the jawlines were similar.

'Circumstantial,' Bullman replied, and Declan realised that if she kept defending him, it'd fall badly on her. She was a good detective; he'd seen that when she came to Beachampton to save DCI Monroe.

He couldn't have her tarred with the same brush.

'It's true,' he said reluctantly.

Sutcliffe turned to face him in shock. 'Say that again?'

'I was with Kendis the night before her death,' Declan admitted. 'But we weren't planning a terrorist attack. We were having an affair. So, that's why I left the house in the morning.'

There was a moment of silence at this revelation.

'What about the fancy-dress cemetery visit?' Sutcliffe asked as Bullman now stared at Declan with what looked like disappointment.

'Kendis was working on an expose of Rattlestone,' Declan explained. 'She told Charles Baker's wife about this, and she died shortly after. It scared Kendis and Rattlestone needed to discredit her.'

'Lies,' Sutcliffe clapped his hands together. 'But a nice confession nevertheless.' He looked out to Frost, rising from his desk. 'Gather your coat, you're taking Mister Walsh to a more secure location!'

He looked back to Billy.

'Do you want to do the honours?' he asked.

Sadly, Billy nodded.

'Declan Walsh, I am arresting you for the murder of

Kendis Taylor, and under the operation of police powers under the Terrorism Act 2000, I'm arresting you for suspected terrorism ...'

Declan didn't hear the rest. The *whooshing* noise had returned.

Kendis was dead. Nasir Gill was dead.

And now Declan Walsh was a *murderer and a terrorist.*

16

RUN RABBIT RUN

'I NEED TO PISS.'

Declan didn't mean to say it like he did, but he knew that this was his only chance before they dragged him away to god knows where.

'What?' Sutcliffe looked back from the door. 'What did you say?'

'I said I need to piss,' Declan repeated, looking to Billy, who'd stopped reading Declan his rights and was now looking back to the DCI for advice. 'Look, I came here this morning, we had a meeting, then the pub which exploded, I went to a shopping centre and then was brought back here. It's been a long day and I haven't relieved myself.'

Sutcliffe opened and shut his mouth a couple of times. 'And this matters to us how?'

'Because if your lad there takes me to wherever we're going, it'll be longer,' Declan explained. 'Then who knows how long it'll take. If this had been a normal station, you could have put me in a cell, and I'd have peed in the toilet there, but this isn't a normal station and there isn't a cell.'

He pointed to the back of the office and the door that led out.

'There's a toilet right there,' he said with a smile. 'I've not been fully read my rights yet, I'm not officially arrested, so how about you let me go do my business and then I'll tell you whatever you want.'

Sutcliffe went to reply, to refuse this request, but Bullman nodded.

'Even suspected terrorists have rights,' she said.

Sutcliffe sighed, looking to Billy. 'Where does that corridor go?' he asked.

'Nowhere,' Billy replied. 'A toilet, one that has three cubicles in, and on the other side is a storeroom.'

Sutcliffe thought long and hard. Eventually he nodded.

'Phone and keys,' he said. Declan was confused at this, but then realised that he still had his items on him; they were so quick to bring him in, they still hadn't searched him.

Which meant that he still had Nasir's Micro SD card in his pocket.

'You'll take care of these for me, right?' he asked as he pulled them out, placing them on the table.

'While we're at it, you can pass me your warrant card,' Sutcliffe continued. 'After all, you won't be needing that ever again.'

Declan paused at this, but eventually reached into his jacket pocket and pulled out the warrant card, placing it on the desk.

'And, I'd like—'

'All I wanted was a piss,' Declan insisted. 'You can have everything I own in a couple of minutes, yeah?'

Sutcliffe glared at Declan. 'Go on,' he hissed, looking out to Frost. 'Monitor him.'

Frost walked over to Declan, grabbing him by the arm.

'I don't need to be escorted,' Declan snapped.

'I beg to differ,' Frost replied as they walked through the back door and into the corridor.

As they reached the toilet door however, Declan smiled as he turned to the man with the rimless glasses. 'Do you need to check it out?' he asked.

Frost pushed him through the door.

Now in the toilet, Declan turned to look back to Frost.

'I know it was you,' he breathed. 'That attacked Monroe. That tried to kill him. There's a recording. He's in the wind now, isn't he? I bet that must weigh on you. If I find it was you that murdered Kendis, I won't be arresting you. I'll kill you myself.'

Frost smiled, but it was a forced one. *He was rattled,* Declan realised.

'Just piss.'

'Can't do it while you're watching,' Declan walked to the cubicle.

'Keep it unlocked,' Frost replied.

Declan pushed the cubicle door closed behind him as he tried to think on his feet quickly. 'Why did you steal the phone?' he asked.

'Your daughter?' Frost was leaning against the sinks now. 'We needed to show you we could get to anyone. It was part of a plan to get you in line, but it all changed when the whore was killed.'

'She's not a whore.'

'Adulterous trollop?' Declan could tell from the tone of the voice that Frost was smiling.

'You didn't kill her?'

'Not us.'

'Who's us, exactly?' Declan continued. 'Rattlestone? Because Nasir was one of yours and you shot him in the head.'

'Nasir was an accident.' Frost's voice was lower now as he moved towards the cubicle. 'You finished yet?'

'Why, in a hurry to take me to a real cell?' Declan leaned across to the cistern, grabbing the lid. 'Or are you going to drive me to a secluded plot of land and shoot me in the head?'

'Which do you think?' Frost was getting bored now.

'So, do you work for Baker or Harrison?' Declan pulled the lid now, wincing as the ceramic clinked loudly.

Suspicious now, Frost pushed the cubicle door open. 'What are you doing anyway—'

He wasn't expecting Declan, the ceramic lid of the cistern held in his hands like a weapon, to slam the lid into his face, his nose exploding in a spray of blood as he staggered back, clutching at it. Declan moved in quickly, swinging hard, connecting again and then for a third time, slamming the heavy lid against the back of Frost's skull, sending him unconscious to the floor.

'Did you let me win that time, you prick?' Declan hissed as he placed the cistern on the floor, listening to see if anyone had heard. Hearing nothing, he quickly rummaged through Frost's pockets, taking his Detective Inspector ID and tucking it into his own inside pocket. There was a noise outside and, not wanting to waste any more time, he rolled the unconscious Frost over, handcuffing him to a sink pipe and turning to the toilet door. It was a U-shaped handle with no lock, and Declan stared at it for a moment as he tried to gather his breath. His chest was tight; for a moment he wondered whether he was having some kind of minor heart attack.

Looking at his reflection in the mirror above the sinks to the left of the door, Declan turned the tap on, splashing water on his face.

Am I really doing this? he thought to himself. If he ran, there was no way that he could walk this back. He would be a fugitive, and every lie thrown on him so far would be taken as the truth.

Every lie thrown on Kendis would be taken as gospel, too.

But, at the same time, if Declan stayed here, accepted the future, there was no way that he'd be able to clear his name. This was his only chance.

He hurried over to the middle cubicle, feeling behind the basin and pulling away the burner phone Trix had left there. He pulled the toilet seat cover down and stood on it, reaching up to the ceiling tile that was above it, pushing up. The tile popped up, and Declan could see that there was a hastily made wooden frame around it, like the hatch of a loft or attic.

'How long were you working on this?' Declan muttered to himself as he jumped up, grabbing the sides of the frame and pulling himself into the crawl space. He couldn't help it; the scrabbling of his feet made a noise, especially when he connected hard with the basin, using it to boost him up. Once in the crawl space, he carefully placed the ceiling tile back in place and tried to get his eyes adjusted to the dark.

The crawl space was mainly filled with insulation and ceiling beams running parallel to each other for the entire length, and only a couple of feet above him were the beams for the next floor. He only had a minimal area with which to crawl, but luckily there were small planks across the beams beneath him, most likely left by Trix.

Who, being smaller and skinnier, probably managed this with ease.

Quickly, he slid across a few feet, pulling up another tile and dropping into the hallway that led to a staircase. He was now effectively in a different building, and he hoped that this would take a while to be discovered as he ran up the stairs. At the top, though, he found he was in another narrow corridor, and for a moment he'd lost his bearings.

Follow the corridor west, to the front-facing windows.

Doing this, he found another narrow corridor heading north, where the windows to the building were situated. Running as far north as he could and then opening the last window, he stared out over Temple Inn.

This was his route out.

Carefully he climbed out of the window, clambering onto the top of it; as the roof was sloped and the window was jutting out, which meant that it had a small square above it he could gain a grip on. From there he reached up to the top of the small, sloped roof, pulling himself up and over, sliding into the channel along the middle of the building. He'd been lucky; the trees outside the offices had blocked people from seeing him do this unless they'd actively been looking for him, and currently the only people doing that were still inside.

The channel ran from north to south, sloped roofing on either side, but to the north was a ladder leading up to the roof of the next building. Declan climbed up and onto the roof, now finally able to run on the flat surface as he covered the fifty yards to the next building with ease, moving onto another sloped roof building before stopping.

The roof was too high to climb; all that he could use was a foot-wide balcony that ran to the left and around the building. It was only around ten yards long, but he would be exposed to anyone looking up and the roof to the left was a sloped one; he'd have to slide to the other side of it to ensure that he wasn't seen, while trying his best not to slide off.

He needn't have worried. Sirens were now blaring in the courtyard as police cars were pulling in, police running into the Temple Inn Crime Unit. They were so convinced that Declan was still there that they weren't spreading out yet. Also, the noise and commotion was enough to distract anyone walking in the courtyard, ensuring that they weren't looking up to the suited, terrified fugitive who now clambered for his life over slippery roof tiles five storeys in the air.

Eventually he reached the next block of buildings, pulling himself gratefully over the sloped roof and down into a walkway. From there it was a twenty yard dash to a white door. He looked around, but couldn't see a keypad.

Trix had said there was a keypad.

Looking north, he realised with a groan that he was at the *wrong door*. Trix had mentioned a jump; he hadn't even reached that part yet. Forcing himself to breathe slowly, he thought back to her words.

West, north, and west again around Old Mitre Court, jump north onto the next building.

'Christ,' he muttered as he moved on, continuing north and clambering around a chimney stack to climb onto yet another roof, this time the one above Mitre Court Buildings. Although sloped, this one had a large flat area to run on and Declan did this, making his way three quarters of the way along before turning to the right and north. There was another building facing him, a channel beside a small, sloped roof, his only opening.

But there was a six-foot gap between them.

A gap that, if he missed, would see him fall five storeys down to his death.

Taking a deep breath, Declan ran down the roof, using the speed to give him momentum as he leapt across the gap.

He didn't make it.

Luckily, however, he landed hard on the edge of the building, his arms scrabbling for purchase on the roof as his legs dangled over the drop. Pulling hard at the guttering that he could grasp, he clambered onto the roof, taking a moment to revel that he wasn't dead.

Come on, move you idiot.

Rising and now on shaky, adrenaline-fuelled legs, Declan made his way north, up the staircase and to the second white door. This one did have a door code and, after entering it, Declan made his way shakily down four flights of stairs and emerging, as Trix had said, next to Messrs Hoare Bankers.

Looking around, Declan realised he only had moments to decide what to do next. He needed to go to ground, to continue investigating the case, while most likely becoming the subject of the biggest terrorist manhunt London had found itself in for years.

Think, Declan.

He couldn't use cards. They'd track him. But maybe that was an idea? Perhaps he could use this to his advantage?

Yes, that would work. It was a half-mile walk to St Paul's, and everything he needed was there.

Turning eastwards down Fleet Street, Declan walked quickly, pulling his lapel up to hide his face. With luck, they'd be searching Temple Inn for a good hour.

That was plenty of time to disappear.

17

DEALS WITH DEVILS

Doctor Marcos had sent DC Davey back to the Crime Unit as soon as they'd escaped the hospital. As far as she was concerned it was a far better plan to keep someone on the inside, to ensure that Sutcliffe and his goons didn't destroy the unit before Monroe returned to gain bloody vengeance.

That said, Monroe still wasn't in that much of a bloody vengeance mood, and the constant moving was bringing on stabbing migraines because of the pressure still on his brain, causing him to almost black out frequently as they made their way out of the hospital and, placing him (with a small amount of fuss) into a black cab that specialised in wheel-chairs, making their way into East London.

Finally able to check her messages, Doctor Marcos quickly realised the severity of the immediate situation. Declan was apparently on the run, outed as the "terrorist handler" that had worked with Kendis, Anjli was still on site at a bomb explosion and DCI Bullman had arrived at Temple Inn, proving to everyone that she was an utter nightmare to be around.

Which was precisely what Doctor Marcos had *asked* her to do.

'Things aren't looking good,' she muttered to Monroe as he sat, half sprawled, on the taxi's back seat. 'Whoever's done this, they've planned it with military precision.'

'Can we find Declan?' Monroe asked, his voice still rough.

Doctor Marcos thought about this for a couple of seconds.

'Not through legal means,' she said.

'What does that mean?' Monroe asked, finally realising that the taxi was even moving. 'Where are we going?'

'Just shut your eyes and leave that to me,' Doctor Marcos placed a tender hand on his forehead, but it was just to check the temperature. Exhausted and too tired to argue, Monroe shut his eyes. Which was good, because it meant that he didn't see that the taxi was driving into Globe Town, the home of Jackie and Johnny Lucas; otherwise known as The Twins.

* * *

At the Temple Inn offices, Anjli stared at the chaos in front of her.

Police cars were parked haphazardly around the entrance, officers were scattering out around Temple Inn and DCI Sutcliffe was standing at the base of the steps of the building, bellowing out orders to seemly anyone who was listening, which at the moment seemed to be only Billy and DI Frost, currently holding a handkerchief to his bleeding nose.

'What's going on?' Anjli asked as she approached. 'Are we being attacked or something?'

'More the or something,' Billy replied. 'Declan's escaped.'

'Escaped from where?' Anjli looked around and saw DCI

Bullman talking to some officers to the north. 'What's she doing here? I was only away an hour or two!'

'Your tardiness may have costs lives,' Sutcliffe snapped. 'Did you know Walsh was a terrorist sympathiser and handler?'

Anjli stood still, unable to reply to this. Sutcliffe took her silence as confusion, and so continued.

'The man in the hat and glasses that's currently on every news screen? Walsh. The man who attacked Monroe last night? Walsh. The man who killed the only surviving witness to link him to the terrorist Kendis Taylor? Walsh.'

'We're not completely sure that he attacked Monroe—' Billy stopped as Sutcliffe glared at him.

'This can't be right,' Anjli looked around imploringly. 'There's no way he's a terrorist!'

'It's time to come back to the real world, Anj,' Billy muttered.

Anjli glared at him for a moment before replying.

'Still the *Judas*, I see,' she snapped. Billy looked at Frost, changing his handkerchief for a less bloody one before replying.

'If being a Judas means working for the greater good, then yeah, call me that,' he replied angrily. 'Declan confessed. He said he'd seen Kendis, that he went to the cemetery, that he lied to us. Then, before we could formerly arrest him, he escaped custody.'

'How?' Anjli's head was aching now.

'Apparently he kicked the shit out of that guy there and disappeared into thin air,' Bullman said, pointing at Frost as she walked over. 'Either that or he's still inside the building, hiding. They're combing the floors as we speak. Hello, DS Kapoor.'

'Ma'am,' Anjli nodded. 'May I ask what brings you to Temple Inn?'

'Came to act as Walsh's Federation Rep, but it seems like he wasn't interested in going that route,' Bullman shrugged.

'So now she'll be buggering off back to Birmingham,' Sutcliffe sneered.

Bullman, however, simply smiled at this.

'I think I'll be hanging round for a while longer,' she said lightly, looking at her fellow DCI. 'After all, when you eventually find him, I'm still his Federation Rep. Also, while you're all running around in circles, someone needs to keep hunting DCI Monroe's attacker.'

'Dat was Walsh!' Frost snapped, his nose still clogged. 'He codfessed do id!'

Bullman looked at the man with the rimless glasses.

'First off, *Detective Inspector* Frost, as a superior rank you either refer to me by the terms 'Ma'am', or 'Guv', or you use my rank if you can even say it properly right now. And second, as one of the four people in the room, I can state with some clarity that the one thing that Declan Walsh didn't do was confess to that attack.' She looked to Anjli.

'Do *you* know who did it?' she asked.

'I have some thoughts,' Anjli replied, looking at Frost as she spoke.

'Excellent,' Bullman patted Anjli on the back. 'We can work the case together.'

'Go wild,' Sutcliffe muttered. 'And while you're at it, see if you can find the dopey bastard too, as he seems to have disappeared with his doctor and DC Davey—'

'Sir? Did you need me?' Davey, standing in a group of forensics officers to the side, wearing their PPE suits looked up. Sutcliffe almost did a double take.

'How long have you been here?' he asked. Davey shrugged.

'Oh, I dunno, about an hour?' she suggested. 'I guess it's hard to see us properly when the suits are on.'

Sutcliffe looked back to Bullman.

'Are you still here?' he snapped. 'Well, go on then! Go solve this bloody case!'

With a final, withering look at Billy, Anjli and Bullman left the scene. Frost, watching this, painfully blew his nose, staring down at the blood and mucus in the ruined handkerchief before turning to Billy.

'She's pissed at you,' he mumbled. 'I don't dink you're friends adymore.'

Billy shrugged.

'I didn't join the force to make friends,' he said. 'I joined to make a difference.'

Frost looked to Sutcliffe, who smiled.

'You're a good copper, Fitzwarren,' he said before walking back to the building, finishing over his shoulder. 'I can see a glorious future for you.'

'Thank you, sir,' Billy said, seemingly grateful. He looked back to Frost. 'So, what now?'

'Now we hunt a terrorist,' muttered the man with the rimless glasses.

———

MONROE OPENED HIS EYES WHEN THE TAXI PULLED TO A STOP.

'Jesus, woman,' he groaned. 'Not here!'

'Yes, here,' Doctor Marcos replied, pulling the wheelchair out of the taxi and, after paying the driver, she stared up at the entrance to the Globe Town Boxing Club. 'Beggars can't be choosers, and you need a day's rest before you fight,' she smiled. 'Besides, haven't you seen *Rocky* movies? They always use a gym like this when they recover from the massive beating they take in Act Two.' Grabbing the handles, she wheeled Monroe through the doors and into the boxing club.

It was an old building, but it seemed to be going through a small renovation as they entered. The walls, the paint at one time stained with nicotine and peeling was now gone, sanded down and primed for a more colourful layer; the heavy bags and the weights were brand new, still in their wrapping as they awaited their installation, and the ring had been given new canvas and ropes. Even the smell, the musty taint of sweat and leather seemed to be missing from the gym.

One decorator looked up as they walked past. He was wearing old clothes but no overalls, and when he spoke, his voice was heavy with an Eastern European accent.

'Not open,' he said, waving back to the door. 'Come back later.'

'We're looking for Johnny or Jackie,' Doctor Marcos said politely. 'I'd prefer the former though.'

Known around East London as a kind of modern-day version of the *Krays*, Johnny and Jackie were, to many, an enigma. They famously never appeared together in public; an agreement allegedly made when they first started so that if one was killed, the other could gain revenge for them. When people turned up to speak with them, they never knew which of the twins they'd meet with, as Johnny and Jackie changed around their schedules constantly to ensure that targeted attacks were impossible. They looked identical. They wore almost identical clothing. Their haircuts were the same, although sometimes mirrored.

The problem was, though, that Johnny and Jackie weren't twins; they were one person with a very particular multiple personality disorder. There was "Johnny", the rational, business-like one and "Jackie", the psychopath.

There was a reason Doctor Marcos wanted the *Johnny* persona. He was more likely to listen to sense and broker a deal. The *Jackie* persona was likely to bury you in the foundations of a motorway.

'Oh, you would, would you?' A voice spoke through the door to the back room and a man emerged, walking out behind a meaty looking man in his forties, tracksuit over a tank top and his hair gelled back. The man who spoke wore a black suit and deep-blue shirt, currently open. His salt and peppered hair was blow-dried back, giving him a little quiff at the front, and he bore an expression of fury.

Shit, thought Doctor Marcos. *The Jackie persona.*

Jackie however stopped when he saw Monroe in the wheelchair. He stared at him for a long moment, taking in the scene.

Then he laughed.

'Oh Jesus, old man,' he said, holding his side. 'I didn't realise it was my birthday.'

Monroe forced a weak smile in response, and Doctor Marcos stepped forward, bringing Jackie's focus back to her.

'We need your help,' she said. 'People want to kill him.'

'Aye,' Jackie grinned, but bore more resemblance to a shark baring its fangs. 'And I'm on that list too.'

He stopped.

'I know you,' he blurted, delight crossing his face. 'You're that forensics bitch! The one who did the Tancredi tea party!'

Doctor Marcos nodded. The reason she was banned from crime scenes for another five months, in fact the reason DCI Alex Monroe was the only person in the police force who would hire her, was because of her unconventional ways when working out murders. The *Tancredi murders* was one such case; they tasked her with working out the timeline of how four Liverpudlian crime lords killed each other while sitting around a circular table. Nobody else had worked it out, but she'd achieved it by convincing her assistant, then-DS Joanne Davey to steal the bodies from the morgue one night and spirit them back to the crime scene, sitting them in their original seats to recreate the moment.

Four dead, naked crime lords being manipulated like dolls did not go down well with the authorities. Davey had been demoted. Doctor Marcos would probably have been fired if it wasn't for the fact that she'd solved the case.

'Yeah,' she nodded. 'I have that honour.'

'I'm a big fan of taxidermy,' Jackie continued. 'When I was a kid, my uncle took me to this weird bloody place in Cornwall. They had stuffed kittens in dresses, and rabbits in suits. Little dioramas named *Kitten's Tea Party* or *Bunny's First Day At School*. Scared the right royal shit out of me. Probably made me the man I am now.'

He considered this.

'I always wanted to make one of my own, you know, out of my enemies.'

'Day's still young,' Doctor Marcos replied. 'Have at it, and all that.'

'I like you,' Jackie said, walking over to Monroe, peering down at him. 'I hate him, but I like you. What happened anyway?'

'Someone slammed my head repeatedly into a glass window until it broke,' Monroe replied, a wry smile on his face. 'Problem you have though, is that technically you're one of the suspects.'

'What, because you arrested one of my men?' Jackie was referring to Danny Martin, recently arrested in Beachampton. 'If I wanted you hurt, I'd do it right.'

'I know,' Monroe tried to sit up in the chair. 'I saw the bastard who did it.'

'This is why you're here?' Jackie looked back to Doctor Marcos. 'Let me guess. The attacker's connected and you can't touch him.'

'A bit like that,' she replied. 'We need to stay off the grid for a day or so. Give Alex a chance to recover, to let the swelling on his brain drop. I figured that because of your past association, this would probably be one of the last places they'd look.'

Jackie nodded, looking back to Monroe. 'I seem to remember though, that the last time we spoke, you said you would *tear down this poxy little boxing club and stick me behind bars so fast I wouldn't even have time to change shirts.*'

'I seem to recall that you replied with an offer to *gut me like a pig and lace me into one of your heavy bags.*' Monroe looked back to the new heavy bags being installed. 'Seems a shame to damage these nice new ones, though.'

'I think you'll find that was Johnny who said that,' Jackie said. 'I would have done it there and then.'

He looked back to Doctor Marcos.

'I could help, I suppose,' he mused. 'But what's in it for me?'

'Haven't we done enough for you?' Doctor Marcos actually laughed at this. 'We just cleared the way for a takeover of North London and Birmingham for you, or whoever you set up. We showed you a traitor in your midst and stopped their attempt to take over your territory. I'd say *you* owe *us* right now.'

Jackie shrugged. 'I need a little more,' he said.

Doctor Marcos leaned in.

'I'm a forensic examiner and Divisional Surgeon,' she whispered. 'I know how to kill a man and never leave a mark. How to torture them to the point of death and then bring them back to life. Years of experience working with bodies and murder scenes. More knowledge than the average hitman. Plus, I'll *owe* you.'

Jackie Lucas held out a hand with a smile.

'Welcome to my home,' he said.

18

DOUBLEBACK

It took Declan around fifteen minutes to make it eastwards to St Paul's. He'd ambled, ensuring that he didn't stand out, keeping his collar high and his head low. Wearing a suit and coat he looked like most of the surrounding people; city folk out for a late lunch, or simply taking a break from their offices. Which in a strange way was exactly what he was doing.

As he walked, he made plans. Declan was a copper through and through, but his time in the *Special Investigations Bureau* of the Military Police had pitted him against some of the best operatives in the armed forces, and hunting them down he'd seen the tricks and routes that they took to avoid capture. Now he was gamekeeper-turned-poacher, these evasion techniques were now ones that he was going to utilise.

The first plan was to set a false trail. That was easy, but more complicated than it should be. He had to give away a series of clues to his location without being too obvious.

While doing that, he needed to work out where his actual destination was.

Nasir Gill had said that Francine Pearce was under house arrest. He could find the location somehow; he was sure of it. Then he had to get in somehow and speak to her. He needed to gain information on Rattlestone, confirm that something connected the murder of Kendis to Charles Baker.

Who, for some reason, was his ally in this.

Was he wrong? Was this not connected to Baker? He knew without a doubt that Rattlestone had killed Kendis, and most likely because of her investigation, but now he needed to prove it. Monroe was in the wind too; no doubt hunting his own nemesis. Declan wished he could help his mentor somehow but knew that if he did, he'd be bringing a most likely national terrorist manhunt with him.

A manhunt that he now needed to evade.

There was a sportswear shop near St Paul's. Declan walked in, quickly picking up a pale-grey zip hoodie, some black tracksuit bottoms, a baseball cap and a dark-brown fake-suede bomber jacket. He bought cheaply, avoiding known brands, picking a small, grey backpack as his last purchase. The total was just over fifty pounds for all the items and they were placed into a large carrier bag. Declan used some notes he'd taken from his father's book safe the previous day. He couldn't believe that it was only yesterday; so much had happened since then.

Declan moved quietly into an optician's two doors down, finding the chunkiest pair of black men's glasses on display and quietly pocketing them as he left. Many opticians had no security for the testing frames, and nobody called out after him, unaware of the simple theft. As he progressed into St Paul's Churchyard, he rubbed at the lens of the glasses, rolling off the sticker that gave the cost of the frames and placing them into his pocket as he walked into his final destination, an outdoors shop specialising in camping equipment.

Here he was less restrained, actively smiling and talking to the receptionist, asking her suggestions for a small sleeping bag and a medium-sized rucksack. He claimed it was for his daughter, going to Hull University and, when he'd picked two suitable items, some men's socks and a fold-up rain cover, he placed the shopping bag and camping items into the rucksack, secured it, placed it over his shoulder and paid for the items with his credit card.

He knew that this would be found. He wanted it to be found.

From there, Declan caught a black cab, paying once more with his card to Kings Cross Station. Pulling up at the front, Declan thanked the driver, ensuring that he saw Declan's face, and made his way into the main concourse, recently renovated with a white-framed diagram roof that arched over the open space below and the shops and upper-level food outlets to the left. He walked over to a payphone, one of the few seemingly left in London and, popping a pound coin in, dialled a number.

Jess answered on the third ring.

'Dad,' she said, her voice worried. 'Are you okay?'

'Yeah, sweetheart,' he replied, looking around as he spoke. 'Is your mum there? It's important.'

There was a pause, and then Lizzie's voice came onto the line. 'Where are you?' she asked as the station announcer went off, giving out the platform and time of the next train to Ipswich.

'Look, I can't explain anything, but you have to trust me,' Declan replied. 'You're going to hear some bad things. Untrue bad things. I'm being framed and I'm on the run.'

'This isn't a joke, is it?' Lizzie said. 'I saw about Alex Monroe. Is this to do with that?'

'Partly,' Declan replied cautiously. 'I can't really talk. I'm on my way to Whitby. Pack some things and get out of there with Jess.'

'I'll go to—'

'Don't tell me where you're going!' Declan exclaimed. 'They might hear this. People died today because of them.'

'Did they take Jessica's phone?' Now Lizzie's voice was darkening with anger.

'Yeah,' Declan looked around again, worrying that he'd spent too long on here already. 'Get out, lie low. Tell Jess I love her lots, and I'm sorry.'

Declan placed the phone back on the cradle, quickly continuing through the crowd to one of the self-service ticket machines. Here, he bought two tickets; the first, a London Travelcard was bought with cash, while the second, an open return to Whitby was paid for with his card. Now moving into the middle of the concourse, Declan checked up at the giant screens that displayed train arrivals and departures. The next train to Whitby wasn't showing, so Declan walked over to a blue-jacketed station official, a young man with floppy blond hair who leaned against a wall.

'Excuse me,' Declan said as the blond man sprung to life. 'How do I get to Whitby?'

The station officer looked up at the giant screens above them.

'You're cutting it close,' he said as he looked at his watch. It matched the screen above, stating that it was twenty past two. 'Catch the two thirty to Northallerton, yeah? Then change to Thornaby, and there you get a third train to

Whitby. I hope you've got a book though as it's a bloody long journey.'

Declan thanked the official and ran for the platform. He needed to not only catch the train, but fulfil other criteria. Sliding his ticket into the machine, he made his way to the train platform, noting that the tracks the other side were empty with a queue of people already waiting for whatever train was arriving. Entering the carriage through the sliding doors, he made his way up it, nodding to people as he passed, knocking a couple accidentally with the rucksack and apologising. Basically, he did everything that a man running from the police and trying to keep a low profile shouldn't do.

At the end of the carriage was an empty toilet. Sliding in, Declan locked the door behind him, opening up the rucksack. Now time was of the essence, as he needed to be off the train before it left, and according to his watch he had less than five minutes.

Quickly and carefully he pulled off his jacket and suit, keeping his shirt on as he removed everything from the pockets. This done, he now pulled on the black jogging bottoms and zip hoodie, zipping it up over the shirt, and letting the hood flop over the collar of the brown suede bomber jacket as he pulled it on. He quickly placed his personal items into the grey backpack that now rested on his shoulder, pulled on his shoes and the baseball cap, and frantically pushed his old clothes into the rucksack, closing it up. Then, with the black-framed glasses now on, he came out of the toilet, placed the rucksack onto the luggage rack and continued down the carriage. Now he was a completely different man; the lenses in the glasses were clear, but distorted his face, the cap hiding his hair. As a train pulled up on the other platform, Declan left his train, walking across to the other side and, as the travellers now at their last destination emerged from the carriages, he joined them in walking back to the barriers. In the rush of commuters, he slid his Whitby return ticket into the machine, passing through as the gates opened. Nobody would realise that he had used it, and only when they found the rucksack would they learn that he'd changed his identity.

By then he'd be far away.

As he walked back through the concourse, heading towards Kings Cross Underground Station, he saw four police cars pulling up outside, the sirens flashing as officers emerged, running towards the concourse. He felt a sudden pang of fear at this.

How had they found him so quickly?

However, he forced himself to slow, to move to the side as they passed him; nothing more than a curious onlooker. They ran for the platforms, but looking at his watch Declan knew they were too late to catch the train. If he was correct, the first stop would be Stevenage, over half an hour's journey away. Even if they stopped the train and started a search through the carriages, it would be about an hour from now before people realised that Declan wasn't there. By then, he'd be on another train, heading in the other direction.

Using the Travelcard, Declan caught a Circle Line train to Paddington where he found another self-service ticket machine and, using almost the last of his cash, he bought an open return to Maidenhead. Running for this train, he almost missed it, clambering in as the doors beeped and closed.

Sat on a seat beside the window, Declan stared out of the window as the train emerged out of the station, following the tracks westward as they took him to safety. He knew he was taking a risk here; the whole point of the subterfuge was to give him time to escape, to become a ghost. But he was heading to a known location, and one they would surely examine. He had no choice, though. This wasn't an escape for him; this was still an active investigation, whether or not he was legally allowed to. He just needed a little time to set up the basics. He knew he'd created a breathing space with the trains, but how long he had, he didn't know.

IT WAS LATE AFTERNOON BY THE TIME DECLAN ARRIVED IN Hurley upon Thames.

He'd caught a taxi in Maidenhead, spending the last of his money on the fee and a small tip, asking to be dropped off outside The Rising Sun pub. From here it was a short walk; one that Declan needed, if only to work out the next part of his plan.

He'd given his keys in before he escaped, so there was no way he could quietly enter his house. He remembered his father had once placed a spare back-door key under a statue in the garden though, and he was relying on this to be his way in. If not, he'd have to break a window to enter, just like someone had done a couple of days ago when they stole his father's iMac.

He also knew that he didn't have long; the rucksack on the train would have been discovered by now, and they'd already be racing to find him. Hurley was a known safe house. It was only a matter of time before they arrived, but he'd expected this when he decided to travel here.

Passing his house, a semi-detached one on the end of a series of similar houses, Declan kept to the fence as he slid around to the side, finding a secluded spot to climb over the wooden slats, landing clumsily in his garden. Skulking through it, monitoring the surrounding houses, Declan walked over to a large statue of Diana, Goddess of the Hunt. Easily five feet in height, it was an ugly bloody thing that Patrick Walsh had loved. As Declan forced it from its long-standing base, creating a small circular motion to spin it around, he saw the old, rusted key sunken into the ground below.

Taking it, he ran to the back door and was overjoyed to see that it still worked; the door unlocking with a solid click. Opening it and slipping inside, Declan closed the door behind him and for the first time in an hour breathed a sigh of relief. For a slight moment, he was safe.

Pulling out the phone that he'd taken from the back of a toilet in what seemed like a lifetime ago, Declan turned it on to see that Trix had been telling the truth. There was only one number in it and, as he walked up the stairs, he dialled it.

Trix answered on the third ring.

'You're popular,' she said. 'They're spitting bullets right now.'

'You can still hear them?' Declan asked, surprised.

'Of course,' Trix replied. 'I've been listening since they brought you in. They had a call from Sutcliffe about fifteen minutes ago and he was close to having a stroke.'

'Then you know what happened,' Declan entered his father's study now, sliding the bookshelf across to reveal the secret room. 'And you know I need Pearce's address.'

'She won't help you,' Trix's voice was distracted, as if she was doing something else while talking. 'She'd rather make a deal with Baker. If she helped you ...'

'I know, but she's the only option I have,' Declan sat on his father's chair. 'I need to prove Kendis right.'

'I'll find the address and send it to you,' Trix said, her tone all business. 'Are you at your father's house?'

'Yeah,' Declan replied. 'How did you know?'

'I said before, cell towers,' Trix could be heard typing. 'I know you think it's safe there, but it's not. Get out now.'

'Why?' Declan was already rising, walking out of the study, moving to the window in the study that looked out over the front garden. 'What do you know?'

'Get out now,' Trix insisted. 'It's why Sutcliffe called the office, to put things in motion. They're blanketing every known location of yours. Liz's house, your old apartment in Tottenham, and Hurley. They're coming for you.'

But it was too late. As Declan looked out of the window, he saw the flash of blue lights and heard the faint sounds of sirens through the glass. As he backed away from view, he saw the cars were already screeching to a halt outside his house and police officers were emerging, spreading out to cover both front and back entrances. Down the street, he could see another officer, a blond Viking of a man, knocking on his neighbour's doors. Disconnecting the call and walking back to his father's desk, Declan listened to the sounds outside; the police officers hammering on the front door, the shouts as they barked orders to each other. Soon they'd find entry into the house, and it was a matter of time before they found him.

He couldn't help himself. He laughed at his immediate situation. He'd thought he would have had at least an hour before he had to leave. Instead, he'd only had a matter of minutes. There was no escape.

Declan was *surrounded.*

19

DOOR TO DOOR

DCI SUTCLIFFE HAD BEEN FURIOUS WHEN FROST LET DECLAN Walsh escape. He was even angrier when he learned, half an hour later that Declan had escaped, not out of the toilet as people believed, but up through the ceiling and somehow onto the roof, an escape verified by some tourists in Temple Inn who had watched "the man running over the roofs" earlier.

They'd worked out that he'd escaped into Fleet Street partly through following the route, but also because twenty minutes later he'd bought supplies by credit card in St Paul's. Sutcliffe had scoffed at this; the man was a fool. How did he not understand that they could track the receipts? He obviously hoped to use speed rather than intellect, to gain distance from London. This was also obvious from the other receipts that they had picked up: the taxi to Kings Cross and the train to Whitby.

Arriving at the station, Sutcliffe and his unit, primarily comprising Frost, his bleeding nose now stemmed and Fitzwarren, sickeningly eager to please, checked with the first responding officers to see what they'd learned. Bullman and Kapoor hadn't joined them, still believing that Alex Monroe had been attacked by someone separate to Walsh, but Sutcliffe didn't care about them. He simply needed to catch Walsh.

The police had arrived moments too late, he'd learned. The train had already left the station by the time they ran onto the platform, but two units were now deployed to the first stop on the route, and the ticket inspectors had been sent an image of Declan to help them identify him as they walked up and down the seven carriages. There was a station officer, a small, scrawny little runt of a man who claimed that Declan had asked him which train to catch, but with this, something felt off here. Who was Walsh visiting in Whitby, and why did he take a sleeping bag?

The more he thought about it, the more he realised that Declan Walsh wasn't the idiot he'd been making out to be. He'd obviously had help escaping, but by who? The only people who'd been on his side were his team, most of whom hadn't been in the room and Charles Baker.

But Baker's office had wanted Declan destroyed.

Sutcliffe had audibly hissed with annoyance, surprising several of the surrounding officers. Frost and Fitzwarren had walked back to him, both with faces of deep disappointment.

'Let me guess, they didn't find him?' Sutcliffe asked. 'CCTV didn't pick him up?'

'Actually, it did, sir,' Fitzwarren spoke up. 'We have him entering the two thirty train on platform eleven.'

'So Stevenage it is,' Sutcliffe suggested. 'We can get there just in time to arrest him if we put our foot down.'

'No,' Frost was still watching around Kings Cross, as if expecting Walsh to be watching him back. 'This feels too easy. He's leaving us a bloody good trail, but he's not that stupid.' He looked to Fitzwarren. 'Is he?'

'He, well, he thinks with his heart,' Fitzwarren replied. 'So there's a chance that he could have done this.'

'You're not just saying this to delay our investigation, are you?' Sutcliffe enquired. 'Some misguided loyalty here?'

Fitzwarren bristled visibly at the accusation. 'You've seen how Anjli and Davey reacted to me,' he said. 'I'm classed as a traitor because I valued my job and my career over loyalty.'

Sutcliffe nodded. 'So, if you were Walsh, where would you go?'

'Maybe his ex-wife's,' Fitzwarren suggested, but Frost cut him off.

'He'll go back to Hurley,' he said. 'It's out of London, it's a sleepy village and he has everything he needs there. It's a bolthole.'

Sutcliffe remembered the house in Hurley very well; the first time he'd ever met Walsh was on the doorstep, as he tried to take a suspect out of the premises.

'We go there,' he said as he looked to his watch. 'If he is doing that, he has to make his way to Paddington, and to Maidenhead. We'll likely miss him at both stations, so let's just cut to the chase and go to his house.'

'Should we pass this on?'

'I'll do it,' Sutcliffe replied. 'Just get to that bloody house before he leaves. I want that bastard back in custody.'

Frost and Fitzwarren left Kings Cross at a run as Sutcliffe pulled out his phone, dialling a number. He knew he needed to let the Crime Unit he currently commanded know about the current plans, while he still had to wait for a response from the Stevenage police once they had searched the Whitby train. Then, after both, he'd need to speak to

Chief Superintendent Bradbury, if only to give him an update.

But before that, he had a more important call to make.

'Charles Baker's office,' he said to the operator who answered. 'Tell him it's DCI Sutcliffe.' He waited a moment, glancing around the station as he did so. Bradbury would probably want to do some kind of televised press conference. He loved doing those bloody things. He was thinking of ways to escape this when the phone answered.

'It's me,' he said. 'Walsh is in the wind. I'll get him back, but I wanted you to know.'

He paused, listening to the voice at the other end of the phone.

'You don't need to worry,' he continued. 'I have this under control. I'd have had it a damn sight better controlled if you'd told me about the operatives you sent after the Muslim.' Another pause as he listened. 'Well, perhaps you—no, of course I'm not questioning you. I'm just saying that there's a lot riding on this, and we need to ...'

One last pause.

'Of course not, sir,' he whispered, his face whitening. 'I'm completely loyal to Rattlestone. And you, of course.'

The call disconnected. Sutcliffe, now looking quite queasy, stared down at his phone as if he genuinely expected it to attack him.

He really needed to find Declan Walsh.

IN HURLEY, PC DE'GEER WAS THE FIRST TO ARRIVE ON SCENE. A tall, muscled man with Scandinavian heritage, he looked like a Viking who'd had his beard trimmed, his hair cut and had then been squeezed into a police constable's uniform. He'd surveyed the house, checked the area and rather than confront a potential terrorist on his own, he had instead knocked on the surrounding doors, speaking to the neighbours, looking for anyone that might have seen Declan Walsh that day. By the time he'd moved to the second door, more police cars had arrived, and more officers were surrounding the house, banging on the front door, peering through the windows.

It stayed like this for another ten minutes; PC De'Geer carried on speaking to the neighbours while his colleagues waited impotently around the house, unsure that the suspect was even in there.

There was a neighbour, a battle-axe of a lady who claimed continually that Walsh was a "bad sort" and that she was sure that she'd seen him on the street less than an hour earlier, but she also claimed that his father had been a spy, had worked with the Russians and even faked his own death, so she was a little unreliable in the witness stakes.

Eventually a Mini screeched to a halt outside the house, and two men climbed out. One was a blond man in a three piece suit, while the other was older, cleaning his rimless glasses as he looked around.

'Who was first to respond?' he shouted.

PC De'Geer walked over. 'I was, sir,' he said.

The man with the rimless glasses nodded. 'I'm DI Frost, this is DC Fitzwarren, and we're taking this over. Why aren't we in the house yet?'

'Because we have no evidence to believe that the suspect is even in there,' PC De'Geer replied. 'The last we heard was that he was on—'

'The train?' Frost interrupted. 'Yeah, that's wrong. We

checked it at Stevenage. All we found was a rucksack with his suit in. Chances are he doubled back just before it left.'

PC De'Geer nodded to this. 'Even so, sir, we have no proof—'

'I'll give you bloody proof,' Frost snapped, walking up to the door, and opening the letterbox.

'Walsh!' he shouted through the hole. 'We know you're in here! Don't make this more difficult for yourself!'

There was a silence as Frost waited. Then, sighing, he straightened, pulling out a small black package from his pocket. Opening it, he pulled out two lock picks.

'I thought I heard someone in danger,' he explained as he picked the lock. 'Best to make sure, eh?'

With that, the lock to the front door clicked open, and DI Frost entered the house.

BILLY HAD ONLY EVER BEEN IN THE HOUSE ONCE, BACK WHEN the last police standoff had occurred, but he'd never had a chance to really look around. That said, he still felt uneasy about entering the premises without due cause or a warrant, but Frost ignored his concerns.

'He's a terrorist,' Frost explained, pulling on his blue latex gloves as they walked up the stairs, the ground floor now completely examined by the officers who joined them as they moved upstairs. 'Rules change when you deal with that.'

'I know,' Billy replied, his own gloves already on. 'But it's different for you. I still see the man I worked with.'

'The man they forced you to work with,' Frost reminded him as they entered the main bedroom, looking around. 'You didn't choose to work with Monroe's band of misfit toys. What did you do that got you transferred, anyway?'

'I was in Cyber Crime,' Billy replied, opening a sliding wardrobe. 'My uncle was running a Ponzi scheme with *shitcoins*. That's a derogatory term for cryptocurrency that doesn't give any worth to the investor.'

'A play on words from *Bitcoin*,' Frost nodded. 'That must have pissed off your family.'

'They disowned me,' Billy pulled aside some suits, peering in. 'I've been trying to rebuild that relationship since. Nothing in here.'

Frost pulled out his phone, looking at it irritatedly.

'Of course he'd live in a piece of shit village with no signal,' he muttered.

Billy looked at his own phone.

'Really?' he asked. 'Mine's on four bars. May I?' He held a hand out. Frost looked at him in confusion 'You probably need to renew your carrier settings,' Billy continued. 'Cyber expert, remember?'

Frost passed Billy the phone and after a couple of minutes tapping on it, Billy passed it back with a smile.

'Three bars,' he said. 'Not quite perfect, but enough for a call.'

Placing the phone back in his pocket with a grudging nod, Frost led Billy out of the bedroom, allowing the officers to carry on, walking across the corridor into a room filled with boxes. A half empty bookshelf was at the other end, and the room looked to all extent like a storeroom.

'Christ,' Frost muttered. 'Minimalist much?'

'He's just moved in,' Billy suggested. 'I don't think he's had time to unpack.'

The Viking-looking officer, PC De'Geer leaned around the door frame, almost dwarfing it.

'Nobody up here, sir,' he said.

'Is there a loft in the house?' Frost retorted. 'He does so love to crawl around in lofts.'

PC De'Geer left to check and Frost looked back to Billy.

'You're wasted in this department,' he said. 'When this is done, I'll see if I can get you transferred to mine.'

'What, DCI Sutcliffe's team?' Billy looked surprised at the offer.

Frost laughed. 'Christ, no,' he said. 'Sutcliffe's a tool to be used. After this, I'll be a DCI myself. I'll have my own department. You can be my first Detective Sergeant.'

Billy smiled. 'A promotion would be nice,' he replied, spying something on one of the boxes. Walking over, he picked up a police issue extending baton.

'Never got the hang of these,' he said. 'Bloody thing's a liability in my hands.'

'You just need the training,' Frost replied, examining another box.

Billy turned to face him. 'You used one on Walsh, didn't you?' he asked. 'When you were undercover?'

Frost nodded. 'I've used one for years.'

'How did you do that?' Billy sat on one box. 'I mean, the whole undercover thing. I couldn't have done it. You were pretending to be working for Pearce, while still being an actual DI ... it would have driven me mad.'

'You get used to it.'

Billy flicked the baton, losing his grip and watching it clatter to the floor beside the bookcase. Frost watched this, shaking his head.

'You need to grip the end,' he said as he flicked his arm

out. His own baton, hidden up his sleeve, now appeared in his hand with the ease of a motion performed many times. With a second flick, the baton extended.

'That was awesome,' Billy said. 'Do you have a secret pocket up there?'

'No, just experience,' Frost passed the baton over. 'You try. Grip the end and flick.'

Billy followed the orders, but again the baton went clattering across the room, landing beside the other baton in front of the bookcase. Picking it up, Billy paused, staring at the bookcase for a moment.

'You okay?' Frost asked.

'Just my pride being dented,' Billy reluctantly passed the baton back to Frost. 'I think I'll stick to computers if that's alright,' he smiled sheepishly.

Frost took the baton, condensing it and replacing it up his sleeve as PC De'Geer returned in the doorway.

'Nobody in the loft space,' he admitted. 'We've looked everywhere.'

'We can't have,' Frost scanned the room now, looking at the boxes, the walls, the bookcase ...

'Maybe he didn't come here,' Billy replied. 'I mean, let's be honest. With all the subterfuge of the train to Whitby and everything, he's hardly going to go to the first place we'd look.'

'He would if there was something here for him,' Frost muttered, half to himself.

'Or maybe he got here after the police did, and it spooked him?'

'Whatever the reason, I'm not wasting any more time here,' Frost muttered, walking out of the room. 'I want two officers outside watching this building until we catch this terrorist. Come on, Fitzwarren, we've got work to do.'

Billy reached down and picked up the other baton. 'I'm going to keep practising,' he said as he followed Frost out. 'I mean, practice makes perfect, right?'

PC De'Geer took one look around and shivered. He couldn't explain why, but he had the uneasy feeling that he was being watched.

Shaking it off, he left the room, following the officers and detectives out of the house, closing the door behind him, and finally leaving it empty.

After a moment's silence, the bookcase moved, sliding slowly to the side.

Declan emerged from the secret study, tiptoeing to the window, staring down at the police as they left.

He'd heard everything. Every comment made by Frost and Billy, listened while kneeling against the back of the bookcase, his ear to the wood. He knew they wouldn't stop looking for him, especially if Frost thought he'd make a career from it.

It was time to go on the offensive.

20

WATCH THE BIRDIE

DECLAN WALKED BACK INTO THE SECRET STUDY, FINALLY ABLE to breathe. He'd heard Frost's last commands to the officers, so he knew they would post a car outside the house, and that it'd be a terrible idea right now to stand near the windows. That said, the police had kindly left half of the lights on in the house when they left, so he wouldn't be stumbling around in the dark.

Declan looked back to the bookcase, now half opened. He'd had plenty of time to work out his hiding strategy when the police had arrived, sliding it back into place and turning off the desk lamp, sending the room into darkness as he waited. Sitting back at the desk, Declan grabbed a large desk notepad and a pen. He needed to think fast; he didn't know how long it would be before someone else came into the house; although that said, he hoped that the simple fact that they were sitting outside would stop any of them from returning into the building.

Unless they needed the toilet, that was. Coppers always needed the toilet when on stakeout.

Pushing the thought out of his head, he looked at the notepad.

There were two issues here. The first was that they had attacked Monroe, and that the attacker, DI Frost, had been trying to look as similar to Declan as he could, in order to frame him.

The second was that Kendis was on to a story that had forced her enemies to brand her a terrorist, and to kill her before she could tell people what she knew. Kendis knew Donna had been a signatory for Rattlestone, but Donna was dead. Kendis had nothing and her source, apparently Francine Pearce, wouldn't risk blowing up any deal she was about to make for freedom.

Which led to Kendis's death, and the problem Declan had here. They could have simply destroyed her journalistic reputation and killed any trust that people had in her with the file that had been on Monroe's laptop. There was no need to kill her.

But someone had. Why?

A memory came to light; something that Trix had said the last time he was in this house.

'Baker wanted Kendis to be ruined, but he didn't want her dead. That's not his style. He also didn't hate Monroe enough to do that. But here's the thing. Adding what happened to Monroe to what I was doing? It was genius, but had to be done by someone who not only knew that Rattlestone had created the file, but that Baker was having me upload it. It became a moment of opportunity, to not only go for you and the Unit, but pin this on Baker.'

Someone connected to Baker, and who had knowledge of what *Rattlestone* was doing.

It could be any of them.

Even Pearce had worked with *Rattlestone* when she was in

charge of *Pearce Associates*. Somehow, Declan needed to speak to her.

Pulling out the burner phone Trix had given him, he opened a browser, googling *Balkan attack militia convoy Kendis*. Nothing came up except for articles on ethnic brawls on buses and some unconnected sites. So, Declan changed his search, narrowing down the words. Eventually he found the attack that Kendis had mentioned. A piece written by her in 2015 flashed onto the screen. Declan read through the page; it was quite pedestrian, keeping simply to the facts that a militant force had attacked a Peacekeeping convoy, and in the ensuing firefight four soldiers had been killed.

A link to another article commented more on this, giving a heartfelt statement by Sir Michael Fallon, the then Secretary of State for Defence, stating that justice would prevail, while a final paragraph commented that Fallon's department, headed up by the Minister of State for the Armed Forces, Malcolm Gladwell, would investigate the matter fully, while Rattlestone Securities were tendering to take over the convoys.

There was nothing about Baker there. So, how was he involved?

After another Google search, Declan found a Parliamentary piece on some blog site from 2014 that stated that Charles Baker was the then Parliamentary Under Secretary for Defence; it was a role that would have meant that his office was technically under Gladwell's remit, although Baker and Gladwell might have never even *met* while in the same building.

However, this also meant that Baker's office would have definitely seen the schedule.

Four soldiers were killed because of a leaked itinerary, all possibly to give a security firm with links to Baker a nice, hefty contract.

Declan leaned back in the chair. In Parliament, you could get away with being blackmailed, or even having kids out of wedlock. But costing soldiers' lives? If that came out, it was political suicide. Somehow, Declan had to find a way of proving a connection.

Leaving the secret study, Declan walked over to the boxes in the room outside, finding one marked BOARDGAMES. Opening it and rummaging through it as quietly as he could, he found what he was looking for, an old *Travel Scrabble* game.

Walking back to the desk, he opened the box, pulling out a green felt bag and emptying the tiny white squares of letters onto the surface. Then, brushing through the pieces, he laid the ones he needed out into a line.

R A T T L E S T O N E

Moving them around, he realised that although he could think up a few six or even seven letter words, he couldn't think of any word that used all eleven. Even googling *anagram solver* and typing the word into a particular site found nothing larger than nine letters.

So not a known word then. A name perhaps?

Declan leaned back from the table, staring at the random collection of words. He didn't even know if all eleven were used here. Gathering the eleven letters together, he placed them into the green bag and put it beside Frost's stolen warrant card.

There was a noise outside. Quietly making his way over to the window, he peeked out. It was just another police car arriving, most likely the next shift. Returning to the desk, Declan stopped, reached into his pocket and pulled out the Micro SD card that he'd taken from Nasir's camera earlier that day. They'd never searched him when he was arrested, and therefore they'd never found it.

Quietly and carefully, Declan went downstairs, methodically making his way over to the side of the living room, and to the waist-high side cupboard beside the drinks cabinet. Opening it up, he found a digital camera nestled at the back of a low shelf, a good decade old and probably unused for years. Opening it up, Declan saw it had a Micro SD slot.

Slipping Nasir's card in and closing up the compartment, Declan opened up the back, replaced the AA batteries and turned the camera on. It wasn't a touch screen, the buttons and dials on the camera moving through the options, but Declan could open the photo library on the card after a couple of attempts. The last five or six images were taken in the shopping centre, general photos of people and places, although a couple at the end were closeups of the team that had been sent to take Nasir out.

One of them, when zoomed to its maximum, showed a gun, likely the same gun that killed Nasir in what looked to be a shoulder holster. Declan took the burner phone and, unable to transfer the image in a traditional sense, simply zoomed in and used his phone's camera to take a picture of the screen.

Starting at the first photo on the card, a countryside shot that looked like it was taken the day before, and then scrolling through the photos on the card, Declan scrolled through images of Brompton Cemetery; artful shots that seemed more for magazine articles than for keeping, and images of the street outside, including the image that was now plastered across every newspaper in the country; the stranger in the cap and aviators, now known to be Declan.

From the way the images flowed, it looked like Nasir had taken a position across the road to take a shot of Declan before entering the cemetery after him, continuing to take shots as he did so. This was shown by images of Kendis talking with Declan now appearing on the photo feed, taken at a distance and before Nasir showed himself.

Scrolling even further forward, Declan trawled through a couple of street photos—

Declan stopped scrolling.

On the screen was an image of Kendis Taylor, in the early evening and sitting on a bench in a City of London park, arguing with a skinny, red-headed man in a suit who sat beside her. It was taken from a distance, but it was definitely her and the man seemed familiar, as if from television.

Declan zoomed in and took a photo of this image too. These latter images gave the impression that Nasir had been tailing her after she'd spoken with him and Declan. Which, if he'd been working for Rattlestone, was incredibly likely. Nasir and Kendis must have parted ways an hour or two before she died though, and Declan rubbed at his chin as he started flicking back through them one more time.

Why did Nasir follow Kendis, and why did he stop?

Placing the camera down, Declan stretched, ensuring that the car out front couldn't see him. He was hungry, and irritated by so many questions that he couldn't answer and so snuck his way into the kitchen, grabbing some bread, ham and butter from the fridge, making a quick sandwich that he ate as he returned upstairs. This was the safest place for him; the police had already examined the location, and they were convinced that nobody was inside. All he had to do was keep quiet and decide what to do next.

He changed out of the cheap clothes.

———

'So where exactly are we, and why the hell did we have to walk here?' Bullman rubbed at her ankle as Anjli looked back to her.

'First, I don't have a car, Ma'am. Second, I didn't want this visit being seen by anyone.'

'Any reason?' Bullman was now stretching her shoulders, shaking some life back into them.

'What, apart from me not trusting anyone in there and all my friends are on the run?' Anjli almost laughed. 'Currently, the only person I trust is you, Ma'am.'

'Well, that's reassuring,' Bullman looked up at the building they were now standing outside of. At the junction of Whitehall Place and Whitehall Court, it was an opulent, white brick neo-gothic building that merged with the surrounding offices and hotels seamlessly, with the corner entrance an elaborate arch over a double wood and glass doorway. A brass plaque to the left of it read:

NATIONAL LIBERAL CLUB

'Is he okay?' she asked quietly.

'Ma'am?'

'Monroe,' Bullman continued. 'I'm guessing you've been in touch with him.'

Anjli shook her head. 'I've got an idea where he is, but I've not seen or heard from him since he awoke.'

'Is that normal?' Bullman watched Anjli, who shrugged.

'To be honest, nothing we're doing right now is normal.'

'So, what are we doing here?'

'We're seeing a friend,' Anjli replied. 'Well, not a friend, but a friendly. It's not technically about Monroe's attack, so I didn't want to mention it until we arrived.'

'Of course,' Bullman replied as Anjli walked to the right-hand side door, pulling it open. 'I mean, I've worked with your boss and your Divisional Surgeon before, how could I assume that you'd be any different?'

Entering through the doors, they turned to the left where, in an alcove marked "Enquiries", an ornate clock above it, was the doorman, currently behind a chest-high counter.

'Is Anthony Farringdon in?' Anjli showed her warrant card. 'We were hoping to have a chat.'

'He's upstairs in the bar,' the doorman replied. 'I could check?'

'Please,' Anjli smiled her most winning smile. 'DS Kapoor and DCI Bullman.'

'And Anthony Farringdon is?' Bullman asked as the doorman moved to his phone, calling upstairs.

'He worked at Westminster for years,' Anjli explained. 'Amazing memory, knows everything. He helped us with the Victoria Davies murder, and I'm hoping he can answer some questions about the Star Chamber.'

'The what Chamber?'

Anjli grimaced. 'Ah yeah, I forgot you wouldn't know.'

'Mister Farringdon will see you now,' the doorman smiled, placing the phone back on its cradle. Anjli smiled back and with Bullman following walked towards the end of the entranceway where the hallway opened into a large rotunda, a huge spiral staircase that ran along the white marbled wall in front of them, an ornate marble banister circling up alongside as it rose towards a beautifully designed glass ceiling.

'I've been here before,' Bullman said as they started up the stairs. 'Sherlock Holmes Society thing. I was a guest speaker.'

'Really?' Anjli was delighted at this. 'I'm a member of that—'

'Hated every second,' Bullman replied, effectively killing the potential bonding session. 'So, tell me about the Star Chamber.'

BILLY SAT AT HIS DESK, ALONE IN THE OFFICE. HE WAS ALONE because everyone else was outside, watching Bradbury hold some kind of press conference that was live on *BBC News*. Billy knew this because he was watching it on the screen. Behind Bradbury, Sutcliffe could be seen to the side, watching him like a bodyguard.

'I repeat, we do not believe that Mister Walsh is a dangerous man, but suggest that anyone who sees him contact the police immediately,' Bradbury was saying. 'We do not know if they radicalised him before or after joining the police—'

Billy turned off the browser, effectively ending the video. Bradbury was just like the others, already convinced that Declan was the villain here. The actual thought of doing any police work was forgotten. Even Anjli and Bullman were elsewhere, working on what was more likely to be a far more interesting case.

But what Billy was doing *was* important. He was solving a heinous crime.

He looked to his notebook, open on the desk where written at the top of the page was the note that Kendis had on her when she died.

TOTTERS LANE
FOB C

What did it mean? Totters Lane was a small Shoreditch street that's only claim to fame was that it was wiped out during a German bombing raid in World War Two. But as for the other …

Reaching over to his jacket, he pulled it open, revealing the extendable baton that he'd taken from the floor of Declan's house. It looked so unobtrusive there, but Billy knew that someone looking like Declan had beaten Monroe with such a weapon.

Grabbing a clear bag from his desk, he wrapped the plastic around the handle and pulled it out of his jacket pocket. It measured about two feet, with a handle of around eleven inches. Carefully placing it in an envelope, Billy sealed it up, writing a name on it. This done, he rose from the desk, grabbing his coat.

It was time to put things in motion.

21

CHAMBER OF STARS

ANTHONY FARRINGDON WAS IN HIS USUAL SPOT IN THE UPSTAIRS bar; a high-ceilinged room, with red marble pillars running along each side, the space between each one either filled with the green wallpaper of the wall, or revealing a floor to ceiling bay window complete with green drapery. Glass-fronted mahogany trophy cabinets were beside several of the pillars, and beside a bust of William Gladstone was a low table with three dark-green leather armchairs, one of which currently held Farringdon as he rose to greet his guests. Wearing the same military blazer that he wore the last time he met Anjli, buttoned over a pair of dark trousers, white shirt and military tie in a Windsor knot, Farringdon was better dressed than either of the detectives that faced him, his white hair neatly parted to the right.

'DS Kapoor,' he smiled, offering his hand to shake. 'And you are ...'

'DCI Bullman,' she replied as she also shook Farringdon's hand.

He indicated for them to sit, and they did so.

'Can I offer you a drink?' he asked, waving to a server.

'Water, please,' Anjli replied to the server who, looking to Bullman, noted her nod in agreement, before leaving.

'I've seen your man Walsh is on the TV,' Farringdon leaned forward, lowering his voice. 'I'm guessing this is about him?'

'In a way,' Anjli admitted. 'It's also about the death of Kendis Taylor.'

'I saw that too,' Farringdon replied, picking up and taking a sip of his own drink. 'Met her a couple of times when I was in Westminster. Never pegged her for a terrorist. I'm guessing she wasn't?'

'That's what we're trying to work out,' Bullman replied cautiously. 'As you can imagine, there are many people out there who want to push that narrative.'

Farringdon nodded at this. 'So, therefore, you're here.'

'You worked in Westminster for decades,' Anjli leaned closer to meet Farringdon now. 'Your memory is incredible. I was hoping you could answer some questions about the Star Chamber.'

That was not the question that Anthony Farringdon was expecting. He thought for a moment and then leaned back.

'Charles Baker,' he mused. 'You're looking at him as a suspect?'

'Why would you think that?' Bullman asked. Farringdon shifted in his seat as he counted off on his fingers.

'Current Chamber is Malcolm Gladwell, Conservative, Tamara Banks, also Conservative, Jerry Robinson, a known Ulster Democrat, Labour's Norman Shipman and Baker. I know that because when he was selected last year, the Lib Dems threw a fit about how it was overweighted on the right wing while they didn't have a say. That said, it was more a whine about the lack of seats they now had, as the spot he took was because of one of their golden boy MPs losing theirs.'

'I thought it wasn't about politics,' Anjli said.

Farringdon smiled. 'It's not supposed to be, but everything is,' he said. 'They're like a secret Privy Council. They work in the shadows and they have complete deniability. In the eighties they were a bit of a black bag organisation and removed more dissidents to Thatcher than MI5 did. Recently they've been more linked to disinformation on campaigns like Remain, Me Too, Black Lives Matter, that sort of thing, mainly as with the UDP and Tories holding four of the five seats, they have a bit of a monopoly.'

'How does it work?' Bullman was writing in her notebook. 'Is it just them?'

'Christ no, that'd be chaos,' Farringdon admitted. 'They have aides and teams that provide them with what they need, and then they decide based on the evidence. Once done, they pass it down the wire. Usually to the Security Service.'

'What if it directly contradicts a Government policy?'

'Then they use non-Governmental contractors,' Farringdon sipped at his drink again, glancing around the room. 'To be honest, everyone's a little concerned about it right now. Tamara joined three months back, Baker last year. That means that for the next four years they've got a voice. Robinson has another year or so and Shipman is in his last five months; the moment he goes, Gladwell takes over as longest server and Chairperson. They'll be unstoppable, no matter who replaces him.'

Anjli looked to Bullman at this, but the older DCI was emotionless.

'Why would they decide to discredit Kendis?' she said.

Farringdon shrugged. 'She's not the first one they'd done this to,' he replied. 'There's been a lot of journos over the years that have been discredited because of these buggers.'

'Would they have killed her?' Bullman finally looked up from the notebook. Farringdon shook his head.

'They might be more right wing than usual, but none of them have the spine for murder,' he considered. 'They'd try everything before something like that happened. Also, I can't see Baker deliberately pushing to remove your man Declan right now unless he'd been given something explosive.'

'Why?'

'Because he's too closely linked to him. The Devington fallout hasn't reached the courts yet. I saw Taylor's piece in *The Guardian*, talking about Andy Mac, so discrediting her is a good idea, but that's not the same.'

'Hypothetically, how would you have done it?' Bullman asked.

Farringdon laughed. 'I'd fake a terrorist folder on her and leak it,' he said. 'Pretty much what they did.'

'The attack on Monroe? Could that have been them?'

'Unlikely,' Farringdon waved to a server for the bill. 'But not impossible.'

'Are Rattlestone connected to the Star Chamber?' Anjli enquired.

Farringdon lowered his voice again. 'They're connected to everything,' he whispered. 'So, I seriously suggest you steer the widest berth that you can there.' He checked his watch. 'I'm sorry, I really need to move soon. I have a dinner appointment.'

Anjli and Bullman rose. 'Thank you for your time,' Bullman said as she once more shook Farringdon's hand.

'If it means anything, I don't think your man's a terrorist,'

Farringdon finished as he shook Anjli's hand. 'I saw him when he came here. He's a zealot.'

'Zealot?' Bullman paused. 'As in a fanatic?'

Farringdon nodded. 'But not in the way you're thinking,' he said. 'He's fanatical about the law. Of justice. You could see it when he spoke, just like his father did. He sees a crime and he'll do whatever it takes to solve it. Someone like that, he's a straight arrow.'

He paused.

'One last thing,' he added. 'Charles Baker. He might be a bugger, but he's not one of the worst ones. Check his voting record; he's quite centrist for the Tories. But he's not leader material.'

'Why do you say that?' Bullman asked.

'He has a nickname amongst the Westminster staff,' Farringdon explained. '*King John.* People think it's because they're likening him to a ruler, even a rather bad one like John, but it isn't. You ever see *Robin Hood*? The Disney one with the foxes?'

Anjli and Bullman both nodded, so Farringdon continued.

'In that film, King John is a Lion, but he's useless. Completely enthralled to his adviser, *Sir Hiss.*'

'You're saying Baker has this nickname because of his adviser?'

Farringdon shrugged. 'Let's just say Will Harrison has many of the properties of a sneaky over-controlling snake and leave it at that. To be honest, considering the little shit's pedigree, I'm surprised he's not an MP himself.'

With the conversation ended, and more to consider, Anjli and Bullman left Anthony Farringdon to his dinner date.

Walking back onto the street, Bullman looked to Anjli.

'Well, as we seem to move to your agenda, what do you want to do now?'

Anjli watched the traffic drive past, as she decided on which path to take. 'You might not like it,' she said.

'That's supposed to entice me?' Bullman smiled.

'Baker's wife committed suicide a few weeks back,' Anjli explained. 'They classed it as suicide, but now I'm starting to wonder.'

'Who ran the case?' Bullman was already looking for a taxi. Anjli shrugged.

'Let's go find out,' she said.

DECLAN HAD CHANGED BACK INTO A SUIT; WHEREAS HE'D WORN a grey one earlier that day, now left on a train heading somewhere north, tonight he wore a navy-blue pinstripe one with a white shirt and dark-grey tie. He didn't want to stand out, but he wanted to not look like someone who was deliberately hiding. His plan was to hide in plain sight, and to use Frost's warrant card to somehow carry on the investigation.

But now he sat upstairs in a dark room, staring out across his front lawn, out at the street and the lone police car that had been watching his house for the last hour. He'd worked out that they changed cars every couple of hours, although this seemed more to keep the eyes fresh than to stick to a routine. Also, once the new team took over, one officer would leave the vehicle and patrol around the block, starting down the footpath between Declan's house and his neighbour, one that went past his house and the one that backed onto it, following around the block and returning around six minutes later. They would re-enter the vehicle and then that was that, for about twenty minutes before the other officer went for the same stroll. Where they were parked gave them an unobstructed view down the footpath, meaning that any attempt to leave the house would be seen unless he clambered over the back fence or the left-hand side one; he knew next door had wireless CCTV covering their garden too, and the chances that this was now being broadcast into the officer's car were incredibly high. It was definitely the first thing that Declan would have done, after all.

He was trapped.

He'd been watching now for most of the evening; it was getting late, time to possibly consider sleeping. However, as much as he knew that while they were outside he was safe inside, he didn't know how *long* this status quo would continue. They could re-enter at any time, or Frost or even Sutcliffe could return and if he was asleep, he'd be caught. Even if he was in the hidden study, there was a chance that Anjli could give him away, or even his daughter could accidentally mention it if they found and questioned her. No, he needed to make some kind of move tonight.

His burner phone beeped; looking at it, he saw an address in Woking had been sent to him. No message, just the details. He smiled.

Trix had come through for a change.

Now he just had to get there, and at the same time get in.

Gathering the small urban backpack once more, Declan filled it with things that he might need; he knew that at any second he would be forced to run, so he wore comfortable shoes in case he needed to sprint anywhere, and placed a change of clothes in the bag. In addition, he took the money from the fake book, the warrant card and the fake glasses. He didn't know what to do with his hair; a cap wouldn't work with the suit, so he gelled it back into a slicked back look with a different side parting, trying to match the image of Frost, hoping that with the glasses, it would suitably alter his face.

He was filling a small aluminium water bottle when his house phone rang, almost causing him to jump out of his skin. He stopped, tiptoeing into the living room. Through the window he could see the officers exiting the police vehicle; they had obviously also heard the faint noise of the phone ringing too and wanted to see if they could hear anything when the message was left. Declan moved to the kitchen door, standing in the dark, listening as the phone went to answerphone.

It was Doctor Marcos.

'Declan,' she said, choosing her words carefully. 'I'm calling all known numbers and hoping this gets to you. Royal Bastard. Gallifrey. Dentist.'

The connection clicked silent, and the answerphone light flashed. Staying in the kitchen, Declan thought over the cryptic message. He knew exactly what it meant, but he hoped that anyone else that heard it would be completely baffled.

What it meant was hope.

What it meant was that Monroe was still alive.

Declan looked at his watch. It was past nine in the evening; he needed to move. He needed to get to Woking, which was a good twenty to thirty miles away and close to an hour through back roads. Besides, to do this, he needed a car.

Luckily, he knew where he could find one.

Watching the police vehicle outside, he waited until the next walk around ended before slipping into the back garden. The last thing he wanted was to have the officer accidentally overhear him as he escaped. This done, Declan made his way quietly to the back wall, using a compost bin placed against it to help him over, dropping quietly into the back garden of his backing neighbour, Karl Schnitter. A mechanic by trade, there was every chance that Karl could find a vehicle that Declan could borrow, if he even believed him.

As it was, Karl was in the kitchen, waiting for Declan as he walked towards the house.

'Get in before they see you,' he whispered, letting Declan pass him. 'I saw you enter the house earlier from my bedroom, and when you weren't brought out in handcuffs, I knew you were still in there.'

'I'm not a terrorist,' Declan said, sitting at the table.

Karl shrugged. 'I know,' he replied. 'And your friend, the one that was pretty? I believe that she was not one either, but she was killed for something. Do you know who killed her?'

'I'm getting close.'

'Good,' Karl rose from his own chair, walking to the fridge. A tall, tanned, robust German in his mid-sixties, Karl had been possibly the most laid back and calm member of the village as long as Declan could remember. 'How can I help?'

'I need to get to Woking,' Declan explained. 'There's someone there that might help.'

'You need a car,' Karl turned back, passing Declan a can of some energy drink. 'Here, you need to stay awake. I will also make coffee.' He walked to the kettle, turning it on.

'I can find you a car,' he said. 'I have a couple of courtesy ones that people who leave their cars with me for long periods of time use.'

'That would be great,' Declan replied.

Karl held up a hand. 'But,' he said, his tone becoming

more sober. 'In return, you must do me something. That Helen Mirren woman?'

Declan nodded. He knew Karl had seen a woman who resembled the actress Helen Mirren visit Patrick Walsh frequently. Declan didn't know who this was, but believed that this could be the mysterious Wintergreen, who had once worked with Patrick Walsh and Alexander Monroe as a Detective Sergeant back in the nineties; someone who now had become a ghost.

'As soon as I find her, I'll inform her of your intentions to court her,' he smiled, trying to be as formal as Karl was.

The German nodded at this, tossing Declan a set of keys.

'Good,' he said. 'Peugeot 308, outside the garage. Half a tank. I expect it back in the same condition.'

Declan took the keys, and the offered coffee, taking a sip. Even though this had been a brief conversation, this was the first normal one he'd had all day. He was almost loath to leave it.

Almost.

22

COLD CASES

THE PRESS CONFERENCE HAD ENDED BY THE TIME THAT ANJLI and Bullman returned to Temple Inn. Bradbury had already left with his entourage behind him, and only Frost, Billy and Sutcliffe remained. Even DC Davey wasn't to be found on the lower levels, a note stating that she'd gone to another forensics laboratory to chase up some supplies.

Entering the upper floor of the offices, Anjli hadn't even made it to her desk before Sutcliffe leaned out of his – no, *Monroe's* office.

'Where the hell have you been?' he snapped. 'We were supposed to have all officers here for the conference.'

'I'm not working your terrorist case, remember?' Anjli replied before reluctantly adding, 'sir.'

'You're working the Monroe attack though, right?' Frost lounged on one chair, his left arm resting lazily on the desk as he turned to face her. 'Declan Walsh attacked him. So yeah, you're working the terrorist case.'

'No proof as yet on that,' Anjli gave a smile to Frost. 'But when we find out who really did it, we'll let you know.'

'Also let us know if you find Monroe,' Sutcliffe muttered, returning into the office as he spoke. 'Bugger going off the grid like that just screams suspicion.'

'I'm just here to print out a form and then we're off again,' Anjli explained, walking over to the printer and collecting some pages that were spitting out into the document feeder. 'Collating witness statements, that sort of thing.'

'Which witnesses?' Billy asked as he looked up from his workstation.

Anjli ignored him, gathering the sheets and then walking over to Bullman.

'Whenever you're ready?' she said, ignoring both Billy and Frost, but feeling their eyes boring into her back. 'There's a bit too much *Judas* in this office for my liking.' She glanced back at the printer, as if concerned that she'd missed a page. Billy seemed to flinch a little at the insult, but kept quiet as Anjli and Bullman, without saying another word, left the offices once more.

The moment they were gone, however, Billy rose from his chair and walked over to the printer.

'Does it bother you?' Frost asked. 'The *Judas* thing?'

'Not really,' Billy replied as he clicked his way through the menu on the printer's screen. 'In fact, every time she says it now, I see it as a kind of call to action, you know?'

The printer spat out pages, and Billy picked up the first one, reading it.

'The thing about Anjli Kapoor is that she's a bit of a Luddite,' he explained. 'She doesn't understand that actions have consequences. For example, when you print across the network, the printer keeps the last file in memory.'

'So you see what she's printed?' Frost waved for Billy to bring it over. 'What is it?'

'I dunno, sir,' Billy admitted. 'I mean, how do the police notes for Donna Baker's death help the Monroe investigation?'

Frost read through the first page as Billy passed him the rest of the printouts; it was indeed the case files for the investigation of Donna Baker's suicide.

'It doesn't,' he said, looking at the door where moments earlier Anjli and Bullman had left with copies. 'Excellent work. We can nip this in the bud before it goes too far.'

Placing the papers on the desk, Frost picked up his phone, dialling a number that he seemed to know by heart.

'It's me,' he said when it answered. 'We have another problem.'

Billy walked back to his desk, smiling at Frost's compliment. Now, back at his workstation, he carried on with what he'd been doing before the two women had arrived. On his screen was the Wikipedia page for Brompton Cemetery. Scrolling down, he couldn't help hearing Frost's conversation.

'You know who they're going to speak to. You should shut her down before she can talk to them.'

Billy typed on his keyboard; Frost, finishing the call, looked over, only to see that Billy was still searching through websites.

'You can shop online later,' he joked.

Billy smiled, looking over. 'Still trying to work out what *FOB C* means,' he said. 'I can't find anything connected to Declan, so I'm going through Kendis's online articles, seeing if she ever wrote it in a piece.'

'Diligent,' Frost nodded as he rose from his chair. 'Keep it up.' With that he walked over to Sutcliffe's office, knocking on the door and then closing it behind him as he entered. Billy, alone in the office, kept searching, pausing as a line on the screen caught his eye.

The Friends of Brompton Cemetery organise Open Days, regular tours, and other public attractions.

Looking back to his pad, he wrote the letters F O B C down one side, while filling in the blanks next to them.

F riends

O f

B rompton

C emetery

There was no way that this was a coincidence. Searching through the records, Billy saw that the Friends of Brompton Cemetery was a group that was independent of the cemetery itself, the official website stating that it *preserved the grounds as a model of a historic cemetery with an active role in modern society* by restoring and maintaining the cemetery's buildings, monuments and landscape. Pulling up the membership lists, Billy could see that many of the members had plots on the cemetery; joining the organisation probably gave them opportunities to get in to tidy the plots up when the cemetery wasn't open.

One name however stood out as he read through it; William Harrison had upper level access to the cemetery because of his family mausoleum being there since 1854. Billy leaned back as he saw this, glancing up to ensure that neither Frost nor Sutcliffe had seen this on his screen. Closing the browser, Billy considered this.

Nobody knew how someone had brought Kendis Taylor's body into the cemetery once it was closed; but Will Harrison had a bloody key.

All Billy had to do now was work out how to continue this line of investigation, while his superiors chased another subject.

THE LAST THING WILL HARRISON HAD EXPECTED TO SEE WHEN he emerged into the octagonal entranceway known as the Central Lobby was the smiling face of DS Anjli Kapoor. But there she stood, a grin plastered across her face.

'Alright, Will?' Anjli said, waving her warrant card. 'You remember me, don't you? DS Kapoor?' She glanced over at one of the eight sides of the chamber where two BBC journalists were comparing notes on something that had happened earlier that day. Will didn't know what it was; so many things happened each day in the corridors of power. What he knew though, and the one thing he knew that DS Kapoor knew, was that the last thing he wanted was the press to gain interest in any of the meetings in the Central Lobby. Especially when they had cameras there.

'Mister Baker is in late night sessions,' he said. 'You'll have to come back tomorrow.'

'Who said I was here to see Charles?'

'Then why are you here?' Will was still smiling as he spoke, but it strained the lines on his face, an act for anyone watching.

'We're hunting a killer,' DS Kapoor whispered conspiratorially and a little too loudly for Will's taste. 'And apparently a terrorist.'

'I thought DCI Sutcliffe had taken over that case?' Will asked politely.

'Oh he is,' DS Kapoor grinned. 'But he's a little distracted, what with being a subversive plant, placed there by someone with an agenda. Allegedly.'

Will nodded as if interested, but secretly wishing this conversation had been in one of the quieter side corridors where he could have called security and had the bloody woman removed, preferably forcibly.

'Well, you'll need to take that up with his superior. Bradbury, I believe?'

'Oh, I will,' DS Kapoor pulled out a notepad. 'While I'm hanging around, do you mind if I ask you a couple of questions?'

'Very much,' Will replied. 'But I don't really have a choice here, do I?'

'Not really,' DS Kapoor looked to the news crew that was now watching them, and gave a little wave. 'How deep is Baker linked to Rattlestone Securities?'

'Rattlestone?' Will shrugged. 'No idea.'

'Come on, his wife was a signatory on the board.'

'Which means nothing,' Will replied. 'What his wife did was nothing to do with Charles. He wasn't a controlling husband. He kept her away from his business, and we both know why.'

He was implying the conspiracy that had come out a couple of months earlier during the Davies Murder, where it was revealed that as well as having a secret love child, Charles Baker had been blackmailed for over two decades by Pearce Associates, believing during this time that he was the murderer of Victoria Davies, but had blanked it out. DS Kapoor simply nodded at this.

'Understandable,' she said. 'Do *you* have any connections?'

'Am I the one under investigation here?' Will asked, his

face sweating a little. He wasn't the fittest of men at the best of times, but the lobby was hot, and the questions were intrusive.

'How long have you worked for Baker?'

'I've worked with Charles since the 2010 Election,' Will replied, emphasising the word *with*.

'Ten years then,' DS Kapoor smiled, but it felt more like a shark testing out their prey. 'Must be hard to always be in the shadows.'

'I like the shadows,' Will replied. 'Is there anything more?'

'You get all sorts of advisors here, don't you?' DS Kapoor was looking around at the busts as she spoke now. 'The Thomas Cromwells, the Alistair Campbells, the Dominic Cummings, all becoming part of the narrative rather than controlling it.' She looked back to Will. 'Which one are you? The quiet unknown like Geoffrey Norris, or a soon to be nail in their boss's coffin one like Cromwell was?'

'The role of senior advisor is one that—'

'Advisors always fall on their swords,' DS Kapoor interrupted. 'Do you have a sword?'

'Does a letter opener count?' It was a weak attempt at a joke, and DS Kapoor ignored it.

'So, are you likely to end your days here walking out of the office with a box of your things, or rather executed for *high treason?*'

The second part of this threw Will, but he didn't have time to reply.

'I know Baker sent a text, telling someone to *flick the switch*, to upload a terrorist dossier on Kendis Taylor onto DCI Monroe's computer,' DS Kapoor continued. 'Then, the following day, there you both were, visiting us.' She leaned in.

'Did you pass the message on?' she asked. 'Did you divert

it? Maybe tell someone to enter our Crime Unit and attempt to murder our Detective Chief Inspector? Did you order the death of Kendis Taylor?'

By now the news crew were stirring, aware that something was going on in the Lobby, and were setting up their cameras. Will was visibly sweating now, looking around as if hunting for allies.

'You don't know what you're talking about,' he snapped. 'You've got nothing on me. You'll regret this.' Caught in a corner, Will was feeling light-headed. He wanted to attack back, to shout, to strike, but he couldn't. Not here.

'Where were you the night that Donna Baker died?' DS Kapoor's tone changed, suddenly conversational. 'Where was Laurie Hooper?'

If Kapoor had expected this to be the killing blow, she was sorely mistaken. Will chuckled. He'd expected this one. He'd been told that Kapoor and her partner, DCI Bullman, had taken the crime report and that Laurie Hooper, Donna's personal assistant, would be their next witness to be questioned.

But that would be difficult.

'Is that your kill shot?' he asked.

DS Kapoor shrugged. 'She around?'

'No,' Will replied calmly. 'She's gone. Left the moment I heard you were starting this witch-hunt.' He gloated now. He knew he shouldn't, but he couldn't help himself. 'You thought you were so clever. But you can't speak to a Government employee on Government property without a warrant.'

'Oh, I know,' DS Kapoor smiled, and Will suddenly felt uncertain that he'd scored the goal he believed he had. 'That's why we ensured you'd be hearing about us gunning for you. We guessed you'd bundle Miss Hooper into a car and pop her out the back entrance of Portcullis House. Interesting thing, though. The moment they go through the gates, they're not on Government property anymore.'

With horror, Will realised why DCI Bullman wasn't there. DS Kapoor, seeing the realisation cross his face, nodded.

'Now we're on the same page,' she said.

Will looked around, trying to find a way out of this. He couldn't use his phone, and he couldn't demand that security remove this bloody woman without cause.

DS Kapoor kept bloody smiling.

'Shall we start again?' she said, opening the notebook. 'Where were you the night Donna died?'

23

LATE NIGHT TRADING

OUTSIDE FAIRLEY HOUSE, A SMALL SCHOOL IN LAMBETH THAT was dedicated to students with learning difficulties, Doctor Marcos climbed out of a taxi, finding herself on the junction of Pratt Walk and Lambeth Road, paying the driver in cash and looking across the street at the four-storey brown-brick and glass building on the corner. Although housing the Metropolitan Police Central Communications Command Centre, it was also the home of the Metropolitan Police Forensic Science Laboratory, where the body of Kendis Taylor currently resided. It was a brutalist style police complex with external concrete staircases, brick infill and a large concrete ventilation shaft that protruded out on the street corner, and Doctor Marcos, familiar with both the inside and the outside of the building was not a fan of it.

To the side though, on the other side of Pratt Walk was a sandwich bar and delicatessen called *The Sandwich Man*; usually closed at this time of night, there was often an unofficial agreement with the police that sometimes the deli would stay open until nine pm some nights. Tonight was one of those nights.

Entering the delicatessen, Doctor Marcos saw it was sparsely filled with police officers, taking a break with a cup of tea, or trying to jolt themselves awake with an espresso or two. At the end though, nodding to her was DC Davey, a foolscap folder in front of her on the table. Ordering a flat white coffee, Doctor Marcos walked over to Davey, sitting opposite her.

'How is he?' Davey asked.

Marcos shrugged. 'Sleeping,' she replied. 'Hopefully the pressure will ease over the next few hours and he'll have fewer headaches.'

'You're sure that he's safe there?'

'If they do anything while I'm not there, they know they'll have me to deal with,' Doctor Marcos smiled; a dark, vicious one that gave no humour. 'I think he'll be fine for the moment. What do you have?'

'I did a second autopsy on Taylor,' Davey pushed the folder over to Doctor Marcos who, before opening it gratefully accepted the flat white from a waitress. Sipping at the coffee, she finally opened the folder, staring down at the photos within.

'Anything different from the official one?' she asked.

Davey shook her head. 'DCI Raghesh did the autopsy, and he seems to have picked up everything,' she replied. 'All I did was probe a little more on certain areas.'

'Like what?' Doctor Marcos looked up from the photos.

'Taylor was stabbed with a long, thin blade,' Davey started. 'Double-sided, about two-and-a-half centimetres wide, half a centimetre in depth at its middle point, and made of Ruthenium. Or at least coated in it.'

'More likely coated,' Doctor Marcos muttered as she flicked through the photos, bringing out the original autopsy report. 'Ruthenium is rare as rocking horse shit, and a blade made of it, although being pointless, is a tad expensive. Did that kill her? I mean, Ruthenium Oxide is toxic and incredibly volatile ...'

'All Ruthenium compounds are regarded as highly toxic and as carcinogenic, so possibly,' DS Davey read from her notes. 'Apparently Russian-born scientist Karl Ernst Claus discovered the element in 1844 at Kazan State University and named Ruthenium in honour of Russia.'

She looked up. 'Could this be a Russian murder? Another Salisbury?'

Doctor Marcos shook her head. 'Ruthenium is mainly mined in North and South America, South Africa and Canada, but sure, let's blame the Russians.'

DC Davey nodded, looking back to the notes. 'Well, she suffocated because of the punctured lung, and *that* killed her,' she said. 'But she'd been tasered as well. Burn marks on the upper torso showed the device had six prongs, set in a three and three circular pattern. It was probably one of those stun torches you can buy on eBay, and she most likely fell the moment it hit, as those buggers packs a punch. I couldn't see any signs of a heart attack, but it wouldn't have helped.'

'What about the cut on the head?'

'Now that's an interesting one,' Davey leaned forwards. 'We know she was brought there, placed by the grave, but the cut had small fragments of some kind of ceramic in it. Like she broke a vase when she struck it with her skull.'

'The graves nearby?' Doctor Marcos rubbed at her eyes. 'She fell, maybe hit something holding flowers?'

'Possibly, but this feels like it was higher. If it was on the floor, we'd have found a different impact shape. Also, we found contaminates in the wound, like stone dust from where it hit the floor.'

Doctor Marcos considered this for a moment.

'Some mausoleums have shelves, and all of them have stone floors.'

DC Davey thought about this for a moment. 'So she was killed in the cemetery, just not where she was found?'

Doctor Marcos nodded as she flicked through a series of images on her phone. 'I think we're narrowing this down,' she replied. 'The moment we do, we'll nail the bastards for this and Monroe's attack.' She stopped at an image.

'You got something?' DC Davey asked. Doctor Marcos turned the phone to show her assistant.

'Google search Ruthenium Blade and you get a few hits,' she said. 'Seventh one is this. *A Montblanc Letter Opener in metal Ruthenium, plated with inlay in black soft calfskin leather.*' She carried on scrolling. '*This letter opener has been crafted out of metal with a Ruthenium-coated finish.*'

'Montblanc is expensive,' DC Davey replied. 'There are easier and cheaper options to use when killing someone.'

'Unless they picked it for a reason,' Doctor Marcos rose from the table, taking the folders as she did so. 'A two to three hundred pound letter opener isn't something you buy if you're worried about the rent. Get hold of one. See if it matches the entry wound, and whether the composition matches.'

She paused before leaving.

'Also find out if there's a way to see who owns one of the bloody things.'

THE GLOBE TOWN BOXING CLUB WASN'T USUALLY OPEN around ten pm on a weekday, but when all was said and done, the Globe Town Boxing Club wasn't a normal club, neither.

The two men who climbed out of the black SUV didn't know any different. To them, it was simply another location to enter and extract from. Their last extraction had gone badly. The taller of the two, an older, stockier man with grey temples and dark, thinning hair now had a vicious-looking scar, stitched together and covered with a dressing on his right temple, from an unfortunate impact with an SLR camera, swung at speed by a terrorist earlier that day. The other man, a younger yet bald man, with a slighter frame than his friend, checked that the pistol that he had under his bomber jacket was still hidden.

'I don't see why I can't have my gun,' the stockier man moaned.

'Mate, you shot a guy in the head,' the bald man replied. 'They don't just let you carry guns after that.'

'They did in Afghanistan,' the stockier man muttered sullenly as they entered the club.

There were two painters, currently priming one wall when the two men walked through the boxing club.

'Anyone here?' the stockier man shouted. 'Wakey wakey!'

There was movement from the back of the club and Johnny Lucas emerged, wiping his hands with a towel.

'We're closed, lads,' he said, relaxed and with an air of calm. Both men reached into their pockets and pulled out warrant cards. Waving them momentarily in Johnny's direction, they placed them away.

'We understand you might have a fugitive staying here,' the bald man said.

'And which fugitive is that?' Johnny asked causally. 'I have so many pass through.'

'Alex Monroe and Rosanna Marcos.'

'I thought that DCI Monroe was a victim?' Johnny asked, slowly moving towards the two men. 'Can I see your IDs again?'

'Why?' the stockier man asked.

'Because you didn't tell me your names,' Johnny replied. 'Coppers always give their names and ranks when meeting for the first time. I think it's taught in copper school.' He stopped only a couple of feet from the two men.

'Which makes me think you didn't go to copper school.'

The stockier man pulled out his card, showing it to Johnny before placing it away again. Johnny nodded, walking back to the door that he'd emerged from.

'They're excellent forgeries,' he said. 'But I've seen better. Hell, I've made better. I'm guessing you're part of Rattlestone then?'

Sick of this, the bald man pulled out his gun, aiming it at Johnny.

'Listen, you little shit,' he hissed. 'It's been a long day and I'm tired. I want to find Alex Monroe and take him into custody. If you won't help me, I'll drop you here and find him myself.'

'I'm more than happy to help you,' Johnny smiled. 'I'm guessing you have a warrant or something?'

'I have this,' the gun was aimed at Johnny's head as the bald man started walking towards him. 'No scrawny bastard like you is gonna stop me passing.'

'Look,' Johnny held his hands up one last time. 'You're not coppers, you're trying to kidnap someone by force and you're threatening my life. I'm sick of you. Turn around, jog on, and piss off out of my club.'

The bald man cocked his gun and then stopped. From the shadows emerged two trainers, both with shotguns and, glancing to the side where the painters were, he saw that they too had removed guns from underneath their overalls.

'Nobody points a gun at me,' Johnny hissed. 'Last chance.'

LAURIE HOOPER KNEW NOTHING.

This was the line that had been repeatedly told to her over the last couple of weeks; that she didn't see what she thought she saw, that she was in shock over Donna's death and that if she tried to reveal anything that happened that night, she'd not only lose the high flying and well paid government job that she'd been moved into immediately following Donna's suicide, but that she'd never work in any form of employment above overnight shelf stacker ever again. If people asked her, she walked away. If people contacted her, she passed it on to Will Harrison and let him deal with it.

Whether she agreed with this was irrelevant. This was how it worked when you played at this level of politics.

The problem was that Laurie Hooper had seen what she thought she saw. As Donna Baker's PA, she'd been on call the night of "the incident". She'd witnessed the argument that Donna had with Will Harrison shortly before her death; but she'd also seen other things. The additional fight that she had with her husband the morning of the death. Also, she'd seen Donna arrange secret meetings with both Malcolm Gladwell and Kendis Taylor, the former of which was …

Well, it was complicated.

Laurie Hooper hadn't mentioned this when asked, though. She was told to "forget everything", and so she did.

Besides, she liked Gladwell more than that fat prick Harrison.

So, when a bald man in a bomber jacket arrived at her office door that evening and told her to gather her things and leave immediately, she thought that this was her time to join Donna.

But instead, as they walked hurriedly down the stairs of Portcullis House to the back entrance on Canon Row, an enclosed street that went nowhere with contractor buildings at one end next to a tall, grey, spiked barrier fence and the stark brown and white brick walls of 1 Parliament Street facing her, she was told that there were detectives coming to speak to her, and it was better for her, better for everyone if she simply wasn't there to speak to them.

Clambering into a black Ford Focus, balancing her brief-case and her hastily gathered paperwork together, Laurie took a moment to check her appearance in the passenger mirror, noticing how tired and scared she looked as the car now drove down Canon Row, turning left into Derby Gate and the exit into Whitehall.

This was usually only a way into Portcullis House, the exit out long blocked, but the bald man seemed to have some kind of sway with the armed police that guarded the gates here and as the Ford Focus approached, the barriers were raised so that the car could move out into the traffic. However, as they passed the second gate and moved onto the section of road that drove beside The Red Lion pub, Laurie was surprised to see a woman walk out of the door and stand in the road in front of them, effectively blocking the way. In her late fifties, her short, blonde hair over a charcoal-grey suit, she seemed nonplussed as the bald man hammered on the car's horn, yelling at her through the side window to get out of the way. Instead, as the armed police at the gate, seeing this altercation made their way out of the gate and towards the car, the woman simply smiled, pulling out a warrant card and waving it to the inhabitants of the car, allowing the head-lights to pick it up.

'DCI Bullman,' she explained, still standing in the way. 'Laurie Hooper, I have some questions for you. Please get out of the car.'

'We're on—' the bald man stopped as he realised they weren't on Government land. So, unable to run this woman over and with armed police now surrounding his car, he turned the engine off and swore.

It was another ten minutes before Anjli made her way from the Houses of Parliament to The Red Lion pub. The car was still there, and the bald man was arguing with Bullman, stating that Miss Hooper couldn't speak to anyone right now, but the moment he turned to the end of the road and saw Anjli approaching, he swore again.

'Hello again,' Anjli said as she walked over. 'I haven't seen you since you drove away from the scene of a terrorist explosion.'

At this comment the armed police standing around raised their rifles, and the bald man leaned against the car.

'Has he been allowed to make a call?' Anjli asked. Bullman shook her head, holding out two phones that were in her hand.

'Stopped them the moment they tried,' she explained. 'With a little help from these guys.'

Anjli looked at Laurie Hooper, still sitting in the car, facing forward, acting as if nothing was happening here.

'This is your chance to tell us everything,' Anjli said.

———

24

CATCHING UP

DECLAN HAD PULLED UP NEAR THE HOUSE IN WOKING AT around half past ten that night, and stared at it through the windscreen for a good ten minutes before finding a better spot to park the car, down a side road a couple of streets away, gained by walking through a narrow pedestrian footpath with a right-turn in the middle and with a clear route out of the area. If everything went fine, it was a slightly longer walk to return to it.

If everything went wrong, however, this could save his life.

It was a detached five-bedroom house, with a hedge around it, a tall, slatted fence at the back and a six-foot-high wooden gate at the front with a buzzer beside it. No camera though, which was a small blessing. Declan pressed the buzzer and waited.

'Yes?' a male voice answered.

'DI Frost,' Declan lied. 'I'm here to speak to Miss Pearce.'

'We don't have a Pearce here,' the voice replied.

'Don't mess me around, laddie,' Declan put on his best

Monroe voice. 'It's late, I'm tired, and it's starting to rain. Open the bloody door.'

'Yes, Guv.' The door buzzed and Declan pushed it open, walking to the front door. His hair was slicked back into a severe side parting, as if he was enabling a comb over to hide a bald patch. His black glasses were on and his overcoat – well, his father's overcoat, as his was in a train somewhere – had the lapels pulled up.

The door opened a crack and a nervous young police officer peered out into the night, staring at Declan, still slightly in the shadows. Declan held up the warrant card momentarily, ensuring that the police officer saw the name and rank, but didn't focus on the image with it.

'Bit late, sir?' the officer asked.

Declan shrugged. 'Crime waits for no man, and we're short staffed,' he explained.

The officer laughed, opening the door wider to let Declan in.

'Story of my life, sir,' he said as Declan entered the house.

'Is she still up?' Declan asked as they walked down the main hallway.

The officer nodded. 'Stays up past midnight. It's like having a bloody teenager when we try to get her to go to bed.'

'We?'

'There's always two of us here, sir. One on the door and the other with Pearce. You know, to ensure she's not trying to get messages out.'

Declan paused. 'Why not put CCTV in the rooms?' he asked. 'I mean, surely that'd make things easier.'

'There're cameras, but we're not allowed sound,' the officer explained as he walked to the living room door, opening it. 'Part of the plea deal her lawyers are working out. You need long?'

'Just a few minutes,' Declan said as he entered the living room. It was white-walled, with a whole wall replaced by full-length windows that looked out into the garden, but were currently covered with slate-grey slatted blinds. A large television, at least sixty inches in size, was on one wall, and underneath it was some kind of console machine and a Blu-ray player. A brown leather sofa faced it, a small glass coffee table blocking the path, and a second leather armchair sat at a ninety-degree angle to them both. Another police officer, a young female PCSO looked up at the door when they entered; the woman on the sofa continued to watch the news on the TV.

'DI Frost needs to ask Miss Pearce some questions,' the police officer beside Declan explained, and Declan prepared himself to attack; the moment Pearce looked at him, the game would be up. She knew who he really was, and all she had to do was say this to the officers in the room.

Declan was hoping, however, that she wouldn't.

'I've told you all I'm willing to say right now—' Francine Pearce said as she turned to look at Declan, her eyes widening with recognition. 'Oh. Now *this* is interesting.'

Declan looked to the female PCSO, now rising from the leather armchair. 'If you could both give us some time alone?' he asked.

The two officers made their way out of the room as Declan walked over to the recently vacated chair, sitting in it. He'd noticed that the camera in the room, a small Wi-Fi ball on a corner shelf was pointed directly at him, but considering the fact that he was impersonating an officer and had two police officers outside who had already seen his face, the moment for hiding his face was long gone, and he was happy to risk this.

Francine Pearce was slim, in her forties and had a black, 1920s bob cut to her hair. Usually at home in business suits and dresses, it seemed strange for her to be in jogging bottoms and a sweatshirt, although her makeup was still on point, her hair set perfectly. It was almost as if they took the head and the body from two different images: one glamorous and swish, the other some kind of lounge-wear catalogue, and photoshopped together.

A smile on her face, she picked up the remote and muted the television.

'Last I saw you, it was on that television,' she commented. 'Nice little piece in the news. Apparently you're a terrorist now or something.'

'Last time I saw you, I remember you shooting me twice in the chest,' Declan retorted.

Pearce laughed. 'Would have been a damn sight more impressive if Donnal had used real bullets instead of blanks,' she replied. 'What do you want, Walsh? I mean, it must be something pretty bloody big for you to waltz in here while the subject of a national manhunt. I wonder how many favours I'd gain if I was to call out and inform them who you are.'

'If you were going to do that, you would have done it the moment you saw me,' Declan replied. 'But if you'd rather watch the TV with your babysitter, I can bring her right back.'

'Christ, no,' Pearce grimaced. 'I'm bored shitless. You're actually a welcome distraction.' She leaned back in her seat. 'So, go on then. Why are you here bothering me?'

'Rattlestone,' Declan replied. 'Also the death of Kendis Taylor.'

'I heard she was a terrorist.'

'I heard you were her source.'

Francine Pearce stopped at that. 'Who told you?' she asked.

Declan shrugged. 'Nasir Gill, right before he was murdered by people who claimed to be Special Branch.'

'Sounds like you had an exciting day,' Francine grinned. 'So tell me what you want to know about Rattlestone, then.'

Declan pulled out his notepad. 'Who runs it?' he asked. 'The only name anyone knows is Donna Baker, but she's dead.'

'Poor woman,' Francine nodded. 'The only fallout of the Davies case that I'm truly sorry for, was her finding out what a total shit her husband was.' She leaned forward, picking up a glass of wine from the coffee table. 'I'd offer you a drink, but to be honest I don't want to.'

'Don't drink while on duty,' Declan replied, almost automatically.

Francine choked on the wine as she laughed. 'You're on the run and excommunicated from the force,' she said, placing the glass back down. 'You're using someone else's warrant card. You're literally cosplaying a copper right now. There's no duty involved.'

Declan bristled but didn't reply, mainly because he knew she was right. Eventually Francine stopped laughing and thought about the question, furrowing her brow as she steepled her fingers together.

'There's a board of directors, but it's all for show,' she said. 'Ex-army types, civil servants who got sick of flying economy, that sort of thing. They get paid a pretty penny for looking the part, but they don't control Rattlestone. They don't shape it. That happened after the Balkans.'

'I've heard about that,' Declan noted this down. 'Was it Baker who leaked the itinerary?'

Francine shook her head. 'As much as he was a craven bastard, he had a kind of moral compass. If it was anyone in his department, it was Will Harrison. He was a sneaky little runt at the best of times.'

'So who controls them now?'

'Last I heard, they were working for the Star Chamber,' Francine offered. 'Black bags always were a part of their remit, after all.'

'What was your connection to Rattlestone?'

'What makes you think I had one?'

'You hired them.'

'My *company* hired them as security consultants,' Francine waggled her finger. 'Not the same as *I* hired them.'

Declan leaned back in the chair, observing Francine for the moment, fidgeting, her right hand on the arm of her chair, tapping tunelessly as she spoke. 'But you knew them,' he said. 'A Rattlestone employee was your driver to Devington Hall, and Shaun Donnal stated the same man on your orders beat him.'

'Oh,' Francine smiled again. 'You mean the undercover officer, DI Frost, who you seem to play the part of right now.'

'Did you know he was undercover?'

'Sweetheart, I didn't even know his name was Frost,' Francine replied. 'DI Frost? Check the warrant card you must hold. If his first name's Jack, you know it's fake.'

'Why?'

Francine shook her head. 'Christ, didn't you watch TV? David Jason? *A Touch of Frost*? He played DI Jack Frost.' She chuckled. 'Good show. But either way, Frost isn't his actual name. I never found it out, and neither will you. By the time you reach him, he'll be gone all over again. Or didn't you think it strange that the moment that you last arrested him, he was instantly whisked away?'

'I thought it strange that he'd break cover and try to beat Alex Monroe to death.'

This genuinely surprised Francine. 'He did it? You're sure?'

'We have him on tape.'

'Sloppy,' Francine mused. 'He doesn't have the sense to do something like that alone. He had to be ordered.'

'Baker?'

'He's Star Chamber, so maybe. Only the Chamber gives kill orders these days.'

'Sutcliffe?'

'He's police, but he has outside influences,' Francine nodded. 'More than happy to assist us when we needed him in Hurley, so I can see him sucking Rattlestone's cock if it gives him a bigger pension.'

'What if Baker passed the order to Will Harrison?'

'Oh, I can see him screwing with orders,' Francine sipped at her wine again. 'Plus he's been in the game since just before the 2010 election.'

'Could Harrison be the genuine power behind Rattlestone?' Declan asked.

Francine almost spat out her wine as she laughed. 'That would be a horror show and no mistake,' she mused. 'But no. They created Rattlestone a good five years before Baker and Harrison barged their way into the party. I was the one who got the two of them in, in fact.'

'If you got them in, then you must know who was at the top.'

Francine stayed silent at this.

'I was told that some unknown guy in the shadows named it with a bombing and some scrabble letters,' Declan replied. 'All I need is his name.'

'I don't play with secrets these days,' Francine mock chided. 'I'm a good girl. That's more for people like Baker and Gladwell.'

Declan paused at the name. 'Gladwell?'

'Sickeningly fit ginger-haired prick.'

Declan pulled out his phone, noting that as he scrolled through the photos on it, Francine was nervously fidgeting again. He found the photo of Kendis and the red-haired man in the park. He showed it to Francine.

'Is that Malcolm Gladwell?' he asked.

Francine's eyes brightened. 'Oh, yes,' she said. 'Interesting. So Gladwell was talking to Kendis Taylor. I wonder why?'

'You tell me,' Declan placed the notebook away, but a gnawing sensation in his gut was telling him he was *missing* something.

Then, just like that, the memory snapped back.

Declan remembered seeing him in The Horse and Guard, sitting with a woman, her dyed-blonde hair pulled back severely.

Kendis had gone there to see her source.

Gladwell. Not Pearce.

Francine was still tapping, but it wasn't fidgeting. It was rhythmic.

'You're not the source,' Declan muttered.

'Oh, Declan,' Francine replied, pausing the incessant tapping the moment he spoke. 'When did I ever say that?'

Declan stared in stark realisation at Francine Pearce. 'Nasir named you.'

'Nasir Gill worked for Rattlestone,' Francine smiled. 'And Nasir Gill sent you to *me*. To tell me who the *source* was.'

Declan thought back to the moment he'd told Francine that he knew she was Kendis Taylor's source. She never denied it, simply asking who told him, and now he'd revealed Malcolm Gladwell.

Idiot idiot get out of here now.

Francine's fingers still tapped on the side of the chair. *The side of the chair facing the CCTV camera.*

'What did you tell them?' Declan rose now, looking at the hand.

Francine shrugged. 'Just morse code,' she replied. 'Saying *get help this is Declan Walsh* repeatedly.'

Declan listened; in the background he could hear police sirens.

'I guess Rattlestone owns you,' he said.

Francine shook her head.

'No, they owe me,' she replied. 'I'm giving them you, after all.'

As Declan turned to the door, it opened and the young police officer entered, a bright yellow X26 taser gun in his hand.

25

THE FUGITIVE

'GET ON THE FLOOR,' THE POLICE OFFICER SAID NERVOUSLY, HIS voice wavering as he raised it to aim at Declan, who stared at the officer, hands slowly raising.

'There's more going on here than you realise,' he suggested, but the officer didn't budge, the taser gun still aimed at him. However, he was nervous, and the taser was wavering a little in Francine's direction.

'Don't point that near me, you bloody idiot!' she snapped as it passed her a third time. As the officer glanced in her direction, pulling the taser away, Declan took the momentary distraction to jump across the sofa, taking the officer down in a tackle, the taser firing off to the side as, now up and running again, Declan ran past the confused PCSO and slammed open the door.

There was no way to leave through the main gates; the police had already arrived, screeching up onto the kerb outside. Luckily though, the gates were closed; the young officer had forgotten to open them before he entered the room, and that gave Declan a moment's respite as the police ran to the gate, frantically hammering on the pad beside it to open it up, watching the man in the suit exit through the front door and stop, unsure where to go next. Deciding, Declan turned to the right, sprinting across the garden in a diagonal direction away from the gate. He knew the police would run around the house, but he hoped that he could get to the gate and climb over it before they reached him. Then he'd try to lose them down the back roads and alleys as he made his way back to the car.

Leaping over the back fence with the help of an apple tree beside it, Declan fell to the pavement on the other side of the wooden slatted wall, looking back up the street to see a young officer sprint around the junction. He was alone, so had obviously already been moving in that direction, but one officer, no matter how large or small could still see where Declan was going. There was a good fifty yards between them so Declan now continued running in the opposite direction, hoping to escape the chasing police, darting down the first side road, turning into the footpath before the second officer could catch him. He could hear the sirens of police cars, but it was too late for them; they would have to take the long way round to reach him.

There was a piece of pallet wood on the floor down the alley; about three to four feet in length and, as Declan grabbed it, hefting it in his hands like a baseball bat and moving against the wall where the path turned, it became a vicious-looking weapon. As the officer ran into view Declan swung it hard, catching the police officer low, under the anti-stab vest and sending him to the floor, clutching at his groin. Declan tossed the pallet away, said a quick 'sorry' and carried on running.

Through the passageway now and with the keys in his hand, he ran to the car loaned to him by Karl and, leaping into the driver's seat, started it up, driving off down the street before he'd even closed the door. He knew the police officer, by now back on his feet would see him drive off, but the street was dark, and Declan had faith that the registration wouldn't be seen.

He drove for two more streets before pulling into a busy pub car park and stopping, parking up between two vans. He could hear the police vehicles as they passed, and so he hunkered down in the seat, with the engine turned off. There was a moment of tension when a police car drove into the car park, looking at the vehicles, but as a torch swept across, Declan stayed low and kept as quiet as a mouse. Having seen nothing, the police car continued on.

Declan gave it an hour before he dared leave the car park; by then the police would have moved the search out of the area.

Finally, with a clear route out of Woking, he placed the car into gear and started back to London.

———

IN WESTMINSTER, IN AN UPSTAIRS ROOM AT THE RED LION PUB, Anjli nursed a glass of wine and stared across the table at DCI Bullman, now drinking a half pint of some obscure pear cider.

'So, what do you think?' she asked.

'I think that it's never dull with you guys,' Bullman replied, staring into her glass as she swirled it. 'Any reason we're not discussing this back at your office?'

'Don't trust the people in it,' Anjli shrugged. 'Stunned we weren't arrested the moment Harrison appeared.'

Will Harrison had appeared a couple of minutes after Anjli had entered the Ford Focus. He was out of breath, sweating and screaming out that this couldn't happen, as the bald-headed driver worked for the government under the *Intelligence Remit of 2016* and was at no liberty to divulge any information to her without a warrant, and the people and items within his car, including Laurie Hooper were covered by the same remit. Anjli had thanked the flustered Will for confirming that the man who apparently blew up a pub in Chelsea was indeed an employee of his; Will then back-tracked, saying that the man, still unnamed, was an employee of the Government, and therefore not just the office of Charles Baker. At this, Anjli had thought for a moment and then nodded, allowing the bald man and Mrs Hooper to leave.

The bald man, unaware that he'd dodged a bullet, or possibly too arrogant to believe that he could be shot at had glared furiously at Anjli as he climbed back into the car, starting it, and with a loud rev of the engine, the Ford Focus had screeched into the late night traffic, scattering onlookers beside The Red Lion pub as he did so.

Anjli had looked at Will right then, noticing his flushed red face. Poor bastard had likely started running here the moment Anjli had left. The only difference was that she was a damn sight fitter.

'Happy?' she had asked.

'Far from it,' Harrison snapped.

'Take it up with your MP,' Bullman then replied, looking to the armed police and nodding thanks. This done, both

Anjli and Bullman had entered the pub, ordered drinks and taken them to a quiet area upstairs.

'So, what did she tell you?' Bullman took a drink after asking.

Anjli glanced out of the window, down at the street below.

'Nothing much,' she replied. 'Stuck to the same story as we had in the report. She'd worked with Donna on the day of her death and didn't know that anything bad would happen. Donna had met with three people that day: Will Harrison, Malcolm Gladwell and a journalist named Kendis Taylor.'

'Why Taylor?'

'She didn't know. But I got the impression that Laurie Hooper knew more about Kendis Taylor than she was letting on.'

'Maybe she was the source that Kendis spoke to Declan about?' Bullman suggested.

Anjli nodded. 'Apparently she was also in the pub that blew up the same night that Kendis and Declan were,' she replied. 'But she wouldn't say who with.'

Anjli pulled out her phone as it beeped, her eyebrows rising as she read the message.

'Anything interesting?' Bullman indicated the message on the phone.

'Doctor Marcos,' Anjli nodded. 'She thinks that the murder weapon could be an incredibly overpriced letter opener.'

'It's Westminster,' Bullman snorted. 'Everything's expensive.' She caught the expression on Anjli's face, however. 'What?'

'Harrison, when I confronted him tonight,' Anjli replied.

'I was goading him, saying that he'd have to fall on his sword. He asked if a letter opener would do.'

'Interesting, but not enough to convict.'

'Yeah, true,' Anjli finished her drink. 'Come on, let's go, Guv. I think we've given Sutcliffe and his crew enough time to dig some holes. Let's go find Monroe.'

MALCOLM GLADWELL HADN'T EXPECTED LAURIE HOOPER TO come back to him that night, although it was a welcome distraction for him. Allowing her access by buzzing her into the building, he met her at the door to his apartment, hugging her tightly as she cried into his arms.

'What happened?' he asked as he brought her into the room, sitting her down on the sofa and walking over to the kitchen counter where, out of a cabinet he found and poured out a generous measure of vodka, walking over and placing it into the crying woman's hands.

'They questioned me,' Laurie mumbled, sipping from the tumbler.

'Who did?' Gladwell felt a twinge of fear run down his spine. 'The police?'

Laurie nodded. 'And Will,' she continued. 'They bundled me out of Westminster in a car, Malcolm. They didn't want me talking about Donna.'

'What did they want to know about Donna?' Gladwell asked. 'Do you mean the police?'

Laurie nodded. 'They wanted to know about her last day. The officer, an Indian woman, she said she didn't believe how Donna died, and she knew I didn't think so either. She *knew*, Malcolm! She knew I was the whistle-blower!'

'Hush, darling,' Gladwell replied, sitting down beside her and placing a protective arm around her shoulders, feeling her lean into him as he continued. 'They don't know that. Only I know that, remember? And I agreed to speak with Kendis for you, so she only ever believed that I was the whistle-blower. You're safe, my dear.'

'What did you speak to Donna about?' Laurie asked softly. 'The day she died?'

If Gladwell was surprised by the question, he didn't show it. 'I was warning her about Will,' he replied. 'That you didn't cross *Sir Hiss* and expect to get away unbloodied. She was angry that they had duped her, and that Rattlestone was being dumped on her shoulders. I was taking it off them.'

'I always wondered if you were having an affair,' Laurie forced a weak smile, sipping again from the tumbler of vodka.

Gladwell laughed out loud at this. 'She's definitely not my type,' he said as he stroked Laurie's hair.

'I'm sorry I came here,' Laurie mumbled, her cheeks reddening, partly from the vodka but also as she flushed. 'I didn't think it was right to go home.'

'I'm glad you came,' Gladwell stood up now, leaving Laurie at the sofa as he walked across the room, picking a small, thin box up from the side cabinet. 'I have news for you.'

'What sort of news?' Laurie was suspicious as Gladwell returned, placing the box on the table. 'Good news?'

'That depends,' Gladwell took the tumbler and placed it on the table next to the box, as he took Laurie's hands, turning her attention to his face. 'I know how Donna died. Will Harrison brutally murdered her. I'll have the full facts texted to me tonight, and we'll go to the police tomorrow.'

'They won't believe us,' Laurie moaned. 'Will? He's protected.'

'True, he'll never be charged with it, but that doesn't mean he can't face justice,' Gladwell picked up the box. 'You see, he made a massive error yesterday. He killed a journalist and tried to blame it on a police officer.'

'Kendis Taylor?' Laurie half rose, but Gladwell's grip kept her in place. 'He killed her? How do you know this?'

'Because thanks to my own assets, I know where he did it, why he did it, how he did it …' Gladwell opened the box, showing the contents; a thin, sharp looking gunmetal grey letter opener, with black leather insets. '… and what he used to do it with,' Malcolm Gladwell finished. 'Tomorrow, Will Harrison is going to find that karma is a bitch.'

'Is he here?' Anjli asked, leaning against one of the heavy bags as Johnny Lucas faced her, his expression one of amusement.

'I should start charging rent,' he replied. 'I've got more coppers here now than boxers.'

He looked at Bullman, currently examining a spot of blood on the floor.

'Boxers, love. Bleed when punched.'

He turned back to Anjli with a broad smile.

'I know I said don't be a stranger, but I never said bring all your pals.'

'Interesting times,' Anjli replied.

'You gonna introduce us?' Johnny indicated Bullman.

'No,' Anjli replied simply as, from the back corridor, Doctor Marcos walked out into the gym, Monroe with her.

'These ones don't have to be kicked out,' he said wearily as he smiled.

'We had some visitors,' Doctor Marcos explained. 'They were quite forceful, but eventually were convinced that they should leave.'

'They're probably trying to gain a warrant for here right now,' Monroe added.

'That won't happen,' Johnny replied, without explaining why he was so sure.

Anjli couldn't help herself, she walked over and embraced Monroe.

'How are you feeling?' she asked.

Monroe shrugged. 'I've been better, but I've also been a hell of a lot worse,' he replied. 'The headaches and the dizziness have gone. But then the adrenaline's also gone, so I'm feeling a little shite right now.'

Doctor Marcos looked to him, her tone softening. 'Alex, when this is over, we need to have a serious discussion.'

'On whether I'm fit to continue?'

'Among other things,' Doctor Marcos turned to Anjli. 'Any news on how Declan's doing?'

'They haven't caught him, so hopefully he's out there fighting. Plus we think we know what the murder weapon is.'

'We might have something for you on that,' Monroe weakly smiled. 'Oh, and did I hear right, that Billy's working with Sutcliffe?'

'Currently, yes,' Bullman stated, still watching the gym, as if expecting to be attacked at any time.

'Billy works for the law,' Monroe replied sagely, sitting on a foldout chair and shutting his eyes. 'He's doing the right thing.'

Anjli nodded. 'We'd better leave,' she said, looking to

Bullman. 'We just wanted to make sure you were okay, although it sounds like we'll need to find you a new place to hide.'

'No need,' Monroe replied, his eyes still closed. 'We'll end this tomorrow.'

Then Monroe, his eyes closed, snored.

'I hope to God you're right, old man,' Anjli whispered.

26

GHOSTS

Billy sat in the black Mercedes, looking nervously out of the window as it made its way through the night-time traffic, heading westwards along the Embankment and towards Westminster. He'd been at his desk and about to log off for the evening when DCI Sutcliffe had left his office and tapped Billy on the shoulder, telling him to grab his coat and follow. Billy had expected them to be heading to a crime scene, or perhaps to a briefing at a different location, but he hadn't expected the address that was given to the driver of New Scotland Yard.

'Am I in trouble?' he asked Sutcliffe, sitting next to him on the back seat, currently reading his phone as they drove.

'Why would you think that?' Sutcliffe looked up at him.

Billy shrugged. 'Because we're in a black Mercedes at eleven at night, and I have no idea where we're going or why we're doing it?'

Sutcliffe snorted. 'That's the problem with you nine to five-ers,' he replied. 'Everything out of the ordinary is an issue.'

Billy bit back the reply that pretty much none of the cases that he'd taken since joining the Last Chance Saloon had been ordinary and sat back in the seat.

'Frost's making a play for you,' he whispered.

This gained Sutcliffe's attention, and he put the phone away as he turned in the seat to face the younger man.

'Say that again,' he ordered.

Billy licked his now dry lips. 'He said you were a tool, and that he was effectively going to replace you,' he replied. 'He offered me a job in his new unit, and a promotion.'

Sutcliffe nodded at this, as if it wasn't a surprise. 'And you're telling me because?'

'I thought I ought to,' Billy said, looking out of the window again. 'You're a higher rank, and even though we work together, I still remember what Frost did.'

'What he did?' There was a note of caution in Sutcliffe's voice.

Billy looked back. 'You know, when he attacked Declan that time.'

'Oh, yes. That.' Sutcliffe's posture relaxed. 'Well, you did good letting me know. Leave it to me, just carry on as if nothing's happened.'

'Is this a Rattlestone thing?' Billy asked.

Sutcliffe's head snapped back to him. 'What do you mean by that?' he asked.

Billy leaned in closer. 'He told me that Rattlestone was the future, that it'd be involved more with police work. Suggested I even consider affiliating myself with it.'

Sutcliffe looked surprised at this.

'Bugger's definitely making a play,' he said. 'He knows he needs Rattlestone on his side if he wants to oust me,' he smiled. 'But Rattlestone and me? We go a long way back, and I know where the secrets are.'

Billy grinned. 'So it's like the Freemasons?'

Sutcliffe looked away, irritated. 'I wouldn't know,' he said. 'They never invited me.'

'Well, that's easy enough to fix,' Billy said, settling back into the seat. 'You get me into Rattlestone, and I'll put a word in with my Lodge for you.'

Sutcliffe mulled this over for a moment.

'Only if you join my team after this,' he suggested. 'If you're a team player, that is.'

Billy nodded. 'There's a reason I gave up Frost to you, sir,' he replied.

The car pulled up outside of New Scotland Yard, and Sutcliffe climbed out of the vehicle, Billy following a moment later, looking up at the white-brick building beside him. Although Temple Inn was technically City Police jurisdiction, it was on the western border of it, and therefore one reason that all the officers now working there had come from the *Metropolitan* Police, of which Scotland Yard or, more officially *New* Scotland Yard was the headquarters of. Billy carried on after Sutcliffe, now walking up to the main entrance and entering without checking on his young companion, hurrying through the foyer, passing through the security checks and entering a lift to the fourth floor. It was only here that Billy realised what the purpose of the meeting was; these were the offices of Chief Superintendent David Bradbury.

As they approached the glass office, using their visitors' passes to enter through a turnstile, Billy saw Bradbury rise from his desk, walking out to greet them.

'Please, come in,' he said as Billy and Sutcliffe entered, sitting in two offered chairs the other side of Bradbury's desk.

'I'm getting pressure from Charles Baker,' Bradbury started, the formalities and pleasantries over. 'He wants to know what's happened with the Declan Walsh investigation.' He looked down at a sheet of paper. 'He's also written a rather lengthy letter to me which states in no uncertain terms that he believes Declan isn't a terrorist, and that if he proves to be correct at the cost of a good man's career, then he will make it his life's purpose to bring down whoever caused it.'

'Baker's got an unpleasant taste in characters,' Sutcliffe muttered. 'Walsh confessed to us before he escaped.'

'Not to being a terrorist, sir,' Billy countered. 'Just to seeing Kendis Taylor.'

'Who's a terrorist,' Sutcliffe argued.

Billy went to speak again, but Bradbury raised a hand.

'This is the problem,' he said to Sutcliffe. 'You were put in charge, against my wishes I'll add, to helm this department. How's that going for you?'

'I'll admit, it's been challenging,' Sutcliffe shifted in his seat. 'There's a lot of loyalty there.'

'Yet one of his old partners sits beside you,' Bradbury looked to Billy. 'How do you see things?'

Billy was now the one to shift. 'The Guv's right,' he said. 'There's a lot of misguided loyalty. I don't know why DCI Monroe ran from the hospital with Doctor Marcos, but it doesn't look good for him. Declan running hasn't helped his case, either. Anjli's going rogue, and the DCI from Birmingham, Bullman? She seems to enable it.'

'But you're loyal,' Bradbury said.

'I'm loyal to the law, sir,' Billy replied.

Bradbury pulled out a sheet of paper, looking down at it.

'Doctor Marcos has been leaving messages for Walsh,' he said. 'Land lines, voicemails, emails, everywhere. Same three phrases. *Royal Bastard. Gallifrey. Dentist.* Do you know what it means?'

Billy nodded. 'I do, sir,' he said. 'It's the location and time tomorrow for a meeting. If we plan it right, we can get them all.'

'Them all?'

'If Doctor Marcos is sending Declan cryptic messages, sir, I think we can safely agree that she's playing for the wrong team,' Billy looked to Sutcliffe, who nodded.

'The boy's right,' he said, reaching for his phone. 'I'll contact my team and ...' he started checking through his pockets. 'My phone ...'

'Did you leave it in the car?' Billy asked as Sutcliffe rose, still searching his coat. He looked to Bradbury. 'If we're done here?'

Bradbury nodded. 'Go find your phone, Detective Chief Inspector,' he replied, looking to Billy. 'I need to speak to DC Fitzwarren quickly about a Detective Sergeant exam you've applied him for.'

As Sutcliffe left at speed to find his phone, Bradbury looked to Billy.

'Now, how about you tell me what's really going on,' he said, coldly.

SUTCLIFFE HAD JUST REACHED THE FOYER AS BILLY, RUNNING, caught up with him waving a phone.

'It was on Bradbury's floor, under the chair,' he said as Sutcliffe, taking the phone, opened it up, checking the apps.

'You didn't look at it, did you?' he asked.

Billy frowned. 'It's passcode and fingerprint locked,' he replied. 'I couldn't if I wanted to.'

Sutcliffe nodded at this, putting the phone away. 'I have a meeting to get to,' he said. 'You can get home from here?'

'I'm returning to the office,' Billy replied. 'I have a lead I want to follow up on.'

Sutcliffe muttered some kind of approving sound and walked over to the Mercedes, getting into the back seat. Billy watched it leave, walking over to a waste bin on the pavement.

There, he rubbed at his thumb, rolling off a thin sheet of silicone.

This removed, he tossed it into the bin and started walking towards Blackfriars Bridge.

DECLAN ARRIVED BACK IN LONDON AFTER MIDNIGHT.

Originally, Declan had considered driving to his old Tottenham apartment; he still had the lease, and it ran out later that week. But there was the police part of his mind, that soft, practical voice that told him what to do that pointed out that if they'd looked for him in Hurley, they'd look for him in Tottenham. The best thing to do right now would be to go to ground, to work out what the next stage was in his plan.

He needed to revisit the crime scene.

He'd driven into Chelsea, parking Karl's borrowed Peugeot on Kempsford Gardens, facing the north entrance of Brompton Cemetery. He sat for a moment, the engine off, staring at the wall across the road, still finding it hard to believe that it wasn't even two days ago that he'd met with Kendis in there for the last time.

When she was still alive.

He knew the cemetery didn't open until seven am, a good six or so hours away, so he settled into the seat, pulling the lapel of his coat up as he closed his eyes. But, after half an hour of small shifts in posture and occasional loud noises outside, he gave up sleeping for the moment and clambered out of the car, stretching his legs. The streets were quiet at this time of the morning, and so Declan risked a walk, a patrol of sorts of the cemetery, as if by doing this, he might get a better idea into what was going on.

Moving out onto the Brompton Road, Declan turned left, walking with the wrought iron bars of the cemetery to his right, looking through them at the gravestones and markers that were only feet away from him as he continued on. A few yards on he turned right at the crossroads, now heading south on the Finborough Road, where modern designed red brick apartments stood next to four-storey Victorian terraces. Passing the now closed Finborough Arms, Declan followed the road to the right as it split off, now walking down Ifield Road as he considered everything he knew so far.

Kendis had been scared, and had received a call to martyrdom letter through her door, a sheet now believed to have been sent by the now dead Nasir Gill. Who it also seemed worked for *Rattlestone* and had been taking photos of Kendis during the day.

Somehow, she'd found her way back into Brompton Cemetery that night. *Why?* Walking around it now, Declan could see that there was no way that you could simply stroll in. Only someone with a key could get in. So who had a key? He remembered a line she had said, when they met.

'Don't belittle the dead. Some of Westminster's biggest and brightest have plots here. That's the one for the Gladwells. Over there is the Harrison family.'

Malcolm Gladwell, who she'd met with earlier in the same day, and could have been her source now that Francine Pearce was out of the picture. Also, Will Harrison, the right hand puppet master of Charles Baker, and most likely moving on the head of Rattlestone, vying for the top position.

So, Kendis had met with Declan, then met with Gladwell and then returned to the cemetery. Had she gained a key from him?

By now Declan was emerging out of Ifield Road onto the Fulham Road, facing a twenty-four-hour service station. Knowing that they would have cameras, Declan hid his face as he turned right, heading westwards along the north side of the road, passing the southern entrance to Brompton Cemetery, a wrought-iron gate flanked by two old style red phone boxes. It was dark, but he could make out the plaque on the other side of the railings, in particular the words at the bottom.

Paid for by the Friends of Brompton Cemetery

Walking on, Declan considered this. Some kind of organisation like that would have ways to enter and exit the park whenever they wanted, and he was sure that the bigger plot holders would likely have a say in the FOBC—

FOB C. The note that Kendis had in her possession when she died. She knew this already, that the person she was hunting was connected. Was that why she met Declan there? Was she, like the night before at The Horse and Guard, using him as a reason to scope the place out?

Talking of The Horse and Guard, Declan realised, as he continued his circuit, that the bombed-out building was only another hundred yards down the road; he hadn't figured out how close it had been the night before. Anyone there would have been able to walk in or out of the cemetery in moments. Was that why Gladwell had met there? Was he nearby, able to enter and exit Brompton Cemetery as he pleased?

They had boarded the windows over, the external frontage burned away and blackened. Declan had seen on a news report that nobody had been injured in the explosion, which was still being classed as an accident. Declan resisted the urge to shudder. It had definitely been no accident. Neither had the meeting inside been an accident the night before, where Kendis and Malcolm Gladwell had spoken.

Gladwell, again.

Gladwell, who was in the Star Chamber with Charles Baker.

Gladwell, who had been Charles Baker's boss during the Balkan massacre, even if they didn't talk during that time.

Gladwell, who was Kendis Taylor's whistle-blower.

But why?

By now Declan had moved on past the burned-out pub, finding his chest tightening as he'd stood there, the moment of the blast striking him again. He continued westwards, towards Stamford Bridge, the legendary home of Chelsea Football Club. Walking past it, he continued along the Fulham Road, passing Fulham Broadway Underground Station and the shopping centre built around it, but he wasn't paying attention to his location anymore. By now he was re-evaluating everything that he'd been told and shown during the investigation. He was so convinced that Frost, Sutcliffe and Baker were behind it, that he hadn't considered the alternatives. He'd taken Baker's arrival after Monroe's beating as a moment of gloating. But what if it wasn't?

Now he was heading north, zigzagging along the back streets, making his way back to the Brompton Road. Turning right, he walked back to where his car was parked, climbing back inside, returning to his overnight observation. It was now almost three in the morning, and Declan felt tired enough for a nap. Shutting his eyes, he tried to drown out the noise of the streets, and the gnawing fear inside his stomach.

What if it was a genuine offer of aid?

27

FRIENDS OF THE DEAD

WILL HARRISON HADN'T SLEPT WELL THAT NIGHT.

After retaining Laurie Hooper, Will had sat in on her debrief; well, more of an interrogation, if he was being brutally honest. He'd made his way to the Rattlestone safe house in Pimlico where his man had taken her, and after a couple of hours had allowed her to leave, safe knowing that she wouldn't be talking to anyone else soon. She'd realised very early in the debrief how easy it was for her to disappear and had been incredibly helpful in her responses.

She'd admitted that she'd seen Donna Baker arguing with Will the day that she died, but Will repeatedly stated that *she was mistaken, that this hadn't happened*, and that she'd be destroyed if she ever suggested this to anyone. She claimed she had told no one, even the Indian police officer, and after the first plea, Will had believed her. What he hadn't known, and what he learned through the debrief, was that Donna had also met with Malcolm Gladwell that same day. Now, Malcolm was a known commodity, and no matter what issues they had with each other he was the trouble-shooter for the Tories right now, but this was several weeks after he'd been trying to push Baker as a leadership contender, a push that had inevitably failed after the Davies Murder case. There was no reason he'd drive out to Charles Baker's house just to speak to Donna, unless it was …

Yes. It had to be because of what that bloody journalist had said.

Laurie said that Donna had been quite distressed when she'd spoken to Gladwell that day, most likely because of the conversations that she'd had with Kendis Taylor earlier that week.

Will sat at his breakfast table, muttering to himself as he mused through this. Kendis Taylor had a source, someone that was feeding her the information. He'd originally assumed that it was Donna herself, but the conversations had continued after Donna had died. Will couldn't work out whether this meant that it had been the same person throughout or someone new, continuing when the original whistle-blower had died. If that was so, there were only a few people who could benefit from this. Only a few people still had guilt from the Balkans incident. Or had any way to profit from it.

Will finished dressing and walked out onto his balcony; he lived on the fifth floor of a luxurious Chelsea apartment complex that looked out onto the Thames, a location way above his pay grade if he'd just relied on his Advisor's salary. Luckily, he had other forms of income. Considering these, he sipped at his Italian roast coffee and decided on what his next plan was to be. He needed to clean up the house before Rattlestone applied for the Ministry of Defence Police tender, as there were too many loose cannons in the wind now. Bloody Frost had royally screwed the pooch when he went rogue and attacked the DCI in his office, and only the fact that Declan Walsh had been outed as a terrorist kept the idiot from too much scrutiny there. Sutcliffe too was a waste of time; since being installed in the Temple Inn office, not only had he lost the prime suspect, but he'd also allowed his detectives to run around performing their own enquiries, something that Will knew only too well from the previous night.

Someone wanted Will out of Rattlestone. It had to be. They had seen his movement, knew he was ambitious. This had to be it. But *who?* They weren't wrong, however; he *was* making a power play. Too many Parliamentarians had a say here—

There was a knock on the door. Walking back into his apartment, Will crossed through the living area and opened it. A blond man in a three-piece suit stood there, a warrant card in his hand. Will didn't need to see the card though, as he knew this officer from the files.

'DC Fitzwarren, City Police,' Fitzwarren said, putting the warrant card away into an inside pocket. 'Any chance of a quick chat?'

'Make it quick, I've got a busy day of meetings,' Will walked back into the apartment, Fitzwarren following. 'You're with Sutcliffe, aren't you? I'm hearing good things about you. He might be a prick, but work ethics are work ethics.'

'Thank you, sir,' Fitzwarren said uncertainly as he looked around the minimalistic design of the apartment. 'I just had a quick question for you.'

'Only one?' Will chuckled. 'Your partner Kapoor had loads last night.'

'Anjli's not my partner,' Fitzwarren said frostily. 'I serve the law, not my vanity.'

'Well said,' Will sat down at the breakfast bar as he faced the young detective. 'What's the question?'

'I saw you're a member of the Friends of Brompton Cemetery.'

'What of it?' Will asked. 'It's been a family thing for generations.'

'I wondered how much access you gain from it,' Fitzwarren continued. 'For example, if there's a way to get in out of hours?'

'Yes, we're given a key to the North Lodge gate, as the *Friends* have offices in the East Wing,' Will replied. It wasn't a secret, and he knew that lying would soon catch him out. 'You can access the cemetery from the cafe garden. Not that we need to, as the bloody place is open from dawn until darkness.'

He smiled.

'I have a grave grant pass too, which means I can drive to my family mausoleum, if that's of interest too.'

'Do you visit the mausoleum much?'

'Christ, no. Morbid, tiny bloody place. I pay people to cover my workload there. You know, tidying it up and all that. Several of us do.'

'Us?'

Will nodded. 'Quite a few MPs have plots there. Malcolm Gladwell, for example.'

He leaned forward.

'You should check into him, DC Fitzwarren. You should tell the others.'

Fitzwarren nodded as if understanding this. 'I will do, sir,' he replied. 'Can you tell me who has access to your key though?'

'My workers have it,' Will replied a little too nonchalantly. 'I get it from them if I need it.'

'Could they have used it the night that Kendis Taylor died?'

'It's possible,' Will considered this. 'But I thought the murderer was Walsh?'

'I'm trying to work out how he got in there,' Fitzwarren admitted. 'Or, why Kendis and Declan hung around for so long after their meeting.'

'Who said they did?'

'Well, going on the evidence—'

Will waved Fitzwarren silent. 'I get it,' he said. 'Look, there's about a hundred members, maybe more, I don't know. You can join on their website. But only a few of us have keys. They're old ones. There's bound to be copies, and some old bastards who have them are in their nineties, so it wouldn't surprise me if a few had disappeared. You know, sold on the dark web or something.'

'Why would keys be sold on the dark web?'

'I dunno,' Will replied, already regretting his flippancy. 'Getting into a graveyard at night and all that?'

Fitzwarren nodded, as if this thought hadn't occurred to him. 'Thank you for your time,' he said. 'One other small thing, and you might know nothing about this. Do you own a Montblanc letter opener?'

'Is this case-related?'

'Is that a yes or a no?'

'I don't know,' Will replied, his expression completely void of any emotion. 'Come to the office sometime and we'll have a rummage. How does that sound?'

'Thank you, sir.' Fitzwarren turned for the door.

'Well, when you hear anything more, please let me know,' Will smiled, rising from the stool.

'Of course,' Fitzwarren walked to the door, but at it he stopped, turning back to Will.

'Between us,' he said conspiratorially. 'Why did you give the order to attack Monroe?'

'I didn't,' Will's smile dropped now. 'And if you suggest to anyone that I did, I'll ensure you'll never work a case again. Understood?'

Fitzwarren nodded, his face unchanged, almost as if he'd expected the response. 'Of course, sir. I had to ask, to ensure I can't be accused of bias. Also, sir, my family has connections to you, I believe. I'd appreciate it if you could put in a kind word for me?'

Will nodded, escorting Fitzwarren to the door. 'Think nothing of it,' he said as he ushered the detective out. Closing the door behind him, he walked over to his coat rack, pulling his phone out of a jacket that hung there.

Dialling a number, he waited.

'It's me,' he said as he walked back into the living area. 'I think I know who's trying to ruin us and I need them stopped.'

OUTSIDE THE APARTMENT COMPLEX, FROST YAWNED AS HE SAT in the driver's seat of the black Lexus that he'd requisitioned the previous day. He'd followed Billy Fitzwarren from his house that morning, through London and had stopped here, across the road, watching him buzz for entry and enter the building. Frost knew who lived there; he knew the addresses of everyone connected to Rattlestone, and this was top of the list. Well, almost. He considered entering himself, of walking in on Fitzwarren, snapping out his baton and smacking the stupid expression off the idiot boy, but before he could decide on the best way to attack, the door opened and Billy emerged again, writing in his notebook as he passed a blonde woman that entered past him, not even paying attention to her as he did so. Frost tutted to himself.

And he called himself a police officer.

The woman had been Laurie Hooper. Frost had met her twice over the last year or so; she'd been Donna's right-hand woman until the unstable bitch offed herself. Since then she'd been Charles Baker's charity case, and the thorn in Will Harrison's arse cheek. Frost watched Fitzwarren enter his stupid little car and for a moment considered following him. But the thought of catching Hooper and Harrison together was an opportunity for both blackmail and promotion.

Climbing out of the car, he checked his pockets to ensure he was armed, and then walked across the road.

WILL WAS PACING IN HIS LIVING SPACE, FRANTIC AND NERVOUS as the doorbell went again. Glancing at the clock on the wall, Will saw that it had been literally two minutes since Fitzwarren had left. The bloody idiot had probably forgotten his way out of the building or something.

'Bloody detectives,' he said as he opened the door, facing his second visitor in as many minutes, locking eyes with them as he spoke. 'What the hell are *you* doing here?'

Laurie Hooper stood there, uncertain, tears streaming down her face.

'I know you killed her,' she said, looking around the

hallway before pushing past Will and entering the living area. 'Malcolm explained it to me.'

'Killed who?' Will observed the woman, wondering whether he should call the police, an ambulance or both. 'Kendis Taylor?'

'Donna!' Laurie hissed.

Will opened and shut his mouth at this.

'You're serious?' he eventually said. 'Donna Baker was a bipolar manic-depressive who realised she was married to Charles Baker! I'm stunned she didn't off herself before!'

The backhand from Laurie was unexpected and surprisingly forceful, and Will staggered backwards across the room, only faintly aware that the door to the apartment was still open. With luck, someone would hear this. Maybe the police officer, Fitzwarren, would return with another question.

But nobody did.

'You convinced her to kill herself!' Laurie continued. '*Sir Hiss*, that's what they call you. The hypnotic snake in Robin Hood has nothing on you, though!'

'You're hysterical,' Will rubbed at his cheek, aware that no matter what happened, people would see this. The mark would be public until it faded. 'Have you taken your meds today? I ask because you're utterly mental, so I'm guessing you take a lot.'

'You killed Donna, and you killed Kendis,' Laurie was on a roll now, her eyes bright and wide.

Will wondered if she'd taken something, maybe a small amount of coke, to give her Dutch courage for the confrontation. Will almost laughed at this.

'You killed them both because of Rattlestone.'

'Well, there you're right,' Will clapped his hands. 'Both of them died because of that. But tell me, how the hell was I supposed to kill Taylor?'

Laurie reached into her pocket and pulled out what looked like a small, gunmetal blade. Will glanced down at it, his eyes widening in horror as he recognised it.

'Where did you get that?' he asked, now backing away from Laurie and the door. 'Seriously, where did you get it?'

'A friend gave it to me,' Laurie was stalking her prey now, licking her lips as she warmed to the task at hand. 'He told me you tried to hide it, that you were foolish to use it because it's easy to track back to you.'

'Look, I'll admit I bought it, but not for myself,' Will insisted. 'I wasn't the last to speak to Donna, either. Malcolm was, and I bought that bloody thing for—'

Will Harrison didn't finish his explanation; as he stared into Laurie's eyes, trying desperately to invoke some kind of empathy from her, she rammed the Montblanc letter opener in metal Ruthenium and plated with a black inlay into his chest.

Holding it, as if trying to pull it out but unable to work out how, Will stared down at the letter opener, his mouth bubbling and filling with hot, sticky blood, spattering out across his shirt front as he tried to form words. But there were none to come from his lips as he slid to his knees, the blood from the wound now pooling on the surrounding carpet. He made one last, faint gurgling, keening sound, his eyes focusing onto the door behind Laurie, as if willing himself to escape, and then he slumped to the floor, his now lifeless eyes staring up at the ceiling.

Laurie stared down at the body for a moment before spitting on it.

'That was for Donna, you prick,' she muttered.

There was a sound behind her, a small scuff of the carpet, and Laurie turned around quickly, scared that someone had walked past the open door and seen her premeditated act.

She saw the figure behind, her eyes widening even further with surprised recognition as the taser torch rammed into her sternum, pulsing the electricity through her and sending her twitching to the floor.

28

GRAVE ROBBING

It wasn't the most comfortable bed he'd ever slept in but he'd had worse, and Declan managed a broken three and a half hours before finally giving up and, rubbing at his bleary eyes tried to move about in his seat to allow his cramped muscles to loosen. He peered down at his watch to see that it was almost seven thirty in the morning; already the rush hour traffic was building on the road ahead, and he could see that the gates to Brompton Cemetery were now open.

Reaching into the back of the car, Declan pulled forward the urban backpack, opening it up and bringing out some items he'd brought with him. He needed a change of shirt, a wipe down with wet wipes and a quick spray of antiperspirant. He took a small swig of mouthwash, swilled and spat out into the gutter beside the car. Then, as freshened up as he could be, he took a mouthful of water from his bottle, grabbed out a lock pick case that he'd barely ever used, zipped the bag back up and left the car, head down, entering the cemetery.

A man in a green jacket, obviously some kind of custodian, looked at him as he entered, so he quickly showed the Frost ID.

'Crime scene follow up,' he explained. The man nodded, waving him past, and Declan carried on down The Avenue, towards where Kendis had been found.

But he didn't go there.

Instead, he made his way down a side road, over to a set of gravestones where, two days earlier, he'd stood with Kendis as she waved her hand around the cemetery.

'That's the one for the Gladwells. Over there is the Harrison family.'

Declan remembered where she had pointed, but needed a reference for it. Here, where he had last seen the longest love of his life alive, he noted the two mausoleums that she had pointed at before his vision blurred as tears filled his eyes.

No. He couldn't break down now. He had to carry on. He had to find her killer.

Walking further down the path, he picked his way through the gravestones to where her body had been found. It was about a hundred yards from Will Harrison's family plot, while only about thirty from Malcolm Gladwell's.

Why had she been here?

There was still incident tape, slivers of blue and white plastic fluttering around in the morning breeze as Declan looked down to the small area of ground where, less than twenty-four hours earlier, he'd found her, placed onto her back and with her arms crossed, as in repose.

'Defensive wounds on her hands and arms, bruising around her neck, as if she was throttled.'

'She was arm-barred during the struggle, I think. Forearm

pressed against the throat. There are taser marks on her upper chest, so I think she tried to fight whatever was happening, and then was zapped. There's a cut to her head where she fell, struck it on something.'

'They stabbed her in the chest. Small, thin blade into the lung. It would have caused an injury-related pneumothorax, a collapse of the lung itself. She would have passed out most likely, suffocated eventually.'

Declan's hands were clenching as he recalled Doctor Marcos's post mortem report. There had been a cut on her head where she'd struck it. In addition, there was no blood.

Somewhere in this cemetery, there was a place with blood.

Declan looked to the Gladwell Mausoleum, purely because it was the closest. He once more walked his way carefully through the graves as he made his way to the eastern wall and the stone building that stood silently under a large and probably old tree. It was square, with a metal door; surrounded by railings, it looked like a tiny house.

Suddenly, he stopped.

There was a wire, running along the side of the mausoleum, about an inch from the lip of the roof. Slowing, Declan carefully walked around the perimeter, checking to see what this could be. As he reached the front though, he realised that something connected the wire to what looked like some kind of motion detector, maybe even a camera, like the doorbells that recorded you when you walked up to the doorstep. There was an antenna at the back, some kind of Wi-Fi extender, perhaps? Billy would know. Declan took a couple of photos of the serial number on the antenna, intending to send them across later. Either way, this looked very much like serious levels of security on a simple mausoleum.

But why? *Resurrectionists* were long gone.

Declan considered leaving the mausoleum, not alerting anyone, but he couldn't walk away. Every nerve in his body cried out that there was something wrong here. He needed to go inside.

Is this how Kendis had died? Had she gone inside and been seen doing so?

Declan needed to keep his identity out of any cameras, so hunted around the base of the tree, finding a broken-off branch, most likely fallen because of a storm a few days ago. Walking to the side of the mausoleum, he used the branch as a hook, yanking the wires out of the extender and then hanging the branch in them, making the act of vandalism look as if the falling branch had simply caught the wire. Then, not knowing how long he had before someone came to look, Declan jumped the railings and, with his lock-pick case, started working on the door. An experienced lock picker could get through such an old lock in seconds, but Declan wasn't that adept, and it took a good few minutes. They were long, worrying minutes where at any point anyone could find him, before he unlocked the door to the mausoleum, opening it up and with his phone's torch as his light source, entered the dark room within.

The mausoleum was square, a corridor on the left and two full-length shelves on the right giving eight square tombstones, four on each shelf where coffins would have been placed in, headfirst. These were covered with small memorial stones, each one explaining which member of the Gladwell family lay in rest there. There were a couple of blank ones; Declan assumed these were empty, held for the next dead members of the family. They didn't look as if they'd been touched in years.

What did look like it'd been disturbed recently was a small table against the back wall, a wrought iron cross on top of it, and a circular mark on the surface, as if something with a circular base had been moved after years, leaving a change in colouration. Shining the torch to the floor, Declan saw shards of a ceramic bowl, shattered into pieces on the floor. When he looked closer, the floor, damp and mouldy, seemed darker here, as if stained with blood.

Kendis died here.

But why? Gladwell was her source. Had Will Harrison found her here? On the opposite wall to the tombstones Declan could see two burn marks, about an inch apart, a ragged line that looked like someone had taken a taser and scraped it along the wall.

'There are taser marks on her upper chest, so I think she tried to fight whatever was happening, and then was zapped.'

Declan fought to breathe, his chest tightening. He needed to get out, but then stopped as he looked at a tombstone inscription on the far left of the top shelf. It read

ARCHIBALD GLADWELL

1875-1941

DIED AGED 66 DURING THE GERMAN BOMBING OF SHOREDITCH

10TH MAY 1941

Declan stared at the inscription. He couldn't explain it, but something felt off here. Something Billy had said about the piece of paper Kendis had held came to mind.

'Totters Lane is in Shoreditch. Nothing of note, got obliterated in the war. People literally vaporised.'

If Archie Gladwell was vaporised, how was there anything to place inside a coffin?

Declan ran a finger around the stone; the others looked wedged in, stuck in place for years, centuries even. This however had a minimum of debris in the grooves, as if someone had removed it recently. Glancing about, Declan picked up the metal cross, noting that one end had been flattened, like a crowbar. Inserting it into the side of the tombstone, Declan levered at it, surprised to see that the stone moved out easily, and with a minimum of fuss. Taking the stone and placing it to the side, Declan stared into the coffin hole.

There was a wrought iron safe facing him.

It was square and old, that was for sure. There was a bronze plaque on the top of it that read

MacNeale & Urban
Hamilton, OH

Declan stared at the old safe for a long moment; it looked like it had been concreted into the space, so there was no way to remove it. As well as that, it looked like an antique, and Declan wondered whether it had been installed there years before, maybe for an earlier member of the family. The one thing that caught Declan's eye though was the dial. Most safes had a tumbler lock that used numbers to unlock the safe, spinning the dial left and right, hitting the number and then moving to the next. The MacNeale & Urban safe however didn't have that. Instead, it had a dial that had twenty-six letters on it; this was a safe that relied on words, not numbers to open it.

Words.

'Half a day, a bomb and a pack of scrabble letters would give me the truth behind Rattlestone.'

Declan turned to the small table. Pulling his backpack off his shoulder, Declan opened it up, removing the green felt bag, opening it up and scattering out the scrabble squares that spelled out *Rattlestone*. Declan rearranged the scrabble letters, stepping back as he stared at the two words facing him. Two words taken from Rattlestone's name.

TOTTERSLANE

Malcolm Gladwell had named Rattlestone after the bombing.

Malcolm Gladwell had named Rattlestone.

Malcolm Gladwell was the true leader of Rattlestone.

So, if Will Harrison had been trying to remove the leader, that meant he'd been taking his shot at Gladwell.

Turning to the dial, Declan moved the first letter to T. Then left, all the way to O. Then right to T and so on, swapping direction every time he reached a letter, hearing a faint click as he did so. Finally, as he reached the final E, there was a click and the safe door eased ajar. Pulling it open, Declan looked inside. There was a metal briefcase in there, the size matching the safes interior exactly. Pulling it out, Declan placed it on the table and opened it, staring down at the files, USB sticks and photos inside.

This was the secret history of Rattlestone. Most likely some kind of blackmail box that if Gladwell was accused of anything would free him.

Pulling out one folder that caught his eye, he read the cover of it: *BALKAN INCURSION 2015*. Opening it up, he read the first few lines and then stopped, whistling.

He now knew who'd given up the schedule to militants; it

was here in black and white. God knows what else would be in this briefcase.

Pulling out his phone, he started taking photos of the pages. Once done, and placing the briefcase back into the safe, Declan stopped, staring at the inside of the safe door. On it, written on a piece of faded and ancient paper, were instructions from 1872 for the safe's owner on how to change the eleven letter combination.

Declan grinned. It seemed a shame to waste such an opportunity.

As he closed and re-locked the safe, placing the tombstone back in place, there was a noise outside; nothing more than an old man cycling past, using the route through the cemetery as a shortcut, but it was enough to remind Declan to get out before anyone arrived to check the wires. Exiting the mausoleum, re-locking the door with more ease than he unlocked it and climbing over the metal fence again, Declan melted back into the gravestones before anyone could see him.

They had murdered Kendis Taylor in Malcolm Gladwell's family mausoleum.

Now he had to work out whether it was by Gladwell himself.

IN FACT, IF DECLAN HAD WAITED ANOTHER TEN MINUTES HE could have asked him, because no sooner had he gone before Malcolm Gladwell entered Brompton Cemetery like a man possessed. Wide-eyed and desperate, he ran to his mausoleum, pulling out his key as he did so. His day had taken a turn for the worse when he received a notification that his motion alarm had been broken. Looking at the building as he arrived, however, he could see that this was apparently because a branch had fallen from the tree above and pulled out the wire. On a normal day, Gladwell might have accepted this, but today was different. He stared at the large metal key in his hand, wondering whether Kendis had copied the key that she'd stolen from him, the one he now had back in his hand. Although, with the cemetery opening earlier now, anyone could have entered.

Entering the mausoleum now, Gladwell paused. Someone had moved the cross on the table. He wasn't sure, and the last time he'd been in here he'd been distracted, but it was angled away from the door, as if replaced haphazardly. Grabbing it, he levered the tombstone away, revealing the antique safe behind it.

His father had told him about the safe one night years earlier, explaining the story behind it, and how his father, Gladwell's grandfather, had positioned the safe in the mausoleum. In a world where digital technology was constantly hacked, the thought of an analogue hideaway was something Gladwell could really get behind.

The safe was closed, and for a moment Gladwell believed he was just being paranoid, that everything was okay, however the voice in the back of his head told him he should check just in case, and so he twisted the dial; first to the T, then the O ...

When he finished, he realised the door hadn't opened. Worried that he'd made a mistake during the eleven letter code, he tried again, and a third time. He fell to his knees, pulling at his hair.

Someone had changed the combination.

Which meant that someone had opened the safe, which meant that someone had learned everything.

Turning and walking silently out of the mausoleum, he pulled out his phone, dialling a number. With Kendis and Harrison dead and Baker scared of his own shadow, there was only one person who could have done this.

He needed to get ahead of this, and fast.

29

CSI: CHELSEA

Billy hadn't expected to return to Will Harrison's apartment so quickly.

'You look like you've seen a ghost,' Frost said with a frown, pulling on his white PPE suit as he did so. 'Let me guess. You've never really been to a solid, gory crime scene before?'

'It's not that at all. It's that I was just here,' Billy replied, pulling on his own PPE suit, zipping it up as he stared through the door at the bodies of Will Harrison and Laurie Hooper. He had been in that very room speaking to Harrison less than two hours earlier.

'What do we have?' Frost asked a forensics officer – a tall, elderly looking man – as they walked past. 'Give us the basics.'

The officer paused, pulling off his mask. Billy didn't recognise him, but then the only forensics he really knew were on the run or back at Temple Inn.

'Name?' he asked.

'DI Frost, this is DC Fitzwarren.' Frost seemed unimpressed at being called out, and had been miserable as sin since they'd arrived. 'And you?'

The forensics officer equally didn't look impressed at the DI in front of him as he pulled his hood off, running a gloved hand through his short, white hair. Billy went to comment on this, but then stopped; he didn't think that commentating that the gloves were now compromised was the right thing to do in this scenario.

'Brightman, Forensic Scene Investigator,' he replied. 'I don't have a fancy rank like you, *Detective Inspector*. What I do have is years of experience on crime scenes, so giving "basics", as you asked for isn't really within my remit.'

'We're happy for more detailed explanations,' Billy quickly interjected. Brightman sniffed at this.

'We think that Mrs Hooper here visited and then fought with Mister Harrison, in the process stabbing him mortally in the chest with a letter opener, but not before he'd tasered her several times with the customised torch.' He showed the taser torch, still in Harrison's dead hand. 'Probably got a few shots in on her before he died, enough to cause her an immense coronary spasm in the process.'

'A what?' Frost looked to Billy.

'A massive heart attack,' the younger man replied. 'Basically Laurie Hooper killed Will Harrison, but he killed her too.' He looked down at the bodies. 'Which morbidly is good for us, I suppose.'

'How in God's name is this good for us?' Frost exclaimed. Billy pointed at the letter opener, still in Will Harrison's chest.

'If she'd escaped alive, we'd most likely be blaming DI Walsh for this as well,' he said. 'I'd stake my salary on betting that's a Montblanc letter opener with a metal Ruthenium finish. DC Davey sent me the reports for Kendis

Taylor's death and she believed *that* was the murder weapon.'

'DC Davey's an idiot,' snapped Frost. 'She couldn't solve a crime scene if we gave her the answers.' He stared down at the bodies. 'So say for a moment that the same blade killed Kendis Taylor. How did Laurie Hooper get it?'

'She might not have arrived with it,' Brightman spoke up now, standing by the sideboard. 'There's a Montblanc box here, and a receipt from a year ago. Bought with a card, but I'm pretty sure the number will match one Will Harrison owns.'

'Leave the detective work to the detectives, okay?' Frost was visibly agitated. Billy watched him.

'Did you know either of the victims, sir?' Billy asked.

Frost went to snap back, but stopped himself.

'I've worked with Harrison before,' he admitted softly. 'When I was undercover, of course.'

'Sorry for your loss,' Billy replied, leaning over the bodies again. 'So Laurie visits Will, which could match considering that last night Anjli and Bullman saved her from being questioned by him.' He looked around the room. 'She comes back here this morning, after I visited ...'

'How can you be sure?' Brightman asked.

'Because he wasn't dead then,' Billy replied.

'She may not have killed him, but she might still have been in the apartment,' Brightman suggested. 'Perhaps they were having an affair?'

'No, she was sleeping with—' Frost stopped himself. 'That is, the rumours were that she was sleeping with someone else. Possibly Malcolm Gladwell.'

'The MP? That's a bit soap opera, isn't it?' Billy looked back to the box on the sideboard. 'So either way, she's here or she comes in later. They have a row, and they fight. She grabs a letter opener from a box on the sideboard. He grabs a taser device that frankly shouldn't be allowed.'

'He works in politics,' Frost was examining the torch now, his blue gloves glowing with a blue light as the end of the taser torch sparked. 'I've seen people carry worse. You never know the crazies you meet out there.'

He stood up. 'Bloody idiot.'

'Sir?'

'If you're right, he should have taken her down well before she stabbed him. One shot is enough to restrain. He could have called – well, he *should* have called for help.'

'Not if it was a surprise attack,' Billy replied. 'They were talking, she stabbed him, he got a shot in before he died.'

'Multiple shots,' Brightman added. 'If he did do this, he spent a good minute repeatedly tasering her before he bled out.'

Billy stepped back, looking around. 'Well, there's one thing this proves,' he said. 'If that's the same weapon, Declan Walsh didn't kill Kendis, but Will Harrison might have. When I spoke to him, he admitted he had a key for Brompton Cemetery, so he could have been in there that night.'

'We need to see where Harrison was on that night,' Frost reluctantly admitted. 'But I'm not counting Walsh out of anything until we have him under questioning.'

Billy nodded, staring down at the bodies. There was something wrong here, out of kilter, as if someone had placed them in this way. Just like Kendis Taylor had been placed back in Brompton Cemetery.

Frost walked out of the apartment and Billy ran to catch him up.

'What's the matter?' he asked quietly.

Frost looked to him, as if weighing up whether he could speak.

'Look, Guv, I've already shown my loyalty to the department,' Billy added. 'If Monroe comes back, I'm first out the door. So I'm tied to you, no matter what. So explain what the issue is.'

Frost looked back to the room. 'I saw her enter,' he mumbled. 'I saw you leave, and I was so busy wondering if I should follow you, I delayed in stopping her.'

'Why were you here?' Billy looked confused.

Frost sighed. 'I was following you,' he explained. 'I heard about your little trip with Sutcliffe last night.'

Billy froze, as if caught in the headlights of a car. 'I was going to speak to you about that,' he said. 'This kind of eclipsed it.'

'He offered you a job, didn't he?' Frost asked.

Billy nodded. 'I didn't say yes,' he replied. 'But you have to understand, I couldn't turn him down or he'd know something was wrong.' Billy looked around the hallway, leaning forward.

'He knows you're making a play for him,' he whispered. 'Said that you're – look, these are his words, not mine – not the sharpest tool in the box, and that you're nowhere near as in to Rattlestone as he is. Said that when this is done he'd jump me up to Detective Inspector in his squad as there's going to be a vacancy, if you know what he means.'

'Treacherous bastard,' Frost muttered. 'You did good in letting me know. Anything else?'

'Yeah,' Billy pulled out his phone. 'He sent me something last night.'

Frost looked at the messages that Billy now showed. It was from Sutcliffe's number.

> Tomorrow, after we arrest Walsh stay by my side. We'll block Frost from the questioning. He's too close, and we can pin this all on him.

> Are you sure, sir?

> He needs to be removed from the equation. Forcibly, if possible.

'Bastard!' Frost hissed. 'He's as deep in this as I am! How dare he throw the blame on me!'

'Deep?'

'Look, you're a bright kid. You've probably worked it out. I work for – well, I worked for – Will Harrison,' Frost said. 'So does Sutcliffe, and a lot of the police, in small ways. *Rattlestone*'s integrated everywhere. Will was the voice behind it.'

'I thought Baker was?' Billy was confused.

Frost smiled for the first time that morning.

'That's what you're supposed to believe,' he replied. 'But it was always Harrison and Gladwell.'

'Malcolm Gladwell?'

'Yeah. He's at the top of the chain, it looks like.' He looked back at the apartment. 'Harrison swung for him and missed.' Frost considered the text message again.

'We need to keep this under wraps until we capture Declan today, okay? We can screw over Sutcliffe afterwards. You're sure of this location for the meeting?'

'Absolutely,' Billy nodded. 'Fitzrovia, two thirty.'

Frost nodded back in reply. 'We capture Walsh and then work out what he did or didn't do,' he explained. 'In the meantime, we let Sutcliffe take the blame for everything.'

CHARLES BAKER WAS SITTING AT HIS DESK, HIS HEAD IN HIS hands, when Malcolm Gladwell burst into his office.

'*Was it you?*' he screamed. 'Did Harrison tell you where the safe was?'

Slowly, his eyes red-rimmed with tears, Charles looked up at Gladwell with a face that was drained of all emotion.

'What the hell are you on about now?' he asked. 'Can't it be sorted later?'

Gladwell paused, rattled by the answer. 'It wasn't you? That broke into my mausoleum. Changed the password?'

'What bloody mausoleum? What bloody safe?' Charles was completely lost. 'What the hell are you talking about?'

'You're not making a run for head of Rattlestone?' Gladwell was now thrown off balance.

'Do I look like I'm in any state to do that?' Charles hissed. 'Will and Laurie are dead! They say he killed Kendis and possibly Donna! When the press gets hold of this, I'm ruined! They'll ask how I didn't see this, how I didn't know!'

Gladwell sat in the chair on the other side of the desk from Charles now, nodding sympathetically, as behind the eyes he tried to work out what was really going on.

'We can get you out of this,' he said. 'We can change the narrative, show that you were trying to stop this, perhaps?'

Charles Baker simply stared at Gladwell, but it felt like he was looking straight through him.

'Maybe it's time for me to resign,' he said. 'Maybe Kendis was right when she wrote about me.'

'You're on the Star Chamber, man!' Gladwell hissed. 'Grow a spine!'

'*To hell with the Star Chamber!*' Charles stood as he

shouted. 'Look at what I've got around me! My Special Advisor killed a journalist! He tried to frame a police officer for terrorist crimes!' He stopped, as if his common sense was finally returning.

'You know, I told him to get you a present back when you said you'd help me with the Leadership,' he whispered. 'Something nice. Rare. Like a Montblanc letter opener in Ruthenium.'

'Did he? I can't remember.'

Charles Baker's face was now dark and foreboding.

'If I find you did anything here, that you were to blame for any of this, I will destroy you,' he hissed. 'We took the flack for your Balkans error, but I still know where the papers are.'

'You do?' Gladwell laughed. 'In a safe in a mausoleum, perhaps? Good for you! Go get them! Let's see how you do!'

'What do you mean?'

'I mean that someone beat us to it!' Gladwell rose now, facing Charles. 'They changed the combination! We can't get into the bloody thing!'

'Walsh,' Charles replied softly. 'He saw Francine last night. He knew Kendis well. Maybe he knew about it?'

Gladwell went to reply, but then stopped.

'Dammit,' he hissed, pulling out his phone. 'I need to make a call.'

'Problems?'

'You could say,' Gladwell muttered, texting as he left the office. 'I'm about to have him *executed*.'

30

THE STING

Declan stood in front of The Fitzroy Tavern, in the heart of Fitzrovia, and took a deep breath.

Royal Bastard. Gallifrey. Dentist.

He'd understood the message the moment he heard it; the Royal Bastard was *Henry Fitzroy,* the first Duke of Grafton and illegitimate child of *King Charles II*; the surname *FitzRoy* was a term meaning "bastard child of a royal".

Fitz-Roy.

His great grandson, Charles Fitzroy, Baron Southampton had bought the Manor of Tottenham Court, building Fitzroy Square to the east, and Fitzroy Street had been named after him, the area gaining a lot of interest from Bohemians in the 1930s, in the process earning the nickname *Fitzrovia.*

Gallifrey was because of Declan's first meeting here with Alex Monroe. When he first joined the force from the Military Police, his father had arranged a drink for Declan with Monroe, then just a DI himself, to go over some basics in the new field. They'd arranged it for an evening during the week, meeting in the downstairs bar only to discover that they'd coincided with the monthly meeting of a group of *Doctor Who* aficionados. They'd not stayed long, but the memory was strong.

Finally *Dentist* could only mean the terrible joke that Doctor Marcos had told him, of *tooth hurty* being the best time for one, and so it was at two thirty in the afternoon that he stood on the junction of Windmill Street and Charlotte Street in Fitzrovia, staring at the bar and willing himself to enter, hoping that it wasn't a setup.

Taking a deep breath, Declan adjusted his coat to cover his face a little and then entered the bar through the side entrance.

ON WHITFIELD STREET, RUNNING PARALLEL TO CHARLOTTE Street and directly attached to Windmill Street, Billy and DI Frost sat in an unmarked police car, watching the pub across the road as a man in a long coat entered.

'Was that him?' Frost asked.

Billy shrugged. 'It could have been, but I couldn't tell for sure,' he replied. 'Maybe we should go in and look?'

'You're sure this is where the meeting was?' Frost picked up a radio as Billy nodded.

'Henry Fitzroy's the Royal Bastard, and *tooth hurty* is the best time for dentists,' he explained. 'Doctor Marcos told me the joke, and she was the one leaving the message.'

'What about the Gallifrey line?'

'They had some kind of monthly comic thing there,' Billy smiled. 'Never was my thing, so when Monroe mentioned it I kinda turned off. But it's definitely the right place, and that has to have been Declan.'

Frost clicked his radio on. 'All units, be prepared. Suspect is believed to have entered the location, and we're going to check it out.'

'That's a negative,' a voice spoke through the radio, surprising Frost. 'Stay in your vehicle until we accurately identify whoever is joining him. I want all of them.'

'This is my sting, DCI Sutcliffe,' Frost replied into the radio. 'I didn't realise you'd be on the frequency.'

'I'm taking this over,' Sutcliffe's voice showed a hint of anger. 'I don't trust your judgement right now.'

Turning the radio off and tossing it onto the dashboard of the car, Frost looked to Billy.

'You were right,' he said. 'He's trying to move me out of the way.'

'Perhaps then we need to ensure that we sort this before he reaches us?' Billy suggested. 'If we get a chance, we should tie up all the loose ends, if you know what I mean.'

Frost nodded.

'We'll give it ten minutes,' he said. 'Then we move in.'

WALKING DOWN THE STAIRS TO THE BASEMENT BAR, DECLAN saw that the door to it had a sign that read *CLOSED – PRIVATE EVENT*. Opening the door and entering, Declan saw a long table by the wall with Monroe, Doctor Marcos, Anjli and DCI Bullman sitting there. Monroe looked tired, but forced a weary smile as Declan walked over, sitting down at the table.

'I didn't order you a drink,' Monroe said softly. 'I didn't know what this new persona of yours would drink.'

Anjli grinned. Declan couldn't help it; he smiled as well.

After a full twenty-four hours of constant fear and tension, to sit with friends was something he sorely needed.

'No Billy or Davey?' he asked.

Doctor Marcos shook her head. 'Billy is with Frost and Sutcliffe,' she replied. 'And Davey is working on something.'

Declan nodded. He'd expected that. 'How long do we have?'

'Not long,' Monroe replied. 'So let's get down to it. What do we have? Declan?'

'Rattlestone was created back in 2010,' Declan started. 'I think it was Malcolm Gladwell who created and named it, and seemed to have the most to gain from it. Over the years he brought on board Francine Pearce, Charles Baker and Will Harrison. Later, Donna Baker, Charles's wife, was placed on the public board, but didn't seem to know what was going on there. In 2015, Rattlestone gained its first Ministry Of Defence contract after a UN Peacekeeping force was attacked in the Balkans, killing four soldiers.'

'The Ministry of Defence leaked that,' Anjli interjected. 'We thought Will Harrison, perhaps.'

Declan shook his head. 'I found files showing that Malcolm Gladwell did it. At the time he was Baker's boss, of sorts. He arranged it to look like it came from Baker's office, though.'

'Why kick off about it now, though?' Bullman asked. 'I mean, that was years ago. What tipped the apple barrel?'

'We did,' Declan explained. 'We brought Baker's past into the limelight. Kendis did more digging. She'd been there in 2015, and this gave her the opportunity to move in on Baker. She got to know Donna, intending to use her as an unwilling source. The problem was that Donna wasn't aware of this and then took this to Baker.'

'It might have been more than that,' Anjli replied as her phone beeped. 'We spoke to Laurie Hooper, Donna's PA, and although she didn't say much, she said that on the night Donna died, she had heated arguments with both Will Harrison and Malcolm Gladwell, who she was with the night that you met with Kendis at The Horse and Guard. We think she was the whistle-blower and spoke to Kendis that night.'

Declan shook his head. 'She met with the whistle-blower, but I don't think it was Laurie,' he replied as he showed the image of Kendis and Gladwell on his phone. 'She met with Gladwell after meeting with me.'

He stopped.

'Gladwell didn't want people to know that he was meeting Laurie there,' he said, thinking. 'It didn't fit his narrative. People might question his motives. That's why The Horse and Guard was destroyed; not to remove the CCTV footage of us, but of *them*.'

'Possible,' mused Anjli.

'Who took this?' Bullman was examining the image now.

'Nasir Gill,' Declan replied. 'I took it from his camera's SD card after he died. He was following Kendis for Rattlestone.'

'Who then killed him.'

'Pretty much,' Declan replied.

'I'd hate to see their retirement package,' Monroe smiled.

Anjli had been reading her phone's message and now looked up. 'I might have something,' she said. 'From the Harrison murder.'

'The what?' Declan asked in surprise.

'Laurie Hooper and Will Harrison killed each other this morning,' Bullman explained. 'Well, we're meant to believe so, anyway. Harrison was stabbed with the same letter opener that Kendis was killed with, and there was a receipt found with the box that proved that he'd bought it on his credit card.'

'How did Laurie die?' Declan leaned forward.

'Some kind of taser torch, held in Harrison's hand,' Bullman replied. 'Why?'

'Kendis Taylor was killed in Malcolm Gladwell's mausoleum,' Declan looked to the table, remembering. 'I found a ceramic vase that had broken, there were bloodstains on the floor and taser marks on the walls from a scuffle.'

'Why was she in Gladwell's mausoleum?' Monroe frowned at this. 'Especially if he was the whistle-blower?'

'Because he had a secret safe in it,' Declan's tone darkened. 'Also, I think Kendis didn't fully believe him. He had a motion detector on the mausoleum, and he would have been alerted that she'd broken in.'

'So Gladwell arrives, they fight and he stabs her with Will Harrison's letter opener? How does that work?' Doctor Marcos asked.

Anjli held a hand up at this.

'I know that one,' she said, showing her phone. 'Anthony Farringdon just came back to me. Parliamentary members must reveal all gifts they receive, yeah? The same week that Will Harrison bought the Montblanc letter opener on his card, Farringdon remembers Malcolm Gladwell registering the same thing as a gift.'

'Thank God for photographic memories,' Monroe whispered to himself.

'So how did it get back to Harrison?' Bullman asked. 'Unless ...'

'Unless Gladwell gave it to Laurie Hooper to kill Harrison with. Maybe even returned with her, and zapped her to ensure that the ends were all tied up,' Anjli replied. 'The whole whistle-blower thing? Maybe she told him she was going to tell Kendis about Donna's death and Gladwell saw an opportunity to remove Harrison and Baker.'

Bullman nodded. 'He agrees to speak to Taylor on her behalf, then pretends to be the source, so that when this all eventually comes out, he's seen as the hero while Baker's department is shown the door, and removed from Rattlestone.'

'You shoot at the king, you'd better not miss,' Anjli mused. 'Harrison did both.'

Declan nodded. 'But how do we prove this?' he asked.

Monroe stroked at his white beard.

'I think we need to be a little more biblical,' he replied.

BILLY LOOKED AT HIS PHONE AND CURSED SOFTLY.

'What now?' Frost asked. Billy looked up, his expression sheepish.

'We're at the wrong pub,' he said, showing the screen of the phone. 'I was worried, so I googled. It's not The Fitzrovia Pub, but The Fitzroy Tavern, just down the street.'

'Christ!' Frost grabbed his radio as he bounded from the car. 'All units! Get to the Fitzroy Tavern! Now!' He looked to Billy, now next to him. 'You're an idiot!' he snapped. 'How could you screw this up!'

'Hey, I fixed it!' Billy exclaimed as they ran. 'That has to account for something!'

In The Fitzroy Tavern, Declan patted Monroe on the arm.

'I'm glad you're doing okay, Guv,' he said. 'It wasn't the same without you. Where did you hide out?'

Monroe looked pained to answer, so Doctor Marcos replied.

'Globe Town Boxing Club.'

'The Twins?' Declan half rose to his feet. 'Are you insane?'

'No, but I was desperate and critical!' Monroe snapped back. 'I had limited options!'

Declan sat back down. 'Did he at least look after you?' he asked.

'Well, he almost killed two men who wanted to kill me,' Monroe smiled. 'Does that count?'

There was a moment of silence as Declan and the others around the table took this revelation in.

'Anyway, Rosanna said you heard Frost on a tape?'

Glad for the change of subject, Declan nodded.

'Trix had it,' he smiled. 'She came through for a change.'

'Always knew that girl was an asset,' Monroe lied with a smile.

'So how do we do this?' Bullman asked.

Monroe looked to her. 'You need to get out of here,' he said. 'You're not part of this. You shouldn't be punished for it.'

'To hell with that,' Bullman replied with a small smile. 'They still haven't decided what to do with me about DI White. They'll probably use you as a character witness, so I need you on my side.'

'The moment you came to help Declan, you gained me as an ally,' Monroe looked back to Declan. 'How did you get out of the offices?'

'Trix, again,' Declan replied. 'She had a backup exit in case she needed to run, but never used it.'

'I have a feeling that we under-used that girl,' Monroe mused. 'And Dec, I'm sorry to hear about Kendis. I might not have been a fan, but you were, and that was enough—'

He stopped as the door to the downstairs bar burst open and armed police swarmed in through it, assault rifles aimed at the lone table.

'*Hands on the table!*' The lead armed officer shouted. '*Hands on the table!*'

Declan slowly placed his hands on the table and watched the door as DI Frost and Billy entered, Billy looking away in what seemed like shame as he did so.

'Judas,' hissed Anjli.

'Always,' Billy replied, looking straight at her. 'But I'm the one working on the side of justice, it seems.'

Frost walked up to Declan, pulling him up by the arm, cuffing his hands behind his back as the armed officers gathered up the others around the table.

'This time there's no clever escape, my little terrorist friend,' Frost snarled. 'This time your life is bloody well *ended.*'

31

KILLED WHILE ESCAPING

THEY'D BEEN ESCORTED OUT OF THE MAIN ENTRANCE AND bundled into a police van that was parked up outside the pub and, with Frost and Billy in the black Lexus that followed, they left Fitzrovia, heading eastwards as they did so. In the back of the van a single armed officer sat with them, his helmet and goggles still on as he kept his distance, as if scared that even being next to these potential terrorists would somehow stain his own reputation.

'Are you still sure that this was a good idea?' Bullman asked.

Declan chuckled.

'I never said it was a good idea,' he replied.

'So, what do you think?' Monroe asked. 'Police station or murder site?'

'Murder site,' Anjli replied. 'Definitely.'

'I say police station,' Doctor Marcos stated optimistically.

'I'll take that bet,' Anjli smiled. 'Tenner do it?'

'And how do I pay you if you win?' Doctor Marcos asked.

'Let's face it, if it is a murder site, we won't be coming out of it to square up.'

'Don't blame me,' Anjli snapped. 'It was the Guv's idea.'

They sat in silence, each now in their own thoughts for the rest of the journey which seemed to be about another thirty minutes. Then, with a sharp turn to the left that threw them off their seats and a bump of the wheels that sent them tumbling about on the metal benches, the truck came to a stop. The armed police officer banged on the back door, and after a moment the doors opened, the two other armed officers who'd entered with Frost and who'd driven the van now standing there, their carbines at the ready. Behind them, emerging from their own car, were Billy and Frost, the former of the two looking confused why they had stopped here.

'Get them out,' Frost said as the armed police manhandled Declan, Anjli, Bullman, Doctor Marcos and Monroe out, lining them up.

They were in an abandoned warehouse, the broken windows and open doors looking out to what looked like the Thames. It looked like an industrial estate, the other buildings around it quiet, and Declan assumed this was more of an abandoned one than a bustling, busy one. The only places he could think that looked like this were on the south bank, maybe between Lambeth and Rotherhithe, but they could have been anywhere. There were mounds of bricks by the pillars, and piles of plasterboard lay unloved in corners. This looked like a place that someone had comprehensive plans for a long time ago, but had never followed through.

Perfect for *executions*.

'You owe me a tenner,' Anjli muttered to Doctor Marcos.

'I'll pay you later,' Doctor Marcos replied with a wry smile.

'Forgive me for asking, but this doesn't look like Scotland Yard,' Monroe said.

Frost laughed at this and then, without warning, punched Monroe hard in the gut, almost doubling him over. There was a unified shout of outrage at this as the others moved to stop this, but the weapons raised by the armed police stopped them.

'You like my personal police force?' Frost asked. 'They're Rattlestone through and through. Given to me by my fairy godfather.'

'I thought your fairy godfather just got skewered by a secretary?' Bullman muttered.

'That was my *old* one. I have a new one now,' Frost replied. 'Also, these guys do whatever I tell them.'

'So, what are you telling them?' Anjli asked.

Frost grinned. 'That terrorists tried to break you out of custody, and you were all killed in the resulting firefight.'

Anjli looked to Billy, who turned away.

'Don't think that he's helping you,' Frost interjected. 'He's learned who's really the power here. He'll go far.'

'So, what, you're going to kill us all here?' Declan looked around the warehouse. 'Not really sporting.'

'No, I'm going to kill them, but leave you alive,' Frost replied, pulling out a silenced pistol. 'My boss needs a password from you.'

'Oh, he found that I'd changed the safe combination then?' Declan laughed. 'Tell you what, Frost. Or whatever your actual name is. How about you let them go and I'll give you the password? You can take all the folders, make your own luck.'

'No thanks,' Frost aimed the gun at Declan. 'I'm loyal.'

'To whom?' Anjli asked. 'Will Harrison or Malcolm Gladwell? I mean, Will gave you the command to attack the Guv, but he's dead now.'

'Curiosity gets you nowhere,' Frost smiled. 'Now, which of you do I shoot first?'

'None of them,' muttered Billy.

Frost shook his head. 'Changed your mind?' he asked. 'Siding with terrorists now?'

'No,' Billy replied. 'I want to see you take down Declan. He was always a smug shit. But he won't tell you if you kill everyone. He's a martyr, with a bleeding heart. You need to hurt them, make him beg you to stop.'

Frost's eyes widened at Billy's response, and Declan could see that he was reassessing the situation.

'Fair point,' he replied. With his pistol in his left hand, he flicked out his right arm, the extendable baton clicking out into his grasp.

'Recognise this, old man?' he asked with a sneer as he turned to face the handcuffed Monroe. 'Maybe I can start with you, finish the job that I started.'

Monroe, instead of backing away however, stepped forward.

'Not sure,' he said. 'Mind if I have a look?'

Frost, confused by this complied, holding the baton up for Monroe to observe. Eventually, shaking his head, Monroe stepped back.

'Nope, not seen that before,' he said.

'Are you blind?' Frost raised the baton, holding it close to Monroe's eyes as he leaned in. 'Do you need a reminder?'

'Yours didn't have DW stencilled on the base,' Monroe replied with a dark smile.

Confused at this statement, Frost looked at the baton,

noticing that the base did indeed have DW stencilled on it. He looked to Billy, who for the first time smiled.

'Why the hell are you grinning like an idiot?' Frost snapped.

'DW stands for Declan Walsh,' Billy explained. 'I gave it to you when we were at the house. I took your one and passed it to forensics. Interestingly, they texted me this morning with the news that they found a whole load of DCI Monroe's blood DNA on it.'

'You're on my side!' Frost hissed. 'You told me about Sutcliffe! You showed me the texts he sent you!'

'Yeah, about that,' Billy shrugged. 'I stole his phone. Used a silicon sheet that DC Davey made me of his thumbprint, unlocked the phone and sent the message to myself, replied and then sent the second one. Took like five seconds. I then deleted the thread, right after sticking in a worm app that took all the data in his phone and forwarded it to my personal server, while also keeping the microphone on, recording everything that happened around him.' He shook his head.

'You really should have listened to me when I told you I was a cyber expert.'

He looked to the armed officer that had ridden in the van with them. 'You picked Sutcliffe up right before the stakeout, didn't you, sir?'

'Indeed, we did,' the armed officer replied as he pulled off the helmet and goggles to reveal the face of Chief Superintendent Bradbury, now turning to Frost. 'Also, we were right beside him when he radioed you.'

The two armed officers, once believed to be Rattlestone, now turned their weapons on Frost, who slowly clapped his hands.

'Very good,' he said. 'I knew this day was going to end bad. But all you have on me is Monroe, and they blackmailed me into doing that.'

'We have more than that,' Billy added. 'Remember when I sorted your phone's carrier settings back in Hurley?'

Frost pulled out his own phone, staring in horror at it as Billy continued.

'Can you guess what I did to your phone as well?'

Declan now stepped forward, his hands now appearing in view, the handcuffs open.

'You might as well tell us everything, Frost,' he suggested. 'It's the last chance you'll get to do a good thing, and if you don't, we'll just ask Sutcliffe.'

As Frost watched, each of the supposed detainees revealed their hands, all having been uncuffed while in the van.

Frost laughed, looking back to Billy.

'All this time?' he asked.

Billy nodded. 'From the start,' he replied. 'Anjli and me, we'd decided to use secret codes in case anything went wrong. She wouldn't let me use *Belgrade*, but *Judas* was a good one.' He pulled out his phone. 'I've recorded every conversation you, me, Sutcliffe ever had. I've placed tracker apps in your phones and know exactly where you were each minute of each day, as well as any burner phones you've called during that time. Like, for example, that I know you went into the apartment after I left. So when we have time to listen to it, we'll hear every single moment of what happened in there, courtesy of your phone's microphone.'

Frost thought for a moment and then physically slumped, as if finally beaten, the baton dropping out of his hand.

But, before anyone could say anything, he brought up the

silenced pistol in the other hand, aiming it point blank at Billy as he fired.

Declan was the closest and had been moving before Frost had. He knew Frost wouldn't go quietly, had watched the trigger hand clench and unclench the grip of the gun, and had intended to push Billy out of the way before Frost fired. However, he was a moment too late and, as Frost fired he'd only moved in front of Billy, blocking the view, the bullet slamming into Declan's shoulder, spinning him around and sending him to the ground as the Armed Response officers fired their carbines at Frost, hitting him centre mass, sending him already dead to the floor.

Doctor Marcos was the first to Declan, checking his shoulder.

'It's gone right through,' she said. 'Lucky bastard.'

'I don't feel lucky,' Declan groaned.

'So what now,' Anjli asked. 'Is Declan cleared yet?'

Bradbury shook his head. 'We have a confession and proof that Walsh didn't attack his DCI, but we still have the fact that he clandestinely met with a potential terrorist, and still could have been connected to her murder, a fact that, with the potential alternatives for the murderer all dead causes a bit of an upset.'

'They're not all dead, sir,' Billy replied, already working his way through Frost's phone. 'Sutcliffe made calls to Gladwell on a burner phone, the same number that sent a message to Frost, demanding that he gain a password from Declan. We have the message here, along with quite a few others.'

'What do we know about this number?' Monroe asked.

'We're getting data on where it's been over the last few

days,' Billy replied. 'We'll know in an hour everywhere it went.'

'Plus we know Gladwell named Rattlestone back at the beginning, and held their secrets,' Declan groaned as they helped him up, holding his shoulder while the officers pulled out a medical pack from the truck. 'He knows I changed the combination. He'll know that I'm after him. He'll try to change the narrative again and there's only one person left he can frame.'

Doctor Marcos was now working on his shoulder with the kit as she spoke. 'Charles Baker.'

Bradbury considered this. 'So, what do you want to do about it?' he asked. Declan forced a smile, but it turned into a wince as Doctor Marcos worked on his shoulder.

'I'd like to – Jesus, woman! – I'd like to be the one that brings him in,' he replied. 'For Kendis. Besides, it's a bit of a ritual now, me saving Charles Baker.'

Bradbury looked to the others. 'I can't in good faith let this man, injured and still suspected of terrorism, go after an elected Parliamentary Official,' he said. 'Unless one of you vouches for him?'

Anjli, Billy, Bullman and Monroe all stepped forward as one.

'They attacked our unit,' Monroe said. 'We all want him.'

'Well,' Bradbury smiled. 'You'd better go find him, then.'

32

DECLAN WALSH

CHARLES BAKER WAS PACING AROUND HIS DESK WHEN MALCOLM Gladwell returned to his office.

'What the hell do you want now?' Gladwell asked, looking around, seeing that the office was empty. 'Do you want people to think we're complicit? Stop bloody calling my office to get me to meet with you! Christ, we've spoken more today than we have since the last election!'

'The press are hounding me!' Charles snapped back. 'The news about Laurie and Will's deaths is out now. I need to divert it away from me.'

Gladwell paused. 'Jesus,' he muttered. 'You're falling apart. Get a grip.'

'Look, all I need is some help with the story I'm saying,' Charles added. 'That's it.'

Gladwell sat in the chair opposite Charles, looking up at the ceiling as he let out a frustrated sigh. 'Pour me a drink then,' he said. 'Let's work it out.'

Charles pulled a bottle of expensive brandy out of his bottom drawer, pouring the amber liquid into two small tumblers. Passing one over to Gladwell, he sat back down, sipping at his drink.

'Give me the issues,' Gladwell said.

'Balkans,' Charles offered.

'Simple. You tell them that Will did it,' Gladwell replied. 'Thought he could gain influence in Rattlestone, told no one, allowed our offices to fight with one another.'

'Did he though?' Charles asked. Gladwell almost spluttered his brandy.

'*Who cares if he did or not?*' he snapped. 'He's dead!'

Charles mulled over the idea, eventually nodding.

'Taylor.'

'Terrorist.'

'Come on, Malcolm—'

'That's what we stick to!' Gladwell exclaimed, almost rising from his chair in anger. 'Look, your man Harrison created the hatchet file on her with Rattlestone resources. That might come out to bite us, but if it does? We claim it was on him. If it doesn't? Then we keep the narrative. Even if she wasn't, she actively began this by speaking to Donna.'

'What about the claims that Donna didn't kill herself?' Charles spoke softer now, calmer, watching Gladwell as he replied.

'Are nothing but claims,' Gladwell leaned forwards in his chair, bringing his voice down to match. 'Look, I had a falling out with Donna that day, and so did Will. She wanted to come clean, go to the press. I felt bad; having you push for the Leadership was my idea. The extra press was because of that, and the Taylor woman turned her brain around. I'm sorry it ended the way it did.'

'Did you kill Taylor?' Charles asked.

'Of course not!' Gladwell decried. 'Will did it! He told me!'

'When?'

Gladwell shifted in his chair. 'We spoke yesterday.'

'The attack on DCI Monroe? Was that Will too?'

Gladwell sat still now, observing Charles.

'This feels more like an interrogation than an ideas exercise,' he intoned, looking around. 'Is there something I should know?'

'Yeah, probably,' Charles slumped back in his chair, turning to a door leading out of the back of his office.

'You might as well come in now,' he said, his voice raised.

Malcolm Gladwell rose as the back door opened and Declan, his right arm in a sling, entered through the door, Monroe following in behind him. 'What the hell is this?' he asked.

'It's time to end this,' Charles replied, looking back to the desk. 'These detectives have some questions for you.'

'I won't answer anything without my brief present,' Gladwell snapped back. Declan shrugged, nodding.

'I guessed you'd say that, so let me instead tell *you* some things,' he suggested. 'How's that?'

As Gladwell reluctantly sat back in the chair, Declan walked into the room now, leaning against the wall as he looked at him.

'I knew Kendis since we were kids,' he started. 'So understand that I'm not going to say that it's nothing personal. It's incredibly personal.'

Gladwell nodded. 'I wondered why Frost hadn't replied to me,' he said. 'He was always a wild card. Going off on his own—'

'Frost, or whatever his name is? He's dead, laddie,' Monroe interjected. 'So I'd shut up if I was you.'

'You can't speak like that to an elected official!' Gladwell looked for support, but Charles Baker was still staring down at his desk.

'Let me tell you a story,' Declan began. 'Ten years ago you create Rattlestone. Even named it after a street where one of your family died. Nice touch. You build up some nice contracts, create a fake board, all of that.'

'Hearsay.'

'I have files in a mausoleum safe that say differently,' Declan replied.

'So there you are, living the life, skimming some nice defence contracts, and then the Balkans incident happens,' Monroe continued. 'You pass the blame onto other departments, but it's swept under the rug and Rattlestone makes a nice hefty chunk of coin. Over thirty pieces of silver, even, considering you climbed over the dead to get it.'

'But here's the problem,' Declan took over. 'Now we're a few years on. You're in the Star Chamber, Baker there is newly admitted, you've got a chance to really do something here, but people are complacent. Will Harrison is using Rattlestone as his stepladder to greatness, and that's pissing you off. Francine Peace is using it as her personal security and there's nothing you can do and Charlie there is taking substantial payments for "lectures".'

'I'm confused,' Gladwell smiled. 'You're saying that I'm the moral one here?'

'It looks it,' Monroe nodded, now sitting against Charles's desk. 'But then the shite hits the fan. Literally. The Davies murder comes out. We learn Pearce has been blackmailing Baker. He has a son, now murdered. Terrible affair. Then from that a journalist, one that was in the Balkans who saw the betrayal first hand, starts digging.'

Declan continued, 'First, she thinks it's Baker, so she aims at him, finding Donna's name on some documents. She pressures her, hoping to gain a source, but Donna doesn't do that. She tells you what she's learned.'

'Donna spoke to me, Will *and* Charles that day.'

'True, and all of you told her to ignore Kendis,' Declan replied. 'But that night she's found dead.'

'I didn't kill her,' Gladwell protested.

Declan shrugged. 'We'll never know,' he replied. 'Besides, that's only the start. At this point Laurie Hooper, Donna's PA, gets involved. She's Donna's confidante, she knows that something smells here. So, she contacts Kendis as an anonymous source. Meanwhile, you each go into protection mode. Harrison creates this fake legend, informing Charles that Kendis is a terrorist sympathiser. Charles, grieving and desperate to focus blame on someone, accepts it as truth. He utilises a government department, maybe one he has connections with through the Star Chamber to get it out there. To "flick the switch", turn on the light, reveal this dissident. But Will Harrison starts his own campaign, sending a text to Frost, telling him to kill DCI Monroe, dressed as me.'

'I never knew about this,' Charles replied. 'I swear.'

'King John never knew he was being played by *Sir Hiss* in the Disney film, either,' Declan muttered, looking back to Gladwell. 'You didn't know any of this because you were planning your *own* political assassination of Harrison and Baker. You started an affair with Laurie, convincing her you were the only one that believed her. On the night of Monroe's attack, you went with her to a meeting at The Horse and Guard with Kendis, ensuring that by the end, Kendis believed that *you*, not Laurie, were the whistle-blower. Maybe you told Laurie that it'd be more believable from an MP; I don't know.

What I do know is that the following day you met with Kendis in St John's Park, playing the part perfectly.'

'How do you know this?' Gladwell asked. 'I mean, I'm not saying I didn't; I felt I had a duty to bring a full transparency—'

'*Shut up!*' Declan shouted, his face filled with anger. 'Enough with the lies! I know because you brought in one of your assets, Nasir Gill. He followed Kendis for you, taking photos. It's how I know you met her. But you had to explain why you needed him to do this, you had to make him think that Francine Pearce was involved, and in the end he had to be taken out before he realised the truth.'

Gladwell sat silently now. Declan took a deep breath, gathering his composure. Monroe, seeing this, continued.

'Personally, I believe you wanted to remove Harrison, maybe even Baker there. Being seen as the man who learned that one of his own colleagues, a man that he had once championed for Leadership had done such a terrible thing, using a force created for good ... nice PR there. You'd have shown how they'd followed you too, taken photos that showed you to be a target as well.'

Still no response from Gladwell, now staring balefully at the two detectives.

'But here it goes off the rails,' Declan, calm again continued. 'I think Kendis took something, maybe your key to get into Brompton. She doesn't trust you, you see. So, she sneaks in once it's closed and goes to have a sniff around. Unaware to her, she sets off your motion alarm. It's three miles to the cemetery from your house. A cab could get you there in ten minutes.'

'I was at home all night,' Gladwell replied. 'You can check my phone records.'

'Oh, we did,' Monroe smiled. 'Not your normal phone though; we looked at the burner phone you used to speak to Sutcliffe and Frost with. You thought that one was safe. So you went to Brompton for about eight pm, according to the cell tower data. The same time that Kendis is believed to have been murdered.'

'I went into your mausoleum,' Declan added. 'There's blood on the floor and also on a broken vase, shards of which I'm sure will match the ones found in Kendis's head. Also, there are scorch marks on the wall, made from a circular taser, the same marks found on her body.'

Gladwell leapt up. 'Conjecture! This is a farce! Will Harrison could easily have killed her there! And he had the taser in his hand when he died!'

'The letter opener that killed her in his chest, too,' Monroe countered. 'Yes, we're aware of that, laddie, and that was a problem. How did the weapon that killed Kendis, a particular weapon that left a rare, easily identifiable residue arrive wedged between his ribs? That was tough until we realised a couple of things.'

'First, although Will bought the item, he gifted it to you,' Declan chimed in. 'You even claimed it.'

'I don't recall this,' Gladwell replied, po-faced. 'My people would have done it, and Will probably lied to them.'

Declan pulled out his phone. 'How did Laurie Hooper get it?'

'From the crime report I read, she found it in a box on his sideboard or something,' Gladwell commented, on stabler ground now. 'Which shows that Will had both weapons and most likely killed Kendis Taylor.' He smiled now, a humourless one that didn't quite reach his eyes.

'If only the dead could speak,' he said.

'But they can,' Declan said, pressing play on his phone. Through the speaker, voices could be heard.

Frost's voice: *Well, well. Hello there. What do we have here?*
Gladwell: *What the hell are you doing here?*
Frost: *I saw her enter. I was coming to see if I could help Mister Harrison. That seems a bit late, though.*
Gladwell: *You're Frost, right? You work for him?*
Frost: *Well, I worked for him. Now that looks a little sketchy. What exactly are you doing here, Mister Gladwell?*
Gladwell: *It's not what it looks like.*
Frost: *Are you sure? Because it looks like you're repeatedly tasering a dead woman.*
Gladwell: *What I'm doing is fixing a problem. And if you help me, I'll be a better benefactor to you than he ever was.*
Frost: *I'm listening. What do you need?*
Gladwell: *Take this box and put it on the sideboard. Make sure the receipt is visible. And then wipe this down and stick it in his hand—*

Declan turned off the recording.

'We recorded everything Frost did for the last twenty-four hours,' he explained.

'Frost's dead. You already told me,' Gladwell, his voice now rising with fear, looked from face to face as he replied. 'This won't stand up in a court of law.'

'No, but we don't need it to,' Declan replied. 'You wiped the knife down, but forgot to wipe the box. We know you had it and we know that ten minutes after arriving at the cemetery, your phone makes its way back to Page Street momentarily before moving back to the mausoleum.' Declan moved closer now, his hands clenching.

'You tasered her. She fell, unconscious, bleeding from the head. You then left her, unconscious and locked in a tomb as you went back to your apartment, found an item that could be blamed on Will Harrison and then returned, stabbing her in the chest.' His voice was breaking now, the emotion raw. 'Then you dumped the body near Harrison's tomb. But you didn't expect him to place his own men, including Frost, into the investigation and you panicked. You needed to create a patsy, and so you groomed Laurie into killing Harrison with the same letter opener.' He grabbed Gladwell by the jacket lapels, pulling the scared man close now. 'I shouldn't arrest you! I should *kill* you!'

'Fun story, but only that,' Gladwell tried to sneer. 'I never had a relationship with Laurie Hooper. You can't prove—'

'I have the footage from The Horse and Guard,' Declan replied. 'You were so busy trying to blow it up, you never checked if they backed onto the cloud.'

He released his grip, letting Gladwell fall back to the chair.

'I might not prove all this, but you'll damn well lose all this,' he hissed. 'And the Balkans file in your safe will send you away for the deaths of innocent soldiers.' He looked to the main door.

'Get this traitorous bastard out of here,' he called out.

Anjli and Billy entered now, handcuffs at the ready. Gladwell, horrified, looked at Charles.

'You set me up?' he exclaimed.

Charles shrugged. 'I made a deal,' he replied, standing now, watching as Monroe, Anjli and Billy led the handcuffed and protesting Malcolm Gladwell out of the office, and into the corridors of power. They wouldn't walk him through the major areas, but the press would hear. They'd locate him as he left. He'd be front page news within the hour.

'I'm genuinely sorry about Miss Taylor,' he continued. 'She was a pain in my arse, but politicians need people like her.'

Declan nodded silently, turning to the door.

'DI Walsh?' Charles said, stopping him. 'We had a deal. You had my help here, and in return ...'

'The combination, sure.' Declan looked back to Charles Baker now. 'Enough people have died because of Rattlestone,' he said. 'I expect you to do the right thing.'

'My wife died because of it,' Charles mused. 'I never want to hear the bloody word again. So, what was it?'

'Two words, eleven letters, a name you'll always remember,' Declan said as he wrote the password onto a piece of paper, passing it to Charles and, without another word, he turned and left the office.

Charles Baker picked up the piece of paper, reading it.

Then he laughed.

'Oh, you arrogant bastard,' he said as he sat down at the desk and made calls.

EPILOGUE

THE FALLOUT FROM THIS, AS EXPECTED, WAS IMMENSE. WITH the information gained from both the phones of DCI Sutcliffe and DI Frost, and the additional evidence gained from the investigation by the Temple Inn Crime Unit, there was more than enough evidence to destroy the career of Malcolm Gladwell, let alone charge him for the murders of Kendis Taylor, Laurie Hooper and by association, Will Harrison. There was a faint chance that he could have been charged with the murder of Donna Baker, but Charles Baker had spoken against that, claiming that his family just wanted closure. He had however sent the police to Gladwell's family mausoleum in Brompton Cemetery where, in an antique safe opened by a combination password was a single folder, one on the 2015 Balkans debacle, which laid the blame for the leaking of the itinerary directly at Malcolm Gladwell's feet, giving four more deaths, British soldiers, that he could be charged with.

There was no briefcase in there.

Charles Baker was as good as his word, and by the end of

the day had launched an investigation into Rattlestone's prac-
tices, in the process effectively closing it down. There was no
mention of the five million that he'd made in the other shell
companies, or what files he'd recently gained that would
assist him in other ways.

As for the detectives of *The Last Chance Saloon*, the fallout
was heavier. DS Anjli Kapoor and DCs Billy Fitzwarren and
Joanna Davey had been spared from the brunt of it, having all
performed their duties under exceptional circumstances, but
that DCI Monroe and Divisional Surgeon Doctor Rosanna
Marcos had deliberately gone to a known crime lord for help
had not sat well with the higher command, who felt that the
team needed more than a DCI, a rogue DCI at that, looking
after them. So, while Monroe was given administrational sick
leave to recover from his injuries, they promised to
completely audit the department, something that worried
everyone involved. Even DCI Bullman, the first to be pulled
in and questioned, didn't comment to anyone what had
happened in the meeting.

DI Declan Walsh had also been targeted; it was pointed
out that his reckless antics over several cases had been part of
the cause of these situations, and that he hadn't revealed his
relationship with Kendis Taylor while actively investigating
her was a major strike against him. That said, that he had
been framed for domestic terrorism and had not only proved
his innocence but solved the case while uncovering a parliamentary conspiracy was a tick in his favour, as were the
glowing recommendations he received, to his surprise, from
both Charles Baker, MP and Chief Superintendent Bradbury.
But no matter what happened, the fact of the matter was that
Declan and his team had, again, embarrassed the Government. Declan knew that there would need to be a scapegoat.

As they placed him on administrative sick leave to heal his shoulder wound, he wondered if he'd ever be allowed to return to duty again.

That he'd lost Kendis too almost broke him.

However, the fallout didn't stop there; Declan had learned that during this, Jessica had been cyberbullied; taunted and painted online as the daughter of a terrorist, and when he'd called, Liz had explained that *now wasn't the best time to speak to her,* and that he should give her a few days.

Declan had met with Monroe a couple of days after that; he'd gone to ensure that the old man was still fighting fit, visiting him in the hospital ward that Monroe had been seconded to under threat of death by Doctor Marcos until he was officially well enough to return to duty.

'She'll forgive you,' Monroe had said.

Declan nodded, not really believing that. 'Have they said when you can get out of here, Guv?'

'Couple of days, no longer,' Monroe leaned his head back against the pillows. 'When you spoke to Trix, did she say anything about the night?'

'What do you mean?'

'Did she see what I was working on?'

Declan understood, now. 'No,' he replied. 'She was uploading, so didn't see the screen. Why?'

Monroe closed his eyes as he spoke. 'I was writing my resignation letter,' he explained.

There was a moment of silence as Declan took this in. 'You're quitting?' he eventually asked.

Monroe, however, shook his head.

'It was right after Birmingham,' he explained. 'I felt that for most of my life I've skirted the edge of the line. Hell, half of my life is on a bloody wall in your house and, after the case, my capture and all that, I worried that I'd lost my edge.'

'And now?' Declan leaned forwards on his chair.

'But now, having literally fought for my life, I'm seeing things differently,' Monroe opened his eyes again, looking directly at Declan. 'But it might be too late. There's a strong chance I'll be pensioned off, and the doors of the Last Chance Saloon will close forever, laddie.'

'They can't pension you off,' Declan forced a smile. 'They'll have me to deal with.'

Monroe smiled, thanked Declan for his friendship and closed his eyes.

Declan returned to Hurley to recover, aware that every face that looked at him wondered whether the rumours were true; whether he was indeed some kind of sleeper terrorist, a danger to be watched or even stopped. So the house that had for the last couple of months felt like home, no longer did so.

———

IT WAS A WEEK AFTER THE ARREST OF MALCOLM GLADWELL that Kendis Taylor was buried.

Even though she'd spent more than half of her life away from the sleepy village, she'd asked in her will to be buried back in Hurley, in the family plot. So, her husband Peter had agreed, holding the ceremony in the graveyard of St Mary The Virgin, the same churchyard that, a couple of months earlier, they had buried Patrick Walsh in.

Declan didn't attend; instead at a distance he stood by some trees, watching the service from afar. It was a minor affair, kept short, and Declan wiped a tear from his eye as he watched the coffin lowered into the ground. With that he'd turned away, and walked over to Patrick Walsh's grave, staring down at it. The ground had settled. It didn't look or feel so out-of-place now.

Now it was Kendis's grave's turn to look like that.

Too many good people are dying, he thought to himself. *Maybe being kicked out of the force is the best thing here.*

There was a rustle of leaves behind him as someone approached, and Declan turned to see Peter walking over to him.

'I'm sorry for your loss—' Declan began, but didn't finish as Peter bunched his fist and, with a heavy right-handed swing, connected hard on Declan's chin, sending him tumbling to the floor.

'Get up, you *bastard*,' Peter hissed.

Declan lay on the ground, sprawled across his father's grave.

'Do what you want,' he replied, shutting his eyes. 'I deserve it.'

Peter leaned over Declan, his face crunched up with anger, his eyes reddened with crying.

'You were just a shag,' he hissed. 'Nothing more than a one-night stand. She loved *me*, Walsh. *Me.*'

He stood up, looking back to the service.

'Pay your respects to my wife,' he said. 'It's the only time you're allowed to. I know people in this village, and they bloody hate you. They tell me everything, and if I hear you've visited her grave at all after that? I'll kill you.'

Peter spat onto Declan, kicking him in the side one more time for good measure and then, turning around, he walked away from Declan without a backward glance.

Declan painfully climbed to his feet, noting that the

exchange had been seen across the graveyard by two of the older residents of Hurley.

Bloody wonderful. As if I hadn't fuelled enough gossip.

Dusting himself down and rubbing at his bruised chin, Declan slowly walked to the now empty graveside, staring down at the coffin that held Kendis Taylor.

'I'm sorry,' was all he could manage in a choked voice, forcing the returning tears back as he spoke. After a couple of moments of silent farewells, he eventually turned and walked out of the churchyard, away from Kendis and his father and back towards his house.

In the church car park there was a woman standing by a nondescript grey van, watching him quietly. In a long grey hoodie and a pair of jeans, she made no movement, no signal of communication, but had positioned herself so that he'd notice her. Recognising her, Declan turned, now walking towards the van.

'Trix,' he said as he stopped in front of the younger woman. 'Third time in Hurley in a month? You'll be renting a place next.'

'I'm sorry for this, Declan,' Trix replied. 'For your loss and all that. But also for being here.' She looked to the front of the van, as if looking to see if anyone on the High Street was watching; as usual for a sleepy village, they were alone. 'I've been trying to sort your Wintergreen problem out.'

'You have?' Declan was surprised at this, and went to speak, but Trix looked back to him, raising a hand.

'You've pissed a lot of people off in Whitehall, Declan. There's a ton of people want you in a box for what you did to Rattlestone, including the bigwigs who control my department. It's really hard to get your name in through any front doors, you know?'

'No, I don't know,' Declan stared at the young woman, confused. 'What do you mean?'

'I mean what I said,' Trix looked away again, as if ashamed. 'I'm sorry for this. But orders are orders.'

Declan went to ask what she meant, to ask why she was being so cryptic, but as he did so he heard the scuff of a boot behind him and, before he could turn around to see who it was, a small black hood was thrown over his head, muffling him as his arms were grabbed from behind. Something was firmly placed over his nose and mouth; a damp cloth, stopping him from shouting as he struggled, a sickly sweet smell coming from it and through the hood that, as he was forced to breathe it in made his limbs feel heavier, slumping as the unconsciousness of sleep took him.

Looking around, Trix opened the side of the van as a man, dark-haired and in his late thirties bundled the unconscious Declan into the back of it, slamming the door shut and checking around one more time to see if this had been observed as he climbed into the driver's seat, nodding silently to Trix as they drove off, south down the High Street, and out of Hurley ...

DI Walsh and the team of the *Last Chance Saloon* will return in their next thriller

Order Now at Amazon:

http://mybook.to/whisperforthereaper

And read on for a sneak preview...

PROLOGUE

CRAIG RANDALL LED A DOUBLE LIFE.

That's what he told everyone that he spoke to; it made him sound like a secret agent, some kind of exciting, enigmatic hero rather than what he really was; a fifteen-year-old bully with a Walter Mitty fantasy.

Craig's double life *wasn't* fake though; it just wasn't what you'd expect to see when asking someone about it. During the week, Craig was just a Year 10 loser, picked upon by the bigger, stupider kids in his year because he wasn't a fan of the same football teams, a teenager who spent a lot of time on his own, and who didn't have that many friends. He wasn't that academic; he wasn't that sporty. In fact, he wasn't that... *anything*. If you looked up the words *academically average* in a school guidebook, you'd probably find a photo of Craig Randall smiling out at you. Or, at least scowling, annoyed that he was being made fun of again.

But on the weekends, oh yes *the weekends,* he was a *God*.

For Craig Randall spent his weekends somewhere else. Not in South East London like the other losers in his class, no; Craig and his family would spend every weekend from Easter until October at a camping and caravan park in *Hurley Upon Thames.*

It'd started when he was eight. His parents, sick of the estate they lived in and desperate to escape from the city, if only for a day or so borrowed a frame tent from a friend, and, with a minimum of camping equipment and experience had muddled their way to Hurley after seeing it mentioned in the back of *Camping and Caravanning* magazine. They'd arrived late on a Friday evening in May and, as Craig and his dad wrestled with the tent, realising very early in the process that they didn't have a manual explaining *which pole went where*, Craig's mum and his sister Ellie went to visit the camp shop, and picked up some fish and chips from a van that had arrived just outside it.

They'd been cramped back then; eight-year-old Craig and five-year-old Ellie had to share one of the two 'bedrooms', nothing more than a cloth divider between their manky sleeping bags on cheap air beds, and their parents' double air bed, with equally battered sleeping bags.

They'd had a BBQ on the Saturday and cooked from a single camp stove the other days. They'd played football. Although they had a small TV to watch things on, they didn't really bother. There was a small boat ramp that led into the Thames, which you could get to by following a path from the first field, or by making your way across a rickety, home made bridge created from wooden pallets over a stream beside the third, furthest away field, and then following the Thames back to it.

He played there a lot. And he built the bridge, too.

It had been a break in every sense of the word; a break from the artificial normality of the world, and a return to an easier time. From that day onwards, the Randalls were *born again weekend campers*, updating their equipment piece by piece while travelling down every Friday evening, often from the moment Craig left school, and returning mid afternoon on the Sunday, just in time for him to prepare for school the following day.

They weren't the only people who did this and over the weeks and months that they lived this double life, Craig had recognised other people, other families, other *children* who also travelled to Hurley on the weekends. And, they met *new* families who were just starting the journeys.

Families and children who didn't know Craig, and had no context of what he was truly like.

And thus the *second* Craig Randall was born.

This Craig was a cool one. He was captain of his school's football team, had a girlfriend who was super hot and two years older than him, and he was doing these new visiting children a favour by hanging out with them. He was the experienced one, the veteran of the camp; he knew the coolest places to play in the woods that surrounded the campsite, the best places to swim, and he always had a story of something amazing that'd happened in the past which was always a story that made him look as *equally* brilliant. In fact, as the years went on and Craig reached his teenage years, he'd spend the weeks waiting for the weekends, when he could go back to Hurley and gain adoration from the smaller kids there, annoyed when the camping season ended in October and he had to wait almost *half the year* to return.

He didn't explain what he did while camping to his weekday friends. They weren't that important to him. They didn't see him in the same way.

They'd adopted a spaniel named Scamper, named after

some book dog his dad had loved as a kid a couple of years into this. Craig wasn't a fan of the spaniel, mainly because he ended up as the *de facto* dog walker, but that said, it seemed to attract girls to him, all wanting to stroke Scamper; and Craig had by then reached an age where girls were very *interesting*.

And then it'd all gone wrong. His parents now had a caravan, and although Ellie still slept with them inside it, they allowed Craig his own three-person tent, which he'd had to save up for. It was like having his own place; he had a double mattress inside it, even if his sleeping bag fitted one person, and a small radio that played CDs. But for the fifteen-year-old Craig, this was a bachelor pad. He was finally becoming a man.

And his attitude to the other kids on the site changed.

He wasn't bothered about playing in the woods like he was five years earlier. He wanted to kiss girls and look cool. He'd just finished his Year 10 mock GCSE exams. You were effectively a *grown up* when you did that.

He bullied the smaller kids in the campsite, mainly because he *could*. That, and it was revenge for the bullies who still attacked him at his own school. He'd also realised that he was no longer the 'veteran' who could show the coolest places to other kids; that was now a position given to his sister, or even other younger children who, arriving years after he had claimed the role were now looking at him as some kind of weird hanger on. And this had angered him.

He'd acted out by hurting the smaller kids; not physically, but mentally.

He'd take things of theirs, left outside the tents at night and throw them into the Thames or break them, leaving them back outside the tents for the owners to find the following morning.

He'd tell stories of the *Grey Lady,* a ghostly woman who hanged herself in *Medmenham Abbey*, a stately home across the Thames and historically infamous as the location of Sir Francis Dashwood's *The Hellfire Club,* who used it for "obscene parodies of religious rites" in the mid-1700s, her ghost walking the banks of the Thames late at night, stealing children's souls.

He'd even pretended to become *possessed* by Dashwood, terrifying the younger children until they cried, now and then finding an intrigued teenage girl who wanted to know more.

He'd never gone too far with *that*, except for that one time.

But now it was summer, school was over, and the Hurley campsite had become a *prison* for Craig. After seven years there, he had built a reputation; one that his parents had often argued with him about. *They were one strike away from being banned because of his antics,* they'd say. He'd laugh and tell them that the ghost of Francis Dashwood had done the terrible things, not him, and then walk out before they could reply. In fact, he'd just done that, walking with Scamper eastwards along the Thames, towards Hurley Lock, a mile or so away.

The Thames was to his left, strangely quiet for the time of day; nobody was fishing, there weren't even any kids playing in the water. It felt wrong, odd, somehow. The bank of the river became an open field to his right, and about fifty yards away a bank of trees showed the woodland copse that bordered the campsite. This was where Scamper was running to, as Craig tried to get his battered old iPod Nano to work. If he'd charged it earlier, he wouldn't have heard the barking.

And that would have changed everything.

As it was, he hadn't charged the iPod, and therefore it wasn't playing music and he heard Scamper barking at something somewhere near the edge of the woods. The bloody dog wouldn't come back after being called, and Craig almost continued on, convinced that Scamper would just follow him, or just do him a favour and leave forever, when he heard the barking cut off abruptly with a *yelp*.

Turning back to the trees, Craig could see that Scamper had run over to the rickety bridge. And, walking towards it, frustrated that Scamper had most likely run into the trees, he stopped about twenty feet away from it, as a man appeared the other side, emerging from the woods.

He was old, maybe in his fifties. He was slim, had short brown hair in a buzz cut, and wore a green *Barbour* jacket. His face was pale, like he didn't get out into the sun that much. And he was smiling.

'Have you lost your dog?' he asked, his voice showing the slightest hint of a European accent. 'He is right here. Come and get him.'

'Nah, it's okay,' Craig said. There was something about this old man that unnerved him. 'I'll just wait.'

'I think he is tangled in nettles,' the man replied. 'You must come and help him.'

'It's cool, I'll wait until you've moved on,' Craig tried to smile, but it came out as a leer. The man however nodded at this.

'Understandable,' he agreed. 'I am a stranger. You are right to be wary. But we are not strangers, are we *Craig*?'

At the sound of his own name, Craig felt an icy wind blowing down his spine. He'd never seen this man before, and he'd sure as hell not given his name away.

'Who are you?' he asked. 'How do you know who I am?'

'I know everything about you,' the man continued to smile as he spoke, and Craig found himself irrationally angry at this. 'I know you have been coming here for years. I know you are a bully. I know *what you did to that girl.*'

'I didn't assault her,' Craig snapped back. 'She came on to me. I didn't do anything.'

'I'm sure you did not,' the man replied, stepping back from the bridge, beckoning Craig in. 'But perhaps we should talk more about this together, rather than shouting it loudly across a stream?' The old man watched Craig, still not moving.

'Your dog is in pain,' he said. 'You will not save him?'

Now terrified, Craig shook his head. The man thought about this for a moment and then pulled something out of his jacket pocket, tossing it over the stream, the item landing at Craig's feet. As Craig bent down to look at it, he could see it was an ivory handle. Picking it up, he realised it was a wickedly sharp cut-throat razor.

'See?' The man smiled. 'Now you have a weapon. If I attacked, you could hurt me. Please, come in, Craig. Come and *play a game* with me.' And as Craig watched, the man walked back into the woods.

With the blade now in his hand, Craig felt more in control of the situation. The man was right; he *could* hurt him and hurt him badly if he tried anything. And, as he crossed the rickety bridge and entered the wooded copse, he saw Scamper, a rope loosely tied to his collar and secured to a tree, wagging his tail with delight at this strange game they were playing. The dog wasn't in pain or in distress at all. Craig looked to the man, angry that he had lied to him, and found him sitting on a fallen tree trunk, with another fallen trunk facing him.

'Sit, please,' the man indicated the other trunk. 'We have much to talk about.'

Now more curious than scared, Craig ignored the dog and walked to the tree, sitting down on it, blade still in his hand, ready to defend himself. Noting this, the man reached into a pocket and pulled out a hip flask with two small metal cups, made of metal bands that clicked into shape when flicked. Into these, he poured a liquid, offering one to Craig, who shook his head.

'And I thought you were almost an adult,' the man sighed, drinking one cup. 'See? Not poisoned. But you will need to drink this, Craig Randall of Gleeson Road.' He held the offered one up again. 'Drink.'

Craig didn't mean to, but the man's voice was so commanding that he couldn't help himself, taking the metal cup and downing the liquid with a cough. It was a sweet, strong taste, like apples.

'Good, yes?' The man smiled. 'Schnapps. With a little benzocaine added to numb the pain.'

Craig coughed as the man pulled out a small, silver coin.

'You know what this is?' the man asked, not waiting for an answer as he explained. 'This is a solid silver East-German Mark.' He twirled it in his fingers. 'See? A number *one* is on this side, that is *heads*, while on the other side is a compass and a hammer; *tails*. I have had this for many years now.' He looked up from the coin now, staring intently at Craig.

'We play a game now,' he explained as he reached into his pocket again, pulling out another cut-throat razor. 'I will flip it. If it lands heads, I will take this razor, this very sharp blade and slash my throat open. If it shows tails, however, you will do this instead, yes?'

'No!' Craig rose now, angry. 'You're mad! I—' he stopped as a heaviness overcame his legs, sending him back to the tree trunk. 'What did you do?'

'I told you,' the man replied. 'Schnapps. With a little benzocaine.'

'I don't want to play,' Craig whined, realising that this was a terrible place to be right now.

'I understand, it is scary,' the man nodded sympathetically. 'But you have been a wicked man, Craig. As have I. And as such we must face *repercussions*.' He rolled the coin over his fingers. 'And you might not get tails. I might lose.'

'I'll scream,' Craig insisted. 'I'll call for help.'

'And that is your right,' the man nodded calmly. 'But know that if you do, I will be gone before anyone arrives. And then, at some point very soon, I will enter your house while your mother, father and dear little sister Ellie are asleep and I will slowly and painfully skin them all alive. And then I will find you and make you watch as I slice pieces off you with this straight razor.'

Craig was crying. 'Please, I'm sorry,' he said. 'I don't want to die.'

The old man smiled.

'Maybe you will not,' he said as he flicked the coin into the air, watching it lazily flip before landing on the back of his hand. 'Let us see, shall we?'

———

DI FREEMAN CLIMBED OUT OF HIS BMW AND LOOKED AROUND the campsite. It was right after the school holidays had started, and there were families and children everywhere. A nightmare to keep a crime scene contained.

There was a perimeter already placed around the entrance to the copse; a couple of police officers ensuring that the small crowd of onlookers couldn't enter.

This was good. They really didn't want to see this.

One onlooker, a young dark-skinned woman with frizzy black hair, waved to him as he approached the police officers, catching his eye. Forcing a smile while silently swearing, Freeman walked over to her.

'Kendis,' he said amiably. 'I didn't think you worked for the Maidenhead Advertiser anymore?'

'I don't,' Kendis Taylor replied, pulling out her voice recorder. 'But I'm visiting mum. It's the Olympic opening ceremony tonight and my cousin's in it. Saw the blues and twos as I was driving to the house.'

Freeman wanted nothing more than to escape. 'You needn't turn that on. There's no story here.'

'You sure?'

Without answering, Freeman walked away from the annoying reporter, showing his ID to the nearest officer and passing under the incident tape, entering the woodland clearing. Here he found more officers, mainly forensics, working the case while other officers kept the public out of sight. Recognising one officer through the white PPE suit she wore, he waved to gain her attention. Regan was a solid SOCO, and he didn't want to piss her off if he could help it, so he kept as far away as he could.

'What've we got?' he asked. Regan walked over to him, glancing back as she did. On the floor, lying on his back, his arms outstretched and his throat slashed, was a teenage boy.

'Craig Randall, fifteen years old, throat slashed from right to left,' she said, making the motion with her hand. 'Went out with the dog two hours back. Dog arrived back in the campsite about an hour ago. Family went looking for him, couldn't find him, tried calling his phone, no answer. Eventually that caravan there heard the ringing and entered the woods, thinking someone had lost a phone. Instead, they found this.'

'Nice,' Freeman stared at the body. 'Cause of death?'

'We think it's some sort of razor,'

'Think?' Freeman looked back to Regan. 'No weapon found?'

'None yet,' Regan admitted. 'But then he could have slashed his throat and then thrown it into the bushes or even the stream.'

'You think this was self inflicted?' This surprised Freeman. Regan waved for him to follow, moving a little closer to the body, but not close enough to contaminate the scene.

'See there? The cut is from right to left,' she explained. 'It's jagged, so it wasn't committed; almost like he started, stopped and then continued through.' She pointed to the left hand, currently against the ground. 'Blood started spurting out on the right-hand side, then spurts to the left as he continues to cut, where it splatters all over his fist and arm. But his palm is absent of any sign of it.'

'Because he was gripping the blade,' Freeman nodded. 'Any reason he'd do this?'

'Apart from the fact that he's apparently a little shit with a bit of a rep for being a bully?' Regan shrugged. 'Better ask the parents.'

'No note?'

Regan pointed to a tree where, on the bark, was etched one word.

SORRY

'That do for you?' she asked.

DI Freeman sighed. 'Anything else?'

'Actually, yes,' Regan waved to an assistant who passed over a clear plastic bag. In it was a piece of card the size of a business card, blank except for one image; a little red man with what looked like a hat on, arms out to the side, and holding a scythe. 'We think this is some kind of collectable—'

'It's *murder*,' Freeman said, his face draining of all colour. 'This wasn't suicide. I need to call Walsh.'

'Walsh? Why does he need to get involved?' Regan was irritated now, aware that she'd missed something, but unaware of what it was.

'Because we've seen that picture before,' Freeman replied, pulling out his phone and dialling. 'Yeah, it's me,' he eventually said into it. 'Get Detective Superintendent Patrick Walsh on the line, now.'

He looked back at the body.

'Tell him we have *another Red Reaper*.'

WHISPER
FOR THE REAPER

Order Now at Amazon:

http://mybook.to/whisperforthereaper

ACKNOWLEDGEMENTS

Although I've been writing for three decades under my real name, these Declan Walsh novels are a first for me; a new name, a new medium and a new lead character.

There are people I need to thank, and they know who they are. To the ones who started me on this path over a coffee during a pandemic to the ones who zoom-called me and gave me advice, the ones on various Facebook groups who encouraged me when I didn't know if I could even do this, who gave advice on cover design and on book formatting all the way to my friends and family, who saw what I was doing not as mad folly, but as something good. Also, I couldn't have done this without my growing army of ARC readers who not only show me where I falter, but also raise awareness of me in the social media world, ensuring that other people learn of my books, and editors and problem catchers like Maureen Webb, Chris Lee and Jacqueline Beard MBE, the latter of whom has copy-edited all four books so far (including the prequel), line by line for me.

But mainly, I tip my hat and thank you. *The reader.* Who took a chance on an unknown author in a pile of Kindle books, and thought you'd give them a chance, whether it was with this book or with my first one.

I write Declan Walsh for you. He (and his team) solves crimes for you. And with luck, he'll keep on solving them for a very long time.

Jack Gatland / Tony Lee,
  London, January 2021

ABOUT THE AUTHOR

Jack Gatland is the pen name of *#1 New York Times Bestselling Author* Tony Lee, who has been writing in all medias for over thirty years, including comics, graphic novels, middle grade books, audio drama, TV and film for *DC Comics, Marvel, BBC, ITV, Random House, Penguin USA, Hachette* and a ton of other publishers and broadcasters.

These have included licenses such as *Doctor Who, Spider Man, X-Men, Star Trek, Battlestar Galactica, MacGyver,* BBC's *Doctors, Wallace and Gromit* and *Shrek*.

As Tony, he's toured the world talking to reluctant readers with his 'Change The Channel' school tours, and lectures on screenwriting and comic scripting for *Raindance* in London.

An introvert West Londoner by heart, he lives with his wife Tracy and dog Fosco, just outside London.

Locations In The Book

The locations that I use in my books are real, if altered slightly for dramatic intent. Here's some more information about a few of them...

The Worshipful Company of Stationers and Newspaper Makers is indeed real, and is one of the many Livery Companies in London that still exist. They often have dinners, but this one was a fictional one. In fact, I do them a disservice, as they're a wonderful organisation who do a lot of work for charities. Charles, as we all know now, is a bit of a bastard, and this whole scene is from his own perspective...

The George Tavern in Southwark is also a real location, and has held meetings for both *The Sherlock Holmes Society* and *The Dracula Society* among many others, in the same back room that the *Star Chamber* meet in my story. Built back in the 1500s, it was badly damaged in the Great Fire of London in 1666, and rebuilt in the 1670s. Charles Dickens was definitely familiar with *The George,* having mentioned the inn by name in his novel *'Little Dorrit'.*

The Boxing Club near Meath Gardens that Johnny and Jackie Lucas allow Monroe to stay in doesn't exist, and neither do the Twins - but the location used is the current **Globe Town Social Club**, within **Green Lens Studios**, a community centre formerly known as Eastbourne House, that I would pass occasionally in my 20s.

Hurley-Upon-Thames is a real village, and one that I visited many times from the age of 8 until 16, as my parents and I would spend our spring and summer weekends at the local campsite. It's a location that means a lot to me, my second home throughout my childhood, and so I've decided that this should be the 'home base' for Declan. And by the time book four comes out, I'll have completely destroyed its reputation!

Brompton Cemetery is a real place, and the organisation the *Friends of Brompton Cemetery* are real people, although I don't know if they actually have keys to enter!

St John's Gardens is a real park in Westminster and was a place I'd visit many times in the nineties, when I (not Gladwell) would visit Page's *Star Trek* Bar; there was free parking on Saturday nights and Sundays beside it. After the bar was closed and turned into apartments I never visited again, but I've passed it on occasions.

The Horse and Guard pub does exist, but under another name; this is *The Chelsea Pensioner* on the Fulham Road. A pub I've been to many times over the years, I didn't have the heart to blow the actual pub up in the story, and so renamed it!

Not so much a location, but **Macneale & Urban** not only existed and were a known safe manufacturer, but they did indeed make one of the only *letter-based combination safes* in existence. That said, they were only four-letter locks, not the *eleven* letter one of the story. Unfortunately, the company ceased manufacturing in 1903, so any safes found with these locks are now incredibly rare.

Finally, **The Fitzroy Tavern** does exist and for many years had a monthly *Doctor Who* fans meet up; in the nineties, when the show wasn't on, you would often find writers such as Russell T Davies and Steven Moffat there, both of whom would go on to showrun the series when it returned years later. The monthly meetings moved though when the pub was updated a few years back, and I'm not sure if they returned when the pub reopened.

If you're interested in seeing what the *real* locations look like, I post 'behind the scenes' location images on my Instagram feed. This will continue through all the books, and I suggest you follow it.

In fact, feel free to follow me on all my social media, by following the links below. They're new, as *I'm* new - but over time it can be a place where we can engage, discuss Declan and put the world to rights.

www.jackgatland.com

Subscribe to my Readers List: **www.subscribepage.com/ jackgatland**

www.facebook.com/jackgatlandbooks
www.twitter.com/jackgatlandbook
ww.instagram.com/jackgatland

Want more books by Jack Gatland? Turn the page...

THE THEFT OF A **PRICELESS** PAINTING...
A GANGSTER WITH A **CRIPPLING DEBT**...
A **BODY COUNT** RISING BY THE HOUR...

AND ELLIE RECKLESS IS CAUGHT IN THE MIDDLE.

JACK GATLAND

PAINT
— THE —
DEAD

A 'COP FOR CRIMINALS' ELLIE RECKLESS NOVEL

A NEW PROCEDURAL CRIME SERIES WITH
A TWIST - FROM THE CREATOR OF THE
BESTSELLING 'DI DECLAN WALSH' SERIES

AVAILABLE ON AMAZON / KINDLE UNLIMITED

THEY TRIED TO KILL HIM...
NOW HE'S OUT FOR **REVENGE.**

NEW YORK TIMES #1 BESTSELLER **TONY LEE** WRITING AS

JACK GATLAND

THE MURDER OF AN **MI5 AGENT**...
A BURNED SPY **ON THE RUN** FROM HIS OWN PEOPLE...
AN ENEMY OUT TO **STOP HIM** AT ANY COST...
AND A **PRESIDENT** ABOUT TO BE **ASSASSINATED**...

SLEEPING
SOLDIERS

A **TOM MARLOWE** THRILLER

BOOK 1 IN A NEW SERIES OF THRILLERS IN THE STYLE OF
JASON BOURNE, JOHN MILTON OR **BURN NOTICE,** AND
SPINNING OUT OF THE **DECLAN WALSH** SERIES OF BOOKS

AVAILABLE ON AMAZON / KINDLE UNLIMITED

" ★★★★★ AN EXCELLENT 'INDIANA JONES' STYLE FAST PACED
CHARGE AROUND ENGLAND THAT WAS RIVETING AND CAPTIVATING."

" ★★★★★ AN ACTION-PACKED YARN... I REALLY ENJOYED
THIS AND LOOK FORWARD TO THE NEXT BOOK IN THE SERIES."

JACK GATLAND

THE LIONHEART CURSE

HUNT THE GREATEST TREASURES
PAY THE GREATEST PRICE

BOOK 1 IN A NEW SERIES OF ADVENTURES
IN THE STYLE OF 'THE DA VINCI CODE'
FROM THE CREATOR OF DECLAN WALSH

AVAILABLE ON AMAZON / KINDLEUNLIMITED

Printed in Great Britain
by Amazon